ALSO BY CLAIRE TOMALIN

The Life and Death of Mary Wollstonecraft

Shelley and His World

Katherine Mansfield: A Secret Life

*The Invisible Woman: The Story of Nelly Ternan and
Charles Dickens*

Mrs Jordan's Profession

Jane Austen: A Life

Maurice,

or the

Fisher's Cot

MARY SHELLEY

Maurice,

or the

Fisher's Cot

A TALE

EDITED WITH AN INTRODUCTION
BY CLAIRE TOMALIN

ALFRED A. KNOPF
NEW YORK
1998

CONTENTS

ACKNOWLEDGEMENTS

My first thanks are to Cristina and Andrea Dazzi and to Signora Giovanna Dazzi, née Farina Cini, for so generously sharing their discovery with me; for allowing me to use and quote from their archives; for all the work they have put into searching for information; and for their many kindnesses, their hospitality and their friendship. Cristina Dazzi especially has been tireless in working on the details of this book.

Nora Crook, General Editor of *Novels and Selected Works of Mary Shelley* and Reader in English at Anglia Polytechnic University, Cambridge, has given me support, encouragement and invaluable advice.

Catherine Payling, Curator of the Keats–Shelley Museum in Rome, has also done a great deal to help at all stages.

Col. A. L. King-Harman gave me valuable information, lent me books, led me to Lady Mountcashell's letters in Brian MacDermot's book, and allowed his portrait of Lady Mountcashell to be photographed for this book.

William St Clair generously allowed me to inspect his collection of books, in particular children's books.

I am grateful also to Dr Bruce-Barker Benfield of the Bodleian Library; to Lord Abinger; to Louis Amigues,

Directeur des Archives et de la Documentation at the Quai d'Orsay; to Daniele Danesi of the Biblioteca Comunale Forteguerriana at Pistoia; to Laura Desideri; to Deborah Jeffs; to Peter Stothard, editor of *The Times*, and to Richard Owen, the paper's Rome correspondent; and to Harriet Cullen, Chairman of the Keats–Shelley Memorial Association.

The British Library, the London Library, the Bodleian and the Gabinetto Vieusseux in Florence have all been of great assistance.

I should also like to acknowledge generous help from the British Council in Italy and British Airways in Italy.

At Viking Penguin I have once again had the benefit of Tony Lacey's editorial advice and Donna Poppy's meticulous attention to the text, this being the fifth book on which we three have very happily worked together. Gráinne Kelly's picture research has been another essential part of the process; and Valentina Rice helped us with some translation.

I have been particularly pleased to be involved with a project that brings together several European countries—Italy, Ireland, England and France—and demonstrates the strength and continuity of our links.

PREFACE

The story that you are about to read was found at the beginning of the summer of 1997.

A few pages written in an orderly handwriting, tied in two thin bindings with a pale blue cover, which did little to please the eye. They were mixed up with a pile of personal letters, school diplomas, poems and dedications, economic and political pamphlets, newspaper cuttings, visiting cards, train tickets, maps and photographs. A bit of everything.

Simply because there was a bit of everything, I went to rummage through that box in the library. I hoped I might find something interesting to be able to take to an exhibition in Pisa in November—an exhibition about the winter of 1827/8 in Pisa, when the poet Leopardi visited the city and met Mrs Mason and her daughter Laurette.

I took the box and started selecting documents, looking only at the dates and to whom they referred, and I found nothing except for the odd letter from husband to wife regarding the rearing of the children, Laurette and Nerina (Nerina, a few years later, became our great-grandmother).

Suddenly, I found this little book in my hands and I read the dedication at the top of the first page: 'To Laurette from her friend Mrs Shelley'. I thought I had misread it and went back to the house in order to be able to transcribe it at my leisure. I knew that the Shelleys had been in Pisa and had seen the Masons and their children, but I never thought that there had been so much affection and intimacy between them!

I'm not an expert on Mary Shelley, and like many of you have read only *Frankenstein*. I was not aware of everything she had published and merely thought this could be one of the many things of hers that I had not heard of.

And so, little by little, I began doing some research, and I began to realize that it could really be hers and previously unpublished, but for months I had no confirmation.

Then, the Keats–Shelley Museum of Rome gave me the addresses of two specialists and I wrote to them.

Splendid! I received confirmation that all was true. The pages that I touched and retouched, to read and transcribe what I could of the nineteenth-century handwriting, were chosen with love by the famous Mary for a child who would become my aunt.

Cristina Dazzi
San Marcello Pistoiese, 1998

INTRODUCTION

I

Returning from a week's holiday in early November 1997, I found in the long loop of faxes delivered during my absence one from Italy. It was handwritten, and the signature at the end meant nothing to me: Cristina Dazzi. She told me she had come upon what she thought was a 'novel autograph unpublished by Mary Shelley'. She gave its title, 'Maurice, or the Fisher's Cot'; and, although her English was not quite perfect, I had no trouble understanding her description of the 'little book of a few pages, sewed with a string and covered by a thicker paper, inside the cover the words "alla Signora Shelley", perhaps it was a paper bundle piece which Mary used to sew the little leaves, and at the top of the first page: "For Laurette from her friend Mrs Shelley".' Signora Dazzi went on to say that her husband's family had been close to the Shelleys in the 1820s; and she asked for my advice.

An unpublished story by Mary Shelley would be an exciting discovery; but a children's story? I knew of none by her. I telephoned Nora Crook, a friend and a fine Shelley scholar, and we talked the subject over. Mary Shelley's Italian journal records that she did write a story 'for Laurette' on 10 August 1820. There is also a letter from

Mary's father, William Godwin, who ran a publishing firm specializing in works for children (the Juvenile Library), telling her that a story she has sent him called *Maurice* is too short for publication. His letter is dated 10 October 1821, and nothing more was heard of the story until 1976, when the American scholar Charles E. Robinson published an edition of Mary Shelley's short stories, and conjectured that the 'story for Laurette' and the lost 'Maurice', 'never located', were one and the same. It looked as if he could be right.[1]

I faxed all these snippets of information to Cristina Dazzi, for whom they were new and welcome. And I went on exploring the background, and thinking about Mary Shelley: the more I read, the better the provenance looked. The Laurette for whom the story was originally written was the daughter of two Irish friends of the Shelleys living in Pisa, George Tighe and Margaret, Lady Mountcashell; and Laurette's younger sister, Nerina, was Signor Dazzi's great-great-grandmother. Cristina Dazzi and I exchanged further faxes, and I decided I ought to go to Italy.

I got out a map to find San Marcello Pistoiese, where the Dazzis lived, a small Tuscan town in the Apennine hills above Pistoia. Then I rang the editor of *The Times*, Peter Stothard, who takes an interest in literary stories. He offered to send me to Italy if I would write about this one, and if I would go there before other papers in England or America were on to it. I agreed, gratefully. His foreign desk booked me on an immediate flight to Florence, and arranged for their correspondent in Rome, Richard Owen, to drive to San Marcello, bringing with him Catherine Payling of the Keats–Shelley Museum to meet me there.

I set off for Gatwick at once, with my husband's farewell warning in my ears: 'Remember the Hitler diaries.' Fortunately Mary Shelley's handwriting is easier to recognize, and to decipher, than Hitler's *Deutsche Schrift*. Still, it felt like an adventure: certainly a change from a day at the British Library. The plane was delayed, the weather menacing, and I arrived in the dark at Florence Airport to find no taxis. When at last I managed to summon one we sped along the motorway and then up into the hills. Sleet was falling, and the road was slippery and rose in sharp bends. At moments I could see lights gleaming on the plain below; then they were lost. There was fog about too. When we reached San Marcello, the driver had to ask for the hotel, Il Cacciatore—'The Hunter'. It was on the road out of town, one of those boxlike modern buildings, but the people were friendly, and Richard and Catherine had just arrived. We ate our pasta together, followed by a dish of local chestnuts—the hillsides are covered with chestnut woods—and we wondered what was in store for us the next day.

I I

Mary Shelley has interested me since the 1970s, when I researched my first book, *The Life and Death of Mary Wollstonecraft*, which was about her mother. I followed this up with a study of Percy Bysshe Shelley; this time Mary

Shelley was a central figure. After this I kept up with whatever was published relating to her, and in 1997 I was a curator for a bicentenary exhibition celebrating mother and daughter. One way and another, I have lived with the family for twenty-five years. They have never lost their fascination for me, and I have seen Mary Shelley emerge slowly from the overshadowing reputation of her poet husband to take her place as one of the key figures of the Romantic movement. There have been several biographies, and her tales and stories were published in 1976, her journals in 1987. Many hitherto unknown letters of hers were tracked down and published in Betty T. Bennett's fine three-volume edition between 1980 and 1988; and in 1996 all of her novels were republished in eight volumes. Her stepsister Claire Clairmont's journals and letters have also been published—in 1968 and 1995 respectively—adding to our knowledge of Mary; and the ongoing publication of volumes in the Carl H. Pforzheimer Library's *Shelley and His Circle* continues to make more manuscript material available.

If there is now almost a Mary Shelley industry, she is still best known for her novel *Frankenstein*. *Frankenstein* was an extraordinary achievement for a twenty-year-old, with its blend of horror, philosophy and scientific speculation: an account of a man who revivifies dead men's bones to make a living creature, and then repents his experiment when he finds he has produced a monster with a will of his own. Shelley went on to write other, less disturbing novels; but *The Last Man* (1826) was another grim fantasy, in which the human race is wiped out by epidemic disease.

If monsters and the annihilation of the human race are surprising subjects for a young wife and mother, they seem less so when you look at the details of her life. Mary Shelley was the child of two outstanding parents, the philosopher and novelist William Godwin, and Mary Wollstonecraft, famous for her pioneering statement of women's rights, and also a novelist; but the birth of the younger Mary killed her mother. This was in 1797. Godwin was left grieving to care for Mary and her three-year-old half-sister Fanny. The children grew up with the portrait of their dead mother looking down from the wall. They were not best pleased when a stepmother, Mrs Clairmont, joined the household, bringing a son and daughter of her own, and there were always tensions within the family. There were also wider problems caused by the backlash against radical ideas, which meant that Mary Wollstonecraft and William Godwin were both more derided than admired as their daughter was growing up.

Godwin was a good father. He expected much of his children, and they enjoyed rare privileges. They had the run of his library and met his many visitors, among them Coleridge, who read his *Ancient Mariner* aloud as they listened from behind the sofa. Godwin realized early that Mary was greatly gifted. In her teens he sent her away for long visits to friends in Scotland, which she enjoyed; otherwise she grew up largely in London. Money was always short in the family home.

When she was sixteen, Mary met Percy Bysshe Shelley. As a radical, a republican and an atheist, he was an enthusiastic admirer of her father, and he also revered

LEFT: *Mary Wollstone-craft, Mary Shelley's mother and governess to Margaret King, later Lady Mount-cashell*

BELOW: *William Godwin, Mary Shelley's father, who raised her after her mother's death* the memory of her mother, approving of her views on the status of women, marriage and divorce. For him, the discovery that these two great thinkers had produced a child as beautiful as she was intelligent was overwhelming. He was only twenty-two, with a wife, Harriet, and a small daughter; but within months, in the summer of 1814, Shelley and Mary eloped, leaving an outraged Godwin and a desperate Harriet, pregnant with her second child.

Mary's bliss lasted barely beyond the Channel crossing. Her first child, born prematurely, died. Shelley, although he had financial expectations as the son of a rich baronet, was tied in a tangle of debts and quarrels with his family, his wife's family and now Godwin also. Mary's stepsister, Claire Clairmont, had become part of their household, and Shelley's devotion to her, and her dependence on him, were a perpetual irritant. Claire involved herself briefly with Byron and became pregnant by him, but it was always Shelley who made himself responsible for her welfare, and many people believed that Mary and Claire shared his sexual attentions. Shelley did believe in sexual freedom, and at one point proposed to share Mary with his best friend from Oxford.

So far, their affairs were merely muddled, but in 1816, when Mary was writing *Frankenstein*, the horrors of life began to vie with those of her imagination. Her half-sister Fanny, depressed and neglected, committed suicide. Almost immediately after this, Shelley's wife Harriet drowned herself, leaving two small children whose custody her family was determined to retain. Shelley married Mary, albeit reluctantly, in the hope of winning custody of his children by Harriet, but the attempt failed.

He and Mary left for Italy in 1818 with their two children, accompanied by Claire and her daughter Allegra. Four years of high poetic achievement and bitter sorrow followed; their children died, and Mary fell into deep depression, which was not dissipated by the birth of another child at the end of 1819. This was the broad background against which *Maurice*, written in the summer of 1820, had to be read.

I I I

Casa Cini, the home of the Dazzis, is in the centre of San Marcello and is well known to all the inhabitants, as we found when we set off to find it in the morning. It's a large, ancient family house, once famous for its hundred rooms, and is still a maze of passages and winding stairs opening into surprising spaces, with paintings, sculptures and books everywhere. The family now occupies only a small part of the Casa, but they have preserved the family archives. It was among these archives that Cristina Dazzi came on Mary Shelley's story, while searching for something quite different at the request of the University of Pisa—papers connected with the poet Giacomo Leopardi, who became a friend of Lady Mountcashell and her daughters a few years after the Shelleys' stay in Pisa.

We were greeted by Andrea and Cristina Dazzi, and offered coffee. Then the manuscript of *Maurice* was brought out and laid in front of me on the table: an alarming moment, because coffee and manuscripts must not occupy the same space. Once we had separated them, I found *Maurice* exactly as Cristina Dazzi had described it.

The first thing to say about this manuscript is that it is an intrinsically attractive object, beautifully written and put together by someone who knew how to delight a child. From a more technical standpoint, the handwriting is easily legible and shows the characteristic letter formations of Mary Shelley. Catherine Payling compared it with other Mary Shelley manuscripts she had brought from the Keats–Shelley Museum, and we both felt there was no doubt of its being the same hand. Later, Nora Crook was able to examine *Maurice* and do what I had not dared, given the fragility of the manuscript, which was to check the watermarks; and she confirmed, in consultation with Dr Bruce Barker-Benfield of the Bodleian Library, that the paper was of the same kind as that used by the Shelleys during their time in Pisa in 1820 and 1821.

The manuscript is divided into two booklets, the whole work only thirty-nine pages long. I read it through as fast as I could, taking a few notes, and copying out only a phrase here and there. Seeing a text for the first time, your brain races as you read. I was trying to relate it to Mary Shelley's other work. I was looking for her literary sources. I was thinking about the circumstances of her life in 1820. I was trying to remember what I knew about Laurette and her family. At the same time, I wanted to read it purely as a piece of writing—to enjoy it as simply as Laurette must have enjoyed it.

Some of my first impressions follow. I noticed that the slim little story is divided into three parts, just like a three-volume adult novel of its time; and I guessed this was a playful touch, intended to please a bookish child. It

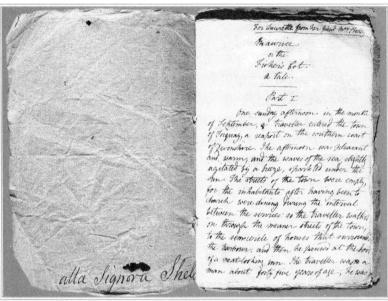

mimics adult novels of the time in another way too, by giving the narrative to several different voices (as in *Frankenstein*). First a countryman sets the scene; then the boy Maurice speaks; next, an unnamed 'Traveller' tells his story. The Traveller also repeats the long confessional story he has heard from a sailor's wife, a crucial element in the plot.

Maurice is the story of a boy who is stolen as a two-year-old from his wealthy parents by a woman who has no child of her own and longs for one—the poor sailor's wife. She brings him up lovingly, but he dimly remembers his other life; and when her husband ill treats him, he runs away with the idea of supporting himself by his own efforts. He gets work on a farm, only to find he is not strong enough to be a labourer; he is turned away and reduced to utter wretchedness. For a while he finds refuge with an old fisherman, Barnet. Barnet's wife, old and infirm as she is, reads her Bible to the village children and tells them stories and ballads, *Goody Two-shoes* and 'Chevy Chase'. She is the one person in this poor community who puts the children in touch with the world of the imagination, something outside their meagre lives: a reminder that Mary Shelley was the daughter of a woman who taught children and cared for the condition of the poor. Maurice learns enough to cry over the Bible stories of Joseph and Absalom, which he can distantly relate to his own experience, and to brood on the histories of great men.

But the modest idyll does not last. Both Dame Barnet and her husband die, and their cottage, which Maurice has come to love, is reclaimed. He is destitute again, and saved only when chance brings his true father, who has been searching for him for years, to discover him and restore him to an easier life.

Maurice is given a natural delicacy and goodness which are unaffected by the harsh conditions in which he is placed; he remains honest, well mannered and ready to trust people through all his ordeals. In *Frankenstein* Mary Shelley suggested that nurture, not nature, made the monster bad; it is an important point that impresses readers. Here she seems to be saying something different, by showing a child whose innate goodness survives ill treatment. Maurice does not seek revenge; if anything he becomes gentler and more careful not to be led into cruelty of any kind himself. He has enough understanding even to forgive the woman who stole him from his sleeping nurse.

Although the story is called *Maurice*, this is not the boy's real name; it is one he chooses for himself, to escape detection when he runs away from the sailor and his wife. His real name is Henry. As far as I know, 'Maurice' is used nowhere else in Mary's work, but Henry was one of the most popular names of the period, and she had already given it to Victor Frankenstein's best friend, Henry Clerval. It was also used by her mother Mary Wollstonecraft for the hero of her first novel, and by Shelley in 1819 in his poem *Rosalind and Helen*.[2] This particular Henry, however, becomes attached to the name Maurice. He makes a point of using it when he revisits his poor friends, as though to demonstrate that, even in his days of good fortune, he continues to value his other self and the memories of his other life of poverty. The fact that he is 'Maurice' in the title supports this loyalty to the poor and the past.

Some of Shelley's views surface in the narrative: a shopkeeper is a heartless and 'money loving man', reflecting his dislike of the mercantile classes. And Maurice, like Shelley, disapproves of people who shoot birds; this, and his decision not to catch fish because he wishes neither to destroy nor to give pain to living things, is a straight echo of Shelley's creed. On the other hand, I was stopped short when I came to the passage in which Maurice is sent to Eton by his true father. What about Shelley's famously unhappy experience of being teased and bullied at his old school? True, he also had cheerful memories of summer picnics on the river at Eton, which he revived in 1821 in 'The Boat on the Serchio'. And Laurette's father was another Etonian; perhaps that was enough to make it the obvious school in Mary's mind.[3]

The setting of *Maurice*, the south coast of Devon, appears nowhere else in Mary Shelley's writing. Ilfracombe, Torquay, Sidmouth, Exeter, Teignmouth and Plymouth are all mentioned; she must have been drawing on her memories of the visit she and Shelley made to south Devon in 1815. It was one of the few periods they ever spent on their own, and no doubt memorable for that reason.[4]

Maurice has a formally happy ending, but what struck me most on this first reading was its melancholy. It starts with a funeral and finishes with the crumbling away of the cottage that has sheltered Maurice. The theme is loss: parents lose their child and seek him year after year; another woman longs for a child so badly that she steals him; the child loses his identity when he changes his name, and is passed through the hands of three sets of parents, his natural ones, his foster-mother and the old couple who take him in and then die, leaving him alone and unprotected. Even writing for a child, Mary Shelley could not escape her melancholy.

There was no more time to read or reflect. The Dazzis offered to show us their library, and we followed them eagerly down to the great shuttered and chilly rooms on the *piano nobile*, lined with shelves crammed to the high ceilings with books from four centuries. First editions of *Adonais* and *Epipsychidion* were placed on a table. The packing case in which Mary Shelley's story had lain for so long stood behind a door.

Before leaving, I was taken to meet Signora Dazzi senior. Her English is perfect, and her memories go back to the early years of this century. She told me that she remembered the husband of Laurette very well, and that his white beard had frightened her as a small child. Could she really mean Laurette's husband, I asked myself? She did. Placido Tardy was Laurette's second husband, a Sicilian who became a professor of mathematics in Genoa; when I returned to San Marcello I found many photographs of him in family albums, confirming that he had lived to be ninety-eight, dying in 1914, thirty-four years after his wife.

This first visit to San Marcello was as intense as it was brief. I had to read and respond to *Maurice* fast. At the same time I was made aware that the family's links with what I thought of as the distant past were much closer than I had imagined. Signora Dazzi senior is the great-granddaughter of Laurette's sister Nerina Tighe and her Italian husband, Bartolomeo Cini; we were in the house to which Nerina came as a bride in 1834, and where her friend Claire Clairmont was also made welcome. Here Nerina's son, Gianni Cini, born in 1840, lived until 1930. Outside the windows of Casa Cini, a vast romantic garden partly planned by Nerina still covers the hillside above the house, with grottoes and fountains rising high in the air, a vast stone-built summer house like a small palace, an ice house and a now decaying rose arbour; the yew trees were planted in honour of Nerina's Irish parentage. A later generation put in a sunken tennis court that was flooded in winter for skating, and used the descending water courses to power an early electricity supply. Thoughts of Henry James, Edward Silsbee and *The Aspern Papers* came into my head; and indeed, American collectors had been here in the 1960s and carried off some of the Cini archive. We were the second wave of barbarians, but now the family had no wish to sell anything; rather, a strong desire to retain their precious inheritance and make it accessible to visiting scholars.

I V

Maurice was produced at the high tide of Romanticism. Mary had already published *Frankenstein*, and had also written a startling novel of father–daughter incest, *Matilda*, a few months before *Maurice*; her father, not surprisingly, advised her against publishing *Matilda*.[5] Shelley was in the full flight of his inspiration, dividing his energies between political and lyrical writing. Byron, also in Italy, had published the first two cantos of *Don Juan* and was working on the next. Keats's odes appeared in print that summer of 1820, and Shelley wrote to him in London, inviting him to join them in Italy; and Keats, knowing himself to be dying of tuberculosis, began to plan a journey to Rome.

From Mary Shelley's account of 1820 we know that she and Shelley also read and admired Wordsworth of the older generation of Romantic poets. 'No man ever admired Wordsworth's poetry more—he read it perpetually, and taught others to appreciate its beauties,' she says; and Wordsworth does seem to preside over *Maurice*, with its clear, straightforward language and its setting among simple people and poor labourers and against elemental backgrounds of rocks and trees, cliffs and seashore.[6] Like Wordsworth, Mary delights in describing the moss and lichens ('yellow, green, white & blue') growing on an old thatched roof, and the wallflowers and honeysuckle round a cottage; and she puts in finely observed detail, such as the way the sea becomes invisible to watchers on the beach when the sky turns dark. Her story is entirely unlike the moral and educational tales popular with publishers and parents of that date (and the staple of her father's publishing firm), directing young readers to the social virtues and away from the vices of vanity, lying and cruelty. *Maurice* has no designs on the reader; it simply tells a human tale, and arouses human sympathy.

It is a small work, but touched with the same spirit as the greater ones it stands among. It is the experience of a child who loses his identity and finds himself isolated in a hostile world. For him, the fisherman's cottage of the title becomes a symbol of security and love; and on the last pages, although he is restored to his true place and name, he sees the cottage destroyed by the natural forces of wind, weather and time. The themes of the story are romantic: the vulnerability of childhood, and of parent-hood; displacement, loss, pain, death and rehabilitation; delight in the natural world; and the power of time both to heal and to destroy.

By a stroke of fate, the history of the manuscript of *Maurice* also embodies some of these same romantic themes. The fragile object, lost for many decades, was found again quite unexpectedly, still within the same family to which it was presented. It came to light in a great and ancient house in the Apennines, itself also threatened by time and change, although preserving in its core a unique collection of family papers, books, documents, letters and poems. Through this archive, and through the story, the life of the early nineteenth century has been kept alive; past and present co-exist.

V

To begin with, there is the matter of lost children. You have only to look at the two households involved in Mary Shelley's gift of *Maurice* to Laurette—the Irish household of the Tighes and the English household of the Shelleys—and tally the children lost to each of them to see how Mary's imagination came to settle on such a theme.

The Shelley household in 1820 consisted of three adults, the poet Percy Bysshe, his wife Mary and her stepsister Claire Clairmont, all in their twenties; with the addition of the Shelleys' infant son Percy Florence. The Tighe household consisted of two adults in their mid-forties, George Tighe and his consort, known either as Lady Mountcashell (her real name) or Mrs Mason (her assumed name), and their two young daughters, ten-year-old Laurette, or Laura, and four-year-old Nerina. On the surface, they were two complete and happy families; but nothing was as it appeared. Margaret Mount-cashell had seven older children who were lost to her. On separating from her husband she had been forced to give them up; the law gave her no right to them at all. Her family with George Tighe was a second start, begun in her mid-thirties; and Laurette and Nerina were brought up to understand that they 'could never expect to be acknowledged by any of their mother's relations'.[7]

The Shelleys were haunted in the same way. Ianthe and Charles, Shelley's children by Harriet, were being brought up by guardians appointed by the Court of Chancery; they were five and three years old when he left England. The three children born to him and Mary in 1815, 1816 and 1817 had died one after another, the first within a few weeks of her birth, Clara aged one in Venice and William aged three in Rome. The next child missing from the household was Claire's three-year-old daughter Allegra, and it is Allegra's fate that was most agonizing during 1820. Claire had given Allegra up to Byron, her father, believing this to be in the best interest of her child, with a promise that she should be allowed to visit her. Now Byron was denying Claire visits and failing to keep her informed of Allegra's whereabouts or health; for six months in 1819 no word of any kind came from him or his servants.

There is still one more child to be noticed. Elena Adelaide Shelley was registered by Shelley in Naples early in 1819 as his own and Mary's newborn daughter, and—almost unbelievably—left in Naples when they set off for Rome, to be collected later. She was not Mary's child, and she was never collected, because in the spring of 1820 she fell ill, and in June she died. She is the seventh lost child of the Shelley household.[8]

When you consider that each family counted seven lost children, Mary's use of a child stolen from its parents as the central figure in her story begins to look like an allusion, conscious or not, to the grief, fear, remorse and mourning of both families. Another likely element was her own history as a child who had lost her mother at birth and acquired a disliked stepmother. Claire too had never known her father, or even his identity. Shelley was estranged from his family; Margaret Mountcashell from hers. To the righteous in England, the Tighes and the Shelleys appeared as the morally dispossessed, taking refuge together in Italy; to themselves, as parents and as children, they must have felt a peculiarly vulnerable group.

V I

After I read *Maurice* I determined to find out everything I could about Laurette, her parents and her history. To begin with, how did an Irish family come to be settled in Italy in 1820? Their story takes us back into the eighteenth century, and there is comedy as well as tragedy in this piece of domestic history. Laurette's mother began life as the Honourable Margaret King, daughter of a viscount, later an earl. In 1786, when she was fourteen, she had a governess who impressed her deeply: Mary Wollstonecraft, whose 'mind appeared more noble & her understanding more cultivated than any others I had known', and who went on to write her great statement of women's rights and to be known as a supporter of radical social reform.[9] So the families were already linked a generation earlier. Margaret King approved and followed many of her governess's views, even after she became a countess through her marriage to the young Earl of Mountcashell.

She thought she could rule her husband, and found she could not. Their politics were opposed, he a Tory, she a republican and democrat, like her governess. She was a supporter—necessarily discreet—of the rising of the United Irishmen in 1798, and was grieved by its failure. When this was followed by the English government's imposition of the Act of Union, dooming Ireland to impotence and aggravating its poverty, she despaired for her country.

She was also dissatisfied with her personal situation. She wanted to do more than give birth to a child every eighteen months and preside over her husband's great house on St Stephen's Green in Dublin or his country mansion in County Cork. She was interested in writing—had written a couple of political pamphlets—and in the study of medicine, although it was closed to women.

LEFT: *Margaret, Countess Mountcashell*

BELOW: *Stephen, Second Earl Mountcashell*

In 1801 she persuaded her husband to take a continental tour. The ending of the war between England and France made travel easier than it had been for a decade, and although she and the Earl agreed on few points, he had no objection to spending his rents on a fashionable Grand Tour. They set off in the style required of their rank and fortune, with a couple of coaches, a woman friend to keep the countess company, four servants and five children and a tutor and governess. First they went to London, where they stayed for two months in the autumn of 1801. Margaret could not visit her former governess, since she had died in childbirth in 1797, but she could and did call on her widower, William Godwin; they had previously met in Dublin in 1800, and then exchanged letters.

Godwin and Margaret Mountcashell shared an interest in child-rearing and education, and she knew he was struggling to care for Mary Wollstonecraft's two daughters, four-year-old Mary and seven-year-old Fanny. 'It would give me great pleasure to see your two little girls,' she wrote in advance of her visit; and it seems likely that the first meeting between Margaret Mountcashell and Mary Godwin (later Shelley) took place at this time.[10] Godwin described his aristocratic friend as handsome but also brawny, with 'gigantic arms, which she commonly folds, naked and exposed almost up to the shoulders'.[11] She did not care about fashion; but she was clever and well read, with the self-confidence bordering on imperiousness of an aristocrat, in spite of her democratic opinions. And she was very tall, with brilliant blue eyes; altogether a striking creature.

At the end of November the Mountcashells proceeded

to Paris, where they visited the sights and were received by the Bonapartes. They gave receptions for all their new acquaintances, from Talleyrand, Lafayette and the painter David to Charles James Fox, Tom Paine, John Kemble, Amelia Opie, Thomas Holcroft and Helen Maria Williams, many of whom had been friends of Mary Wollstonecraft.[12]

During this long stay in Paris, Margaret gave birth to another son, Richard. In September 1802 they travelled on to Italy, where, after none months in Naples, Rome and Florence, Margaret fell ill. By the time she was better, war had broken out again between England and France, blocking their homeward journey. They returned to Rome; she was pregnant again. This would be her eighth child, one having died in infancy; but now in Rome her life changed course. A sheaf of poems in her hand, some inscribed 'Rome 1804 M. M.', show her overwhelmed by a new experience: she had fallen in love. She writes of a 'bright dream', of 'romantic visions', of a man who has 'taught my heart unknown delights', and 'made me prove each fine degree / From joyful love to maddening jealousy'. 'Would thou coudst feel a passion strong as mine,' she urges him. 'Beloved beyond existence, health or fame.'[13]

The man she addressed was George Tighe. He was at first a friend of her husband. They had the common background of the Anglo-Irish Ascendancy, and Tighe was an Etonian; but he was not rich, had no title or great position in society and had inherited as many debts as acres of Irish land. He was, however, a poet and a classical scholar. He had served as an officer in the mid-1790s, when so many young men took commissions in the militia raised to defend Britain from the French threat; then, finding himself heir to his father's estates, and at something of a loose end, he decided to see Italy. In Rome he joined a literary society, the Arcadi Pastori, of which Goethe was a member, and dreamed of the simple life.

Some of his poems have survived, too, in which he addresses Margaret by the Petrarchan name of Laura. His Laura was a formidable mistress, four years older than him and a countess, rich and highly placed in society, as well as pregnant by her husband. Their mutual absorption was noticed by the Anglo-Irish community in Rome, and Lord Mountcashell's jealousy was aroused. At this stage Margaret did not intend to put her marriage at risk. After the birth of her third daughter, Elizabeth, in August 1804, she set off with her husband and family for the long return journey to Ireland.

France being enemy territory, their path lay through Germany; and in Germany Margaret had second thoughts about continuing homewards. The Earl went ahead with the older boys, and she remained with her three daughters and Richard. By her own account, she had decided to return to the south for her health before eventually returning to Ireland. She said nothing about Tighe, but it is clear from Tighe's papers and her own later statement that he joined her in Germany. They wandered from one place to another; there are mentions of Dresden, Munich, Ratisbon, Carslbad, Eger and Jena. The fact that Napoleon's armies were fighting all over the territory must have made things difficult and sometimes dangerous, even for a countess. In October 1805 the French defeated the Austrians at Ulm; it was the same month in which Nelson defeated the French navy at

Trafalgar. In December, Napoleon crushed the Austrians and the Russians at Austerlitz, and in October 1806 he did the same to the Prussian army at Jena.

Throughout this period Margaret and George Tighe were in Germany. She sent her two elder daughters and Richard back to England from Dresden in the summer of 1806, keeping baby Eliza with her. At this point Lord Mountcashell became angry and wrote 'ordering me to return to England immediately to sign articles of separation & to give up my youngest child to him, threatening in case of non-compliance to stop my remittances & to find means of taking the child by force'.[14]

His threats prompted her to write to her lawyer in Ireland, asking 'whether Lord M can take her [baby] from me by force (that is whether the law would authorize such a step) at her age, and whether I have only dreamt that a mother can keep her child with her in spite of the father till seven years old?'[15] She was prepared to fight for her youngest child, and said her heart ached when she thought of the others; and that she had no wish for a separation, 'as I should endure much for the sake of our children and indeed have done so for some years'. She was also careful to tell the lawyer, 'I hope soon to be in French territories (either Italy or France I am not sure which) and suppose it will not be in the power of anyone to molest me there—In perfect solitude and tranquillity I hope to recover my health—I shall seek no society.'[16]

Lord Mountcashell must have reasoned that she was effectively separating herself from him, and probably with her lover; and since he had control of the money, he could dictate terms. For the moment, she and Tighe remained in Germany, living on credit. She later told her daughters that she followed medical lectures at Jena, disguising herself in men's clothes to gain admittance. Jena was renowned for its democratic student body, its openness to new ideas, a teaching faculty that included Hegel and Schiller, and an enlightened ruler who was Goethe's patron. A poem by Tighe describing the battle of Jena suggests he was there to witness the event.

Yet Tighe was in two minds about their future. One of her poems, written in Dresden in 1806, ends,

> Why thought I madly of an equal flame,
> When dying embers only seem to glow;
> Where the exhausted spirit knows the name
> Of Love; but passions' force forgets to know?
> Vesuvius' self no longer is the same,
> And soon the liquid fire must cease to flow.[17]

If Tighe was no longer a Vesuvius, two poems of his, written in Jena in September of the same year—just before the battle—give some account of his private conflict. The first appears to be ending his relationship with his Laura:

> Yes, Laura, our summer is o'er
> And chill blows the heart-piercing blast;
> Alas must we also deplore
> That the Summer of Love it is past?
> . . . Thy fancys, caprices, & fears
> No emotions but anger impart;
> And the storms of reproaches & tears
> Have wither'd this desolate heart.

But the second, 'Palinode' (which means 'recantation'), is intended to reassure:

> Yes Laura our summer is o'er
> But let us not mourn for the past;
> If the blossoms of Love are no more
> Let Friendship's fair ever-green last.
>
> . . . No more shall thy fancys & fears
> Emotions of anger impart:
> Oh come let me wipe off those tears.
> And press thee once more to my Heart.[18]

Reassured by Tighe, Margaret still had to face the battle for custody of her children; and, having no legal rights, she soon lost the youngest along with the others. As a married woman she possessed nothing, and her brothers did not offer to assist her, so the Earl was able to force her to comply by applying financial pressure. In 1807 she went to London and then Dublin, which is probably where she handed over three-year-old Eliza. She never saw her again.

Her friend Lady Moira said she thought the Earl intended a divorce; and went on, 'I am convinced of her [Margaret's] uprightness and real purity of mind—but her minor errors as to judgement I cannot close my eyes upon.' Her 'frank & generous disposition' sometimes misled her, and although Lady Moira would not join with her 'enemies and maligners', she had harsh things to say about Tighe. 'I am grieved to learn . . . that Mr Tighe, once Ld MC's friend & favorite till he assumed &

professed a jealousy of him, is a man of insignificance in every mental quality, & of a vanity to make a parade of being the cause of such a disagreement.'[19]

There was no divorce, but the lovers were ostracized by Dublin and London society alike.

Margaret did, however, renew her friendship with William Godwin, now married to a Mrs Clairmont and running their Juvenile Library in Holborn. At the end of the year they published Lady Mountcashell's *Stories of Old Daniel*: the book became one of the Juvenile Library's biggest successes, went into many editions and was followed by *Continuation of the Stories of Old Daniel*. It was not, of course, put out under Lady Mountcashell's name; she had in any case stopped using it. According to what she later told Claire Clairmont, this was at the insistence of Tighe; and since he did not want her to take his name either, she chose to be called 'Mrs Mason', the name of the good governess in the children's stories by her own well-remembered governess, Mary Wollstonecraft.

Five years after the birth of Eliza Mountcashell, Mrs Mason bore a daughter to George Tighe, on 19 July 1809. The long gap may be a tribute to her medical knowledge; it certainly suggests they deliberated before allowing themselves a child to replace those lost to her. Anna Laura Georgina was always known as Laurette or Laura, her name surely an allusion to the Petrarchan poems her father wrote for her mother. Without a divorce, Mrs Mason and Tighe could not marry; and it appears that the birth took place in Vienna, since Tighe had money sent to him there in 1810, and Laurette's obituary states that was where she was born. They were back in England by 1812; but when the Earl agreed to allow Margaret £800 a year, and to settle the debts she had run up abroad, they decided to start another life in Italy.

In 1814 Europe was at peace again after the defeat of Napoleon. In March the Allies entered Paris, in May Louis XVIII followed, and in August Tighe, Mrs Mason and Laurette left England and travelled to Italy through France. Pisa was chosen as a quiet town with a university and a good medical school, sea and the mountains at hand, and not so far south as to be unbearably hot in summer. It is also close to Florence; but Mrs Mason would always avoid Florence for fear of encountering English visitors. The Tighes took a house south of the River Arno, Casa Silva, and there in Pisa their second daughter was born on 20 June 1815. She was always known as Nerina, although her formal name was Catherine Elizabeth Raniera. Margaret watched over the second family with the most anxious attention; Laurette slept either in her room or next door to it, and Margaret was unwilling to be separated from her.

Tighe remained a reader and occasional writer, and between them they collected an impressive library. He also took up agricultural studies, with a particular interest in cultivating potatoes, not at that time much appreciated in Tuscany; in the family he was known as 'Tatty'. Friends at home got him a Civil List pension of £400 a year, and he had another £200 from his Irish rents, so that by local standards Mr Tighe and Mrs Mason were rich. She continued to be interested in medicine and did good work among the poor of Pisa, dispensing medicines and good advice.

He was a loving father, but both he and Mrs Mason

ABOVE: *Lady Mountcashell, from a physionotrace engraving made when
she was in Paris with her husband in 1802*
BELOW: *Pisa in an 1818 engraving, where Lady Mountcashell—now calling
herself 'Mrs Mason'—settled with George Tighe*

were ambivalent about what they had done, as his account makes clear: 'after many storms we now enjoy as much happiness as falls to the lot of most people. But let it be remembered that this has been gained after many years of doubt and anxiety & that generally speaking an illegitimate connection is as miserable as it is criminal.'[20] She too ended a note written for her daughters in 1818 with the warning words quoted earlier, insisting that they could never expect to be acknowledged by any of her relations. Her statement shows how absolute was the social rejection brought by her adultery, and how entirely she accepted it; in the same note she wrote, 'Misfortune must ever be the lot of those who transgress the laws of social life.'[21] More cheerfully, she welcomed her escape from the aristocracy and her new position 'in that middle rank of life for which I always sighed'.[22]

Neither she nor Tighe returned to England, and at what point Laurette and Nerina became aware of the existence of their seven half-brothers and sisters is not clear. They grew up speaking and writing English and Italian with equal fluency, but never visited England or Ireland; and when Laurette decided to become a novelist and essayist she chose to write in Italian.

V I I

The year in which George Tighe and Margaret Mount-cashell left England for Italy, 1814, was also the year in which Mary Godwin ran away from their parents' house in Holborn and crossed the Channel with the poet Shelley and her stepsister Claire. The three of them—the girls hardly more than children—had worked themselves into a state in which they were oblivious of everything but their mutual intoxication. They made their first trip together across France, through Switzerland and back down the Rhine. They returned to England to face severe difficulties. Both Shelley's wife Harriet and Mary were now pregnant, and he was pursued by creditors. Harriet bore a son, Charles, who lived. Mary's child, a premature daughter, died at a few weeks. A summary must do for the well-known facts that follow. In 1816 Mary had a son, William; very soon after this Claire entangled herself with Byron. If she was silly, he was careless; she pursued him and was soon pregnant. She remained, however, a part of the Shelley household. In 1816 they summered with Byron on the shores of Lac Léman, where the idea for *Frankenstein* came to Mary. That autumn saw the suicides of Fanny and Harriet.

Claire's daughter Allegra was loved by Shelley as much as his own children, and William and Allegra were playmates in their shared household; indeed, despite Mary's resentment at Claire's presence, the children of the double family were equally loved by them all. Mary's daughter Clara was born in September 1817, and early in 1818 they all set off for Italy together. Shelley hoped his health would improve in a southern climate, and the plan was that the Shelleys' Swiss maid Elise should take Allegra to Byron in Venice. He had agreed to be responsible for her upbringing, and, painful as this was to Claire, she believed it would give her child the best chance in life, as the acknowledged daughter of a peer. 'I have sent you

LEFT: *A posthumous portrait of Mary Shelley by Reginald Easton*
BELOW: *Percy Bysshe Shelley, painted by Amelia Curran in 1819*

my child because I love her too well to keep her,' she wrote to him.[23] Heartbreaking words.

Allegra, fifteen months old and never before parted from her mother, was sent to Byron in Venice in April 1818. As the summer went by, Claire became worried about her, getting scant news from Elise, but she eventually learned that she had been put into the care of the British Consul, Richard Hoppner and his Swiss wife. Mrs Hoppner wrote coolly to Mary Shelley about Allegra wetting her bed and losing her gaiety of spirit.[24] As the acknowledged daughter of a peer she was important; her unhappiness as a child was not. In August Claire asked Shelley to take her to Venice to see Allegra. Mary stayed behind at Bagni di Lucca, but when Shelley met Byron he told him the whole family party was with him. Byron allowed Allegra to go to her mother, and lent them his villa at Este; and Shelley had to send for Mary to come at all speed to make his story stand up. Mary set off; baby Clara was not well, and the journey did not improve her condition. After two weeks at Este, they decided to take her to a doctor in Venice; by the time they reached Venice, Clara was dying.

Clara was buried, with Claire looking after Allegra and William. She was allowed to keep Allegra with her until the end of October, when Byron insisted on having her back. The Shelleys then travelled south with Claire. Mary was sunk in depression; perhaps she held Shelley and Claire partly responsible for the death of Clara. Shelley was also depressed.

As we have seen, Shelley registered the birth of another daughter to himself and Mary that winter in Naples, Elena Adelaide, giving her birth date as 27

LEFT: *Claire Clairmont, painted by Amelia Curran in 1819*
BELOW: *Lord Byron, c. 1818, in an engraving after a painting by G. H. Harlow*

Two of the children whose loss lies behind the story of Maurice: William Shelley *(left) and Claire Clairmont's daughter Allegra* (below)

December 1818. Mary appears to have known nothing about her at this stage, and no one has yet given a satisfactory explanation of her parentage.[25] The Shelleys moved to Rome, leaving Elena in the care of a humble family, and intending to return. In Rome they suffered their most devastating blow yet when three-year-old William died after a few days' illness. Mary had now lost all three of her children. As she wrote at the beginning of her new journal in August 1819, 'to have won, & then cruelly have lost, the associations of four years is not an accident to which the human mind can bend without much suffering'.[26] Her depression darkened, and never entirely lifted again; Shelley spoke of it as a form of torture which she inflicted on him as well as on herself.

Claire grieved with Mary and Shelley; and she had a further cause for misery in Byron's refusal to allow visits or to keep her informed about Allegra's whereabouts or health. She grew frightened for her daughter.

The only gleam of hope among them was that Mary was pregnant again. Her child was due in November, and they agreed that Florence would be a good place for the birth. On their way to Florence they stopped in Pisa and took a letter of introduction from Godwin to Lady Mountcashell—or rather, Mrs Mason; and in this way Mary Wollstonecraft's pupil became the friend of the daughter Mary Wollstonecraft never knew.

With such links the two families were well disposed towards one another. Friendship sprang up at once. The Tighes had their library to share with the Shelleys; like them, they devoted much of their time to reading classical and modern literature. Tighe and Margaret were poets and writers, as the Shelleys were. Both groups considered themselves democrats, republicans and free-thinkers; the Tighes had a supply of subversive political pamphlets from England, and there were borrowings and lendings on both sides. Finally, both families were refugees from the intense disapproval of their compatriots.

Claire later described Mrs Mason as possessed of a 'lofty and calm presence', and always cheerful—unlike both Byron and Shelley, she added; and Laurette and Nerina were delighted to have new friends in Mary, Claire and Shelley, who responded warmly to them.[27] The Shelleys went on to Florence, from which Mary wrote to Mrs Mason praising Laurette's 'simplicity and frankness', and Mrs Mason wrote back that Laurette wanted to know whether 'that lady had yet *made her child*'.[28] After the birth on 11 November, Mrs Mason wrote congratulating them, with messages from her daughters: 'Your kind remembrance of Laurette flatters her parents extremely—she is rejoiced to hear of the birth of the little child, which she longs to see, and desires me to tell you to come here soon.' Laurette was also practising the pianoforte with more than usual attention in hopes of 'amazing' the musical Claire, and 'my little Nerina often asks *"Dove son quegli Signori Inglesi?"*'[29]

Mary and Shelley's child, Percy Florence, was born without trouble. He was small but vigorous, and Mary fed him herself. It was Shelley who grumbled about his own health, with a pain in his side—that standard nineteenth-century complaint—and occasional fevers. They did not stop him from writing: the 'Ode to the West Wind' was composed in Florence that autumn. Then the weather turned bitter—*scellerato* and *stravagantissimo,* Mrs Mason called it—and the winter of 1819/20 became the coldest Tuscany had experienced for seventy years. Tighe was also afflicted with rheumatism, and kept to his bed in Pisa. In spite of the weather, and difficulties with servants, when Mary's baby was two months old she invited Laurette to come and stay in Florence. Mrs Mason's reply, dated 14 January, was an apologetic refusal: 'You will perhaps think me very weak when I confess to you that, accustomed as I am to have her always sleeping in my room or the next to it, I fear when on wakening in the night should recollect that she was far from me, it would at this moment have too strong an effect on my shattered nerves.'[30] When Laurette was older she might stay with them, but for the moment she could not be parted from her. The serenity and good spirits noted by Claire were evidently not the whole picture.

On 26 January 1820, after what Claire described myste-riously as a 'half baptism' for Percy Florence, the Shelleys moved by boat and carriage to Pisa, where they took a house. 'Walk with—S—about the town seeking Lodg-ings. Call on Mrs Mason and the pretty Laurette—The Weather most exquisitely warm & sunny—Read an Irish pamphlet,' wrote Claire in her diary the next day.[31] After this she was in and out of Casa Silva, becoming more intimate with the family than Mary and acting like an elder sister to Laurette. She walked and rode with her on the banks of the Arno, took her to enjoy the Carnival fes-tivities and went with her to the opera several times, to hear Rossini's *Cenerentola* on one occasion and the renowned soprano Angelica Catalini on another. Mr Tighe was less in evidence; Claire did not meet him until the end of April. Meanwhile baby Percy caught a light case of measles from four-year-old Nerina, and both quickly recovered. Mrs Mason advised Mary about the hiring of servants and the importance of keeping calm while nursing a baby; she also expressed her admiration of *Frankenstein*. She told Claire stories of her past, and discussed politics with Shelley. She even wrote an admiring humorous poem about him, 'Twelve Cogent Reasons for Supposing P. B. Sh—ll—y to be the D—v—l Inc—rn—t—', listing his devilish qualities—sensitivity, tolerance, linguistic ability, charity to the poor, a preference for justice rather than wealth [the text appears here as the Appendix, pp. 155–159]. He in turn wrote 'The Sensitive Plant', which some think alluded to Mrs Mason's garden.

That summer of 1820, the Shelleys were moving between Pisa, the nearby spa of San Giuliano, and Livorno, where they were lent a house by English friends, the Gisbornes. They enjoyed the sea coast, with its dramatically changing skies and myrtle hedges full of fireflies. Shelley wrote his 'To a Skylark' at Livorno. He turned to satire, with an eye on English politics and George IV's undignified struggle to rid himself of Queen Caroline; the verse drama *Swellfoot the Tyrant*, with its chorus of pigs, was the result. He also began a prose *Philosophical View of Reform*, in which he attacked the merchant aristocracy of England and urged the poor to protest. Mary got on with research into the history of a prince of the neighbouring town of Lucca for a historical novel, *Valperga*.

At the end of April, Claire wrote to Byron in Ravenna, asking to have Allegra for the summer—she had not seen

Livorno

her for eighteen months—and pointing out that the child's health had already suffered from the climate and conditions of eastern Italy. She ended her letter, 'Though I can scarcely believe it possible you will refuse my just requests yet I beg you to remember that I did not part with her at Milan until I had received your formal & explicit declaration that I should see my child at proper intervals.' The postscript reads, 'Pray kiss my dear child many times for me.'[32] Byron sent a roughly worded message that he would not let Allegra go to the Shelley household, citing its bad record for child mortality (nor, he added, did he wish her to 'be taught to believe that there is no Deity'). Claire wrote again, offering to take Allegra on her own: 'My letter is an appeal to your Justice . . . I have exerted myself to remove your objections &

my claim is bare & obvious . . . I can find no words to express my gratitude to all those who have been kind to my Allegra.'[33]

On 4 May she drafted another letter, urging him not to put Allegra into a convent, as he now threatened. So the months went by, Claire pleading, Byron ignoring her pleas. He could not stomach her having any claim on his attention or their child; besides this, he was absorbed in his love affair with Countess Teresa Guiccioli. Mary was impatient with Claire, and still jealous of her share of Shelley's love, so they quarrelled regularly; but she could not be unaware of her suffering. And for all Mary's ambivalence about Claire, the shadow of Allegra falls as closely on her story of a child ill used, and longed for by a loving parent, as the memory of her own lost William.

The tangle of tragedies knots tighter. Shelley heard that Elena was ill in Naples, and wrote to their friends the Gisbornes saying he expected her to die; her memory would torture him, he said. The Shelleys' former maid Elise and her Italian husband began a blackmail attempt, alleging that Elena was Claire's child by Shelley. With the help of a lawyer, he put off the blackmail attempt. Then came news of Elena's death.

None of the Shelley household could be content, but Claire at least had her consoling friendship with Mrs Mason and her family. In July she was reading Mrs Mason's *Continuation of the Stories of Old Daniel*.[34] She spent Laurette's eleventh birthday with her in Pisa; the next day they rode to Livorno to spend the day with Mary, setting off at five in the morning, and making an expedition along the coast. This is the likely spark for Mary's story for Laurette, set on a different coast. Three weeks later Laurette was presented with *Maurice*, perhaps as a late birthday present.[35]

The manuscript is clearly a fair copy, with very few second thoughts. At some point Mary made another copy, which she submitted to her father; his rejection was the last of it as far as she was concerned, nor is there any mention of it in any papers of Laurette's that I have seen. But there can be no doubt that Laurette prized it and kept it among her treasures. As she grew up, she began to write herself; later she asked advice and help of Mary Shelley, whose example and success as a writer, alongside that of her mother, encouraged her to follow the same path.

VIII

The two families maintained their friendship over the next two years. Mary's letters remain cheerless. It could hardly have been otherwise. She was arranging a gravestone for William in Rome, tending her remaining son, and working at her novel. In her spare time she took Greek lessons. Claire, advised by Mrs Mason, went to Florence, lodging with the family of Dr Antonio Bojti, physician and friend to the Grand Duke Ferdinand; his German mother-in-law gave Claire German lessons, while Claire taught the Bojti children English. She was industrious but could not be happy, and her diary records her hopes and dreams of being allowed to see her child again, and her perpetual disappointment.

News of the death of Keats in Rome brought sorrow to them all. Shelley wrote his lament *Adonais*, in which he seems to be mourning his own fate as much as that of Keats. Missing Claire, he interested himself in other women, first Emilia Viviani, kept in a convent by her parents, then Jane Williams, who arrived with her lover in Pisa in 1821.

In March 1821 Claire learnt that Byron, breaking another promise, had placed Allegra in a convent. She was the youngest child to be admitted. When Shelley visited the convent without telling Claire, he was worried enough by what he saw to ask Mary, 'Do you think Mrs Mason could be prevailed upon to *propose* to take charge of her?' He added, 'I fear not,' and no more was heard of the idea.[36] And although he called Mr Tighe 'seriously my friend', Shelley was now of two minds about Mrs Mason, whom he described as annoyingly perverse, perhaps because she had too much influence over Claire and encouraged her to seek an independent life.

When Byron came to Pisa in November 1821, he and Shelley drew close again. Shelley found his charm irresistible, but he did not introduce him to the Tighes, and Tighe is said to have referred to Byron as Bluebeard, or Henry VIII. Claire, in Florence, became desperate about Allegra's isolation from both her parents. She thought of kidnapping her, and later said Lady Mountcashell had offered to give her the means to emigrate to Australia with her child. The Shelleys urged her to continue to accept the convent placement in the hope that Byron would presently lose interest in his daughter. 'Nothing remains constant, something may happen—things cannot be worse,' wrote Mary to Claire.[37] If she meant to be kind in advising Claire, assuring her that the convent was healthy, she also conceded that Byron's 'hypocrisy & cruelty rouse one's soul from its depths' and that 'as soon as possible A. ought to be taken out of the hands of one as remorseless as he is unprincipled'.[38] Yet the Shelleys did nothing.

Claire's last plea to Byron was made in February 1822. 'My dear Friend, I conjure you do not make the world dark to me, as if my Allegra were dead. In the happiness her sight will cause me I shall gain restoration and strength to enable me to bear the mortifications and displeasures to which a poor and unhappy person is exposed in the world. I wish you every happiness.'[39] She got no answer, and in April she expressed her disquiet about Allegra's health to Mary: 'I fear she is sick.'[40] Within two weeks, her child was dead.[41]

Claire responded to the news with the dignity of someone who has nothing more to fear. A few weeks later Shelley was dead too, drowned while sailing off the coast. Mary and Claire were both now without protection or money, since Shelley's allowance stopped, there was doubt about the legality of his will, and without a will his son Charles was his heir. Claire set off almost at once for Vienna, where her brother was, to seek work, only to find that her connection with Shelley and Byron made her suspect to Metternich's police; no one would employ her, and she fell seriously ill. Hearing of this, Mrs Mason wrote to Byron to suggest he might settle a small annuity on the mother of Allegra, since Claire was 'now destitute of the means of subsistence; chiefly in consequence of the unfortunate connection which permits the tongue of malice to join her humble name with one of high celebrity'.[42] She wrote politely, but she considered it a 'claim not of charity but of justice', echoing the words of Mary Wollstonecraft: 'It is justice, not charity, that is wanting in the world.'[43] Byron refused, and rudely. At this Mrs Mason wrote to Mary Shelley, 'I will read no more of his poetry, for I shall always think of him as "a counterfeit & no true man"—He may roll in riches & get drunk with fame, but he will never be happy.'[44]

Claire had to fend for herself, and went as far afield as Russia to work as a governess. Mary took her son to England. She refused to hand him over to Shelley's father, and was allowed only a pittance; so she wrote to occupy her mind, but also to make a living. The death of Shelley's son Charles in 1826 made Percy heir to the baronetcy, but he did not inherit until 1844, when both Mary and Claire benefited from Shelley's will at last.

Byron went his way to Greece, and died at Missolonghi in April 1824. On hearing of his death, Mrs Mason wrote to Mary Shelley, 'Your account of Lord B's sufferings make me pity him . . . Do you remember my last letter to Lord B. & what I said of "the sleepless bed of pain"? It appears to have been prophetic.' She added, 'I regret having written it, as it was to no purpose—but my motive was good.'[45]

I X

Respectability overtook Mrs Mason at last in 1826, when she married Tighe, three years after the death of Mountcashell; but since the girls remained illegitimate, their mother remained suspicious of English prudery. 'For many reasons I have made it a rule to receive no English,'

*Lady Mountcashell in 1835, shortly before her
death, painted by her sister Diana*

she wrote to Mary in 1827, adding that 'Nerina is quite an
Italian ... indeed so is Laurette also.'[46] Marriage did not
improve relations between Tighe and his consort. He dis-
approved of the way in which she took the girls out into
Pisan society, and accused her of spending all her money
without consulting him. She took little notice of these
complaints, continuing serenely along her own course,
and they occupied separate houses for much of the time,
lunching *en famille* on Sundays, when she would have 'a
respectable plumb pudding' ready for him.[47] The girls
loved him and adored her.

She set an impressive example for them, keeping up
her medical work among the poor; a shelf of books wit-

nessed to her success as a writer, not only *Old Daniel* but *Advice to Young Mothers* 'by a Grandmother' (1823), which was translated into several languages. Her novel *The Sisters of Nansfield* was also published in England in 1824 and translated into Italian; but she had no great opinion of it herself, and her story of two sisters in a country village, complete with curate and silly old ladies, reads like Jane Austen drained of everything that makes her worth reading. More brilliantly, she organized a literary society in 1827, the Accademia dei Lunatici, of which she was president and Laurette secretary. Members had to swear they were lunatics upon joining, and they read humorous papers and poems. Most were young men from the university; the whimsicality may have provided a cover for political interests at a time when Tuscany was ruled by an Austrian archduke. Many of the members went on to take part in the struggle for a united Italy.

When Claire arrived back in Pisa in 1831, the Accademia de Lunatici was still going, but it did not last much longer. Claire was invited to live with the family. 'Nothing can equal Mrs Mason's kindness to me. Hers is the only house except my mother's, in which all my life I have ever felt at home. With her I am as her child,' she wrote to Mary.[48] Although Mrs Mason pressed money on her, Claire promptly passed it on to Mary, and earned her own living as a daily governess in an English family. She also resumed the role of elder sister to Laurette and Nerina; the great topic had become Laurette's wish to marry a man everyone else considered disastrously unsuitable. Laurette's portrait, done at this time, shows her with dark hair in a great elaborate pile on top of her head, and

The Tighe sisters, c. 1830: Laurette (left), *for whom* Maurice *was written, and Nerina* (below), *whose descendants preserved the manuscript*

a low-cut dress with a tightly belted waist and huge puff sleeves. Her eyes were blue like her mother's, and she was much admired.

Adolphe Dominique Galloni d'Istria, the man so keen to marry her, claimed to be a prince, but his file in the French diplomatic archives makes it clear he was not.[49] His father was an infantry officer in Corsica, and young Galloni entered the French consular service in 1830 through the patronage of a Count Pozzo de Borgo. He was *'sujet à de violentes colères'*, according to his employers, and wooed Laurette with passion and, in Mary's account, 'at the dagger's point'.[50] He got himself posted to Genoa in 1831 with the plea that he was hoping to marry into a family resident in Italy, and he was determined to succeed. Laurette's parents were united in their horror at the prospect of such a husband. Tighe wrote to her objecting to the proposed marriage, 'of which I was casually informed as a circumstance likely to take place, without the slightest reference to my wishes or opinions', and continued, 'I now beg leave to repeat that nobody in their senses could properly give their consent to such a marriage'.[51] Mrs Mason also 'tried every means to hinder it', according to Claire. 'She cannot disguise her dislike of Galloni—he having nearly killed her with his scenes . . . It is the first time the mother and daughter were ever divided in opinion.'[52] Nerina hated Galloni too, foresaw a cruel fate for her sister, and declared that patriotism was a better cause for women than matrimony. She poured out her thoughts to Claire, after which the two of them would laugh 'at the ridiculous figures human beings cut in struggling all their might and main against a destiny which forces millions and millions of planets on their way and against which all struggling is useless.'[53]

Claire described Galloni at various times as a beast, and as having 'vulgarity of the senses very strongly marked in his countenance, and strong passions'; but Laurette was set on the marriage, and it took place in November 1832.[54] In Claire's account again, the bride came home shortly after the wedding 'pale worn and sad' and took to her bed for three weeks. Then she returned to Genoa and insisted she was happy, 'but as she would not confess it, were it otherwise, we have doubts on the subject'.[55] In the autumn of 1833 Claire mentioned that 'Laurette is in the family way—to Mrs M's horror'; if she was, she lost the baby.[56]

Nerina's marriage was the happy one, in 1834, to one of the Lunatici, Bartolomeo Cini, 'the best & most delightful Pistoian', in Mary's words.[57] The Cinis were an old landowning family, able and respected; Nerina's father-in-law set up a paper mill in San Marcello, providing jobs for the people as well as profits for the family. Mrs Mason approved thoroughly; but her health was failing, and she lived only to see Nerina's first child born. She died in January 1835 and was buried in the Protestant cemetery at Livorno. Neither her married name of Tighe nor her chosen name of Mrs Mason was on the gravestone, which read 'Margaret Jane Countess of Mount Cashell'. Tighe must have decided it was after all the most appropriate form for his consort of thirty years.

Nerina had become a Catholic on marrying; Laurette was an atheist, as Claire explained to Mary, complaining that she was expected to console Laurette for the loss of her mother by insisting on the immortality of the soul, which she did not believe in herself. She pitied Laurette's grief, the more so since 'it is now clear to every body, she does not love her husband one particle'.[58]

Glimpses of Laurette's life and opinions appear in the letters she wrote her father in the last two years of his life—he survived his wife for only that long. At first she followed Galloni wherever his consular appointments took him, and, when he was sent to Majorca in 1836, they travelled by way of Barcelona, arriving in mid-revolution; Laura described the city illuminated after the shooting of the Governor-General, and watched from her hotel window as his body was dragged through the streets to be burnt, to shouts of triumph from the people. The next day troops were brought in, and the Gallonis set sail for Palma. She detested Majorca and its people, finding the nobility profligate and the rest vulgar, and shut herself indoors: 'I retrench myself in my fortress,' she wrote.[59] 'I lead a sort of school girls life having set myself a task for almost every hour.'[60] The tasks were learning Spanish and reading Roman history; she also read Byron, Shakespeare, Dante and, as soon as her Spanish was good enough, Cervantes. Her programme reminds you of Mary Shelley's reading habits; but in the evenings Laurette's husband taught her to shoot, and she boasted that she rarely missed 'the circumference of an orange at a distance of 95 paces'.[61] It seems to have been the one thing she enjoyed doing with him.

In January 1836 she had a visit from 'the only person I have liked for six months'.[62] This was Captain Henry Codrington, in command of the *Orestes*, which put in at Palma. He was the six-foot-tall son of an admiral and a future admiral himself; he was also musical and blessed with a fine voice, and he and Laurette were soon singing duets at the piano and confiding to one another how much they detested garlic and bad oils and longed for good potatoes. 'I have not yet myself learned to enjoy the charms of garlick or to smoke a Cigar,' she confessed. The Gallonis were invited to dine aboard the *Orestes*, and, the weather being rough, Laura had to lie down on a sofa, 'which rather shocked me before an Englishman'.[63] Did she mean her bad sea legs, or the indecorum of lying down? Codrington liked her well enough to call again and sing some last duets before sailing on. It was a charming encounter between a gallant officer in William IV's navy and the blue-eyed beauty stranded in Majorca, ill married to a Corsican. She had hardly met an Englishman in her life, and he was not to know that Madame Galloni was the daughter of an Irish countess: or perhaps she told him. One wants to hear more.

Majorca was a short posting. Galloni had no money, only debts; they were living on his small salary and £100 a year from her father, and Galloni pestered her to ask for more. She had to pass on her father's explanations that he had nothing left but his pension. After a while she wrote to him, 'you must forgive me if I decline entering further into money matters . . . While unmarried a woman has of course nothing to do with such affairs; once married, as you know, the husband takes the fortune great or small into his hands, and acts with it according as he thinks best; so that a wife has as little to do with money matters after, as before, marriage. So much I think it necessary to say in my own defence—not to pass for a complete fool.'[64] Since her husband was beyond control, her father was given the benefit of her crisp summary of the evils of the position of women, with its echo of Mary Wollstonecraft.

Galloni was offered another temporary posting at Civitavecchia. Laurette found the situation on the Italian coast near Rome agreeable; there was no company, and nothing to do but bathe, read and write letters, she said. This was in August 1836, and the records show that Galloni was replacing the regular consul, Henri Beyle, otherwise known as Stendhal. A few years earlier, Mary had refused to review his book on Rome: 'M. Beyle's book is so trite so unentertaining—so *very* common place that I have found it quite impossible to do anything with it.'[65] It is a pity he and Laurette did not come face to face, since he was an admirer of beautiful women, an Anglophile and a man who knew a good deal about unhappiness in love; but he had taken leave to work on his Italian novel, *La Chartreuse de Parme*. It was published in 1839, a marvellous, complex book that moves from the battlefield of Waterloo to the political and amorous intrigues of life at an Italian court in the 1820s; there are extraordinary prison scenes, and the hero is driven to kidnap his own young son, who then falls ill and dies. It is one of the great novels of the nineteenth century; and if Galloni did nothing else good in his life, at least his taking over of Monsieur Beyle's tedious consular duties allowed him to concentrate on finishing *La Chartreuse de Parme*.

Laurette was beginning to think of attempting fiction herself. She was glad to be childless; what she had seen of the trials and tribulations of motherhood would not have encouraged her. 'Every day I thank my evil stars for this one good turn they have done me in life, leaving me without children,' she wrote to her father.[66] She worried about Nerina's babies; some of them flourished, but half of them died, and Nerina, once so blooming, was losing her health. Laurette wrote to her father again, 'I am afraid dearest Tatty I have little confidence left me in the good things of this world.'[67] She wrote this from Rome, and was there when her father died. Then her husband's work took him to Perugia, to Crete for two years, to Sardinia and, in 1839, to Venice.

Laurette kept in touch with Claire, who was away from Italy, working in England, France and Germany during the 1840s, and with Mary in England. When Mary toured Italy in 1842/3 with her newly adult son Percy, she spent enough time with Laurette to see that she was deeply unhappy in her marriage, and seemingly hopeless of any change for the better. 'Much as I abhor & shrink from a public life for women it would be better than the present state of things,' she wrote to a friend; and to Claire, 'she mourns over herself helplessly, bitterly'.[68] 'Unless one murdered Galloni & married her to a Prince I do not see how one could render her happier.'[69] Galloni was in Paris at this point, under investigation by the authorities for alleged mishandling of public money. Claire, also in Paris, observed him living 'in the first style'. 'Poor Laura—what have you ever done to deserve so hard a fate?' she asked.[70]

Glad as Mary was to see Laurette, she found her chilly; but it may have been discretion rather than a cold heart that made her guarded. There was something she may not have told Mary: the existence of a Sicilian admirer. In truth she was in Sicily for considerable periods from 1843

L E F T : *Laurette in the late 1840s when, separated from her first husband, she began writing novels, with Mary Shelley's encouragement*
B E L O W : *Placido Tardy, photographed in the late 1840s a few years before his marriage to Laurette*

until 1847. Her admirer was Placido Tardy, a mathematician, a few years younger than she; he was everything Galloni was not, highly intelligent, disinterested, politically congenial and devoted to her. Galloni's acquittal in 1844 did not restore his wife to him. A French police report of 1848 said he was married to an Italian '*issue de parents riches*' but had spent all her money and run up debts; and in 1849 he was sent to Moscow. Claire decided he was to be a spy there, and was very likely right. By then Laurette was living more or less openly with Tardy, who left Sicily after the uprising of 1847 and moved to Florence. The Cinis approved and welcomed them to San Marcello; and they were sharing lodgings in Florence in the summer of 1849.

Now Laurette in her turn became a writer. She wrote to Mary asking for help and advice about becoming a novelist, and when her first attempt, *Inez de Medine*, was published in Naples in 1846, Mary offered to help her find an English publisher. Mary also wrote to a friend, 'I hope & trust, highly gifted as she is—that her work will be such as to bear the impress of her intellect—If it does! How a million times delighted I shall be—It may happen with all her talents she may want a something—& her productions may fail . . . so till one has seen the work highly as I think of Laura, I know it is a lottery.'[71] Mary was right to be cautious. She began to translate *Inez*. Two chapters among her papers in the Bodleian must have been enough to dismay her, and her translation falls into every cliché, including the famous one Jane Austen warned aspiring novelists against. A Don Juan abducts Inez, who is rescued by the French navy; in Barcelona, Don Juan's sister Dolores lures Inez's brother into 'a very

Richard Rothwell's portrait of the widowed Mary Shelley,
painted sometime before she revisited Italy in 1840

vortex of pleasure and dissipation', while Inez goes mad in Paris. *Inez* did not appear in English, and nothing more was heard of it, or of its successor, *Dolore e Vendetta*.

Laurette was never published in England; she lost her only hope when Mary died in 1851. But in other ways her life took a dramatic turn for the better. In 1852 Galloni was appointed to Puerto Rico. By now Tardy had been given a chair at Genoa by Cavour; and when news came of Galloni's death early the following year, of 'gout of the stomach and brain', Laurette and Tardy were at last able to marry. Happy and settled, she took up her writing again, using the pseudonym 'Sara'. Dismissing her early books as apprentice work, she described *Una Madre* as her first novel in 1857. It is dedicated to her mother's memory, and pays tribute to Countess Mountcashell in the character of a good Venetian Countess Melin, who visits the poor, provides them with medical advice, cares nothing for fashion or appearances, and gives exceptional love and support to her two daughters; sadly, she is otherwise not much like Lady Mountcashell. Laurette Tardy still held to the belief that fiction required melodrama: the Countess is kept busy preserving both of her married daughters from the same vile seducer, and is driven to attack him with a knife when one daughter kills herself in despair after giving birth to his child. All this is played out against the Venetian rising of 1848, in which the Countess's younger son loses his life fighting the Austrians. The elder son has chosen to live in England and dissipated the family fortune gambling, leaving his mother to make ends meet by letting out their palazzo on the Grand Canal to wealthy foreigners. So it goes on, the brew too rich, the characters too thin.

In another story Laurette adds Gothic elements to the theme of marital villainy: a Sardinian count, acting at the behest of his mistress, hires an assassin to kill his young wife in their remote mountain castle. The wife is wounded, and when she recovers she flees Sardinia with her child and faithful maid. They are shipwrecked, arrive penniless in France and settle in a peasant house near Nîmes. A mysterious hermit in a black hood is seen in the neighbourhood, and arrives just in time to save them from a band of rioting socialists. He turns out to be the suitor she had rejected for the evil count, who opportunely dies, leaving them free to marry. I cannot help thinking that if Laurette had only written from her own experience, she would have produced something more interesting.

The story of Sardinia and the French socialists was printed at the end of a collection of essays reprinted from newspapers and magazines, women's themes alternating with essays on Democracy, Conscience and the importance of Truth-telling: they are decent but not exceptional. At least they testify to her capacity for hard work; four volumes of these were published in Milan in 1868 under the title *La Spettatrice*—a reminder of the old volumes of *The Spectator* in her parents' library.

Before starting to read Laurette Tardy's work I hoped she might turn out to be an Italian George Eliot. I was wildly off the mark. But she did address herself to the situation of women, and not just women of the upper classes; there are servants and actresses as well as countesses in her stories. She also took an interest in the politics of her country during the years of the Risorgimento. She was clearly an intelligent woman; she simply did not

Laurette in later life, now established as a journalist and novelist under the pen name 'Sara'. After her death in 1880, her husband Placido (below) made his home with her sister Nerina's family, and lived to be nearly one hundred.

How the manuscript of Maurice *was found*

light on a form that allowed her to say anything original, or a living voice for her characters. Her letters, written in English, have twice the life of her Italian fiction. Perhaps she should have written in English. Finding copies of her novels proved so difficult that I have not seen them all, and there may yet be a jewel I have missed. I can't help hoping so, not least because Laurette is the intellectual grandchild of Mary Wollstonecraft as well as the friend of Mary Shelley.

Laurette and Nerina kept up their friendships with Mary and Claire. Claire returned to Tuscany in 1859 and lived the last twenty years of her life there, in close contact with the Cinis. They had become her family, the most stable point in her long and difficult life: 'Laura, Nerina and Cini are from now onwards (with the exception of my little nephew [Percy]) the beings most dear to me in the whole world,' she wrote after the death of Mrs Mason.[72] She asked Bartolomeo Cini to be her executor, and although she outlived both him and Nerina, one of her last letters is to their daughter Margherita, asking for news of Laurette.

Claire died in 1879, Laurette only a year after her. Upon her death Tardy left Genoa and moved to San Marcello, welcomed by Nerina and Bartolomeo's son, Giovanni Cosimo Cini. The house was so big that Tardy was able to take all Laurette's possessions with him, and stack them away out of sight; among them was the manuscript of Mary's *Maurice*. There it remained, and there he remained too, a neat, white-bearded figure wearing a white suit in the San Marcello photograph albums, watching the next generation grow up, and then the next; and frightening little Giovanna with his beard. When he died in 1914 there were other things to think about than going through his boxes; and after the First World War came political upheavals, another war and losses and tragedies in the family. Even when American scholars and collectors arrived in the 1950s and 1960s, Laurette's boxes remained undisturbed. Then Casa Cini was divided, a whole wing sold and turned into offices and flats; in clearing that wing, Laurette's boxes were moved to the library. So it was that only in 1997, exactly two hundred years after Mary Shelley's birth, was Mary's story brought to light by Cristina Dazzi, the wife of Lady Mountcashell's great-great-great-grandson.

NOTE ON THE TEXT

The text of *Maurice* appears twice in this edition. The first version is corrected and slightly modernized for ease of reading. The second shows Mary Shelley's original lineation, pagination, spelling, punctuation, corrections and emendations; only the old double 's' has been modernized. The manuscript has been re-set line for line, with vertical rules indicating the original page breaks.

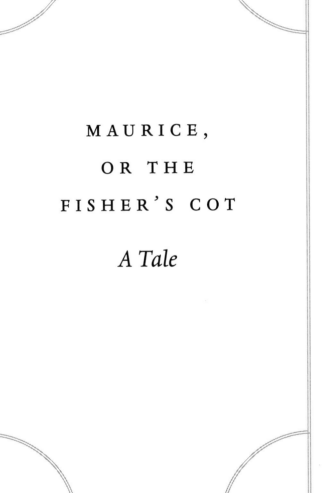

MAURICE,

OR THE

FISHER'S COT

A Tale

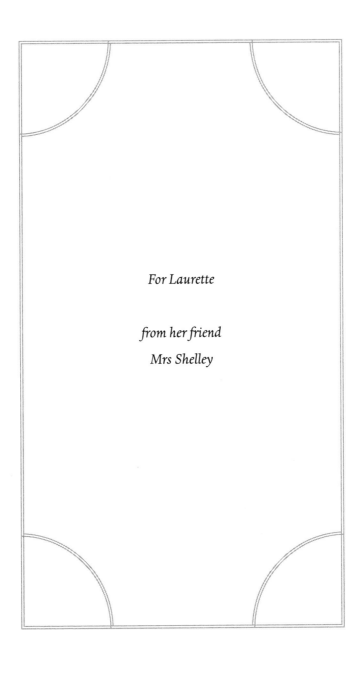

For Laurette

from her friend
Mrs Shelley

PART ONE

One Sunday afternoon in the month of September, a traveller entered the town of Torquay, a seaport on the southern coast of Devonshire. The afternoon was pleasant and warm, and the waves of the sea, slightly agitated by a breeze, sparkled under the sun. The streets of the town were empty, for the inhabitants after having been to church were dining during the interval between the services: so the traveller walked on through the meaner streets of the town, to the semicircle of houses that surrounds the harbour; and then he paused at the door of a neat-looking inn. The traveller was a man about forty-five years of age; he was remarkably erect in his person; alert and even graceful in his walk; his hair was black and curly, although a little fallen from his temples; he was handsome, but somewhat sun-burnt, and when he smiled he looked so good-tempered and kind that you could not see him without loving him. In dress and manner he had the appearance of one who had seen better days, but who was now poor; and he seemed serious, though not depressed by poverty. His clothes were coarse and covered with dust; he was on foot, and had a wallet buckled on his back.

He entered the inn, and asking for dinner, unbuckled his wallet,* and sat down to rest himself near the door. While he was thus sitting a funeral passed by: it was evidently the funeral of a poor person; the coffin was carried by some peasants, and four mourners followed. Three of these, although serious, looked careless and indifferent; the fourth was a boy of about thirteen years of age; he was crying, and was so much taken up by his own distress that he did not observe anything that passed near him. Something in this boy's appearance attracted the traveller's attention; and once, when he ceased crying and looked round towards the inn door, the traveller thought that he had seldom seen so beautiful a youth. He turned to the landlady, and asked, whose was that funeral? And who was the boy that accompanied it?

"That," replied the woman, "is the funeral of old

*_wallet_ in the old sense of a traveller's bag or knapsack.

Barnet, the fisherman: and that boy was a kind of servant or apprentice who lived with him after the death of the old dame, his wife."—

"Does he belong to this town?"—

"He does not; nor do I know from whence he comes: he is the child of poor people or his parents would never have sent him to live in the cottage of old Barnet. The neighbours says he is a good boy, but I know nothing about him."

The traveller sighed and said: "This poor boy can be nothing to me, yet I am much pleased with his appearance and manner."—A young countryman who was dining at a table in a corner of the room now rose, and said: "I live near old Barnet's cottage, and know this boy well; he is the best creature in the world, and all who know him love him: as you, sir, appear inquisitive about him, I will, if you please, relate all I know concerning him."—The traveller expressed his assent and the countryman began thus:—

"Old Barnet's cottage is situated about three miles from this town at the foot of the cliff and overhung by a few trees; it is very solitary and very poor; the spring tide comes up almost to the steps of the door; and when the wind blows the spray of the sea is dashed against the windows. We neighbours often wondered how so old a cot could stand the stress of weather; or being so near the sea that some high south winds do not blow the waves entirely over it; but it is sheltered by the crag, and being built on ground somewhat higher than the shore, out of the reach of the most tempestuous waves, it stands there, as I have known it stand ever since I was born, an old weather-beaten cot, the roof covered with lichens and moss. Beside it is a little cove where the fishing boat is kept, and there is an outhouse where the nets and sails were placed when the old man returned from the sea. A little freshwater brook trickles from the cliff, close to it, down into the sea, and when I was a boy I used often to go and place paper boats in this rill and watch them sailing down to the sea where they were soon lost in the great waves.*

"Old Barnet and his dame lived here. He was a most hard-working old man; early and late you saw his little skiff at sea, and often when no other boats ventured out Barnet would go and come back with fine, fresh fish for the Torquay market. His dame was so lame that she seldom moved from the old, worsted, high-backed armchair where she used to sit mending the nets, and hearing a few children read, who came to her

*Sailing paper boats was a favourite sport of Shelley's.

from the neighbouring farmhouses. Our farm is only half a mile distant from the cot and I am one of those who learned to read in Dame Barnet's great bible. She would not be paid for this, calling it merely a good neighbourly turn; but every Sunday I used to bring her a basket of vegetables and fruits, and every autumn she had a dozen of our best cider.

"Well about a year ago this good woman died, and all the children about wept at her funeral: for besides hearing them read, which she always did without scolding them (her only punishment was not allowing us to visit her), she would make nice worsted balls for them and tell them stories of Goody Two-shoes and the Babes in the Wood, or sing to them the ballad of Chevy Chase and many others which pleased us who were older as well as the children.* Besides she would

---

Goody Two-shoes is a moralistic children's story, believed to be by Oliver Goldsmith (1730–74). 'The Babes in the Wood' is a ballad telling the story of a brother and sister whose uncle decides to murder them and hires killers, who take them to a wood. One repents and kills the other, but he then abandons the children, and they die of exposure and hunger in the wood, where the birds cover their bodies with leaves. The ballad was already old when T. Percy printed it in his *Reliques of Ancient English Poetry* (1765). 'Chevy Chase' is also a very early and popular ballad in which the English Earl of Northumberland, Percy, decides to hunt over the land of his Scottish neighbour, Earl Douglas, without asking leave. A fight follows, and both lords are killed.

do them a thousand services of mending their clothes
when torn by accident and a thousand other little services which made her a great favourite with all. Barnet
was very much grieved when she died: she was of little
help to him not being able to move from her armchair
without great difficulty; but when he came home wet
from fishing, during the stormy winter days when
every wave almost broke over his boat, she would contrive to have the fire lighted for him and the little old
cottage set in order for his supper. But after her death
when he returned from sea he was obliged to go hungry and sometimes dripping wet to the market at this
town; and when he returned he was not handy at
cooking his food or cleaning his room: besides he was
now obliged to mend his nets for himself, and that
took up a great deal of his time so that he did not catch
so much fish as before. All these things made him
melancholy; and he came about two months after his
dame's death to our farm with tears in his eyes, and
said he thought he should give up his fishing and go up
the country to seek his fortune, for that the old cottage
under the cliff had become quite hateful to him since
his dame's death. He was a hale old man, but his hair
was as white as snow, and his back bent with age, so
that it was a piteous thing to hear him talk of leaving

his cot, and his boat, and all that he had in the world to seek his fortune among strangers. My father comforted him, and made him dine with us, and promised to send my sister Betsy sometimes to put his cottage in order: so he went home with a lighter heart than he came.

"The next day the wind blew into shore, and the old man, not being able to go out with his boat, sat down on a piece of rock that formed a kind of seat near his cot, and began to mend his nets. While he was thus employed this same boy of whom we speak, whose name is Maurice, came and sat down on the rock near him. The boy was a stranger in this part of the country, so after having saluted one another they both remained silent for some time; at length Maurice said:—'I think I could help you in that work and as I have nothing to do I wish you would let me try.'—

"'Try, and welcome,' said Barnet; 'but how is it that you have nothing to do? Good boys ought to work; you do not belong to these parts, and it is not well to see a boy of your age wandering about the country alone.'—'My parents are poor,' replied Maurice, 'and not being able to maintain me, I have tried to earn my own livelihood; I have been brought up to no trade, and have always been weakly and unable to work hard.

When I left home I came with a man I knew to a farm not far distant, where they gave me work in plenty in the fields, the stables and the barns. I worked hard, for my master was severe, so at length I fell ill; then when I could work no longer they turned me away, and think I should have died had not a poor woman taken care of me. She was so poor that I would not be a burden to her any longer than was necessary, but now I am too weak to work for my old master, so I am thrown on the wide world, and would be much obliged to anyone who would help me either by giving me such work as I can do, or advising me where I can go to get it; for I am willing, and although I say it myself, I am honest and have always been considered handy and industrious.'

"Old Barnet looked up in the boy's face; you know how pretty a lad he is; he was then sickly-looking and that made him a fitter object for compassion: he has the sweetest voice in the world and all that he said seemed to go the old man's heart. He thought:—I have no child upon earth: my only relation is a brother who disdains a poor old fisherman like me. My name is dead, and I am alone without anyone to help me if I am sick or to say a cheerful, 'Good bye, God send you luck!' when I go a fishing. Surely this boy seems sent by heaven to me, and it seems to me that I love him already as if he were my own son. He shall stay with me; I can maintain him as I maintained my poor wife who is gone: he can put my cottage in order, mend my sails and nets, and on windy evenings who knows but he may be able to read the bible to me as my dame used.'

"This was a lucky thought; the bargain was soon struck, and ever since Maurice has lived with old Barnet in his cottage. He is a good boy, honest, handy and clever: when we came to know him all our house loved him; he is able to read very tolerably, so my little brothers went to him to learn every Sunday as they used to go to the Dame, and no one can be more good-tempered. He made the old cottage quite another thing, cleaning it, and mending the old chairs; white-washing the grate, and furbishing up the pans and saucepans; and laying them in neat rows. He was always merry, always at work, always ready to do a good turn for the poor as well as the rich. Old Barnet loved him better and better, and often thanked God for the day when he first came to the cottage. Out at sea the old man saw through the day the trees wave over his cottage roof, and at night he could distinguish the candle which Maurice placed at the window to direct him where to steer. When he came to shore the boy was always waiting there to help him draw his boat up to the cove. Then in winter he found a nice fire ready to dress his supper, and the table spread with a coarse, old, but clean cloth. In the morning when he went to market, Maurice heaved the water out of his boat, mended his nets, put his sails in order, and said a smiling, 'God give you luck!' when he went to sea. They lived several months in this manner very happily, and now a week ago old Barnet died."—

The countryman paused, and the traveller asked, "What will become of the boy?"—"I do not know; but he is so much loved that I do not think he will come to want. For my part I am now leaving the country for a few weeks, for I am going to visit my grandmother who lives at Sidmouth; but when I return the first question I shall ask is what is become of Maurice. I have told you a long story, sir, but I hope you will excuse me; you have now finished your dinner, and I will detain you no longer. Good bye!"—"Thank you heartily. Good-day, and a pleasant journey to you," was the reply, and the young man left the inn.

The traveller remained some time leaning his head on his hand, thinking what he should do. He wanted very much to make further enquiry about Maurice, but when he thought of the business he had at Exeter he could not resolve to delay his journey: so after resting himself another hour, he strapped on his wallet and left the inn, following the Exeter road.

The next morning he arrived at this city. By and by I shall explain what his business there was; but at present I shall only say that having passed three anxious days, he was obliged to give up his business, and to determine to return whence he came, that he might enquire whether something had not happened in the mean time that might help him; at the same time he resolved on his way back to visit old Barnet's cottage, and to enquire what had become of Maurice, and to offer his services in placing him in some suitable situation, where he might honestly get his livelihood without being worked too hard. And now leaving him to walk with his wallet on his back along the road which leads from Exeter to Torquay, let us take a peep into the cottage under the cliff; and see what has become of Maurice and what help he is likely to get in his misfortunes.

PART SECOND

The three other mourners who had followed Old Barnet's funeral were the brother of whom the countryman had spoken, and his two sons. After the funeral this brother, who was a shopkeeper at Torquay and a money-loving man, spoke thus to Maurice:— "You, it seems, were maintained by my poor brother, and lived in his cottage: now you know by the laws that since my brother died without a will, all he was worth, the cottage and its furniture, the boat and his nets are mine. If they were not you are too young to follow his trade, so there is no possible reason why you should remain in the cottage. The neighbours say you are an honest lad so I would not be too hard upon you; you may stay in the cottage one week, and you can employ yourself in seeking for a place: at the end of that time a friend of mine with his three sons will come and live there, and having bought the boat will carry on the fishing; they will not want you for a servant, so by that time you must remove. You are honest and therefore I need hardly tell you that nothing in the cottage belongs to you, except what you brought yourself, and that you will not be allowed to take anything away with you."—

Maurice thanked his old friend's brother for allowing him to stay a week in the cottage; he intended to have asked his advice about what he ought to do, but there was something so dry and forbidding in his manner that he could not make up his mind to speak, but went away, walking sorrowfully along the shore towards the old cottage. When he arrived he thought that it looked so desolate and strange, that he had not the heart to enter but sat down near the little fresh-water brook, and watched the waves of the sea breaking at his feet. For the first time for several months he was idle; for it was no use to mend the nets when his old protector could not use them, or to get supper ready when he felt his heart too full to eat. He cried for the loss of his dear Barnet till he was quite tired, and then watched the sun set in the blue sea; and half imagined that perhaps Barnet was not dead, but out fishing and that he could perceive his white sail far out at sea: but turning round he saw the boat lying empty in the cove, and then he knew it must be true that his only friend was dead, and that he was now alone in the world. At length quite exhausted by sorrow, and feeling cold as the evening breeze arose and whitened the sea with foam, he got up and opening the cottage door, without eating any supper or striking a light, he knelt down and said his prayers and then went to bed.

Several days passed in this manner, and at length he began to think that he ought not to live this idle life any longer. The week was almost gone when he must quit the cottage, and then what should he do to earn bread to eat? Sometimes he thought he would return to his parents, but that he quickly determined not to do; and at length he resolved to go to farmer Benson, the father of the countryman who related his story to the traveller at Torquay. As he determined this he sat on his accustomed stone near the freshwater rill, and looked at the ocean which was unbroken by waves, and the sky where the sun had set, and the evening star gleamed in the golden light he had left behind him: the air was quite calm and the murmuring of the tide, which was going out, just broke the silence, while a few seagulls flew to their nests in the cliff over his head. Maurice heard a step near him, and turning round saw approach a kind, good-looking man who was indeed the traveller whom I described at the beginning of my story. The boy was much surprised, for a stranger had never before visited the cottage, which was two miles from any road: rising with his usual good nature, he asked him whether he had lost his way, and offered to show him the way to the nearest town.

"I have not lost my way," said the traveller, "I came to this cottage on purpose. I have particular reasons for wishing to see it, and would be much obliged to you if you could afford me a bed tonight."—"You are very welcome; the cottage is poor, but as the bed is clean perhaps you will be content."—"I have travelled too much, my good boy, not to be easily satisfied. But do not rise; for the present let us enjoy this pleasant evening here at the seaside, watching the waves that leave so smooth a beach behind them. Your cottage is built in a very pretty place."—"I think so indeed, and although it is poor and very old, yet taking it altogether I do not think there is a prettier in all the country round. The trees fall over and shelter it, a number of pretty flowers grow beside the brook which comes running down from the tall, red cliff. And nothing to my mind can be more beautiful than the moss and lichens, yellow, green, white and blue, that grow on the old thatched roof, making it look finer than a slated roof could possibly be. In the spring yellow wallflowers grow there, and the green before the door is covered with daisies. Besides if you come round to the other side where the cottage faces the hill you will find a pretty lattice grown over with honeysuckles and several geraniums in the stand outside the window. The geraniums were the great favourite of old Barnet's dame, and he loved them for her sake. Mr Gregory Barnet says that I must take nothing from the cottage, and that I know very well; but if farmer Benson will take me into his service I will spend two shillings that I have in buying geraniums, if the man who is coming to live here will be kind enough to sell them."—"You intend then to leave this cottage?"—"I must. I am not strong enough to manage the boat and go out to sea, and so it is let to some fisherman; next Sunday I go away; but I hope I shall get work hereabouts, and I do not think I shall be unhappy, for I have seldom cried about my own misfortunes when I have been very ill-used indeed; and I do not dislike work when it does not make me ill. I loved old Barnet and liked my life here with him and I cried very much when he died—but if I can get work about a farmyard, I hope in a month or two to sing as cheerfully as I used when I saw his white sail among the other boats which you see out at sea."

Maurice did not say all this at once, but the stranger smiled so kindly, and asked so many questions in so affectionate a manner, that the boy was easily induced to open his whole heart to him, and to talk about his affairs as to an old friend. "I shall not return to my parents," said he, "for I left determining never more to see them till I could earn my own bread. My father works hard and wages are low, so being hardly able to get sufficient food for himself he was angry that he had to maintain an idle boy, and my mother is sufficiently vexed by him without my misfortunes being added to her cares. Unfortunately I am a delicate boy and unable to work as he would have me and have often been confined to my bed with fevers. My father never would believe I was really ill and would beat me and send me to bed without my supper when I could hardly stand. I do not mean to complain of him, and although I have told all this to you who are so kind, pray do not mention it to anyone else."

Thus they chatted till the evening star had set, and the sea became invisible through darkness, except indeed the white heads of the waves that broke near them; for the tide was coming in and the rock on which they sat began to be wetted by the spray: so they entered the cottage and supping on bread and salad, they presently after went to bed, the traveller telling the boy that he would both breakfast and dine with him the following day.

Maurice awoke before light, and leaving his guest sleeping soundly in bed he ran as fast as he could to Torquay to buy some white bread, and potatoes and meat for their breakfast and dinner. He was obliged to spend for this provision the two shillings with which he had intended to purchase his dear geraniums, and this made him a little sorrowful: but he was a cheerful, happy-tempered boy, and consoled himself with think-ing that he would work doubly hard to earn this money before the next spring, and that he would entreat the future tenant of the cottage to take care of these pretty shrubs until that time.

When he arrived at the cottage he found the trav-eller seated on the rock on the beach; they greeted one another kindly, and Maurice, at the request of his guest, brought out a little table on the sands, and placed their breakfast on it in the open air; for it was a fine warm morning without a cloud in the sky. Their breakfast was plain and countrified, consisting of bread, a piece of cheese and a basin of that nice clouted cream that they make in Devonshire;* and our two friends ate so heartily of what was there that very little remained. They then continued sitting on the rock talking of the pleasure of living in the country, of seeing the pretty flowers grow in the hedges and among the green grass; of the beauty of the little birds, and the cruelty of those who kill them: and the sweet life it would be to take care of a nice farm, not working too hard, but sufficient to become healthy and strong through exercise; and in the evening to read entertaining books, telling them of how the earth is cultivated, and how various countries bring forth various fruits: of the sea, and how different voyages and discoveries have been made on it: of the sky, and how the beautiful stars which we see at night move, and the signs they make of winter and summer. The traveller told Maurice that there were books more delightful than these which told of what good and wise men had done a great many years ago; how some had died to serve their fellow creatures, and how through the exer-

*clouted cream is cream thickened by being heated, now known as clotted cream.

tions of these men everyone had become better, wiser and happier. Maurice said that he had never read any book of that kind except the bible, and that he had often cried over the distress of Joseph, when he was sold to slavery, and over the sorrow of David, when his son Absalom revolted against him.

At length, after a pause, the traveller said:—"You talk, my dear Maurice, of going to seek for work at farmer Benson's: now what say you if instead of this, you came and lived with me. I would not task you too hard, but would give you some of these pretty books to read, and would do my best to make you happy."— Maurice looked up at the kind stranger and saw him smiling benevolently after him. "How good you are!"—he replied.—"I will be good to you," said his guest, "but I am a stranger and you may be afraid to go away with one whom you never saw before. It is late now for we have talked a long time, so let us go in and prepare our dinner, and afterwards we will come and sit here again and I will tell you who I am; why I am travelling on foot about the country; what my disappointments have been, and what my hopes are."—

They did as he said. They made a good fire and placed their meat and potatoes to boil. Maurice filled a jug with clear water from the brook, and the traveller took a small bottle of good wine from his wallet. By noon the dinner was ready, and after they had finished they sat down on the rock, and the traveller began his relation.

PART THIRD

"I am the son of a professor of mathematics at the University of Oxford; my father was not rich but he gave me an excellent education, and I was exceedingly industrious and fond of learning. As long as I can remember I never went about without a book in my pocket, and loved to take long, solitary walks, and then to sit and read for hours together under the shade of trees, and beside the river; when I did not as an idler go to sleep, lulled by its murmuring, but I used to study and reflect with great earnestness and curiosity. Everything about me appeared wonderful to my eyes, and I wanted to know why the water of the river always ran and never became less; how the sun was governed as it passed along the sky, and why the moon changed as it did, and sometimes appeared round, and full, and yellow, and at other times only a little silver crescent.

There was also another thing which delighted me extremely, which was to examine three large volumes of prints of beautiful ancient temples that my father possessed. I spent whole days in looking at these, and reading the accounts of their dimensions and how they were built; for I thought I should be the happiest creature in the world if ever I should be able to build such beautiful edifices as I saw represented in these books. As I grew older I became fonder and fonder of architecture, and as no knowledge is gained without application I passed my whole time in learning mathematics and those sciences which best teach us how to erect edifices such as the ancients used to build. When I was five and twenty my kind father sent me abroad to Asia, Italy and Greece to visit the remains of the old temples that still exist, and I passed five years in this happy manner, dwelling among foreign nations, often in desert places where the people do not live by sowing and reaping corn and taking care of farms, as they do here, but depend upon hunting for their livelihood, leaving their native villages for months together in search of game, and living a wild life among the woods and mountains, while their wives and daughters remain at home spinning their own clothes, sitting in the open air, where the winters are so mild that they have neither frost or snow.*

"When I returned to England I applied to business, and being a good architect I soon became rich. When I thought I had money enough I gave up my business and applied myself to country labours and all kinds of study, which I liked better than building churches and bridges where the people have too little taste or too little money to allow them to be built in the beautiful manner I wished.

"I married at this time a lady, whom you will soon see, my dear Maurice, and then you will know how wise and good she is. Soon after our marriage we had a little boy of whom we were dotingly fond. All our joy was in watching this little creature, who was as beautiful and good as it was possible to be. When he was two years old we made a journey during the summer and stayed for a month at Ilfracombe, a seaport more than fifty miles' distance from this place, and here a misfortune happened to us since which we have never been perfectly contented. It is now eleven years ago, but I can never think of that time without being unhappy.

*Mary Shelley is possibly drawing on Byron's accounts of his travels for the traveller's observations of life in Asia, Italy and Greece.

"We used often to ride out, my wife and I, and a servant with our baby; and when we came to a pretty place we used to leave the nurse and child with the carriage while we took long walks in the country. One day we rode until we came to the banks of a very pretty river; and telling the nurse to wait for us, we walked on for several miles, enjoying the pleasant weather, listening to the singing of the birds in the elm trees which hung over the river, and watching the little insects with wings of purple, green and gold that flew on the surface of the water.

"When we returned we were dreadfully frightened to find the nurse asleep among some hay and no child near her. We awoke the woman and she became pale with fear and trembled all over when she found the child gone; since he had gone to sleep in her arms, and she, without thinking of the danger, and lulled to sleep by the sun, had at last fallen asleep also. The first thing we did was to run to the river;—but I will not describe to you, my little friend, the great grief we felt during this search. We did not find our child, or see any remains of him near the water; on the contrary we found one of his little shoes in a field about a mile from the river, and this made us think that perhaps he was stolen. We spent many months in searching the whole country, but in vain, we could not hear any tidings of our dear, lost boy.

"For my part I have never given up hope that I shall one day find him again, for I always felt convinced that he was not drowned. So every year I spend two months in Devonshire going over the whole county looking for him. I dress myself meanly that I may enter the cottages with greater freedom and make enquiries of the country people in a familiar manner; I walk about from village to village, and never pass a solitary cottage without looking at the children, and asking questions concerning them.

"A fortnight ago I passed by a cottage about five miles from Ilfracombe, at the door of which stood a woman crying and wringing her hands: I stopped and asked her what was the matter, and she told me that her husband had died two days before, and that her only son had been away a year and a half and she did not know what had become of him. I tried to console her, and told her that I also was unhappy and had lost my only child while a baby and had never found him again. I then related to her my misfortune and was much surprised to find her more distressed than before, and when I described to her the great grief of my wife, she cried out, "I am the cause of this! I am the wicked woman who stole your child!" I started at these words, and as soon as I could speak I asked her what had become of my poor dear boy. She then began to cry again, and said that it was him she lamented when she told me that she had not seen her only son for nearly two years. She cried so much and appeared so distressed that I was obliged to spend almost an hour before I could console her, and then she told me how all had happened.

"Her husband had been a sailor and they had lived several years together and had had no children: he was a bad man, and would beat and reproach her for not having a child, which made her very unhappy, and she thought that she would be perfectly happy if heaven would bless her with a son. At length once when her husband went on a long voyage, she wrote to him a month after his departure and told him that she was with child. He stayed away a long time, and she continued to write and to tell falsehoods, how the child was born and was thriving; and she did this foolishly without thinking of the consequences, or what her husband would say when he returned and found no child. He was a sailor on board a king's ship, and getting a wound in a battle which disabled him for a long time he wrote to her who was then living in London, to go down to his native place at Ilfracombe, for that he would leave his ship and go and live there the rest of his days.

"She went down with a sorrowful heart, not knowing what she should say about her pretended child; and, not liking to go among his relations, who all expected to see a fine stout boy about two years old, she took a mean lodging in a town some miles off and went by a false name. She passed two months in a very unhappy state of mind, strolling about the country and not able to determine as to what she would do, when one day for our great misfortune she determined to walk towards Ilfracombe to find out whether her husband had arrived, and on her way she found our poor baby asleep in the arms of his careless nurse.

"One wicked thing brings on another; and she who had deceived her husband, and for two years written a number of falsehoods, and had become to have the habit of feeling guilty and wrong, now made up her mind to steal this child, not caring for the unhappiness of its parents. She took him gently out of the nurse's arms, and ran with him across the fields towards the town where she had been living for the last two months. When she came near the town she hid the child under some straw in a barn, and went as fast as she could to her lodgings. She paid for them and taking her bundle of clothes she went back to the child and hid herself in the barn all day. At night she began her journey. She resolved to go to Plymouth and wait for her husband, whose ship was expected in that port, and thus to quit the country near Ilfracombe until her theft should be forgotten. She walked all day and hid herself at night for fear of being discovered. She burned the child's good clothes and made it others out of her own, preserving only a little coral necklace with his Christian name engraved on the clasp and the remaining shoe, whose fellow we found in the field and which we have ever kept with great affection. She lived six months at Plymouth before her husband arrived and then they went together and settled themselves in the cottage where I found them. The woman soon loved our poor boy as if he had been her own and took all possible care of it—caressing and tending on him with the tenderness of a mother.

"But people who do that which they ought not to do seldom find that good comes from the crimes they commit which they expect. Our poor boy had been accustomed to delicate fare and gentle nursing; and whether it was that he was now fed poorly and neglected (not through unkindness, but because she had not leisure to give him the attention to which he had been accustomed with us), whether it were on these accounts I know not, but our little Henry became sickly and delicate, and lost that fine bloom which first tempted her to the wicked action of stealing him. Her husband, who was a bad man and who had before grumbled that he had no child, now became more cross than ever, saying that the sickly brat would never come to good, and that he was obliged to maintain him by the sweat of his brow when he would never be able to do the like for him when he was old.

"The woman then said to me:—'I have been very miserable as well as wicked: for not only I felt great repentance at having taken this baby from his parents, but I found my husband unkinder than ever, and that instead of loving, he perfectly disliked the poor child. Besides the dear fellow lost his health and although the best creature in the world and the most willing and clever, yet he could do no hard work, and often had fevers and other illnesses when my husband grudged the doctor, and I used to sit crying by his bedside thinking that if his rich parents had still kept him he would not lie without help on his sickbed.

"'As he grew older my husband grew unkinder and

sometimes beat him because he could not work, and treated him in so cruel a manner that I dare not relate to you who are his father, so one day Henry (for so I called him as by his broken words I found his parents had named him) came to me, and told me that farmer Jackson had promised to get work for him, and that he was determined to go and try if he could not gain his own livelihood. I cried bitterly, but could not alter his purpose, though then I would have given all I had in the world to find out who his rich parents were, that I might restore him. I gave him my blessing and he went away and I have never heard of him since!'

"I will not tire you, my little friend, with the account of my walks and anxieties for this last fortnight; during which I have been employed in going all over Devonshire tracing my lost child; my labours have been unsuccessful. I am now going to return to Dame Smithson to ask whether he has returned to her. This is my story; do you consent to come and live with me? If I never find my darling boy you shall be a son to me, and if I do find him——"

Maurice had listened to this relation very attentively, and near the end his eyes had streamed with tears and he showed every sign of interest and impatience: and now when the traveller said these words he threw him-

· 1 1 0 ·

self into his arms and sobbed out—"I am your son! Daddy Smithson is not my father! I am your lost boy!"—And then he told him how he had always considered Dame Smithson his mother, and how kind to him and fond of him she was; and how her husband had made him perfectly miserable so that he had determined never to go home again until he should be able to earn his bread for himself. He said that he had called himself Maurice because he was afraid that the cruel man whom he thought his father might come to that part of the country and find him out and beat and ill-use him as he used to do at home.

Now nothing could be happier than the traveller and his dear son as they sat together by the seaside, talking about what they would do and the joy of his poor mother when she should see him again. Henry cried for joy when he thought of the happy life they should lead, reading delightful books, living with a kind father and mother, and having no care upon earth but that of obeying them and making them happy. They went that very evening to Torquay, and hiring a chaise they rode towards the traveller's home; and never rested until they arrived and Henry was in his mother's arms.

And what became of the old moss-roofed cottage

by the seaside? Why, at Henry's request his father bought it, and the boat, and the geraniums, and all that belonged to it from Mr Gregory Barnet. They could not live there because Henry was obliged to go to Eton* to school; and his father's house was near Windsor park, close to the school, so that he always lived with his dear parents. But in the Whitsuntide and Bartholomewtide holidays† they went down to Devonshire to visit the pretty cottage and lived in it two months every year. It was too small for any servants to come with them, so Henry put on a coarse country dress, and his father clothed himself as he used when he travelled about the country to seek for his child. They took care of the garden, bought their own food, cooked their own dinner; and when the weather was fine and the sun shone they sat on the rock near the freshwater rill and talked about all the beautiful things they had seen or would one day see, or read delightful books whose knowledge and

---

*Eton College, near Windsor, is England's foremost school for boys, founded by King Henry VI for sons of noblemen and scholars who traditionally went on to study at King's College, Cambridge. Eton was attended by both Shelley and by George Tighe, Laurette's father.
†Whitsunday is the seventh Sunday after Easter, coming in late May or early June. Bartholomew Day was celebrated on 24 August, so both were suitable times for seaside holidays.

lessons made them both wiser and happier. When they were at this cottage Henry always went by the name of Maurice, and he would go about among his friends whom he had known when he lived with old Barnet, helping and consoling them if they were sick or afflicted, and doing all the good a little boy could do, or by the help of his father making people happy when poverty or misfortune had made them miserable.

In the fine evenings they would sail out to sea in the old fishing boat; they did not fish, for they did not like to give pain to, and to destroy animals, but they would observe the dancing waves, and the rocky shores; and if they stayed out long after sunset they saw how the stars came out one by one till the whole sky was covered with them.

During the other part of the year Dame Smithson lived in the old cottage. She was very sorry for what she had done, and loved Henry very much; and Henry never forgot that he had loved her once as a dear, good mother.

Many hears after, Henry grew older and went abroad to foreign countries, and saw many beautiful scenes of rocks, and mountains, and trees, and rivers; yet he always loved in his heart his pretty cottage and thought it the most delightful place he had ever seen. It was very old, as I have said before; and some time after when Dame Smithson died some of the moss-covered thatch fell off and let the water into the cottage during the rainy weather; it was too old to be repaired, and by degrees it fell all to pieces, and the sea washed it away as it fell, so that it quite disappeared.

When Henry returned from his travels he found his pretty cottage gone, his geraniums dead, and no wall left on which the sweet-smelling, yellow wallflowers could grow; this grieved him very much, yet he was pleased to find the red cliff, the waving tress, the fresh-water rill, and the rock upon which he and his father used so often to sit—remained just the same as when he left them: though the boat had fallen to pieces in the cove, and the garden had run wild. He would not build another cottage there for it would have been too unlike old Barnet's that he loved so well. But he built a house not far off where he placed to live a poor fisher-man and his two children, who having lost his boat in a storm some months before and scarcely saved from drowning himself, was in great want and poverty. He built another boat for the little cove and often during his life came to visit the cliff, and the trees, and the rock; where he would sit and reflect on the life he had led while a little boy with old Barnet in the pretty, old, fisher's cot; and how his father came to visit and assist him when he was poor and helpless, not knowing him to be his son; and how on that very rock he had first discovered that he belonged to good, kind parents; with whom he now lived in content and happiness.

The End

MAURICE

Showing the Author's
Original Lineation,
Pagination, Spelling,
Corrections and
Emendations

Maurice
or the
Fisher's Cot.

a tale.

PART I.

One sunday afternoon in the month
of September, a traveller entered the town
of Torquay, a seaport on the southern coast
of Devonshire. The afternoon was pleasant
and warm, and the waves of the sea, slightly
agitated by a breeze, sparkled under the
sun. The streets of the town were empty,
for the inhabitants after having been to
church were dining during the interval
between the services: so the traveller walked
on through the meaner streets of the town,
to the semicercle of houses that surrounds
the harbour; and then he paused at the door
of a neat-looking inn. The traveller was a
man about forty five years of age; he was |
remarkably erect in his person; alert and
even graceful in his walk; his hair was
black and curly, although a little fallen from
his temples; he was handsome, but somewhat
sun-burnt, & when he smiled he looked so
goodtempered and kind that you could not
see him without loving him. In dress and
manner he had the appearance of one

Torquay, the setting for Maurice

who had seen better days, ~~w~~ but who was
now poor; and he seemed serious, though
not depressed by poverty. His clothes were
coarse and covered with dust; he was on foot,
and had a wallet buckled on his back.

   He entered the inn, and asking for din
ner, unbuckled his wallet, & sat down
to rest himself near the door. While he
was thus sitting a funeral passed by~~e~~:
it was evidently the funeral of a poor
person; the coffin was carried by some
peasants, and four mourners followed. ~~Thre~~
Three of these although serious, looked care
less and indifferent; the fourth was a boy |
of about thirteen years of age; he was
crying, & was so much taken up by his
own distress that he did not observe any

thing that passed near him. Somthing in
this boy's appearance attracted the traveller's
attention; and once when he ceased crying
and looked round towards the inndoor, the
traveller thought that he had seldom seen
so beautiful a youth. He turned to the land
lady, and asked,—"whose ~~wh~~ was that fu
neral? And who was the boy that accompa
nied it?"—

"That," replied the woman, "is the funeral
of old Barnet, the fisherman: and that boy
was a kind of servant or apprentice who
lived with him after the death of the old
dame, his wife."—

"Does he belong to this town?"—

"He does not; nor do I know from whence
he comes: he is the child of poor people or
his parents would never have sent him
to live in the cottage of old Barnet. The
neighbours say he is a good boy, but I know |
nothing about him.

The traveller sighed and said: "This
poor boy can be nothing to me, yet I
am much pleased with his appearance
and manner."—A young country man
who was dining at a table in a corner of
the room now rose, and said: "I live near
old Barnet's cottage, and know this boy
well; he is the best creature in the world,
and all who know him love him: as
you, sir, appear inquisitive about him,
I will, if you please, relate all I know
concerning him."—The traveller expressed
his assent and the country man began
thus:—

"Old Barnet's cottage is situated about
three miles from this town at the

foot of the cliff and overhung by a
few trees; it is very solitary and very
poor; the spring-tide comes up almost
to the steps of the door; & when the
wind blows the spray of the sea is dashed
against the windows. We neighbours often |
wondered how so old a cot could stand the stress of
weather; or being so near the sea that some
high ~~north~~ ^{south} winds do not blow the waves entirely
over it; but it is sheltered by the crag, and
being built on a ground somewhat higher
than the shore, out of the reach of the
most tempestuous waves, it stands there, as I
have known it stand ever since I was born,
an old weather beaten cot, the roof covered
with lichens and moss. Beside it is a little cove
where the fishing boat is kept, and there is an
out house where the nets and sails are ^{were}∧
placed when the old man returned from the
sea. A little fresh-water brook trickles from
the cliff, close to it, down into the sea, and
when I was a boy I used often to go and place
paper boats in this rill and watch them sailing
down to the sea where they were soon lost in
the great waves.

     "Old Barnet and his dame lived here. He was
a most hardworking old man; early and late
you saw his little skiff at sea, and often
when no other boats s ventured out Barnet
would go and come back with fine, fresh fish for
the Torquay market. His dame was so lame that
she seldom moved ∧^{from} the old, worsted, highbacked
armchair where she used to sit mending the |
nets, and hearing a few children read, who
came to her from the neighbouring farm
houses. Our farm is only half a mile distant
from the cot and I am one of those who

learned to read in Dame Barnet's great bible.
She would not be paid for this, calling it merely
a good neighbourly turn; but every sunday I
used to bring her a basket of vegetables and
fruits, and every autumn she had a dozen
of our best cider.

    "Well about ~~two~~ years ago this good woman
died, and all the children about wept at
her funeral: for besides hearing them read, which
she always did without scolding them (her only
punishment was not allowing us to visit her)
she would make nice worsted balls for them
and tell them stories of Goody Two Shoes & the
babes in the Wood, or sing to them the ballad~~s~~
of Chevy Chase and many others which pleased
us who were older as ~~w~~ well as the children.
Besides she would do them a thousand services of
mending their clothes when torn by ~~accieden~~
accident and a thousand other little services
which made her a great favourite with all.
Barnet was very much grieved when she died:
she was of little help to him not being able to |
move from her arm chair without great diffi
culty; but when he came home ~~from~~ wet from
fishing, during the stormy winter days when every
wave almost broke over his boat, she would
contrive to have the fire lighted for him and the
little old cottage set in order for his ~~suff~~ supper.
But after her death when he returned from sea
he was obliged to go hungry and sometimes dripping wet
to the market at this town; and when he returned
he was not handy at cooking his food or cleaning
his room: besides he was now obliged to mend his
nets for himself, and that took up a great deal of
his time so that he did not catch so much fish
as before. All these things made him melancholy;
and he came about two months after his dame's

death to our farm with tears in his eyes, and
said he thought he should give up his fishing
and go up to this country to seek his fortune, for
that the old cottage under the cliff a had become
quite hateful to him since his dame's death.
He was a hale old man, but his hair was as
white as snow, and his back bent with age, so
that it was a piteous thing to hear him talk
of leaving his cot, and his boat, and t all that
he had in the world to seek his fortune among
strangers. My father comforted him, and made
him dine with us, & promised to send my sister |
Betsy sometimes to put his cottage in order:
so he went home with a lighter heart than
he came.

    "The next day the wind blew into shore, and
the old man not being able to go out with his
boat, sat down on ~~the rock~~ a piece of rock
that formed a kind of seat near his cot, and
began to mend his nets. While he was thus em
ployed this same boy of whom we speak, whose
name is Maurice, came and sat down on the
rock near him. The boy was a stranger in this
part of the country, so after having saluted one
another they both remained silent for some time;
at length Maurice said:—"I think I could help
you in that work and as I have nothing ł to
do I wish you would let me try."

    "Try, and welcome," said Barnet; "but how
is it that you have nothing to do? Good boys
ought to work; you do not belong to these
parts, and it is not well to see a boy of your
age wandering about the country alone."—"My
parents are poor," replied Maurice, "and not
being able to maintain me, I have tried to earn
my own livelihood; I have been brought up
to no trade, and have always been weakly &

unable to work hard. When I left home I |
came with a man I knew to a farm not far
distant, where they gave me work in plenty in
the fields, the stables and the barns. I worked hard
for my master was severe, so at length I fell
ill; then when I could work no longer they turned
me away, and I think I should have died had not
a poor woman taken care of me. She was so
poor that I would not be a burthen to her
any longer than was necessary, and now I am too
weak to work for my old master, so I am thrown
on the wide world, and would be much obliged to
any one who would help me either by giving
me such work as I ~~could~~ can do, or advising
me where I can go to get it; for I am willing,
and although I say it my self, I am honest and
have always been considered handy & ~~und~~ industrious."

 "Old Barnet looked up in the boy's face;
you know how pretty a lad he is; he was then
sickly-looking and that made him a fitter object
for compassion: he has the sweetest voice in the
world and ~~th~~ all that he said seemed to go the
old man's heart. He thought;—I have no child ~~of~~
~~my own~~ upon earth: my only relation is a
brother who disdains a poor old fisherman
like me. My dame is dead, and I am alone
without anyone to help me if I am sick or to
say a cheerful, Good bye, God send you luck! when
I go a fishing. Surely this boy seems sent by heaven |
to me, and it seems to me that I love him
already as if he were my own son. He shall
stay with me; I can maintain him as I
maintained my poor wife who is gone: he
can put my cottage in order, mend my sails
& nets, and on windy evenings who knows
but he may be able to read the bible to me as
my dame used.

"This was a lucky thought; the bargain
was soon struck, and ever since Maurice
has lived with old Barnet in his cottage. He
is a good boy, honest, handy & clever: when
we came to know him all our house loved
him; he is able to read very tolerably, so
my little brothers went to him to learn
every sunday as they used to go to the Dame,
& no one can be more good tempered. He
made the old cottage quite another thing, clean
ing it, and mending the old chairs; white
washing the grate, and furbishing up the
pans & saucepans, & laying them in
~~or~~ neat rows. He was always merry, always
at work, always ready to do a good turn for
the poor as well as the rich. Old Barnet
loved him better & better, and often thanked
God for the day when he first came to the |
cottage. Out at sea the old man saw through
the day the trees wave over his cottage roof,
and at night he could distinguish the candle
which Maurice placed at the window to
direct him where to steer. When he came to
shore the boy was always waiting there to help
him draw his boat up to the cove. Then in
winter he found a nice fire ready to dress his
supper, and the table spread with a coarse, old,
but clean cloth. In the morning when he went
to market, Maurice ~~clean~~ heaved the water
out of his boat, mended his nets, put his sails
in order, and said a smiling, "God give you
luck!" when he went to sea. They lived seve
ral months in this manner very happily,
and now a week ago old Barnet died."—

The countryman paused, and the travel
ler asked, "What will become of the boy?"—"I
do not know; but he ~~is~~ is so much loved that

I do not think he will come to want. For my
part I am now leaving the country for a few
weeks, for I am going to visit my grandmother
who lives at Sidmouth; but when I return the
first question I shall ask is what is become of
Maurice. I have told you a long story, Sir, but
I hope you will excuse me; you have now |
finished your dinner, and I will detain you
no longer. Good bye!"—"Thank you heartily.
Good day, and a pleasant journey to you,"—
was the reply, and the young man left the
inn.

The traveller remained sometime leaning
his head on his hand, thinking what he ~~shud~~
should do. He wanted very much to make
further enquiry about Maurice, but when
he thought of the business he had at Exeter
he could not resolve to delay his journey:
so after resting himself another hour, he
strapped on his wallet and left the inn,
following the Exeter road.

The next morning he arrived at this
city. By and bye I shall explain what
his business there was; but at present I
shall only say that having passed three
anxious days, he was obliged to give up his
business, and to determine to return whence
he came, that he might enquire whether
somthing had not happened in the mean
time that might help him; at the same
time he resolved on his way back, to visit
old Barnet's cottage, and to enquire what had |
become of Maurice, and to offer his ser
vices in placing him in some suitable
situation, where he might honestly get his
livelihood without being worked too hard.
And now leaving him to walk with his

wallet on his back along the road which
leads from Exeter to Torquay, let us take
a peep into the cottage under the cliff;
and see what has become of Maurice
and what help he is likely to get in his
misfortunes.

PART SECOND.

The three other mourners who had fol
lowed Old Barnet's funeral were the brother
of whom the country man had spoken, and
his two sons. After the funeral this brother,
who was a shopkeeper at Torquay and a money
loving man, spoke thus to Maurice:—"You,
it seems, were maintained by my poor brother,
and lived in his cottage: now you know by
the laws that since my brother died without
a will, all he was worth, the cottage and its
furniture, the boat and his nets are mine.
If they were not you are too young to follow
his trade, so there is no possible reason why you
should remain in the cottage. The neighbours
say you are an honest lad so I would not
be too hard upon you; you may stay in the
cottage one week, and you can employ ~~that~~
~~time~~ in seeking for a place: at the end of
that time a friend of mine with his three
sons will come and live there, and having
bought the ~~ba~~ boat will carry on the fishing;
they will not want you for a servant, so
by that time you must remove. You are |
honest and therefore I need hardly
tell you that nothing in the cottage be-

longs to you, except what you brought
yourself, and that you will not be
allowed to take any thing away with you."—
    Maurice thanked his old friend's brother
for allowing him to stay a week in the
cottage; he intended to have asked his
advise about what he ought to do, but
there was somthing so dry and forbidding
in his manner that he could not make
up his mind to speak, but went away,
walking sorrowfully along the shore
towards the old cottage. When he arrived he
thought that it looked so ~~det~~ desolate and
strange, that he had not the heart to enter
but sat down near the little fresh-water
brook, and watched the waves of the sea
breaking at his feet. For the first time for
several months he was idle; for it was no
use to mend the nets when his old protector
could not use them, or to get supper ~~b~~ ready
when he felt his heart too full to eat. He
cried for the loss of his dear Barnet till he
was quite tired, and then watched the sun
set in the blue sea; and half imagined that
perhaps Barnet was not dead, but out
fishing and that he could perceive his |
white sail far out at sea: but turning round
he saw the boat lying empty in the cove, &
then he knew it must be true that his only
friend was dead, and that he was ~~quite~~ now alone in
the world. At length quite exhausted by sorrow,
and feeling cold as the evening breeze arose and
whitened the sea with foam, he got up and
~~b~~ opening the cottage door, without eating any
supper or striking a light, he knelt down &
said his prayers and then went to bed.
    Several days passed in this manner, and at

length he began to think that he ought not to live this idle life any longer. The week ~~would soon pass~~ ^{was almost gone} when he must quit the cottage, and then what should he do to earn bread to eat. Sometimes he thought he would return to his parents, but that he quickly determined not to do; and at length he resolved to go to farmer Benson; the father of the country man who related his story to the traveller at Torquay. As he determined this he sat on his accustomed stone near the fresh-water rill, and looked at the ocean which was unbroken by waves, and the sky where the sun had set, and the evening star gleamed in the golden light he had left behind him: the air was quite calm and the murmuring of the tide, which was going out, just broke the silence, while a few sea- | gulls flew to their nests in the cliff over his head. Maurice heard a step near him, and turning round saw approach a kind, good-looking man who was indeed the traveller whom I described at the beginning of my story. The boy was much surprised, for a stranger had never before visited the cottage which was two miles from any road: rising with his usual goodnature, he asked him whether he had lost his way, and offered to shew him the way to the nearest town.

   "I have not lost my way," said the traveller, "I came to this cottage on purpose. I have particular reasons for wishing to see it, and would be much obliged to you if you could afford me a bed to night."—"You are very welcome; the cottage is poor, but as the bed is clean perhaps you will be content."—"I have travelled too much, my good boy, not to be easily satisfied. But do not rise; for the present let us enjoy this pleasant evening here at the sea

side, watching the waves that leave so ~~smo~~
smooth a beach behind them. Your cottage is
built in a very pretty place."—"I think so
indeed, and although it is poor and very old yet
taking it altogether I do not think there is a
prettier in all the country round. The trees fall |
over & shelter it, a number of pretty flowers
grow beside the brook which comes running down
from the tall, red cliff. And nothing to my mind
can be more beautiful than the moss & lichens
yellow, green, white & blue that grow on the
old thatched roof, making it look finer than a
slated roof could possibly be. In the spring yellow
wall-flowers grow there, and the green before the
door is covered with da[i]sies. Besides if you come
round to the other side where the cottage faces the
hill you will find a pretty lattice ~~with~~ grown
over with honeysuckles and several geraniums
in ~~th~~ a stand outside the window. The geraniums
were the great favourite of old Barnet's dame,
and he loved them for her sake. Mr Gregory
Barnet says that I must take nothing from
the cottage, and that I know very well; but if
farmer Benson will take me into his service
I will spend two shillings that I have in buying
the geraniums, if the man who is com~~m~~ing to
live here will be kind enough to sell them."—
"You intend then to leave this cottage?"—"I must.
I am not strong enough to manage the boat
and go out to sea, and so it is let to some fisherman,
next Sunday I go away; but I hope I shall get
work hereabouts; and I do not think I shall be |
unhappy, for I have seldom cried about my
own misfortunes when I have been ~~v~~ very
illused indeed; and I do not dislike work
when it does not make me ill. I loved old
Barnet and liked my life here with him

and I cried very much when he died—but
if I can get work about a farm yard, I
hope in a month or two to sing as cheerfully
as I used when I saw his white sail among
the other boats which you ^see^ out at sea."

Maurice did not say all this at once,
but the stranger smiled so kindly, and asked
so many questions in so affectionate a manner,
that the boy was easily induced to open his
whole heart to him, and to talk about his
affairs as to an old friend. "I shall not
return to my parents," said he, "for I left deter
mining never more to see them till I could
earn my own bread. My father works hard and
wages are low, so being hardly able to get suffi
cient food for himself he ~~thinks~~ ^was^ angry that he
had to maintain an idle boy, ^and^ my mother
is sufficiently vexed by him without my misfor
tunes being added to her cares. Unfortunately I
am a delicate boy and unable to work as he would
have me and have often been confined to
my bed with fevers. My father never would be
lieve I was really ill & would beat me and |
and send me to bed without my supper when I
could hardly stand. I do not mean to complain of
him, and though I have told all this to you who
are so kind, pray do not mention it to any one else.

Thus they chatted till the evening star had
set, and the sea became invisible through
darkness, except indeed the white heads of the
waves that broke near them; for the tide was
coming in and the rock on which they sat
began to be wetted by the spray: so they entered the
cottage & supping on bread and salad, they presently after went to bed, the traveller telling the
boy that he would both break fast and dine
with him the following day.

unhappy, for I have seldom cried about my own misfortunes when I have been ~~very~~ ill used indeed; and I do not dislike work when it does not make me ill. I loved old Barnet and liked my life here with him and I cried very much when he died—but if I can get work about a farm yard, I hope in a month or two to sing as cheerfully as I used when I saw his white sail among the other boats which you see out at sea.

Maurice did not say all this at once but the stranger smiled so kindly, and asked so many questions in so affectionate a manner, that the boy was easily induced to open his whole heart to him, and to talk about his affairs as to an old friend. "I shall not return to my parents," said he, "for I left them meaning never more to see them till I could earn my own bread. My father works hard and wages are low, so being hardly able to get sufficient food for himself he ~~thinks~~ was angry that he had to maintain an idle boy, and my mother is sufficiently vexed by him without my misfortunes being added to her cares. Unfortunately I am a delicate boy and unable to work as he would have me and have often been confined to my bed with fevers. My father never would believe I was really ill & would beat me and

and send me to bed without my supper when I could hardly stand. I do not mean to complain of him, and though I have told all this to you who are so kind, pray do not mention it to anyone else.

Thus they chatted till the evening star had set, and the sea became invisible through darkness, except indeed the white heads of the waves that broke near them; for the tide was coming in and the rock on which they sat began to be wetted by the spray: so they entered the cottage & supping on bread and salad, they presently after went to bed, the traveller telling the boy that he would both break fast and dine with him the following day.

Maurice awoke before light, and leaving his guest sleeping soundly in bed he ran as fast as he could to Torquay to buy some white bread and potatoes and meat for their breakfast and dinner. He was obliged to spend for this provision the two shillings with which he had intended to purchase his dear geraniums, and this made him a little sorrowful but he was a cheerful, happy-tempered boy, & consoled himself with thinking that he would work doubly hard to earn this money before the next spring, and that he would entreat the future tenant of the cottage to take care of these pretty shrubs untill that time.

Maurice awoke before light, and leaving his
guest sleeping soundly in bed he ran as fast as
he could to Torquay to buy some white bread,
and potatoes and meat for the breakfast and
dinner. He was obliged to spend for this provision
the two shillings with which he had intended to
purchase his dear geraniums, and this made him
a little sorrowful: but he was a cheerful,
happy-tempered boy, & consoled himself with think
ing that he would work doubly hard to earn this
money before the next spring, and that he would
entreat the future tenant of the cottage to
take care of these pretty shrubs until this time. |
When he arrived at the cottage he found
the traveller seated on the rock on the beach;
they greeted one another kindly, and Maurice, at
the request of his guest, brought out a little
table on the sands, and placed their breakfast
on it in the open air; for it was a fine
warm morning without a cloud in the sky.
Their break fast was plain and countryfied
consisting of bread, a piece of cheese and a
basin of that nice clouted cream that they
make in Devonshire; and our two friends ate
so heartily of what was there that very
little remained. They then continued sitting on
the rock talking together of the pleasure of
living in the country, of seeing the pretty flowers
grow in the hedges and among the green grass; of
the beauty of the little birds, and the cruelty
of those who kill them: and the sweet life
it would be to take care of a nice farm,
not working too hard, but sufficient to become
healthy and strong through exercise; and in the
evening to read entertaining books, telling them of
how the earth is cultivated, and how various
countries bring forth various fruits: of the sea,

and how different voyages and discoveries have
been made on it: of the sky, and how the beau |
tiful stars which we see at night move, &
the signs they make of winter and summer.
The traveller told Maurice that there were
books more delightful than these which told
of what good and wise men had done a great
many years ago; how some had died to serve
their fellow creatures, and how ~~though~~ through
the exertions of these men every one had become
better, wiser and happier. Maurice said that
he had never read any book of that kind except
the bible, and that he had often cried over the
distress of Joseph, when he was sold to slavery,
and over the sorrow of David, when his son
Absolom revolted against him.

At length, after a pause, the traveller said
—"You talk my dear Maurice, of going to seek
for work at farmer Benson's: now what say
you if instead of this, you came and lived with
me. I would not task you too hard, but would
give you some of these pretty books to read, &
would do my best to make you happy."—Mau
rice looked up at the kind stranger and saw
him smiling benevolently upon him, "How good
you are!"—he replied.—"I will be good to you,"
said his guest, "but I am a stranger and |
you may be afraid to go away with ~~me~~ one
whom you ~~nene~~ never saw before. It is
late now for we have talked a long time, so
let us go in and ~~pl~~ prepare our dinner, and
afterwards ^we^ will come and sit here again and
I will tell you who I am; why I am travelling
on foot about the country; what my ~~hopes~~ ^disappointments^
have been, and what my hopes are."—

They did as he said. They made a good fire and
placed their meat and potatoes to boil. Maurice

filled a jug with clear water from the brook, and
the traveller took a small bottle of good wine
from his wallet. By noon the dinner was ready,
and after they had finished they sat down on
the rock, and the traveller q began his relation.

PART THIRD

I am the son of a professor of Mathe
matics at the university of Oxford; my father was not rich but he gave me an excel
lent education, and I was exceedingly indus
-trious and fond of learning. As long as I can
remember I never went about without a
book in my pocket, and loved to take long,
solitary walks, and then to sit and read
for hours together under the shade of trees,
and beside the river; when I did not as an
idler go to sleep, lulled by its murmuring,
but I used to study and reflect with great
earnestness and curiosity. Every thing about me
appeared wonderful to my eyes, and I wanted
to know why the water of the river always
ran and never became less; how the sun
was ~~govered~~ governed as it passed along the sky,
and why the moon changed as it did, and some
times appeared round, and full, and yellow,
and at othertimes only a little silver crescent.
There was also another thing which delighted
me extremely, which was to examine three
large volumes of prints of beautiful antient
temples that my father possessed. I spent whole |
days in looking at these, and reading the accounts

of their dimensions and how they were built; for
I thought I should be the happiest creature in
the world if ever I should be able to build such
beautiful edifices as I saw represented in these
books. As I grew older I became fonder and
fonder of architecture, and as no knowledge is
gained without application I passed my whole
time in learning mathematics and those sciences
which best reach us how to erect edifices
such as the antients used to build. When I was
five and twenty my kind father sent me
abroad to ~~visit~~ Asia, Italy and Greece to visit
the remains of the old temples that still exist,
and I passed five years in this happy manner
dwelling among foreign nations, often in desart
places where the people do not live by sowing
& reaping corn and taking care of farms, as they
do here, but depend upon hunting for their
livelihood, leaving their native villages for months
together in search of game, and living a wild
life among the woods and mountains, while their
wives and daughters _{remain} ~~sit~~ at ~~hop~~ home spinning
their own clothes, sitting in the open air, where
the winters are so mild that they have neither
frost or snow.

    "When I returned to England I applied to |
business, and being and good architect I soon
became rich. When I thought I had money
enough I gave up my business and applied
my self to country labours and all kinds of
study, which I liked better than building churches
and bridges where the people have too little
taste or too little money to allow them to be
built in the beautiful manner I wished.

    "I married at this time a lady, whom you
will soon see, my dear Maurice, and then you
will know how wise and good she is. Soon after

Ilfracombe

our marriage we had a little boy of whom we were doatingly fond. All our joy was in watching this little creature, who was as beautiful and good as it was possible to be. When he was two years old we made a journey during the summer and ~~f~~ staid for a month at ~~Teignmouth~~ ˙Ilfracombe. a sea port ~~about~~ more than fifty miles distance from this place, and here a misfortune hap pened to us since which we have never been perfectly contented. It is now eleven years ago, but I can never think of that time without being unhappy.

"We used often to ride out my wife and I, and a servant with our baby; and when we came to a pretty place we used to leave the nurse and child with the carriage while we took long walks in the | country. One day we rode until we came to

the banks of a very pretty river; and telling the
nurse to wait for us, we walked on for several
miles, enjoying the pleasant weather, listening to the
singing of the birds in the elm trees which hung
over the river, and watching the little insects with
~~wh~~ wings of purple, green and gold that flew on
the surface of the water.

"When we returned we were dreadfully frighten
ed to find the nurse asleep among some hay and
no child near her. We awoke the woman and she
became pale with fear and trembled all over when
she found the child gone; since he had gone to sleep
in her arms, and she, without thinking of the
danger, and lulled to sleep by the sun, had at last
fallen asleep also. The first thing we did was to
run to the river;—but I will not describe, to
you, my little friend, the great grief we felt
during this search. We did not find our child, or
~~fin~~ see any remains of him near the water; on
the contrary we found one of his little shoes in a
field about a mile from the river, and this
made us think that perhaps he was stolen. We
spent many months in searching the whole country,
but in vain, we could not hear any tidings of
our dear, lost boy.

"For my part I have never given up hope |
that I shall one day find him again, for I
always felt convinced that he was not drowned.
So every year I spend two months in Devonshire
going over the whole county looking for him. I
dress myself meanly that I may enter the cottages
with greater freedom and make enquiries of
the country people in a familiar manner;
I walk about from village to village, and
never passe a solitary cottage without looking
at the children, and asking questions concern
-ing them.

"A fortnight ago I passed by a cottage
about five miles from Ilfracombe, at the
door of which stood a woman crying and
wringing her hands: I stopped and asked her what
was the matter, and she told me that her hus
band had died two days before, and that her only
son had been away ~~ne~~ a year and a half and
she did not know what had become of him. I
tried to console her, and told her that I also
was unhappy and had lost my only child while
a baby and had never found him again. I then
related to her my misfortune and was much
surprised to find her more distressed than
before, and when I described to her the great
grief of my wife, she cried out, "I am the cause of |
this! I am the wicked woman who stole your child!
I started at these words, and as soon as I could speak
I asked her what had become of my poor dear boy.
She then began to cry again, and said that it was
him she lamented when she told me that she
had not seen her only son for nearly two years.
She cried so much and appeared so distressed that
I was obliged to spend almost an hour before I
could console her, and then she told me how all
had happened.

"Her husband had been a sailor and they had
lived several years together and had had no children:
he was a bad man, and would beat and reproach
her for not having a child which made her very
unhappy, and she thought that she would be
perfectly happy ~~w~~ if heaven would bless her with
a son. At length once when her husband
went on a long voyage, she wrote to him a
month after his departure and told him that
she was with child. He staid away a long time,
and she continued to write and to tell falsehoods, how
the child was born and was thriving; and she did this

foolishly without thinking of the consequences, or
what her husband would say when he returned and
found no child. He was a sailor on board a king's
ship, and getting a wound in a battle which dis- |
abled him for a long time ~~w~~ he wrote to her
who was then living in London, to go down to
his native place at Ilfracombe, for that he
would leave his ship and go and live there the
rest of his days.

"She went down with a sorrowful heart not
knowing what she should say about her preten
ded child; and not liking to go among his relations,
who all expected to see a fine stout boy about
two years old, she took a mean lodging in a town
some miles off and went by a false name. She
passed two months in a very unhappy state of
mind, strolling about the country and not able
to determine as to what she would do, when one
day for our great misfortune she determined
to walk towards Ilfracombe to find out whether
her husband had arrived, and on her way she
found ~~t~~ our poor baby asleep in the arms of
his careless nurse.

"One wicked thing brings on another; and
she who had deceived her husband, and for two
years written a number of falsehoods, and
had become to have the habit of feeling guilty
and wrong, now made up her mind to steal this
child, not caring for the unhappiness of its parents.
She took him gently out of the nurse's ~~ha~~ arms,
and ran with him across the fields towards the |
town whcrc [she] had been living for the last
two months. When she came near the town
she hid ~~this my ownern~~ the child under
some straw in a barn, and went as fast as
she could to her lodgings. She paid for them
and taking her ~~mend~~ bundle of clothes she went

back to the child and hid herself in the barn
all day. At night she began her journey. She
resolved to go to Plymouth and wait for
her husband whose ship was expected in that
port, and thus to quit the country near
Ilfracombe until her theft should be
forgotten. She walked all day and hid herself
at night for fear of being discovered. She
burned the child's good clothes and made it others
out of her own, preserving only a little coral
neck lace with his ~~n~~ christian name engraved
on the clasp and the remaining shoe whose
fellow we found in the field and which we
have ever kept with great affection. She
lived six months at Plymouth before her
husband arrived and then they went together
and settled themselves in the cottage where
I found them. The woman soon loved our
poor boy as if it had been her own and |
took all possible care of it—caressing and tending
on ^{him} with the ~~af~~ tenderness of a mother.

    "But people who ~~are~~ do that which they ought
not to do seldom find that good come from
the crimes they commit which they expect. Our
poor boy had been accustomed to delicate fare
and gentle nursing; and whether it was that he
was now fed poorly and neglected (not through unkind
ness, but because she had not leisure to give him
the attention to which ^{he} had been accustomed with
us) whether it were on these accounts I know
not, but our little Henry became sickly and
delicate, and lost the fine bloom which first
tempted her to the ^{wicked} action of stealing him. Her hus
band who was a bad man and who had before
grumbled that he had no child, now became more
cross than ever, saying that the sickly brat would
never come to good, and that he was obliged to

maintain him by the sweat of his brow when
he would never be able to do the like for him
when he was old.

"The woman then said to me:—"I have
been very miserable as well as wicked: for
not only I felt great repentance at having |
taken this baby from his parents, but I found
my husband unkinder than ever, and that
instead of loving, he perfectly disliked the poor
child. Besides the dear fellow lost his health
and although the best creature in the
world and the ~~was~~ most willing and clever,
yet he could do no hard work, and often had
fevers and other illnesses when my husband
grudged the doctor, and I used to sit crying by
his bedside thinking that if his rich parents had
still kept him he would not lie without help
on his sick bed.

"As he grew older my husband grew unkinder
and sometimes beat him because he could not
work, and treated him in so cruel a manner
that I dare not relate to you who are his father,
so one day Henry (for so I called him as by his broken
words I found his parents had named him) came
to me, and told me that farmer Jackson
had promised to get work for him, and that
he was determined to go and try if he could not
gain his own livelihood. I cried bitterly, but
could not alter his purpose, though then I
would have given all I had in the world to
find out who his rich parents were, that I |
might restore him. I gave him my blessing
and he went away and I have never heard
of him since!

"I will not tire you, my little friend,
with the account of my walks and anxieties
for this last fortnight; during which ~~Now~~ I have been

employed in going all over Devonshire tra
cing my lost child; my labours have been
unsuccessful. I am now going to return
to Dame Smithson to ask whether he has
returned to her. This is my story; do you consent
to come and live with me? If I never find
my darling boy you shall be a son to me,
and if I do find him——"

Maurice had listened to this relation
very attentively, and near the end his
eyes had streamed with tears and he shewed
every sign of interest and impatience: and
now when the traveller said these words he
threw himself into the arms and sobbed out—
"I am your son! Daddy Smithson is not
my father! I am your lost boy!"—And then
he told him how he had always considered |
Dame Smithson his mother, and how kind
to him and fond of him she was; and
how her husband had made him perfectly
miserable so that he had determined never
to go home again until he should be able
to earn his bread for himself. He said that
he had called himself Maurice because
he was afraid that the cruel man whom
he ~~called~~ thought his father might come to that
part of the country and find him out and
beat and illuse him as he used to do at
home.

Now nothing could be happier than the
traveller and his dear son as they sat
together by the sea-side, talking about
what they would do and the joy of his poor
mother when she should see him again.
Henry cried for joy when he thought of
the happy life they should lead, reading
delightful books, living with a kind

father and mother, and having no care
upon earth but that of obeying them
and making them happy. They went that
very evening to Torquay, and hiring a chaise
they rode towards the traveller's home; and |
never rested until they arrived and Henry
was in his mother's arms.

And what became of the old moss~~ed~~-roofed
cottage by the sea-side? Why, at Henry's request
his father bought it, and the ~~ba~~ boat, and
the geraniums, and all that belonged to it from
Mr Gregory Barnet. They could not live there
because Henry was obliged to go to Eton to
school; and his father's house was near Windsor
park, close to the school, so that he always
lived with his dear parents. But in the
Whitsuntide and Ba[r]tholomewtide holidays they
~~wend~~ went down to Devonshire to visit
the pretty cottage and lived in it two months
every ~~p~~ year. It was too small for any ser
vants to come with them, so Henry put on
a coarse country dress, and his father clothed
himself as he used when he travelled about the
country to seek for his child. ~~Thh~~ They took care of
the garden, bought their own food, ~~coock~~ cooked
their own dinner; and when the weather was
fine and the ~~sun~~ sun shone they sat on
the rock near the fresh-water rill and talked
about all the ~~de~~ beautiful things they had seen |
or would one day see, or read delightful
books whose knowledge and lessons made them
both wiser ~~hand~~ and happier. When they
were at this cottage Henry always went by
the name of Maurice, and he would go
about among his ~~old~~ friends whom he had
known when he lived with old Barnet helping
and consoling them if they were sick or

Eton College

afflicted, and doing all the good a little boy
could do, or by the help of his father making
people happy when poverty or misfortune
had made them miserable.

In the fine evenings they would sail out to
sea in the old fishing boat; they did not fish
for they did not like to give pain to, and to
destroy animals, but they would observe the
dancing waves, and the rocky shores; and if they
staid out long after sunset they saw how the
stars came out one by one till the whole
sky was covered with them.

During the other part of the year Dame
Smithson lived in the old cottage. She was
very sorry for what she had done, and loved
Henry very much; and Henry never forgot

and ~~when~~ went abroad to foreign countries, &
saw many beautiful scenes of rocks, and
mountains, and trees, and rivers; yet he al
ways loved in his heart, his pretty cottage
and thought it the most ~~beautiful~~ delightful place he
had ever seen. It was very old as I have
said ~~before~~; and some time after when
Dame Smithson died some of the moss-covered
thatch fell off and let the water into the
cottage during the rainy ~~we~~ weather; it was
too old to be repaired, and by ~~de~~ degrees it fell
all to pieces, and the sea washed it away
as it fell, so that it quite disappeared.

When Henry returned from his travels
he found his pretty cottage gone, his gerani
-ums dead, and no wall left on which
the sweet-smelling, yellow wall-flowers could
grow; this grieved him very much, yet he
was pleased to find the red cliff, the waving
trees, the fresh-water rill, and the rock upon
which he and his father used so often to
sit — remained just the same as ~~before~~
when he left them: though the boat had
fallen to pieces in the cove, and the garden

39) had run wild. He would not build ano
ther cottage there for it would have been
too unlike old Barnets that he had loved
so well. But he built a house not far
off where he placed to live a poor fisherman
and his two children, who had lost his boat
in a storm some months before; and ~~who~~
~~& upon poor ~~ himself, was in great
want and poverty. He built another boat
for the little cove and often during his life
came to visit the cliff, and the trees, and
the rock; where he would sit and reflect
on the life he had led while a little boy
with old Barnet in the pretty, old, fisher's
cot; and how his father came to visit
and assist him when he was poor and
helpless, not knowing him to be his son,
and how on that very rock he had first
discovered that he belonged to good, kind
parents; with whom he now lived in
content and happiness.

The End

that he had loved her once as a dear, good
mother.

Many years after, when Henry grew older |
and went abroad to foreign countries, &
saw many beautiful scenes of rocks, and
mountains, and trees, and rivers; yet he al
ways loved in his heart his pretty cottage
and thought it the most ~~beautiful~~ ^{delightful} place he
had ever seen. It was very old as I have
said before; and some time after when
Dame Smithson died some of the moss-covered
thatch fell off and let the water into the
cottage during the rainy ~~we~~ weather; it was
too old to be repaired, and by ~~de~~ degrees it fell
all to pieces, and the sea washed it away
as it fell, so that it quite disappeared.

When Henry returned from his travels
he found his pretty cottage gone, his gerani
-ums dead, and no wall left on which
the sweet-smelling, yellow wall-flowers could
grow; this grieved him very much, yet he
was pleased to find the red cliff, the waving
trees, the fresh-water rill, and the rock upon
which he and his father used so often to
sit—remained just the same as ~~before~~
when he left them: though the boat had
fallen to pieces in the cove, and the garden |
had run wild. He would not build ~~an~~ ano
-ther cottage there for it would have been
too unlike old Barnet's that he had loved
so well. But he built a house not far
off where he placed to live a poor fisherman
and his two children, who had lost his boat
in a storm some months before, ~~and scarcely
h saved from drowning himself~~, was in great
want and poverty. He built another boat
for the little cove and often during his life

came to visit the cliff, and the trees, and
the rock; where he would sit and reflect
on the life he had led while a little boy
with old Barnet in the pretty, old, fisher's
Cot; and how his father came to visit
and assist him when he was poor and
helpless, not knowing him to be his son;
and how on that very rock he had first
discovered that he belonged to good, kind
parents; with whom he now lived in
content and happiness.

The End

APPENDIX:

'TWELVE COGENT REASONS FOR
SUPPOSING P. B. SH—LL—Y
TO BE THE D—V—L INC—RN—T—'
BY LADY MOUNTCASHELL*

'Tis often thought by learned men
that Satan walks the earth again;
And some ev'n go so far's to say
He ne'er one hour has been away
Since first to Eden's garden went he
As Dame Eve's Cavalier Servente;
But always in one form or other
Contrives the Lord's elect to bother.
I oft with holy zeal had tried
To find him out; but he defied
My efforts almost half a century,
And (though I scarcely dared to venture) I
Still sometimes thought a doubtful matter
This Devil, who makes such a clatter

*This text is taken from a typed transcript in the Cini archive.

Among the Saints & the Saintesses.
And teaches them such pranks (God bless us!)
As frighten unbelieving sinners,
And give the holy priests good dinners.
I must confess, for want of persons
(Who in this popish land are scarce ones)
Churches with pews (for *pews* here none add)
Un-Crucifixed & un-Madonna'd,
Free from the sad abomination
Of odorif'rous exhalation;
Breathing alone such vapours pure,
As pious Protestants endure,
To shew their faith in holy writ;
In Luther's or in Calvin's wit.
For want of all these saving aids
I thought (how conscience me upbraids!)
That Satan was a mere non-entity,
A shadow which had no identity,
The blind caprice of troubled rain
Seeking for something wise in vain.
Such were my silly dreams when first
Conviction met me, and disperst
All doubts; shewing that but too well I
Might see the Devil in P. B. Shelley.
Of this sad truth are proofs abundant,
To write one half would be redundant;
But twelve I will select, to shew
That Satan still walks to & fro,
And without doubt's the cause of all
The ills which Kings & *Queens* befall.

Proof 1st   First, all who see his face, observe
A sensibility of nerve
That's quite unnnatural to man,
And shews the Devil soon began
To make his nest in Shelley's gizzard,
Who straight became a-dreadful, wizard.

Proof 2nd   Seeking good Christians to devour,
                He clapped his claw in early hour
                On orthodoxy's lulling preacher;
                Made him a philosophic teacher,
                To lead his pious flock astray
                In toleration's wicked way.

Proof 3rd   Then set gold traps for honour'd sage,
                And filled his mind with Mammon's rage,
                So that the voice which gained applause
                While erst employed in virtue's cause,
                And oft so well of *Justice* spoke,
                Can now no power but Wealth invoke,

Proof 4th   Next good dull folks (in *Study* small)
                Frugal in food, *in hats*, in all,
                He lends *three hundred* foul temptations;
                So wafts them off to distant nations,
                To *cut a dash in Paris* town,
                Which surely marks them for his own–

Proof 5th   Who hears him talk of Hell's delights,
                (That red hot furnace which affrights
                Those worthy souls whose faith ne'er fails
                In fire & brimstone, horns & tails)
                And sees him chuckle at the thought
                Of myriads, who must there be brought,
                Can never question that his home
                Is somewhere near that dev'lisht dome.

Proof 6th   All unknown tongues he speaks at will;
                And this another proof is still,
                For Satan ever has been known
                To strange outlandish lingos prone:
                And when exorcised by a Priest,
                Has always talked Latin at least.

Proof 7th   Oft he cajoleth simple souls
                When with kind soothing lacks, he strolls
                About, and helps the sick & poor;
                Feeds one & pays for t'others cure.

Little they know the reason why:
He fears lest these *in grace* should die,
And so to Heaven from him escape,
Though Hell with all its might should gape.

Proof 8th   Whene'er he meets with folks so wicked
That such black crimes they do not stick at
As living without visit-paying,
Or daily gossipping, or praying;
Who laugh at holy priests & kings
And queens & other sacred things;
With these he feels in near relation,
Brothers & sisters of damnation–

Proof 9th   But when he meets the Lord's elect
None who behold but must suspect
That poetry puts him in pain
For, as if he were a snake again
He twists & winds about, & tries
To shun the gaze of Christian eyes;
And when no other means avail
Springs from his chair & turns his tail.

Proof 10th   With learning of a Grecian sage,
And genius of an Attic age,
No mark of arrogance he shews,
As would the mortal wight disclose.
So 'tis not possible that he
Can other than old Satan be–

Proof 11th   In holy places ev'n he lurks
To carry on his sinful works.
With looks as harmless as a child,
And words of blasphemy so mild,
Corrupts the spouses of the Lord
And makes them speak in tongues abhorred–
All mischief quietly he plans,
The flame of every ill he fans;
Makes nubile spinsters lose their beauty:

Proof 12th   And matrons old forget their duty.
Witness alas! this dogg'rel rhyme;

Whose writer should have at this time
Been otherwise employed: and now
Can only wish it had been so–
But when the Devil drives, they say
No mortal can direct the way–

NOTES

1. *Mary Shelley: Collected Tales and Stories*, edited by Charles E. Robinson, was published by the Johns Hopkins University Press in 1976.
2. According to J. M. S. Tompkins's study of the late eighteenth-century novel, Henry was by far the most popular name for writers of fiction of the period: 'eighty per cent of the heroes are called Henry'. It seems extraordinary, but see her *The Popular Novel in England 1770–1800* (1932; repr. 1969), pp. 57–8n. She adds, 'William, on the other hand, is a name of dubious, often villainous, complexion.' Mary's choice of names for her characters is sometimes surprising, as when, for instance, she uses her own infant son William's name for the little William who is murdered in *Frankenstein*.
3. Mary forgave Eton's treatment of her husband enough to later make it her first choice for their son Percy Florence, although she was dissuaded by Shelley's father on the grounds that the boy might be teased there—like his father. She sent him to Harrow.

4. We know nothing about this 1815 visit beyond that it was made. Mary used the Cornish coast in her last novel, *Falkner*, in which an orphaned child lives beside the sea with a poor foster-mother before being rescued by a father-figure. The Cornish coast was also used in her story of 1833, *The Smuggler and His Family*, in which a father tries to make his son follow him into smuggling. It was written especially for a fund-raising publication, and is nothing like *Maurice* in subject or tone.

5. *Matilda* remained unpublished until 1959.

6. The 'Note on Peter Bell the Third', written by Mary Shelley in 1839 for the second edition of her husband's poems, mentions that 'a critique on Wordsworth's *Peter Bell* reached us at Leghorn' in 1820, and that 'no man ever admired Wordsworth's poetry more;—he read it perpetually, and taught others to appreciate its beauties'.

7. Document written by Lady Mountcashell in Pisa in April 1818. It is reproduced in Edward C. McAleer, *The Sensitive Plant* (1958), p. 8.

8. The evidence for the existence of Elena Adelaide Shelley was found by Professor Alberto Tortagolione, searching in Naples on behalf of the Shelley biographer Newman Ivey White, in 1936. There is a birth registration, signed by Shelley and naming himself as father and Mary as mother, and giving her birth as 27 December 1818; a baptismal certificate for 27 February 1819, again naming Shelley and Mary as her parents, and naming the midwife also; and a certificate of death, saying that 'Elena Schelly of Naples' died on 9 June 1820, aged fifteen months and twelve days, at her home. The informants were a cheesemonger and a potteryman, and the child is described as the daughter of 'Bercy Schelly' and 'Maria Gebuin', both domiciled at Leghorn.

9. Lady Mountcashell's words about Mary Wollstonecraft—whom she does not name—are also taken from the document quoted above, written in 1818. They appear on p. 5 of McAleer's *The Sensitive Plant*.

10. Lady Mountchashell to William Godwin, 8 Sept. [n.y. but 1801], unpub. MS, Abinger deposit, c. 507/5, Bodleian Library.

11. Charles Kegan Paul, *William Godwin, His Friends and Contemporaries* (1876), pp. 369–70.

12. Information from Catherine Wilmot's journal, printed in *An Irish Peer on the Continent 1801–3*, Thomas U. Sadleir, ed. (1920).

13. Unpub. MS poems in Cini archive.

14. Lady Mountcashell to Denys Scully, 27 July 1806, Munich, letter 149, Brian MacDermot, *The Catholic Question in Ireland and England 1798–1882: The Papers of Denys Scully* (1988), p. 133.

15. ibid.

16. ibid., pp. 133–4.

17. Unpub. MS, Cini archive.

18. Unpub. MS, Cini archive.

19. Lady Moira to Denys Scully, 17 Sept. 1807, letter 158, McDermot, *The Catholic Question in England and Ireland 1798–1882*, pp. 145–6.

20. Cini archive, only partly published in McAleer, *The Sensitive Plant*, p. 199.

21. Lady Mountcashell's document of Apr. 1818; these words, McAleer, *The Sensitive Plant*, p. 7.

22. McAleer, *The Sensitive Plant*, p. 7–8.

23. Claire Clairmont to Lord Byron, 27 for 26 Apr. 1818, *The Clairmont Correspondence*, Marion Kingston Stocking, ed. (1995), vol. I, p. 115.

24. 8 Jan. 1819, MS letter in French in Abinger deposit, c. 811/3,

Bodleian Library, only partly published: *'je ne pouvais accoutumer la petite a ne pas se salir la nuit . . . Allegra est devenue tranquille et sérieuse comme une petite vieille, ce qui nous peine beaucoup.'*

25. Marion Kingston Stocking suggests a new possibility in an appendix to her *The Clairmont Correspondence*. The suggestion is that Shelley had a passing sexual fling, just before leaving London in the spring of 1818, with a young English lady who pursued him with her admiration, became pregnant as a result, and followed him to Italy. Adelaide Constance Campbell *may* have been travelling in Italy with her mother Lady Charlotte Campbell, but this is uncertain. What is certain is that in March 1818 Lady Charlotte married her chaplain, the Reverend Edward John Bury, who, as it happens, graduated from Oxford in 1811, the year Shelley was expelled from the university for atheism. The possibility of a link is there, and the name is good, but nothing has been proved. The sources for the story of Shelley's 'scrape' are Claire Clairmont's remarks in old age to Edward Silsbee, and Shelley's cousin Thomas Medwin.

The affair remains wrapped in mystery. Not surprisingly, Shelley did his best to conceal whatever happened. Accused by blackmailing servants of fathering Elena with Claire, he denied it vehemently. Mary also firmly denied this version, when he asked her to do so; but neither of them offered any explanation as to the child's real parentage, and Shelley cuts a curious figure when he protests that he would never commit the 'unutterable crime' of 'abandoning a child'. It is, after all, exactly what he did in this case.

26. 4 Aug. 1819, *The Journals of Mary Shelley*, Paula R. Feldman and Diana Scott-Kilvert, eds. (1987), vol. I, p. 293.

27. Claire Clairmont, cited in McAleer, *The Sensitive Plant*, pp.

NOTES

3–4, giving as his source Edward Dowden, *The Life of Percy Bysshe Shelley* (1887), vol. II, p. 317.

28. 14 Nov. [1819], unpub. MS, Abinger deposit, c. 517/2, Bodleian Library.

29. Both from Lady Mountcashell to Percy Bysshe Shelley, 14 Nov. 1819, unpub. MS, Abinger deposit, c. 517/1, Bodleian Library.

30. Lady Mountcashell to Mary Shelley, Friday 14 [Jan. 1820], letter 7, unpub. MS, Abinger deposit, c. 517/2, Bodleian Library.

31. Thursday, 27 Jan. 1820, *The Journals of Claire Clairmont*, Marion Kingston Stocking, ed. (1968), p. 119.

32. Claire Clairmont to Lord Byron, 23 Apr. 1820, *The Clairmont Correspondence*, vol. I, p. 143.

33. Claire Clairmont to Lord Byron, 1 May 1820, *The Clairmont Correspondence*, vol. I, p. 145.

34. This was published in 1820. Claire Clairmont was reading it in Pisa on 18 July, two days before she rode with Laurette to visit Mary at Livorno.

35. Nora Crook points out that Mary Shelley made no entries in her journal between 6 and 9 August, and that her habit of summarizing the activities of blank days on the day she resumes her journal could indicate that she had been writing and copying out *Maurice* over a five-day period. I am sure this is right, and that 'Wrote a story for Laurette' on 10 August covers the previous days' work on it. The story is too carefully composed to be the work of a single day.

36. Percy Bysshe Shelley to Mary Shelley, 15 Aug. 1821, cited by McAleer, *The Sensitive Plant*, p. 161.

37. Mary Shelley to Claire Clairmont, Mar. 1822, *The Letters of Mary Wollstonecraft Shelley*, Betty T. Bennett, ed. (1980–88), vol. I, p. 226.

38. ibid.

• 1 6 5 •

39. Claire Clairmont to Lord Byron, 18 Feb. 1822, *The Clairmont Correspondence*, vol. I, p. 170.

40. Claire Clairmont to Mary Shelley, 9 Apr. 1822, *The Clairmont Correspondence*, vol. I, p. 171.

41. I was struck by the fact that different authorities give *three* different dates for the death of Allegra in April 1822. Rosalind Glynn Grylls (*Mary Shelley*, 1938) gives 19 April, as does Newman Ivey White (*Shelley*, New York 1940, London 1947), repeated by Robert Gittings (*Claire Clairmont and the Shelleys*, 1992), Betty T. Bennett (*The Letters of Mary Wollstonecraft Shelley*, vol. I), Marion Kingston Stocking (*The Journals of Claire Clairmont* and *The Clairmont Correspondence*) and Mario Curelli (*Una Certa Signora Mason*, 1997). Iris Origo (*A Measure of Love*, 1957) gives 21 April, repeated by Phyllis Grosskurth (*Byron: The Flawed Angel*, 1997); Grosskurth follows Doris Langley Moore (*Lord Byron: Accounts Rendered*, 1994) in saying Byron received the news of his daughter's death on the 22nd. Byron himself asked to have '20th April' inscribed on Allegra's gravestone. Peter Quennell (*Byron: A Self-Portrait*, 1950), Leslie Marchand (*Byron: A Biography*, 1957), Michael Foot (*The Politics of Paradise*, 1988) and the catalogue to the Victoria & Albert *Byron* exhibition of 1974 repeat 20 April. In vol. VII of the Carl H. Pforzheimer Library's *Shelley and His Circle* (8 vols., 1961–86), Doucet Devin Fischer gives 20 April also, with a time, 10 p.m., but no source. 20 April certainly seems the most likely date. Fischer refers to a manuscript letter from Teresa Guiccioli to Byron, which tells him she has given the news to Mary Shelley on the 23rd, for Mary to pass on to Shelley; and, indeed, Mary Shelley's *Journal* has 'Evil news' on the 23rd.

The discrepancies in the dating of an event at the centre of the lives of Byron and the Shelley circle, so often worked over by scholars, are curious. As Langley

Moore wrote, 'Infant life was cheap': and perhaps the dating of infant death still seems relatively unimportant. There has perhaps also been a reluctance to cast blame on Byron for his neglect and his refusal to heed Claire's warnings; or to give her credit for the efforts she made to save Allegra.

42. Lady Mountcashell to Lord Byron, early 1823, cited in McAleer, *The Sensitive Plant*, p. 174.

43. Lady Mountcashell to Mary Shelley, 13 Jan. 1823, unpub. MS, Abinger deposit, c. 517, Bodleian Library.

44. Lady Mountcashell to Mary Shelley, 25 Feb. 1823, unpub. MS, Abinger deposit, c. 517, Bodleian Library.

45. Lady Mountcashell to Mary Shelley, spring 1824, cited in McAleer, *The Sensitive Plant*, p. 191.

46. Lady Mountcashell to Mary Shelley, cited in McAleer, *The Sensitive Plant*, p. 202.

47. Cited in McAleer, p. 200, from the Cini MSS.

48. Claire Clairmont to Mary Shelley, 26 Oct. 1832, *The Clairmont Correspondence*, vol. I, p. 290.

49. I am grateful to the Director of the Archives of the French Diplomatic Service at the Quai d'Orsai for sending me the file on Galloni.

50. Archives of the Quai d'Orsay; Mary Shelley to Maria Gisborne, 17 July 1834, *The Letters of Mary Wollstonecraft Shelley*, vol. II, p. 210.

51. William Tighe to Laurette Tighe, 1831, unpub. MS, Cini archive.

52. Claire Clairmont to Mary Shelley, 26 Oct. 1832, *The Clairmont Correspondence*, vol. I, p. 291.

53. ibid.

54. Claire Clairmont to Mary Shelley, 13 July 1845, *The Clairmont Correspondence*, vol. II, p. 452.

55. Claire Clairmont to Jane Hogg, 1 Feb. 1833, *The Clairmont Correspondence*, vol. I, p. 296.

56. Claire Clairmont to Mary Shelley, 15 Sept. 1833, *The Clairmont Correspondence*, vol. I, p. 301.

57. Mary Shelley to Maria Gisborne, 17 July 1834, *The Letters of Mary Wollstonecraft Shelley*, vol. II, p. 210.

58. Claire Clairmont to Mary Shelley, 2 June 1835, *The Clairmont Correspondence*, vol. II, p. 320.

59. Laurette Galloni to William Tighe, 17 Dec. 1835, unpub. MS, Cini archive.

60. Laurette Galloni to William Tighe, 9 Oct. 1835, unpub. MS, Cini archive.

62. ibid.

62. Laurette Galloni to William Tighe, 29 Jan. 1836, unpub. MS, Cini archive.

63. ibid.

64. Laurette Galloni to William Tighe, 16 Feb. 1837, unpub. MS, Cini archive.

65. Mary Shelley to John Cochrane, 22 Dec. 1829, *The Letters of Mary Wollstonecraft Shelley*, vol. II, p. 97. Stendhal made his own version of the story of the Cenci, which he took from sixteenth- and seventeenth-century manuscripts he found when he was at Civitavecchia in 1834. *Les Cenci* was published only after his death (and Mary Shelley's), in 1855, together with other Italian stories from the manuscripts, *Vittoria Accoramboni*, *L'Abbesse de Castro*, etc., under the title of *Chroniques italiennes*.

66. Laurette Galloni to William Tighe, 2 Sept. 1836, unpub. MS, Cini archive.

67. Laurette Galloni to William Tighe, 9 Dec. 1836, unpub. MS, Cini archive.

68. Mary Shelley to Mariana Hammond, 23 Jan. 1843, *The Letters of Mary Wollstonecraft Shelley*, vol. III, p. 56; Mary Shelley to Claire Clairmont, *The Letters of Mary Wollstonecraft Shelley*, vol. III, p. 62.

69. Mary Shelley to Claire Clairmont, 15 Apr. 1843, *The Letters of Mary Wollstonecraft Shelley*, vol. III, p. 69.

70. Claire Clairmont to Mary Shelley, 2 June 1843, *The Clairmont Correspondence*, vol. II, p. 377.

71. Mary Shelley to Marianna Hammond, Mar. 1846, *The Letters of Mary Wollstonecraft Shelley*, vol. III, p. 281.

72. English translation of Claire Clairmont to Bartolomeo Cini, 22 Feb. 1835, *The Clairmont Correspondence*, vol. II, pp. 317–18.

BIBLIOGRAPHICAL NOTE

My point of departure was Mary Shelley. I consulted unpublished letters to her, as well as her papers in the Abinger deposit in the Bodleian Library in Oxford. Of published works, I used her biographical notes to P. B. Shelley's *Poetical Works* (Oxford edition, 1970). Betty T. Bennett's three volumes of *The Letters of Mary Wollstonecraft Shelley* (1980–88) were indispensable sources of information, as were the two volumes of *The Journals of Mary Shelley*, edited by Paula R. Feldman and Diana Scott-Kilvert (1987). I also relied on the eight volumes of *The Selected Works of Mary Shelley*, edited by Nora Crook (1996); *The Collected Tales and Stories of Mary Shelley*, edited by Charles E. Robinson (1976), and the Carl H. Pforzheimer Library's eight-volume *Shelley and His Circle* (1961–86). Marilyn Butler's introduction to the Penguin edition of *Frankenstein* (1994) is a useful one.

Edward Dowden's two-volume *Life of Percy Bysshe Shelley* (1886), Newman Ivey White's *Shelley* (2 vols., New York, 1940; London 1947) and Richard Holmes's *Shelley: The Pursuit* (1974) were all helpful. Charles Kegan Paul's *William Godwin, His Friends and Contemporaries* (1876) remains a good source of information and letters relating to Mary Shelley's childhood. There is also Rosalind Glynn Grylls's *Mary Shelley* (1938) and Muriel Spark's *Child of Light: A Reassessment of Mary Shelley*, a pioneering book when it appeared in 1951; a revised edition came out in 1987.

On Lady Mountcashell, the Cini archive is a rich source of unpublished letters, poems and papers. There is only one biography of her, Edward C. McAleer's *The Sensitive Plant* (1958). Kegan Paul's *Godwin* has some material on her. *An Irish Peer on the Continent 1801–3* (the journal of Catherine Wilmot), edited by Thomas U. Sadleir (1920), is informative about the early part of the Mountcashells' continental tour. Some of her letters appear in Brian MacDermot's *The Catholic Question in Ireland and England 1798–1822: The Papers of Denys Scully* (1988). Mario Curelli's *Una Certa Signora Mason* (1997) has a good account of some of her unpublished fiction. Her *The Sisters of Nansfield* (1824) is, at the time of writing, catalogued under 'Anon? Charles Lamb' in the British Library.

On Claire Clairmont I used Marion Kingston Stocking's fine edition of *The Journals of Claire Clairmont* (1968)—one of the books that awoke my interest in the history of the group—and her two-volume *The Clairmont Correspondence* (1995). I also referred to Rosalind Glynn Grylls's biography *Claire Clairmont* (1939) and Robert Gittings's and Jo Manton's *Claire Clairmont and the Shelleys* (1992), although sadly this is not entirely reliable.

On Allegra I consulted Iris Origo's essay in *A Measure of Love* (1957), Leslie Marchand's *Byron's Letters and Journals* (12 vols., 1973–82), and many biographies of Byron.

For Laurette Tighe's history I have drawn extensively on the Cini archive again, guided by Cristina Dazzi's expert knowledge of it. For Laurette's husband Galloni's career and life, I consulted the Archives of the French Diplomatic Service at the Quai d'Orsay. Of her works, I have been able to read *La Spettatrice* by 'Sara' (4 vols., Milan, 1868), containing essays and a novella, *L'Ideale et la Scelta; Una Madre* (1857); *Le Due Fidanzate* (1864): and *Debole e Tristo* (1875).

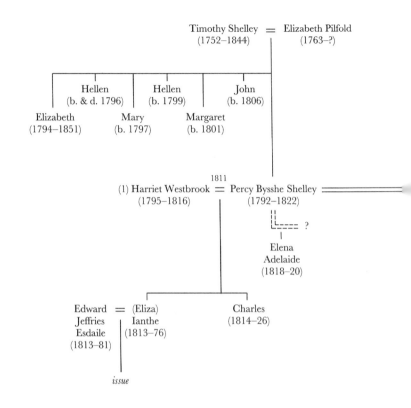

Timothy Shelley = Elizabeth Pilfold
(1752–1844)   (1763–?)

Elizabeth   Hellen   Hellen   Mary   Margaret   John
(1794–1851)   (b. & d. 1796)   (b. 1799)   (b. 1797)   (b. 1801)   (b. 1806)

1811
(1) Harriet Westbrook = Percy Bysshe Shelley
(1795–1816)   (1792–1822)

                                             ?

                                            Elena
                                           Adelaide
                                          (1818–20)

Edward = (Eliza)   Charles
Jeffries   Ianthe   (1814–26)
Esdaile   (1813–76)
(1813–81)

issue

THE FAMILY TREE OF MARY SHELLEY

1791

(1) Stephen Moore, = Margaret (King) Moore, ==
2nd Earl of Mountcashell   (**COUNTESS**
(1770–1822)   **MOUNTCASHELL**)
('Mrs Mason') (1772–1835)

Stephen   Helena   Edward   Richard
(1792–1883)   (1795–1859)   (1798–1876)   (1802–93)
(3rd Earl of
Mountcashell) Robert   Jane   Francis   Eliza
              (1793–1856)   (1796–1847)   (b. & d. 1800)   (1804–92)

│
issue

Margherita   Giorgine   Marianne   Giovanni
(1834–7)   (1836–8)   (1838–48)   ('Gianni') Cosimo
                                                (1840–1930)
                                                (d. w. i.)

THE FAMILY TREE OF LADY MOUNTCASHELL

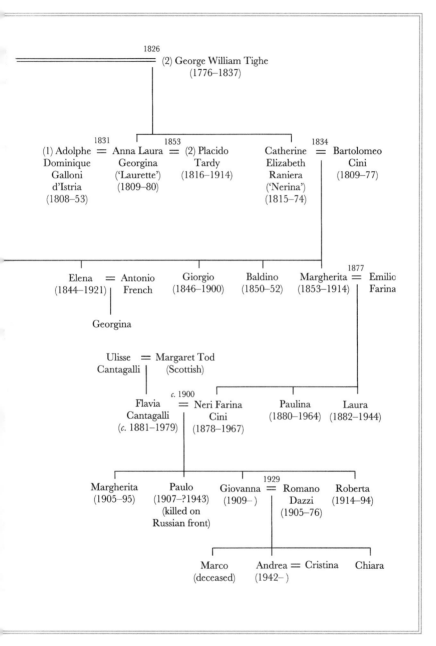

```
                                    1826
        ================================  (2) George William Tighe
                                          (1776–1837)
                                            |
                  1831              1853                              1834
        (1) Adolphe  =  Anna Laura  =  (2) Placido     Catherine     =  Bartolomeo
        Dominique       Georgina        Tardy          Elizabeth        Cini
        Galloni         ('Laurette')    (1816–1914)    Raniera          (1809–77)
        d'Istria        (1809–80)                      ('Nerina')
        (1808–53)                                      (1815–74)
                                                          |
                                                                              1877
        Elena    =  Antonio      Giorgio       Baldino      Margherita  =  Emilio
        (1844–1921)  French      (1846–1900)   (1850–52)    (1853–1914)    Farina
               |
           Georgina


           Ulisse     =  Margaret Tod
           Cantagalli  |  (Scottish)
                       |
                       |        c. 1900
                    Flavia      =  Neri Farina    Paulina       Laura
                    Cantagalli     Cini           (1880–1964)   (1882–1944)
                    (c. 1881–1979) (1878–1967)
                       |
                                          1929
        Margherita    Paulo      Giovanna  =  Romano     Roberta
        (1905–95)     (1907–?1943)  (1909– )   Dazzi       (1914–94)
                      (killed on              (1905–76)
                      Russian front)
                               |
                         Marco       Andrea  =  Cristina    Chiara
                         (deceased)  (1942– )
```

PAGE 8: Mary Wollstonecraft, engraving by J. Chapman after an unknown artist, published 1798 (private collection); William Godwin, 1802, oil on canvas by James Northcote (National Portrait Gallery, London)

12: *Maurice,* Part One, page 1 of the original manuscript (Cini archive, San Marcello Pistoiese); *Maurice,* Part Third, page 24 of the original manuscript (Cini archive, San Marcello Pistoiese)

23: Lady Mountcashell, from a miniature attributed to Charles Robertson (1759–1821) (Cini archive, San Marcello Pistoiese); Lord Mountcashell, later Earl, miniature on ivory by Charles Robertson (© The Board of Trustees of the Victoria and Albert Museum)

32: Lady Mountcashell, from a physionotrace engraving made in Paris by Edme Queneday (1756–1830) (The Carl H. Pforzheimer Collection of *Shelley and His Circle,* The New York Public Library. Astor, Lenox and Tilden Foundations); Pisa, engraving by C. Heath after a drawing by E. F. Batty, published 1818 (Hulton Getty)

35: Posthumous portrait of Mary Shelley by Reginald Easton (1807–93) (The Bodleian Library, Oxford); Percy Bysshe Shelley, 1819, oil on canvas by Amelia Curran (National Portrait Gallery, London

37: Claire Clairmont, 1819, oil on canvas by Amelia Curran (City of Nottingham Museums, Newstead Abbey); Lord Byron, *c.* 1818, engraving after G. H. Harlow (John Murray Collection)

38: William Shelley, Rome, 1819, oil on canvas by Amelia Curran (The Carl H. Pforzheimer Collection of *Shelley and His Circle,* The New York Public Library. Astor, Lenox and Tilden Foundations); Allegra, Venice, 1818, unknown artist (John Murray Collection)

43: Livorno, engraving by Giuseppe Maria Terreni (1739–1811) (Biblioteca Nazionale, Florence [Scala])

49: Lady Mountcashell, 1835, watercolor by Diana King (courtesy of Col. A. L. King-Harman)

51: Laurette Tighe, *c.* 1830, from a drawing by an unknown artist (The Carl H. Pforzheimer Collection of *Shelley and His*

Circle, The New York Public Library. Astor, Lenox and Tilden Foundations); Nerina Tighe, *c.* 1830, from a drawing by an unknown artist (The Carl H. Pforzheimer Collection of *Shelley and His Circle,* The New York Public Library. Astor, Lenox and Tilden Foundations)

58: Laurette, late 1840s, photograph (Cini archive, San Marcello Pistoiese); Placido Tardy, late 1840s, photograph (Cini archive, San Marcello Pistoiese)

60: Mary Shelley, exhibited 1840, oil on canvas by Richard Rothwell (National Portrait Gallery, London)

63: Laurette, *c.* 1870, photograph (Cini archive, San Marcello Pistoiese); Placido Tardy, *c.* 1870, photograph (Cini archive, San Marcello Pistoiese)

64: Archive box in which the manuscript was found in San Marcello Pistoiese, Italy (Cini archive, San Marcello Pistoiese)

120: Torquay, Devon, early nineteenth-century engraving, artist unknown (Hulton Getty)

134: Page 19 of the original manuscript (Cini archive, San Marcello Pistoiese)

135: Page 20 of the original manuscript (Cini archive, San Marcello Pistoiese)

141: Ilfracombe, Devon, early nineteenth-century engraving, artist unknown (Hulton Getty)

149: Eton, *c.* 1830–40, engraving by William Evans of Eton (Hulton Getty)

150: Page 38 of the original manuscript (Cini archive, San Marcello Pistoiese)

151: Page 39 of the original manuscript (Cini archive, San Marcello Pistoiese)

Renewed
for
Murder

Also available by Victoria Gilbert

Booklover's B&B Mystery
Reserved for Murder
Booked for Death

The Blue Ridge Library Mysteries
A Deadly Edition
Bound for Murder
Past Due for Murder
Shelved Under Murder
A Murder for the Books

Mirror of Immortality Series
Scepter of Fire
Crown of Ice

Renewed
for
Murder

A BLUE RIDGE LIBRARY
MYSTERY

Victoria Gilbert

CROOKED
LANE

NEW YORK

Copyright © 2021 by Vicki L. Weavil

Published in the United States by Crooked Lane Books, an imprint of The Quick Brown Fox & Company LLC.

Crooked Lane Books and its logo are trademarks of The Quick Brown Fox & Company LLC.

Library of Congress Catalog-in-Publication data available upon request.

ISBN (hardcover): 978-1-64385-786-2
ISBN (ebook): 978-1-64385-787-9

Cover design by Griesbach/Martucci

Printed in the United States.

www.crookedlanebooks.com

Crooked Lane Books
34 West 27th St., 10th Floor
New York, NY 10001

First Edition: December 2021

10 9 8 7 6 5 4 3 2 1

Dedicated to all the authors
who have enriched my life
with their books, poetry, and stories.

Chapter One

O ne thing I loved about being married to someone who jumped out of bed wide awake was that he often made coffee before I even stumbled downstairs. I was less appreciative when he tried to talk to me before I'd ingested any of that caffeine.

"I'll be home early," Richard said, polishing off his own mug of coffee before I'd taken my first sip. "Since classes don't start until next week, all I have today are meetings with the dance faculty and some course planning. I also have an appointment with Emily Moore to discuss using a piece of her poetry in the folklore project, but that shouldn't take too long. So I can start dinner if you want."

"Uh-huh," I muttered, casting my bleary-eyed gaze around the kitchen. Renovated to honor its farmhouse origins, it featured whitewashed cabinets, soapstone countertops, and a tall, narrow oak table that functioned as an island. In one corner, where adjacent windows created a sunny nook, a round oak table served as a casual dining space.

As my gaze swept back to Richard, I noticed his beautiful gray eyes were sparkling with good humor. Enjoying the

warmth that radiated from his smile, I once again marveled at the surprising turn my life had taken. Three years ago, I'd been a disillusioned thirty-two-year-old who'd fled a university library position and a failed romance to take over as the director of small public library. I willingly admitted that moving to Taylorsford, Virginia, had been driven by a need to escape my past.

Fortunately, I was happy in my new career. Taylorsford, my mother's hometown, was a beautiful and historic village situated at the foot of the Blue Ridge Mountains. I'd grown to love its eclectic community, and the move had allowed me to spend more time with my best friend, Sunshine "Sunny" Fields. I'd also relished the opportunity to live with my Aunt Lydia, who'd offered to share her three-story Queen Anne revival home. The move had settled me into a comfortable, if uneventful, life.

Then Richard Muir, a celebrated contemporary dancer and choreographer, had decided to renovate the house next door to us—a 1920s two-story his mother had inherited from her uncle, novelist Paul Dassin. Having taken a teaching job at nearby Clarion University, Richard also traveled to continue to choreograph and dance professionally.

Although I'd liked him from the start, the last thing I'd expected was that my new neighbor would become my husband after only two years of dating. But here we were, married for almost three months. It was, I confessed as I blew on my steaming coffee, the best decision I'd ever made. Even if Richard *was* far too chipper in the morning.

Richard pointed and circled one foot in an unconscious dance move as he ran his fingers through his dark hair. "Hello,

earth to Amy. You never answered my question. Do you want me to fix dinner, or should I pick something up?"

"Either is fine." I clutched the handle of my ceramic mug like a lifeline, still disgruntled over a dream where someone had rearranged all the books in the library by spine color instead of our regular classification system.

"You're not working late today, are you?" Richard bounded over to the kitchen's apron-front sink.

"No, eight to five today." I took a long swallow of my coffee. "I can actually help with dinner, if you choose a recipe and make sure we have all the ingredients."

"No problem." Richard glanced over his shoulder as he rinsed out his mug. "You're still half-asleep, aren't you?"

I offered him a wan smile. "More like seventy-five percent."

"Well, I think it's adorable. You look like a sleepy kitten." Richard jabbed his thumb toward one of our cats, a tortoiseshell named Loie, who was curled up on one of the wooden ladderback chairs at the kitchen table.

With the caffeine kicking in, I was finally able to formulate a proper response. "But Loie and Fosse never stumble around like zombies. They're always graceful, even when they've just woken up. They're more like you than me."

Richard grinned. "Dancers and cats do have a lot in common."

"Yeah, like their annoying habit of being deeply asleep one minute and leaping about the room the next." I shook my head. "How do you do that?"

Richard spread out his hands. "Don't know. I've always been able to wake up quickly. A gift, I guess."

"Well, it's also adorable, I suppose. In an annoying sort of way." I wrinkled my nose at him. "Anyway, now that I've reached something resembling consciousness, I'll confirm it'd be great if you'd start dinner."

"That's the plan then," Richard said. "I assume you're walking to work today?"

"Absolutely. The weather is supposed to be good. And, unlike you, I need the exercise."

Richard shrugged. "I need it just as much. But it's easier for me to fit it into my schedule. I mean, it's basically a part of my job. Besides, I have to stay in shape. It's hard enough to continue to dance at my advanced age . . ."

I snorted. "You're only thirty-seven."

Richard's bright expression faded a little. "Like I said, an advanced age, at least for a dancer."

I examined him for a moment. Even if he spent more time these days on his teaching and choreography, I knew how much he still loved to dance. "Oh, I expect you'll be leaping about when you're ninety. You're insufferably fit, you know."

Richard reached me in three long strides and pulled me into a close embrace. "Are you complaining?"

"Of course not," I said, my words muffled by the folds of his white cotton shirt. Although Richard was of average height for a man, I was rather short, which meant the top of my head only reached his shoulders. I leaned back and looked up into his amused face. "Which is one reason I feel compelled to walk more now. I have to stay somewhat in shape if I hope to keep up with you."

"You're fine, just as you are," Richard said, before kissing me again.

A gentle knock on the door interrupted this enjoyable interlude. Stepping back, Richard turned and called out, "Come on in. Must be Lydia," he added, turning to me. "No one else uses the back-porch door."

"Or would show up so early," I said, frowning. "I hope nothing's wrong."

The door swung open to reveal my aunt, frozen in place, as an orange-striped tabby wound his way around her slender ankles.

"Hello there." Aunt Lydia held out a basket filled with muffins. "I just finished baking and thought I'd share. If Fosse will allow me to enter, that is."

"He's taken it upon himself to be the welcoming committee, I'm afraid." Richard bent down to scoop up the cat, who snuggled into his arms and shot my aunt a triumphant, golden-eyed stare. "I knew putting in that cat door was a mistake."

Aunt Lydia crossed over to the kitchen island to set down her basket. "I disagree. It gives the cats access to the screened porch, which provides them with fresh air without allowing them to roam outside. Which the birds in my garden appreciate."

"It protects the cats from the wild critters wandering the woods in back of our houses too," I said.

"Not to mention the cars out front." Richard set Fosse down on the wood-grained vinyl plank floor. "Run along, you rascal. Join your sister on the kitchen chairs." Straightening, Richard cast Aunt Lydia a warm smile. "We usually have to dump them off before we sit down to eat."

"Which is one of the reasons my pants are always covered in cat hair." I leaned over the island to inhale the spicy aroma of the muffins. "Mmmm, cinnamon and ginger?"

"My famous whole-wheat spice recipe." Aunt Lydia's smile lit up her lovely face. Always elegant, her smooth complexion and brilliant blue eyes belied her sixty-seven years, even if her hair had turned completely gray.

But gleaming and smooth as liquid silver, I thought, returning her smile. "Thanks for bringing us breakfast, but I suspect there's something else motivating this visit. You don't usually stop by so early."

"Not that we mind." Richard plucked a muffin from the basket. "Especially when you come bearing gifts."

Aunt Lydia leaned forward, pressing her palms against the top of the oak island. "It's Zelda. I'm a little worried about her."

"Whatever for?" I grabbed two small paper plates from the pantry cabinet. Handing one to Richard, I plopped one of the muffins on the other before pulling a knife from the caddy we kept on the counter. "Butter?" I asked, waving the knife at Richard.

"Nope. Have to watch my figure, you know," he replied, before taking a bite from the muffin.

"Hah, as if." I pulled a plastic tub of whipped butter from the fridge. "Anyway, what's all this about Zelda? She always seems like the happiest person on earth. I can't imagine why you'd worry about her."

I caught Aunt Lydia's frown as soon as I turned around. "She has her troubles, like everyone else."

Zelda Shoemaker had been my aunt's best friend since elementary school. A cheery widow who owned a lovely bungalow on the edge of town, Zelda was also a regular volunteer at the library. Although we weren't as close as she and my aunt were, I

still considered Zelda a friend. Observing the worry lines wrinkling Aunt Lydia's brow, I shared a concerned look with Richard. "What's going on? Are she and Walt having problems?"

"Nothing like that," my aunt said, with a flick of her fine-boned hand. "But she seemed so anxious and preoccupied when I saw her yesterday. It isn't like her, as you know."

I split open my muffin and buttered it. "Did she explain what was bothering her?"

"No, which was also strange. You know how chatty Zelda usually is. She isn't one to keep secrets, even when you want her to." Aunt Lydia flashed me a wry smile. "But yesterday she kept saying everything was fine, even though I'm sure it isn't."

"Maybe it does have something to do with Walt? She knows you're also his friend. She might not have wanted to put you in the middle of things," Richard said, before polishing off his muffin.

"I don't think so. I asked her that directly and believe her disclaimer was genuine. No"—Aunt Lydia squared her slender shoulders—"I think this has to do with something else. There was a stranger who scurried away when I arrived at the house—an older woman who looked about the same age as Zelda and me. She resembled Zelda, if I'm honest. Same build and similar curly blonde hair."

"Dyed blonde, you mean," I said, thinking of Zelda's perfectly tinted locks. She always urged my aunt to color her gray hair, with no success.

"Of course. Although I think she, like Zelda, was probably a blonde in her youth. You can tell, you know. The eyebrows and complexion give it away." Aunt Lydia frowned. "Come to

think of it, she had the same light brown eyes as Zelda, too. I suspect they might've looked quite a bit alike when they were young."

"But not now?" Richard asked, with a lift of his dark eyebrows.

"Not really. Zelda isn't all wrinkled, like this woman was. I suspect she was a smoker, or maybe spent too much time outdoors without sunscreen." My aunt slid two fingers along her own smooth-skinned jawline. "Amy's mom and I used to make such a fuss because Grandma Rose wouldn't allow us to sunbathe like so many of our friends. They spent hours baking in the sun, slathered in nothing but baby oil. Now we're grateful."

"One good thing she did," I said, as thoughts of some of her not-so-great acts spooled through my mind.

"She had her moments." Aunt Lydia tapped the polyurethane-sealed oak with her short but well-groomed fingernails. "Anyway, the really odd thing is, when I asked Zelda about the woman, I got no response, other than a squint-eyed stare. I could tell Zelda didn't want to discuss her visitor, which I found extremely peculiar. Since when does Zelda refuse to talk?"

"Never, at least as long as I've known her," Richard said.

Aunt Lydia's lips thinned. "Exactly."

"Maybe she was out of sorts for some other reason," I said, after taking a bite of my muffin.

Aunt Lydia lifted her golden eyebrows. She didn't have to say a word to express her opinion of talking while eating. "To be honest, Amy, that was one reason why I wanted to stop by before you headed off to work. I know Zelda is scheduled to volunteer at the library today. I thought you could engage her

in some friendly conversation and find out what, if anything, is bothering her."

I wiped a few crumbs from my lips with a napkin before replying. "Conduct a little interrogation, you mean."

"Perhaps not quite that intense," my aunt said mildly. "And don't think I can't spy that sparkle in your eyes. It's been a few months since your last opportunity to assist the sheriff's office. I bet you'd enjoy a little sleuthing, wouldn't you?"

"She does love to investigate things." Richard slid his arm around my shoulders. "I've learned to allow her to pursue the truth, even if it ends up turning my hair white."

"Nothing wrong with white hair." Aunt Lydia offered him a smile. "But we do have to make sure Amy doesn't put herself in danger again. That seems to be an unfortunate side effect of her amateur sleuthing."

"Now wait a minute." I squirmed under Richard's arm, which just made him tighten his hold. "I think I've proven I can take care of myself. Besides, talking to Zelda is hardly the most dangerous activity I can imagine."

"I don't know." Richard leaned in to brush a kiss against my temple. "It seems to be the simplest mysteries that spiral out of control."

"Not this time," I said. "I'm sure this will be a piece of cake."

My aunt, who was not at all superstitious, rapped the leg of the oak table.

Chapter Two

B y the time Aunt Lydia left, it was seven thirty. I swore and dashed out of the kitchen, almost tripping over Fosse in my rush.

Richard called out a cheery "Bye, sweetheart, see you later," as I ran up the stairs. I paused to wish him a good day before he left the house.

Somehow, I managed to take a shower and throw on some clothes in time to grab two muffins from the basket Aunt Lydia had brought over. They'd have to do for lunch, since I'd forgotten to pack anything again. Wrapping them in a napkin, I shoved the muffins into my soft-sided briefcase and grabbed my sunglasses from a living room side table. I also determined the location of both cats before dashing outside. I'd recently come home from work to discover Loie had been accidently shut up in a closet, which had resulted in the destruction of a few mittens and a knitted hat, as well as a furious cat.

As I strode past Aunt Lydia's house, I made a mental note to carve out a little more time for my aunt. She might be lonely, now that she was once again living alone in her big old house.

Glancing up at the dusty canopy of leaves that shadowed the sidewalk, I shook my head. What was I thinking? Aunt Lydia had lived alone for many years before I'd moved in with her, and besides, she was a supremely independent woman who had plenty of friends. She was also busy with a number of volunteer activities, and had plenty to do keeping up her house and garden, along with all her cooking and baking.

Not to mention she has a significant other to keep her company most weekends, I reminded myself, smiling at the thought of the intelligent and charming Hugh Chen, art appraiser and historian. Aunt Lydia had lost her adored husband, Andrew Talbot, after only a few years of marriage. She'd carried a torch for Andrew for decades, never looking at another man until Hugh had come along. Fortunately, he'd convinced her to take a chance on love again.

I picked up my pace as I drew closer to the stone building that housed the Taylorsford Public Library. Built in 1919 with a Carnegie grant, it retained its original period details throughout much of the structure, although a utilitarian addition had been built in the 1960s to house the Children's Room and staff lounge.

Surprisingly, there were already people loitering on the sidewalk near the front doors. We didn't typically encounter many patrons so early, but it seemed this day might prove the exception.

Of course, I thought as I circled around to the side of the building. *People would naturally show up early on the one morning you're late.*

I slipped past the thick cluster of forsythia bushes that screened the library staff entrance from the street. Unlocking a

side door that opened into the workroom, I dumped my purse and briefcase onto the large wooden table at the center of the room before poking my head around the door that led to the area behind the circulation desk. Thankfully, Sunny was already at the desk, firing up the circulation system computer.

"Sorry I'm late," I said.

Sunny glanced at her watch. "Not really. It's still two minutes till." She flashed me a smile, her blue eyes sparkling. "I figured maybe Richard distracted you this morning, since you're basically still in the honeymoon phase."

I rolled my eyes. "Really, we aren't teenagers. We do know how to control ourselves." *Although,* I thought, with a little twitch of my lips, *that's not always true.* But I wasn't about to say anything that would offer my friend more ammunition for her teasing.

Sunny arched her golden eyebrows. "If you say so. Anyway, it's not a problem. I've checked over the building and turned on the public computers. We just need to unlock the doors."

"There are already a few people waiting outside," I called through the open workroom door as I pulled the muffins from my briefcase.

Sunny used both hands to flip her long blonde hair behind her shoulders. "I think I can handle a couple of early birds, but you should probably cart your lunch back to the lounge before I unlock the doors."

I followed Sunny's advice. Even though the muffins could've simply sat on a shelf, I preferred not to leave any food in the workroom. No use encouraging mice or bugs to move into our historic building.

By the time I returned, two ladies were loitering at the circulation desk, chatting with Sunny. As I looked them over, I realized I didn't recognize either of the women. The other patrons who'd been waiting outside, some of our regulars, had apparently already spread out throughout the library.

Sunny motioned toward me as I joined her behind the desk. "And this is our director, Amy Webber. Oh, sorry"—she cast me an apologetic smile—"It's Amy Muir. I keep forgetting to use your new name."

"That's okay, so do I sometimes." I focused my gaze on one of the visitors, a lanky woman who was the taller of the two by a good eight inches. "I just got married back in May, so I'm still getting used to the change."

The taller woman locked gazes with me and widened her light blue eyes. "Are you related to Lydia Litton by any chance? Or Lydia Talbot, I suppose I should say. Her younger sister married a Webber, if I remember correctly."

I nodded. "She's my aunt, and her sister, Debbie, is my mom."

"I thought so. You resemble your mother quite a bit." The woman tipped her head as she continued to examine me. "You look nothing like Lydia, but then those sisters always were complete opposites. Heard them called 'Rose Red' and 'Rose White' more than once, and it fit. Debbie was short and curvy and had the most beautiful deep brown eyes and dark hair, while Lydia was taller, slender, and quite fair." The woman extended her hand over the desk. "I'm Gwen Ohlson, by the way. Your mom and aunt might remember me from high school."

I offered her a smile as I shook her hand. Like Sunny, Gwen Ohlson was blonde, but her hair was cropped short, in a feathered

pixie cut that softened her angular face. And, unlike Sunny's naturally golden tresses, I suspected Gwen's ash blonde hair was dyed, probably in an attempt to cover any recalcitrant grays. In contrast to my aunt's relatively smooth complexion, a fan of wrinkles surrounded Gwen's eyes and deep lines bracketed her mouth.

"So you went to Leeland? You must've grown up in Taylorsford then, or at least in the county." I allowed my gaze to flit to Gwen's companion. "Are you back for a reunion or something?"

"In a way," said the shorter woman, whose shoulder-length hair was dyed a matte black and teased and sprayed into a frothy confection of waves. "I'm Olivia Rader, but your mom and aunt would probably remember me as Olivia Bell."

"We're here for the arts festival," Gwen said. "The one being held at Leeland High School this weekend."

"Really? My husband's involved with that. He's going to be the primary judge for the dance competition."

Gwen's jaw dropped. "You're married to Richard Muir? I heard he was going to be involved with the festival, but I never imagined . . ." Gwen closed her lips over whatever words she was about to say. She blinked and flashed a bright smile. "I confess to being a fan. I've seen him dance several times, and simply adore his work. I even caught that fabulous piece he choreographed a year or so ago. He had to fill in for the lead male dancer at the last minute as I recall. Not that anyone complained. I can't quite remember the title of the piece—*Rendezvous* or something?"

"*Return*." Warmth rose in my cheeks as I remembered my own trip to New York City to see Richard perform in that production of one of his choreographic works. "It was based on Orpheus and Eurydice."

Gwen pressed her palms together in a silent clap. "That's the one. Brilliant."

"I totally agree." I glanced at Olivia Rader. "Are you former dancers, then? I didn't realize Leeland High had a dance team in the past, although I know they have a good one now."

Olivia squared her plump shoulders. "No, we're here to sing. Not in competition, of course, because that's for the young people. We're performing at the awards ceremony."

Gwen flicked a tiny piece of lint from her navy and white striped cotton blouse. "It's a fiftieth reunion of the Leeland High School chamber choir."

"Fifty years from when we won the state choir competition," Olivia said, her chestnut brown eyes lighting up with obvious pride.

"Impressive." I flashed both women a smile. "I guess you were invited to perform because of the anniversary?"

"That's right. We were asked back by Martin Stover, who's now the choral teacher and director of the arts programs at Leeland," Gwen said. "Of course, the entire original choir couldn't make it. Some live too far away now, and sadly, some have passed. But we were able to gather enough of the original crew to perform a couple of our old pieces."

"I look forward to hearing you," I said.

"Are you staying in the area?" Sunny cast the women a disarming smile. "Sorry if I'm coming across as nosy, but I'm also the mayor. I'm always happy to see Taylorsford attracting visitors."

"Those that live too far, like Gwen, are lodging at the Taylorsford Inn. Fortunately, I still live close enough to drive in

from home." Olivia patted her stiff waves. "I never left the area; just moved the next county over when I married."

Gwen shrugged. "I don't actually live that far away, just on the other side of D.C. I often drive into the Taylorsford area for things like arts events at Clarion or the fall festival. I just thought, with rehearsals every day this week, it would be easier for me to stay at the inn."

Sunny clasped her hands on the desktop. "Well, it's nice you could all get together again. I bet it's fun to catch up with everyone."

"Of course, although a lot of our time is spent rehearsing. It's not that easy to recapture the old magic," Gwen said.

Olivia shot her a sharp look. "I think we sound splendid, all things considered."

"Sure, but the years have taken their toll on some of our voices," Gwen said, with a rueful smile. "Anyway, we won't take up any more of your time. We mainly dropped by because I wanted to see the library again. I used to visit often when I was young. Doesn't look like much has changed, although of course you now have computers."

"We'd be happy to give you a tour," Sunny said.

Gwen waved this aside. "Oh no, it's fine. We'll head out now and allow you to get on with your work." She nudged Olivia, who frowned for a second, then plastered on a distinctly plastic smile.

Gwen thanked Sunny and me before heading for the exit, with Olivia trailing her.

"I didn't realize what a big deal this festival was," Sunny said, as the two women disappeared through the front doors. "I thought

it was just something to do with the high school, but apparently it involves arts programs from several different counties."

"I'm surprised you don't already know all about it. It's an end-of-summer extravaganza, where all the students involved in regional summer performing or visual arts programs compete for awards." I fiddled with the pencils stuffed into a black mesh holder. "This year the competition and the final performances by the winners are being held at Leeland High, but it involves more than one school."

"That makes sense, and explains why I've heard ads for the final performance event Saturday night on the local TV news as well as the radio station."

"They are hyping it quite a bit. I think that has to do with the guy Gwen Ohlson mentioned, Martin Stover. He seems to have put an extraordinary amount of effort into the festival, based on what I hear from Richard."

"I suppose I should've been more aware of this, being mayor, but I honestly thought it had more to do with some adjacent counties." Sunny cast me a sidelong glance. "I guess you're going, if Richard is involved in the judging."

"You're welcome to join us if you want. And Fred too, of course." I studied Sunny's lovely profile, noting the curve of her lips when I mentioned her boyfriend, Fred Nash, a former police detective turned private investigator who often worked for Hugh Chen. Sunny always claimed she had no interest in marriage, but I suspected Fred would eventually change her mind.

Sunny tossed her head. "Fred's out of town for a few weeks. Some sort of assignment. You know how it is—he gets sent off on these mysterious missions with little warning."

"Something he's working on for Hugh? He appears to be out of town as well. At least I assume so, since he didn't visit Aunt Lydia this weekend." A quick glance over the area behind the desk revealed two full carts of returned books. "Wasn't Zelda supposed to come in this morning?" I motioned toward the carts.

"To answer both your questions—yes, Fred is partnering with Hugh on some investigation into art theft or forgery or something, and no, Zelda hasn't shown up yet." Sunny shrugged. "You know she sometimes forgets. I can give her a call if you want."

"Don't bother. I just assumed she'd already be shelving if she was here. She never lets full carts sit around too long." I plucked one of the pens from the holder and tapped it against my palm. It looked like I was going to disappoint my aunt. I wouldn't get the chance to find out what was bothering Zelda, unless she breezed in later.

Sunny's bright gaze clouded as she stared at the carts. "True. I guess we can wait for her to show up, or I can go ahead and shelve them myself."

"That's not necessary. Denise is coming in this afternoon. It can wait until then." I cast Sunny a smile. "We need useful jobs to keep the volunteers busy, you know. Otherwise they might not continue to show up."

"Well, I'm happy to leave the shelving to Denise," Sunny said, pulling a comical face.

I didn't bother to hide my smile. "Figured as much."

Chapter Three

When I got home after work, I was greeted by both cats, who demanded pets before I headed to the kitchen to help Richard whip up a simple tomato sauce to serve over pasta.

"Zelda never did show up today," I told him as I sliced baby portobello mushrooms.

"Which means you didn't get a chance to question her. Lydia will be disappointed." Richard tasted a spoonful of the sauce. "Needs more garlic."

"You always want to add more." I made a face at him. "I guess as long as we both eat it, no one will be offended."

"Mmmm, garlic breath," Richard said, before leaning in to kiss me.

I allowed a peck on the lips before waving him off. "Behave."

"Never!" he proclaimed, brandishing the spoon like a sword. "I refuse to bow to your cruel dictates, Madame Spoilsport." He pressed the spoon to his chest. "Give me misbehavior or give me . . . more garlic."

"You're going to ruin that shirt," I said mildly, before bumping his elbow with mine. "You seem to be in fine form tonight. Did you get good news today?"

"As a matter of fact, I did." Richard shot me a glance from under his thick black lashes. "I was going to wait to tell you after dinner, but it seems your talent for sniffing out information has ruined my plan."

"It isn't hard to tell when you're harboring a secret. A positive one, I mean. You get all giddy." I dumped the sliced mushrooms into the saucepot. "No offense, darling, but good news turns you as bouncy as a kid at Christmas."

Richard grabbed a larger spoon to stir the sauce. "I was an adorable little boy, I'll have you know."

"I'm sure you were. You're still pretty irresistible." I blew him a kiss. "But now you're being cagey, trying to distract me from your news."

"So that didn't work either?" Richard exhaled a dramatic sigh. "What's a man to do with such an inquisitive wife?"

"I can think of a few things," I replied with a grin but held up my hand to keep him from moving any closer. "Later, or we'll burn dinner. For now, you can spill the secret that's got you so excited."

Richard placed the spoon on the ceramic holder on the stove. "It's about the folklore project." He turned to me with a broad smile. "Not only is Emily Moore willing to allow us to use some of her poetry, she's also offered to kick in some additional funding."

I clapped my hands. "Wonderful! You and Karla have dreamed of taking the project to the next level for so long."

"And now it can happen sooner rather than later. This help from Emily, on top of Kurt's contribution and the smaller donations from other sponsors, also means we can afford to bring in additional professional dancers for the lead roles."

"But you're still planning to use some of Karla's students?"

"Of course, along with some of mine. But a few professionals will be a bigger draw, which will raise more money for Karla's studio, among other things." Richard turned down the heat under the saucepot. "Let it simmer," he said, before pulling me into a close embrace.

"Better stir the pot," I said, after a rather lengthy kiss.

"A talent of yours, I thought," Richard murmured into my ear.

I pulled away, wrinkling my nose at him. "Very funny. Take care of that sauce, mister, or you'll be running out to buy us dinner."

"Aye, aye, Captain." Richard gave me a little salute before turning back to the stove.

"I'll get the pasta," I said, as I crossed to the pantry.

But before I could grab a box of spaghetti and another pot, the doorbell chime rang throughout the house. "You watch the sauce, I'll see who it is," I called out before I hurried down the hall.

I opened the front door to find Aunt Lydia pacing the porch.

"Thank goodness you're home," she said, her blue eyes glazed with unshed tears.

"What's going on?" I stared out over the yard and the road in front of our house, afraid an accident or some other tragic event had befallen one of our neighbors.

"It's Zelda," my aunt said. "She just called and claimed something bad has happened in her garden. Something that obviously sent her into a panic."

"She should've called the sheriff's department, not you." Richard, wiping his hands on a kitchen towel, stepped up beside me.

"That's what I said, but she refused." Aunt Lydia pressed her hand to her forehead. "Zelda sounded so unlike herself. She wasn't making a lot of sense, to be honest. Her words were all slurred and halting. I'm afraid she might be ill."

"A stroke, maybe?" Richard slung the towel over his shoulder. "Hold on, I'm going to turn off the stove, then Amy and I will drive you over Zelda's house."

"Are you sure we shouldn't call emergency services or something?" I asked my aunt, as Richard ran back to the kitchen. "They could get there before we do, and if she needs immediate help . . ."

"She made me swear not to," Aunt Lydia said. "Let's drive over and see what's going on and decide from there what should be done."

"Did you try to contact Walt?" I asked as Richard reappeared with his keys dangling from his fingers.

"No point." Aunt Lydia led the way to our car, tapping her foot against the paved driveway as Richard locked up the house before jogging over to join us. "He's out of town until Wednesday, visiting his daughter and her family."

I frowned. Walter Adams, Zelda's significant other, would've been the person I'd want to oversee any medical emergency involving Zelda. She didn't have children of her own, or any family in the area.

We drove across town without speaking. Richard's earlier buoyant spirits had been replaced by grim silence, while Aunt Lydia kept taking deep breaths to calm her obviously frayed nerves.

Zelda's charming home was a one-story brick bungalow that featured a covered porch with white posts and railings. Lush baskets of ferns swung from chains hung above the balustrades, while metal brackets that hooked over the top rail supported wooden boxes filled with a rainbow of flowers.

As soon as Richard parked, all three of us sprang out of the car and rushed up the concrete porch steps to reach the front door. When there was no response to Aunt Lydia repeatedly jabbing the doorbell with her forefinger, I rapped the door several times, to no avail.

"I don't care what you promised Zelda, I'm calling the police," I said, pulling out my cell phone.

"Wait." Aunt Lydia laid a hand on my arm. "Let's try the garden first."

We circled around the house, passing Zelda's car.

"Seems she's here, unless she decided to walk somewhere," Richard said, as we reached the gate leading into Zelda's picket fence–enclosed backyard.

Unlike my aunt's more formal garden, with its geometric grid of flower and herb beds separated by pea-gravel paths, Zelda's garden was an exuberant explosion of plants. Grass pathways curved around irregular islands of shrubs and flowers like green rivers winding through a jungle. In the center of this lush landscape, a white gazebo gleamed, its domed roof supported by carved posts and elegant latticework.

Aunt Lydia flung out her hand. "I spy some movement there, near the gazebo." She took off at a swift walk. Richard and I followed close behind, batting aside trailing vines and fountains of decorative grasses that spilled over the winding path. Focused on the gazebo, I stepped on a loosened loop of one of my laces, pulling it free. I waved Richard forward as I paused to tie my shoe.

Aunt Lydia's shriek made me throw up my head and dash toward the gazebo, where I found Richard clutching my aunt's arm as to keep her on her feet.

"What is it?" I asked as I reached them.

Aunt Lydia pointed a trembling finger toward the interior of the gazebo.

My gaze followed, and I gasped. On the wooden floor of the open-air building lay a prone figure.

A short, plump woman, lying face down, with a spreading shadow haloing her short blonde curls.

I blinked and looked again, realizing the shadow was actually a pool of liquid.

Blood, I thought, realizing we'd discovered another dead body.

Chapter Four

I shared a shocked glance with Richard. "Is that . . . ?"

"No, no, no," Aunt Lydia said, shaking her arm free from Richard's grip. She ran into the gazebo before either of us could stop her, but halted a foot from the body. "It can't be Zelda. She would never wear something like that."

I stepped forward to join Aunt Lydia, staring at the pearl buttons running down the back of the victim's blouse. My aunt was right—the polyester blouse's ruffled collar and delicate pastel floral pattern didn't match Zelda's typical attire. Nor did the full, pale pink skirt and beige pumps.

"Who could it be, then?" Richard asked, as he moved to stand by my side.

I glanced at my aunt's ashen face. "The woman you saw the other day?"

"Perhaps." Aunt Lydia pointed at one of the wooden benches lining the inside of the gazebo's walls. "Garden gloves. Those are Zelda's. I've seen her wear them before. But she'd never leave them lying out here like that, unless . . ." She lifted her head and scanned the area around the gazebo.

Following her gaze, I stared at the buddleia, more commonly known as a butterfly bush, pressed against the opposite side of the gazebo. The spiky purple blossoms shook, sending a cloud of orange and black butterflies sailing off in all directions. Aunt Lydia and I turned in unison and headed back outside, where I discovered Richard holding his cell phone to his ear.

"Calling 911," he said.

My aunt shot him a sharp look before she circled around the gazebo and made a beeline for the butterfly bush.

I paused, waiting to hear the status of Richard's call, but when he gave me a thumb's up, I followed my aunt. I found her pulling Zelda to her feet. Judging from the broken limbs at the base of the buddleia, I suspected Zelda had stumbled and fallen into the shrub.

"Thank goodness you're alive," I said, examining Zelda with a critical eye. In contrast to her typically stylish attire, she was wearing a worn floral housecoat and a pair of scruffy slippers. A tattered and stained towel was pinned around her shoulders, and her blonde curls were damp.

She was coloring her hair, I thought, as Aunt Lydia slid her hand up Zelda's bare forearm. *Before something, or someone, drew her outside . . .*

Aunt Lydia gave Zelda's arm a little shake. "Are you okay?" she asked, sharing a worried glance with me.

I could understand my aunt's concern. Zelda looked as if she'd been sleepwalking. Her eyes were clouded and her bare face lacked its usual rosy glow.

Sliding her arm around Zelda's shoulders, Aunt Lydia drew her friend close to her side. "What are you doing out here? Did

you run outside because you heard whoever was in the gazebo with that poor woman?"

Zelda's lips worked, but she made no sound. I framed a query about her discovery of the body, but sirens drowned out my question before Zelda could even attempt an answer. The squeal of car wheels spewing gravel told us the authorities had arrived.

"Over here," Richard called out, directing Chief Deputy Brad Tucker and several other sheriff's deputies to the gazebo.

"I'm starting to think the department shouldn't accept messages from any of you guys." Brad, a tall, well-built man in his early forties pushed his hat back from his forehead. "It always seems to lead us to a dead body."

Zelda, who still hadn't spoken a word, was pried from my aunt's arms by one of the female deputies and led out of the garden.

Aunt Lydia crossed her arms over her chest and favored the chief deputy with one of her regal stares. "Please don't be flippant, Brad."

I glanced at the yellow tape other deputies were stretching to establish a perimeter around the gazebo before meeting Brad's cool blue-eyed gaze. "What's it this time?"

Brad grimaced. "Gunshot at close range. Not a pretty sight, so I'd stay back if I were you."

"But who is the woman?" Aunt Lydia's eyes narrowed. "It is a woman, isn't it?"

"Yeah, older female." Brad yanked his hat back down over his broad forehead. "And that's all I'm going to say at this point."

Before we'd been pushed back by the deputies, I'd sneaked another glimpse of the woman's hair, which was eerily similar to Zelda's own golden curls. All I could think of was the woman my aunt had seen visiting Zelda recently, the one Zelda wouldn't talk about. "You can't say who she is?"

"We don't know yet, and no, I couldn't say anything even if we did." Brad's expression took on the stoniness I knew meant he was not about to share any more information with me. He pulled a small notebook and pen from the pocket of his uniform jacket. "Just to confirm, when you arrived, Ms. Shoemaker was already outside?"

"Yes, collapsed beside that butterfly bush," Aunt Lydia said. "I assume she was knocked aside by the perpetrator when they fled the scene. You can see where the shrub is broken from her fall."

"I wouldn't assume anything." Brad squinted as he gazed down at the open pages of the notebook. "According to these preliminary notes, you said she called you some time before your arrival."

"She did, but . . ." Aunt Lydia closed her lips over whatever she'd been about to say next.

"And she seemed very upset and even incoherent during that call?" Brad glanced up from his notes and focused his gaze on my aunt.

"As I've already stated, yes."

"Lydia stopped by our house about twenty minutes ago," Richard said. "She told us she was concerned because of the phone call from Zelda, and we headed here almost immediately thereafter."

"You didn't think to call 911 before driving across town?" Brad scribbled something in the notebook before looking back up at us. "If Ms. Shoemaker appeared irrational, she could've been suffering from a serious medical emergency that might've benefited from immediate help."

"We thought about it, but . . ." I glanced at my aunt, who refused to meet my gaze. Her attention was still fixed on Brad. "Aunt Lydia thought it best to check out the situation first."

Richard's grip tightened around my fingers. "The truth is, Zelda asked Lydia not to involve any emergency services."

Aunt Lydia shot him a glance that could have frozen mercury. "I'm sure she simply wanted to avoid a fuss."

Richard shrugged. "Sorry, Lydia, but finding a dead body in your own backyard is guaranteed to require assistance from the authorities. I'm not sure why Zelda would've nixed that, unless . . ."

"Unless what?" Aunt Lydia snapped.

"Unless she truly was in shock. Which would be understandable," Richard said. "But that also requires special attention."

"I was trying to accommodate her wishes." Aunt Lydia's tone was as icy as her eyes. "And naturally, I wasn't anticipating the fact that she'd stumbled over a dead body in her gazebo."

Brad pocketed the notebook and pen before meeting my aunt's imperious gaze. "Of course not. It's just, Ms. Shoemaker calling you, and not the sheriff's department, is a little odd, don't you think? Even if she was knocked down, it seems she had the presence of mind to phone you, so why not call 911 as well?"

My aunt lifted her chin. "If she truly was in shock, she might not have been thinking clearly."

Richard leaned in to whisper in my ear, "It's like *High Noon*. Killer stares at twenty paces. Maybe we should encourage Lydia to leave?"

I squeezed his hand and nodded. "Can we go, Brad? We're happy to give more detailed statements later, if you want, but I think it might be helpful if we could leave and let you and your team get on with your work."

Brad yanked his gaze off my aunt to look at me and Richard. I bobbed my head toward Aunt Lydia, trying to indicate our willingness to escort her out of the way.

"Sounds like a good plan." Brad rocked back on his heels as he looked the three of us up and down. "I'll have someone give you a call tomorrow if we need more information."

Aunt Lydia stepped back and looked around the scene. "Where's Zelda? I don't intend to leave until I know what's happening with her."

Brad whipped off his hat. Holding it in front of him like a shield, he shook his head. "The EMS crew is checking her out. I suspect they may want to take her in for a more thorough exam, to make sure she has no injuries or didn't suffer a minor stroke or anything like that. I'm sure you agree that's the proper plan, Ms. Talbot."

"It's Ms. Talbot now, is it?" Aunt Lydia, her arms still crossed, tapped her clenched forearms with her fingers. "Don't try to fool me, young man. I know you want to check her hands for gunshot residue or some such thing as well. Which is ridiculous. To my knowledge, Zelda has never owned a gun."

"We'll check into that, of course," Brad said, softening his tone. "But it's just procedure. I have to follow the rules, regardless of who's involved."

Aunt Lydia bit her lower lip and studied Brad's face for a second before replying. "Yes, yes, I know. I just don't want Zelda to automatically become the prime suspect simply because the murder occurred on her property."

Brad popped his hat back over his short blond hair. "That isn't how things work, at least not during my investigations. You should know that, Lydia. I follow the facts, and until we find the gun . . ."

Brad's comment was cut off by one of the other deputies calling his name. Glancing over at the gazebo, I noticed the deputy, whose own hands were encased in plastic gloves, waving the gardening gloves Aunt Lydia had noticed earlier.

"Something you need to see," the deputy called out.

Brad excused himself and jogged over to the gazebo.

"So they found gardening gloves in a garden," Aunt Lydia said with a sniff. "Not such a surprise."

"Maybe it's something the killer used? To prevent fingerprints, I mean." Richard released his grip on my fingers and took a few steps forward. Shading his eyes with one hand, he peered toward the gazebo. "Could they have stolen the gloves from Zelda's garden shed?"

"Possibly," I said, as he turned back to face us.

Aunt Lydia shook her head. "I doubt it. Zelda's kept the shed locked ever since she had tools stolen a few months ago. Although, to be fair, she's forgotten to do that once or twice."

"Or she accidentally left her gloves in the gazebo when she was working in the garden recently." I met my aunt's narrowed gaze. "I know you say she wouldn't do that either, but she does lose track of things at work, and even occasionally forgets to show up for her volunteer shifts. So maybe . . ."

Strain deepened the lines bracketing Aunt Lydia's taut lips. "I suppose it's possible."

"Doesn't mean she's losing it or anything. Heck, I misplace stuff all the time. Found my car keys on the floor the other day," Richard said.

I bit back a comment, remembering that it was Fosse who'd knocked them off the dresser. "Anyway, I think it's strange this woman showed up here again today. You said you saw her leaving Zelda's house the other day, Aunt Lydia. The question is, why did she return? Was she meeting Zelda, or did she just turn up hoping to talk to her again?"

"And if so, why?" Aunt Lydia tapped her fingers against her temple. "I guess I need to tell Brad or one of the other deputies about that previous encounter, don't I?"

Laying a hand on her arm, I offered her a reassuring smile. "I'm afraid you have to. But don't worry, surely Zelda had nothing to do with this stranger's death. She doesn't even like to kill insects, for goodness sake," I added, swatting away a hovering fly.

"True," Aunt Lydia said. "And even if they find gunshot residue on those gloves, that doesn't prove anything."

I squeezed her forearm gently before lifting my hand. "It certainly doesn't mean Zelda was the one wearing them. Like we said, maybe she did leave them lying in the gazebo and the killer just grabbed them to cover their own prints."

"Exactly," Richard said. "Not to mention no one's said any-thing about finding the murder weapon. I bet the killer took it with them. I mean, if Zelda was the shooter, wouldn't the gun have been dropped in the garden? In the state she was in, it would've likely been dumped near where we found her, close to that bush."

Aunt Lydia's face brightened. "Good point. She did seem to be in shock, or at least in no condition to have carefully hidden any weapon."

"Not to mention it looked like she'd run outside right after coloring her hair," I said. "I doubt anyone would take the time to dye their hair when they were planning a premeditated murder."

"I suspect she heard something and ran outside." Aunt Lydia's tone grew more forceful. "And that would've had to have been the gunshot, wouldn't it? What else could she have heard from inside the house?"

She could've heard shouting, I thought, *or she could've been called outside by someone who'd demanded to see her.* But I didn't voice these alternative theories aloud.

As we made our way out of the garden, Richard cast his gaze over the surrounding area. "What about the neighbors? They would have to have heard something as well, wouldn't they?"

"I'm sure Brad will have them questioned, but honestly"—Aunt Lydia swept her hair away from her damp forehead with one hand—"the people on either side and across the street all work late hours or night shifts, so unfortunately, they probably weren't at home."

"Which explains why no one came running over, even with a gunshot," I said, speaking slowly as my mind cataloged this information. "I bet the killer knew."

"You mean, you think they knew Zelda's schedule, as well when her neighbors would be gone?" Aunt Lydia dropped her hand and sighed. "That would mean someone planned this carefully. But why? Zelda has no enemies, or at least none I know of."

"It doesn't make sense," I agreed, as we reached Richard's car. "But I'm sure everything will be sorted out as soon as the detectives gather all the info from Zelda."

"I hope so," my aunt said, frowning as she stared out over the busy scene. Zelda's garden was overrun with detectives and other officials. "They're going to destroy half of her plants if they keep this up."

"Just doing their job." I climbed into the back seat to allow Aunt Lydia to ride up front. "Although it is a shame to see so much of her hard work trampled to pieces."

Aunt Lydia kept her eyes focused on the front windshield as Richard turned the key in the ignition. "As long as that's all they trample, I suppose it will be all right." She tapped the dashboard. "I know you'd probably like to go home, but could we head to the hospital instead? I want to check on Zelda and make sure she hasn't suffered some physical trauma."

I sat back and fastened my seat belt as Richard shot me a glance in the rearview mirror. I could guess what he was thinking—we'd both had enough experiences with emergency rooms to know that we'd probably be stuck at the hospital for some time.

But gentleman that he was, he simply nodded and told my aunt, "Hospital it is."

Chapter Five

Sunny was working a part-time shift at the library on Tuesday afternoon. Not surprisingly, with the library fairly quiet, we ended up discussing the latest murder.

"The news identified the victim as Claudia Everhart. Have you ever heard of her?" I asked as I examined reports on the circulation desk computer. Although we didn't charge fines for turning in library materials late, we did send notices to remind patrons to return items. Not only was it a courtesy; it also prevented them from receiving a bill for replacing any materials that were more than two months overdue.

"Never heard of her, but that's not too surprising. She lived a couple of counties over, and was only in town for the arts festival. Didn't you hear she was part of another reunited choral group participating in the final performance show?"

I glanced away from the screen to meet Sunny's sparkling gaze. "No, I just caught her name. Richard wanted to stream a new foreign film we'd been waiting to see, so we didn't watch much news last night."

"Well, I did, and they said Claudia Everhart's old high school choir is scheduled to perform at the festival event Saturday night. Apparently, they also won first place in the competition fifty years ago. They tied with the Leeland chorus."

"Which neither of our two library visitors happened to mention," I said thoughtfully.

Sunny circled her hand through the air, spinning the stack of gold and silver bangles on her wrist. "No, they didn't, and I think that's a little odd. Made me wonder if someone from the Leeland choir could've been the killer."

"They shot Claudia Everhart because of a rivalry from decades ago?" I raised my eyebrows. "Doesn't sound too likely."

Sunny shrugged. "Who knows? We've run across some pretty weird reasons for murder before."

"True enough," I said, casting her a rueful smile.

Sunny flashed me a grin before her expression sobered. "You said you went to the hospital with Richard and Lydia. Did any of you get a chance to speak with Zelda?"

"No, the medical team said *family only*, and wouldn't listen when we explained that Aunt Lydia was the closest thing Zelda had to family, at least around here." I absently rolled the mouse back and forth on the pad beside the desk computer. "There's Walt, of course, but he was out of town. Even though he rushed back from his daughter's house, he didn't get into town until several hours after Zelda was driven home by the authorities."

Sunny pulled a few returned items from the interior book drop and stacked them on the desk. "Such a mess. Not that I think for a minute Zelda would kill anyone, but to have

someone shot in your garden has to be traumatic, no matter how innocent you are."

I grabbed the top book from the pile and scanned it with the barcode reader. "And it looks bad, because it was Zelda's private garden, which isn't a place where one would typically find a stranger. So I can understand why the sheriff's department would question Zelda intently. I mean, why would someone just happen to be there? And the worst thing is, the victim was someone Zelda must've known, at least casually, since Aunt Lydia saw the same woman talking with Zelda a day or so ago."

"Lydia didn't recognize her?" Sunny asked, fanning her face with a thin paperback.

"No, but she said the stranger resembled Zelda, which is why she immediately recognized her as the victim in the gazebo." I slid another book under the barcode reader before placing it on the returns cart. "Despite her reservations, Aunt Lydia drove over to the sheriff's department today to share that information with Brad. She thought it might be relevant."

"Maybe the woman was supposed to meet Zelda again and that's why she was loitering in the garden." Obviously lost in thought, Sunny rubbed the side of her nose as she stared blankly at the library entrance. "She could've arrived too early for a planned meeting and was waiting in the garden before she knocked on Zelda's door."

"Maybe, but why would someone then shoot her in the gazebo?" I followed the direction of Sunny's gaze and noticed an older African American man striding in from the lobby.

"If the victim was being trailed by someone who wanted her dead . . ." Sunny snapped her fingers. "Hey, you know, she

could've been looking for help. Zelda does have a soft spot for people in trouble."

I pressed my fingers to my lips. "Walt's here," I murmured as I dropped my hand.

Sunny widened her blue eyes and flashed a smile as Walter Adams approached the desk. Recently retired from the Government Accountability Office in D.C., Walt was a tall, lanky, sixty-six-year-old who'd been friends with Aunt Lydia and Zelda since childhood. It was only after they'd both lost their spouses that he and Zelda had finally admitted their love for one another and become more than friends.

"Hello," I said, when Walt reached the desk. "How are you doing? I know this business with Zelda must be stressful."

"That's why I wanted to stop by today." Walt ran one hand through his short, silver-frosted, black hair. "I thought you could help." He nodded at Sunny. "Both of you, maybe."

"Happy to do anything I can," Sunny said.

"Me too, although I'm not sure what sort of aid I can offer, other than moral support," I said.

Walt pressed his palms against the worn wooden surface of the desk and leaned forward. "I was thinking you could do some research, like a little digging into that dead woman's past and . . . a few other things."

Sunny gestured toward me. "You want Amy then. I'm decent at uncovering info, but she's the real expert."

"Works for me." Walt stepped back and clasped his hands together at his chest. "I'd rather not talk out here, though. It may sound silly, but I don't want to share too much in public."

Sunny nodded. "Totally understandable. Honestly, I can watch the desk if you two want to talk in private."

"That sounds like a good plan, if Amy agrees," Walt said.

I motioned toward the workroom. "Come on around and we'll head in there. If we shut the door, no one should be able to overhear us, except maybe Sunny."

"I promise not to press my ear to the door," Sunny said.

Walt's gaze swept over the area near the desk as he circled around to join us. "I don't mind if Sunny hears anything. Just not anyone else."

After we entered the workroom and closed the door, I motioned for Walt to take a seat at the worktable. "Is there more news? I hope it's nothing bad. I can tell you're distressed."

"There are some new developments, and they aren't good." Walt sank down onto a rolling task chair, stretching out his long legs.

After taking a seat at the other side of the table, I shoved the book press we used when repairing broken spines to one side so I could face him without any obstructions. "Oh dear, what now?"

Walt squared his hunched shoulders. "For one thing, there seems to be gunshot residue on Zel's garden gloves. The ones they found in the gazebo."

"But that doesn't mean Zelda was the one wearing them." I lifted a pencil from the table. "She could've left them out there by accident and the killer took advantage of the opportunity."

"True, and the investigators suggested as much to Zel when they questioned her. They did press her pretty hard on where she last remembered leaving the gloves, but she told them, and me, she has no idea. She thought she'd stored them in the shed."

I rolled the pencil between my fingers as I studied Walt's face. A muscle was twitching in his cheek. "Wasn't the shed locked, though?"

Walt shook his head. "The combination lock was hanging in the latch, with the door ajar. Zel's afraid she left it like that the last time she retrieved something from the shed. She remembers getting a phone call that distracted her as she was locking up."

"So the killer could've grabbed those gloves out of the shed as well as discovered them in the gazebo."

"It's possible. Zel always keeps those gloves on a hook inside the shed door. Of course, the sheriff's department also has to consider whether Zel grabbed the gloves herself. So that in itself doesn't exonerate her."

"But it also doesn't prove she was the one wearing the gloves at the time of the shooting." I tossed the pencil into a box containing materials we used in processing new books. "They haven't found the murder weapon yet, have they?"

"Not from what I can figure out, but they might be keeping that under wraps." Walt sat back in his chair and stared up at the fluorescent light fixture hanging over the table. "Of course, Zel was questioned about having a gun, and she initially claimed she didn't. She now admits that was a big mistake."

I leaned forward, resting my elbows on the table. "What do you mean? Aunt Lydia's convinced Zelda wouldn't ever purchase a gun, much less fire one."

"From what she's told me, she didn't, and hasn't. But"— Walt's dark eyes were filled with pain—"it seems her late husband did have a license for a Smith and Wesson revolver."

I threw up my hands. "What of it? That would've been years ago."

"Exactly, which is why Zel forgot all about it and told the deputies she didn't keep a gun in the house. But when they brought up that license, she had to change her story." Walt grimaced. "Which never looks good, especially when dealing with law enforcement."

"I wouldn't worry too much. When they check her husband's old gun, they'll undoubtedly see it hasn't been fired."

"That's the problem—they haven't found it." Walt leaned forward again, gripping his hands together on the tabletop. "The truth is, Zel honestly has no idea where her husband stashed the thing. She said when she told the detectives that fact, they doubled down on their questioning."

I sniffed derisively. "Because they think she used the gun to shoot Claudia Everhart and then ditched it somewhere?"

"That was Zel's impression. She said they started eyeing her with more suspicion at that point."

I sat back in my chair. "But they still have to match the murder weapon to the revolver Zelda's husband supposedly owned. I mean, with the ballistics testing and all that. I doubt it will turn out to be the same type of gun."

"I hope not, but we don't know anything yet." Walt's sigh rattled up from deep in his chest. "Or at least, we haven't been told anything."

I pushed back my chair and rose to my feet. "This is all circumstantial evidence." I paced the short distance between the staff entrance and the door to the circulation desk. "I mean, what reason could Zelda possibly have to kill anyone? It's not like she has a criminal background."

Walt cleared his throat. "Unfortunately, there does seem to be one possible motive, at least in the eyes of the authorities. Zel told me the investigators asked her a lot of questions about whether she had enemies and that sort of thing, but really homed in on the topic of blackmail."

"As in, someone was blackmailing Zelda?" I stopped pacing to stare directly into Walt's eyes. "Whatever for?"

"I have no idea, but the thing is, there's a reason the detectives were pressing Zel over that idea." Walt met my intent gaze and held it. "When I accompanied Zel back to the sheriff's department for more questioning this morning, I happened to overhear some chatter from a couple of the junior deputies. Apparently, a blackmail note was discovered in the victim's pocket. Not addressed to Zel, or anyone in particular," Walt added, waving one hand dismissively in response to my gasp. "But it was obviously intended as a way to extort money, in order to keep some past crime or indiscretion a secret. At least, that's what I deduced from my eavesdropping."

I pressed my palms against the tabletop to still their sudden shaking. "Did you ask Zelda about that when you were alone?"

"I tried. But she didn't want to discuss it. Which was odd in itself. When have you ever known Zel to clam up about anything?" Walt flashed me a humorless smile. "She simply insisted, over and over, that there was nothing in her past to warrant blackmail of any kind."

I examined Walt's drawn face for a moment. "I get the feeling you don't entirely believe her."

"I hate to say it, but I don't. And not just because she was so quick to change the subject." Walt, pressing his hands together

42

as if in prayer, tapped the tips of his fingers against his chin. "She also refused to talk about the victim. She wouldn't tell me why the woman had visited her, not once but twice. To me that means they had something serious to discuss. But all Zel would say was that they crossed paths long ago, when they were involved in rival high school choral groups."

"I didn't realize Zelda sang in high school." I was sincerely puzzled by this new development. Zelda, like my aunt and Walt, had attended Leeland High, and always seemed happy to share memories of their time at the school. *How did being part of a chamber choir never come up in conversation? It seems like something Zelda would've been more than happy to share.* I frowned. *And, come to think of it, why has Aunt Lydia never mentioned that fact? That's almost as strange.*

"She never talks about it now, but she was in the chamber choir that's holding a reunion this week. I heard they were invited to sing during the final performance event at the arts festival at Leeland," Walt said. "Along with the victim's choir, apparently."

I stared at him, widening my eyes. This was an unexpected wrinkle. "But why isn't Zelda performing, if she was part of the group that won? I would've thought she'd love being involved."

Walt's gaze locked with mine. "That's what I want you to investigate. What might've happened back in 1970 that made Zel drop out of chorus halfway through our senior year."

"She left the chamber choir before the end of the school year?"

"Yes, not long after they won first place in the state competition." Walt rubbed the back of his neck with one hand.

"Lydia and I both thought it was peculiar at the time. I mean, Zel fought like a fiend to get into that group, to then up and quit before her final semester. And she'd never say why. Not to Lydia, not to me, not to anyone, as far as I know."

"It is odd." I stepped back from the table. "I thought she would've told her closest friends something like that. Her reasons for leaving must've been pretty serious for her to give up something she seemed to really love."

Walt glanced over my shoulder, staring at the supplies stored on the shelves behind me as if they could unravel this puzzle. "Honestly, at that point, we weren't very close. Remember the times—it wasn't such an issue for a black boy and two white girls to be friends in elementary school, but when we got older, things changed. We saw each other occasionally, but only when we knew no one else was around. We weren't told to stay apart." Walt shrugged. "We'd simply all absorbed enough systematic racism to feel it was better for everyone if we weren't seen hanging out in public."

"I'm sorry you had to go through that," I said. "I know it was tough back then."

Walt's eyes narrowed. "It isn't as different today as it should be, but that's another discussion for another day. Right now, I'm focused on finding out why Claudia Everhart showed up at Zel's house after all these years. I've thought maybe Ms. Everhart was seeking help, but why would she look to Zel?"

"That's the real question—how are they connected?"

"I know, and I'm so frustrated Zel isn't willing to talk." Walt leaned forward, pressing his palms against the tabletop. "My theory is that Ms. Everhart shared some information Zel

44

swore she wouldn't divulge. You know how she is—always eager to share news, unless she really has promised not to spill some serious, life-altering secret. Then her loyalty overcomes her love of gossip."

I nodded. "I can believe that. She's never spoken to me about my uncle in terms of his struggles with addiction, and I'm sure she must've known."

"Exactly. She's never mentioned anything like that concerning Andrew Talbot to me either. She just talks about what a great artist he was, and how much Lydia loved him."

I examined his face for a moment, noting that exhaustion had deepened the hollows under his high cheekbones. "I suppose it's possible Zelda is protecting Claudia Everhart's secrets by not sharing more information, but why? Zelda is close to Aunt Lydia, so she'd naturally want to keep her confidences, but this woman seems to have been little more than a stranger."

"I know, but there has to be some connection." Walt exhaled an audible sigh. "I also thought if we could uncover any reasons why someone else would want to kill the victim, we could take the spotlight of suspicion off Zel."

"I assume you want me to see what I can find online or in the archives," I said.

Walt nodded. "I thought there might at least be some mention of that old arts competition in the papers, or in some documents recording events in the area. Anything at all would be a big help."

I leaned back against the metal shelving. "We do have digitized copies of the local paper, so I can check those files. And it's

possible there could be a mention in the town council minutes, especially since the local high school choir was one of the statewide winners. We store those records in the archives, so I can look into that too."

"Thank you. I don't know how much coverage there might've been, but I expect any local organization achieving such a thing would've been seen as a big deal." Walt clutched the back of the rolling chair. "Which is another weird aspect of all this, to tell you the truth. I vaguely recall hearing about the chamber choir winning a state competition, but Zel never mentions that either, even when we're reminiscing about the past."

"They did tie with another choir for top honors," I said. "But it's still strange Zelda isn't proud of the win. You'd think she'd love to talk about it."

Walt lifted one hand and swept it through the air. "It was a big deal, from what I remember. I didn't pay too much attention back then; too involved with my basketball career. But"— Walt's fingers dug into the worn upholstery of the chair—"Zel fought so hard to get into that group. She even ignored your aunt for a long time, just to be accepted by the other members of the chamber choir. It really hurt Lydia, too. The choir kids were very cliquish and demanded most of Zel's time and attention. She had to choose between spending time with Lydia or with the choir folks."

"And she chose the choir?"

"Sadly, yes. Lydia came to me, crying over that, once. And you know Lydia." Walt raised his dark eyebrows. "She wasn't a crier."

"Still isn't," I said.

"True enough," Walt said with a smile. "Anyway, she felt Zel was spurning her. It was a pretty big betrayal, in Lydia's eyes."

I considered this new information, mentally agreeing with Walt that it didn't make any sense for Zelda to have gone so far as to dump her best friend to get into a choral group, and then abandon the group after they'd earned statewide recognition.

Given those circumstances, I'd have expected her to stay with the choir until the end of her senior year. "But they made up, it seems."

"Right after Zel quit the choir. She was truly repentant, and when she apologized to Lydia, they became close friends again." Walt straightened to his full, imposing height. "But she never told either of us why she left the chorus."

"Who would've thought there'd be any mystery in Zelda's past," I mused, speaking more to myself than Walt. Looking up to meet his steady gaze, I added, "I'll see what I can find out, including any information about Claudia Everhart."

"Thanks, I appreciate you trying to dig up anything that might be out there."

"I'm happy to help, you know that." I offered Walt a reassuring smile. "We both know Zelda is innocent, and I'm sure the authorities will come to the same conclusion soon enough, with or without our help. But it won't hurt to look into some of these mysteries from the past."

Walt's eyes clouded over. "I hope it won't, anyway."

"You actually think there might be something in Zelda's past that would be a motive for murder?"

He shook his head. "Not really, it's just that her silence over her connection to this Everhart woman, along with her refusal

to share any details about their recent conversations, has me worried."

"It's probably the shock." I ignored the little voice in my head that whispered doubts. "I bet she'll spill everything over the next few days."

Walt's lips tightened. "Let's hope so."

"I mean, she's not going to stay silent about such a thing forever," I said, with a bravado I didn't feel.

Walt simply thanked me again and left the room, without assuaging my doubts.

Chapter Six

Acting on impulse, I decided to call someone I thought might have knowledge of events that had occurred in the 1970s.

Although wealthy art dealer Kurt Kendrick had fled the home of his foster father, Paul Dassin, as soon as he turned eighteen in 1963, I knew he'd remained in the general area and had secretly stayed in touch with his best friend, Andrew Talbot. He'd also transacted business in the region during the sixties and early seventies. The fact that his business had involved dealing drugs was the major reason he'd not only changed his name from Karl Klass, but had also never contacted Paul Dassin again.

Kurt claimed to have left his illegal activities behind when he switched to dealing art instead of drugs. I wasn't entirely convinced all his business practices were on the up and up, but had decided to overlook that issue after he'd proven to be a good friend to me, Richard, and our respective families over the last few years.

Knowing he usually only spent weekends at his local estate, I was surprised when he told me he was actually at Highview for the week.

"I'm taking a little break between buying trips," he said, after I'd suggested meeting sometime soon. "You can stop by after work today or tomorrow if you wish. I have no other plans."

"This afternoon would be best," I replied. "I'm working until five today instead of eight, like tomorrow. And I wasn't planning to make dinner this evening, since Richard will be getting home late. He's rehearsing with Karla, one of the pieces they're choreographing together."

"For the folklore project?" Kurt asked, his obvious interest reminding me he'd made a significant donation to support that choreographic suite.

"Yes, and I have some more news I'll share with you when we talk. Is five thirty okay?"

"Perfect," Kurt said. "I look forward to seeing you, Amy. It's been a while."

"I know." A wave of embarrassment swept over me. Kurt's wedding gift to Richard and me—plane tickets, spending money, and a stay at a friend's beautiful Italian villa—had provided us with the perfect honeymoon. Despite our busy schedules, I should've made more of an effort to stay in touch once we'd gotten back. We'd met with Kurt once since then, to share photos from the honeymoon, but that had been two months ago. "Anyway, I'll catch you up on all the news later."

"My dear, I already know all the news." Kurt's tone clearly expressed his amusement.

Of course he did. He employed a network of spies or, as he liked to call them, "little birds," who kept him informed about everything going on in Taylorsford, as well as throughout his business empire.

After wishing him a good day, I turned my attention to the interlibrary loans piled up in the workroom. With my other library assistant, Samantha Green, working the circulation desk, I spent the rest of the afternoon processing the ILLs we needed to send out or return to other libraries, as well as submitting requests to obtain items.

At five I hurried home to borrow the car I shared with Aunt Lydia. Driving outside of town, I turned onto a bumpy gravel road leading up into the mountains.

Unlike the county road, Kurt's driveway was paved. I paused at the two stone pillars flanking a metal gate to buzz the house, calling out my name when Kurt's voice crackled over the intercom. The gate opened onto the blacktopped drive, which was shaded by an arching canopy of leafy branches. At the base of the trees lining the drive, azaleas and rhododendrons merged to create a living fence.

As I rounded the final corner of the winding drive, sunlight flooded the car, forcing me to blink. Set in the middle of a large clearing surrounded by woods, the beauty of Kurt's home impressed me every time I visited. The three-story central section, which had been built in the eighteenth century, was constructed from variegated fieldstone pulled from local meadows. Tall windows, fitted with wavy handblown glass, were sunk into the mottled gray stones. The two-story wood-framed wings were painted a pale jade green and studded with smaller windows flanked by black shutters, while a lacy veil of ivy draped the largest of the stone chimneys.

I parked in the circle at the end of the driveway, staying clear of the entrance to a smaller lane curving around behind

the house. I knew it led to the garage where Kurt stored his elegant black Jaguar sedan.

Climbing out of my own, much less expensive car, I headed for the house, pausing for a moment to admire the riot of color offered by the picket fence–enclosed cottage garden.

The home's porch was smaller than many that graced the Victorian or Craftsman-style houses in town, but its simple stone platform was enhanced by Grecian-style pillars supporting a curved barrel roof. Before I could raise my hand to ring the bell, the forest green front door opened and I came face to face with Kurt.

Or rather, I faced his chest, since Kurt was so tall, his thick head of white hair almost touched the lintel. "Hello, Amy. Do come in," he said, turning on his heel to lead the way inside.

In his youth, Kurt had been called "The Viking." The nickname still suited him. His imposing build was all bone and muscle, and his shaggy mane of white hair was cut a little longer than was fashionable. With his icy blue eyes and rugged features, I could definitely imagine him stepping out of a longboat on some distant northern shore.

I trotted behind Kurt as he strode down his wide main hall, which was filled with an array of antique furniture, artwork, and other decorative objects more commonly found in a museum than a private home. We headed into his living room, an expansive space filled with leather sofas and upholstered chairs anchored by worn Persian rugs. A stone fireplace with a reclaimed beam mantel dominated one outside wall, and an entire gallery's worth of paintings covered the other, pale ivory walls.

I crossed to a sofa facing an Arts and Crafts–style armchair. Kurt waited until I was seated before he sank down into the sturdy wood-framed chair.

"What brings you out to my humble home today, Amy? Over the phone you mentioned wanting to ask me a few questions about the past, but that covers a lot of territory." As Kurt stretched out his long legs, his expensive leather loafers drew a line in the pile of the rug covering the hardwood floor between his seat and mine.

"Humble home?" I said, not bothering to temper the sarcasm in my tone.

"Give me a little credit. I did resist the impulse to add gilt and mirrors." Kurt flashed me one of his wolfish grins. "Now, what was the news you wanted to share?"

"Oh, right." I absently drummed my fingers against the padded arm of my chair. "I just wanted to let you know that Richard has received another donation for the folklore suite. It's from Emily Moore, who's also agreed to contribute some poetry as part of the spoken word component of the project."

"That's great, but I think you could've simply shared that over the phone." Kurt fixed me with his piercing gaze. "I know you actually want information from me, rather than the other way around, so shall we get down to it? I suspect this visit has been prompted by Zelda Shoemaker and the unfortunate murder in her gazebo. Am I on target?"

"You've hit the bull's-eye, as always."

Kurt's brilliant blue gaze swept over me. "Let me guess—you want to know if my little birds have uncovered any information that could prove beneficial in clearing Ms. Shoemaker's name."

"Not exactly. Of course, if they've turned up anything, I would love to know it. Although"—I placed my hands in my lap, crossing one over the other demurely—"perhaps it would be better if you shared such intel directly with the sheriff's department."

"Always happy to help law enforcement. These days, anyway." Kurt's laconic tone was belied by the twinkle in his eyes. "But no, I haven't heard anything. Not for lack of trying, believe me."

"It's okay. That wasn't the main thing I wanted to ask you about." I took a deep breath. "Walt came to see me at the library today. He has some questions about this victim, Claudia Everhart, and her connection to Zelda."

"I'm afraid I don't know the woman. There are numerous Everharts in the area, and I admit I have run up on some of them. Just not this one."

"But you were in the area in 1970, right? At least from time to time."

"I was, but from what I've read about the victim, she was in high school. Not a milieu I was mingling with, for all my faults."

I met his amused gaze with a lift of my chin. "I don't expect you would've concerned yourself with anything as wholesome as a school choir, but apparently both Zelda and this Claudia person were in choral groups at rival high schools. Walt thinks something happened in 1970 that caused Zelda to quit her choir, right after both ensembles tied for first place in some statewide competition, and I wondered . . ."

"If I'd heard any rumors about something untoward happening around that time?" Kurt's bushy eyebrows disappeared

under the fringe of hair falling over his broad forehead. "Let me think for a second. Memory's not quite what it used to be," he added, tapping his temple with his forefinger.

I rolled my eyes. "Right, because you're such a feeble old man."

"Age takes its toll on us all, my dear," he said, baring his large, white teeth in another grin.

"Uh-huh. Anyway, if you could summon the mental capacity to recall any scandal or traumatic event that occurred in the area in 1970, I'd be most appreciative."

"Around the time of some statewide arts event, you say?" Kurt closed his eyes for a moment. "There is something tickling at my memory, but I can't imagine why it would have murderous repercussions decades later."

I slid forward on the buttery leather seat of the sofa. "Doesn't matter. Any little thing might help kickstart my research efforts."

"Ah, so this is part of one of your Nancy Drew escapades?" Kurt rested his elbows on the wooden chair arms as he templed his hands. "Are you sure it's wise to jump into another murder investigation, especially after your recent experiences?"

"Wise or not, I want to help Zelda."

"Very well, then. I'll share what I remember, or at least anything with any relevance. Not that it's much," he said, with a warning shake of his finger. "But I do recall some sort of flap associated with an arts competition back in the early seventies. Andrew told me about it. He was one of visual arts judges for the event."

"Aunt Lydia should also know about that, then." I sat back, puzzling over this connection. If my aunt had any recollection

of a past event involving both Zelda and Claudia Everhart, she certainly hadn't shared it with me.

"I'm sure she does. But whether she's connected it to these recent events"—Kurt shrugged—"is debatable. Since she was still in high school, she probably heard rumors or even some news reports, but she wouldn't have gotten the information straight from Andrew."

"Oh, right. They were just friends at that point." Calculating in my head, I realized Andrew would've been around twenty-four in 1970, while Aunt Lydia would've been only eighteen.

"Casual friends. They'd met when Andrew used to hang out with me at Paul's house, next door to Lydia's home. But he was older and thought of her as just a kid." Kurt's expression hardened. "Until he didn't."

Having no desire to explore the dynamic of this tangle of relationships, I shifted the conversation back on track. "So what was the scandal or whatever at the arts festival? Not something to do with manipulation of the results of the competition, I hope. I know Leeland High's chamber choir tied for first place with Claudia Everhart's choral group from Stonebridge High."

"Nothing like that. It had to do with some kid getting sick." Kurt stared up at the high ceiling, his eyes narrowed in concentration. "Let's see, what was it exactly? Ah yes"—he dropped his gaze to focus on my face—"a serious allergic reaction. There was a boy who went into anaphylactic shock after he ate something laced with peanut butter. Andrew said it was a big deal because, according to the vocal music judges, the young man was very proactive about telling people about his allergy to peanuts. He

would've questioned the contents of any food handed to him, so whoever slipped him the offending item had to have lied to him about its ingredients."

"You mean someone wanted to deliberately trigger his allergy?" I widened my eyes. "But that could've killed him."

"Almost did, from what I was told. Which was why it was such a major flap at the time, at least among the local high schoolers and their families. Not, as I said, that I was connected to the high school crowd"—Kurt flashed a wry smile—"but Andrew led some art workshops at Leeland from time to time, so he knew several of the students. He was very upset about the whole thing."

"Who was the boy who almost died?" I asked.

"I don't know." Kurt waved his hand dismissively. "I'm sure Andrew told me, but it didn't register."

"I bet I can find out in the papers from the time, or something else in the archives."

"No doubt." Kurt leaned forward, gripping his knees with his hands. "Is that enough to go on, then? I really can't think of anything else directly linked to any arts competition around the time, and that seems to be the most significant thread connecting Ms. Shoemaker to the murder victim."

"It's actually a big help. Maybe just digging into the allergy story will give me an answer, or, if not, will lead me onto the right path." I shrugged. "That's how it works with research sometimes. Even a false lead can eventually turn up something useful." After giving Kurt a grateful smile, I glanced over his shoulder, my attention captured by a painting on the opposite wall. "Is that a Christina Quarles?"

Kurt twisted around to follow my gaze. "Yes. I picked it up on my last buying trip. It was meant for the Georgetown gallery, but I decided I couldn't part with it."

I studied the colorful and convoluted curves of bodies filling the canvas. "I only recognize it because I recently read an article on her work. It talked about how she likes to examine and confront constructions of race, gender, and sexual identity."

"Perfect for my collection then, wouldn't you say?" Kurt cast me a wicked grin.

"You do have eclectic tastes," I said mildly.

"Correction—I have excellent taste," he replied, looking me over. "Which you should appreciate, since I include you among the relatively few people I admire."

I didn't rise to this bait, offering him a bob of the head before remarking, "Along with Richard, of course."

"Absolutely, and not just because of his tremendous talent and great personality. To be honest, as the great-nephew of Paul Dassin, he's as close to family as I've got."

"Well, there is Paul's niece, Fiona," I said, unable to contain an impish grin as I considered my husband's imperious mother.

Kurt raised his eyebrows. "Indeed. How is Fiona these days, by the way? Have you kept more in touch? I sensed a slight thaw in the iceberg at the wedding."

I met his sardonic expression with a lift of my hands. "Fiona is still Fiona. But we do seem to have come to some sort of détente. Richard's dad, on the other hand . . ."

"Is an ass," Kurt said.

Since he was right, I didn't correct him. "Actually, Fiona has visited us a few times since the wedding, without Jim. She

always says he's on a business trip and, honestly, no one cares if that's true or not."

"I'm sure Jim is at least delighted by one thing—that Richard has finally married." Kurt's eyes sparkled with humor.

"And a woman, too," I said dryly, earning a guffaw from Kurt.

"Jim Muir must love you," he said, wiping a tear from the corner of his eye.

I snorted. "Yeah, we've gotten to be great pals, as you can imagine."

"You are exactly what he deserves, after the way he treated Richard all those years," Kurt said, his expression sobering. "A woman who won't put up with his bigoted, narrow-minded nonsense."

"I'm sure he loves you too," I said.

Kurt chuckled. "Not after that talk we had at the wedding. Oh, you hadn't heard? I guess he didn't share the details with you or Richard."

"Did you read him the riot act or something?" I asked, with a lift of my eyebrows.

"No, just reiterated my support of Richard's dance and choreographic career, and cut him off when he started on his familiar 'that's nice, but if he'd only gone into finance' diatribe." Kurt brushed the swoop of hair away from his forehead. "I may have responded with a rather harsh comment on his fathering skills. I'm afraid I couldn't help myself."

"It happens," I said with a smile. "All right then, I should probably go. I think I'll stop by the new Indian restaurant outside of town and pick up some takeout for later. Richard is always starving after a rehearsal."

"Not surprising, considering how much energy a dancer expends." Kurt rose to his feet. "I hope my tidbit of information will help you with your research, Amy. If I hear anything else that could prove beneficial to Ms. Shoemaker's cause, I'll certainly let you know."

As I stood to face him my leg bumped the edge of an end table next to the couch. The jolt knocked a couple of books from the table to the floor. "Sorry, how clumsy of me." I bent down to retrieve the books. "You can obviously tell I'm not the dancer in the family."

"It's no problem," Kurt said. "I should probably keep those on a shelf in the study anyway."

One of the books caught my attention and I held onto it after placing the others back on the end table. It was a slim volume bound in buttery forest green leather, its spine and cover tooled with gold lettering. "This is lovely. Oh, *The Portrait of Dorian Gray* by Oscar Wilde. Nice." As I flipped open the cover, I heard Kurt clear his throat. Glancing at the title page, I thought I knew why. There was an inscription. *No, a dedication*, I realized as I deciphered the elegant cursive writing—*To my dearest friend, who isn't nearly as wicked as he thinks.*

Kurt's piercing gaze met mine as I looked up. I recognized the signature in the book, of course. I'd seen it on numerous paintings belonging to Aunt Lydia.

"Uncle Andrew gave you this."

"Yes, and strangely, around the time he was judging that state arts competition." Kurt motioned toward my feet. "I think something fell out."

I glanced down at an old color photograph lying face-up on the rug. Before I could pick it up, Kurt swooped in and grabbed it.

"Ah yes, I remember this. Andrew had offered to paint some scenery for a local community theater production the summer before he volunteered as a judge for the arts competition." Kurt held out the photo so I could take a look at it. "*Brigadoon*, I think it was."

I examined the painted scenery behind a cluster of young women in what appeared to be Scottish dress. "Looks like it. And I can definitely tell it was Uncle Andrew's work."

Kurt pulled back the photo. "That's another odd coincidence," he said after close scrutiny of the picture. "Can you guess who one of the girls might be?"

I took the photograph from him and peered at the image. "Wait, I think I met her recently. Her name is Gwen Ohlson. And the girl next to her is her friend, Olivia Rader—or Olivia Bell, as she would've been known back then." I widened my eyes. Even after fifty years, I could clearly see the resemblance to the women they'd become. I tapped the photo against my palm. "I don't recognize the third girl."

"The one who seems to be one of the leads, judging by her costume and placement in the scene?" Kurt shook his head. "I don't recognize her either."

As I handed the photo back to him, I realized he hadn't confessed to not knowing any of the girls. "Okay, now I'm a little spooked. This is one of those strange occurrences that make one question reality a little bit, don't you think?"

"Because we were talking about the arts event back in '70?" Kurt raised his bushy eyebrows. "I'm not sure I follow."

"Because two of the girls in this photo were involved in that vocal competition fifty years ago. And they have now shown up in Taylorsford. What are the odds?"

"It's just one of life's strange coincidences." Kurt's tone was light, but the glitter in his eyes told me more was going on.

He knows more than he's admitting about one or both of those women, I thought, keeping my gaze locked on his face. "Anyway, thanks in advance for any information you can uncover that might help Zelda. Even if it doesn't seem useful, please share. I want to get to the truth."

"Always your goal, isn't it?" Kurt asked, as he escorted me out into the hall. At the front door, he looked down at me with a sardonic smile. "You seem to want to know the truth, no matter what. Except perhaps where I'm concerned."

"Oh, I want it but have accepted I many never have it," I replied, before wishing him a good evening and heading outside.

"Take care, Amy," he called after me. "And if you find yourself in trouble, you know who to contact for help."

"Yeah, Brad Tucker," I replied.

Kurt's laughter followed me to my car.

Chapter Seven

I was working the late shift on Wednesday, so I didn't arrive at the library until eleven. Coming out of the staff lounge, where I'd dropped off the food I'd packed for lunch and dinner, I was stopped by one of our regular patrons, Mrs. Dinterman.

"Do you have any news about this latest murder?" she asked, her dark eyes bright as polished buttons.

"Not really." I looked out over the Children's Room, which was filling up with youngsters and parents in anticipation of story hour. "And maybe we should take any discussion to the desk? I don't want to talk about such things in front of the children, and I need to relieve Samantha."

"Of course, of course," Mrs. Dinterman said, as she trotted at my heels. She kept quiet until we reached the circulation desk, but as soon as Samantha left to go lead story hour, she started chattering again. "It's awful they suspect dear Zelda. She's just the sweetest thing, don't you think? I can't imagine her hurting anyone."

I fought the urge to chuckle over Mrs. Dinterman's description of Zelda. Yes, she was charming and caring, but she

certainly wasn't the type of person I'd call *the sweetest thing*. She was far too voluble and full of vitality for that. Of course, Mrs. Dinterman was over eighty, so she regarded Zelda as a young girl.

"I'm sure it's all a terrible misunderstanding," I said, as I logged my credentials into our circulation system. "The murder happened on Zelda's property, so naturally she'd be questioned. But I doubt the authorities seriously consider her a suspect."

When Mrs. Dinterman bobbed her head, her matte black hair, sprayed within an inch of its life, moved as one piece. "I don't know about that. I heard some deputies chatting at the Heapin' Plate and one of them mentioned something about Zelda owning the same sort of gun as the one used to kill that Everhart woman."

I frowned. This was certainly not the news I'd hoped to hear. "They shouldn't have been discussing such things in the diner, at least not so anyone could overhear."

Mrs. Dinterman waved one of her plump hands. "Oh, they weren't so very loud. I was simply seated rather close."

You mean you scooted your chair over to where you could hear, I thought, offering her a tight smile. Mrs. Dinterman and her husband lived across the street from Aunt Lydia and catty-corner from Richard and me. It didn't take great sleuthing skills to observe how often they managed to be on their porch when people were coming and going from our houses. *Especially Hugh visiting Aunt Lydia*, I thought. I was sure the older couple had some thoughts on that subject, but despite her efforts, I always refused to allow Mrs. Dinterman to share any opinions about Aunt Lydia's boyfriend.

"I assume it will all be sorted out soon. Honestly, Zelda has confessed she has no idea where her late husband kept his revolver, and she hasn't seen it in years. Maybe the killer stole it from somewhere on Zelda's property beforehand." I glanced away from Mrs. Dinterman's inquisitive gaze to focus on tidying a display of flyers advertising local sites and events. If my neighbor was going to gossip, why not give her a more positive theory to share?

Mrs. Dinterman sniffed. "Could be, I suppose. Lord knows Zelda always seems to have people coming and going from her house."

I looked up, a query as to how she knew such a thing trembled on the tip of my tongue, but I thought better of asking that question. "Zelda does host a lot of volunteer groups at her home, as well as garden club talks and get-togethers. It's possible a stranger could've shown up at one of those events and Zelda thought they were the friend of a friend."

"Very likely. Anyway, I suppose I should run along. I just stopped in to while away a little time while my husband gets the lawnmower checked over by Pete O'Malley. Not that there's ever any rush, of course. That fellow works slower than molasses climbing up a hill in January." Mrs. Dinterman patted her helmet of hair. "But maybe I'll go take a peek in the new shop in town. The Garden Gate, they call it. Have you checked it out yet? Lots of decorative stuff for gardens, it looks like. Thought you might like it since you're setting up a new home and all."

"Not yet, although I plan to check it out soon," I said mildly, not bothering to make the point that Richard had already done a lot of work in our backyard. Based on her husband, Mrs.

Dinterman probably couldn't imagine a man doing much more than mowing or perhaps running a weed whacker, and assumed I'd have to take on everything related to flowers or decorative garden pieces. Which wasn't true—Richard had installed some latticework arches, a wooden pergola, and created several flower beds before we were married.

"Good day, Amy. I hope we hear better news about our friend Zelda soon," Mrs. Dinterman said, before bustling out of the library.

I watched her exit before turning back to the computer to check some statistics.

"That woman don't know nuthin'," said another regular patron, the eccentric older woman we called "The Nightingale" due to her tendency to "help" the library staff by reshelving books.

I looked up to meet her watery gaze. She was tall and bony, with straggling gray hair she wore in a variety of styles depending on her mood. Today she'd created two thin braids wrapped around her head like a crown.

"She just likes to share news," I said, aware The Nightingale also had a tendency to gossip. "Although in this case, not necessarily something proven to be true."

The Nightingale snorted. "I know what she's been saying. Claims she heard the gun that killed that stranger in Zelda Shoemaker's gazebo belonged to Zelda's husband. Well, maybe it did, and maybe it didn't. But it don't make Zelda no murderer."

"No, it doesn't," I replied, offering her a smile. "I bet you've known Zelda a long time, haven't you?"

"Long enough to know she ain't one for guns." The Nightingale clasped her knobby-knuckled hands together and pressed

them against the desktop. "Zelda's smarter than that, too. She knows all about garden stuff, so I'm betting if she did want to off someone, she'd use a poison from a plant or somethin'. Quiet and clever, you know? Not some noisy gun."

I eyed her, taking a deep breath before answering. "I don't believe Zelda capable of killing anyone, but I see your point."

The Nightingale leaned forward until her gaunt face was close to mine. "Anybody can kill. I'd of thought you'd have figured that out by now, what with you stumbling over all those dead bodies over the last few years."

I took a step back. "It's true I've observed that all types of people commit murder, for any number of reasons, but I still don't believe Zelda would do such a thing."

"Anybody." The Nightingale wagged her finger at me. "And don't you forget it. 'Less you want to become the next victim."

I didn't reply, simply watched silently as she spun around and stalked off toward the stacks.

Which we'd have to check later, to make sure she hadn't reshelved auto manuals in the Young Adult section again.

*   *   *

When Samantha returned to the desk, I suggested she go ahead and take her lunch hour. "I'm sure you could use a break after wrangling the kiddos," I said, as a hoard of children and parents filed by the desk, headed for the lobby.

"Thanks, a little quiet would be nice," Samantha said, flashing a grin. She ran her fingers through her short Afro. "No additional gray hairs visible, I hope?"

"None at all," I replied, with a smile. Samantha and her daughter Shay had been regular patrons at the library before I'd hired her as a part-time assistant. She covered the hours Sunny couldn't work when she'd become mayor of Taylorsford. Samantha, whose college degree had been in elementary education, was a great help with all of the children's programs, as well as an excellent circulation desk assistant. "How's Shay these days? I see her in here sometimes, but not as much as I used to."

Samantha shrugged. "Now that she's ten, she's gotten so involved in extracurricular activities, she doesn't have much time for the library. She does use the one at her school, though, and I take home books, so she's still reading."

"That's good." I waited until Samantha checked out several items to a few patrons before posing another question. "I recall you saying Shay's taking dance classes at Karla Tansen's studio. How does she like it?"

"Oh, she loves those classes, and Karla too." Samantha beamed. "You know Shay isn't one of those skinny girls, so she always thought studying dance seriously was out of the question. But Karla tells her it doesn't matter, and of course, provides the perfect role model backing up those words."

An image of my husband's friend and dance partner flashed through my mind. Told she was too tall and big-boned to succeed as a professional dancer, despite her tremendous talent, Karla had eventually turned to teaching. She'd run several studios. Her latest was located outside of Taylorsford, between the town and nearby Clarion University.

"And, of course, Shay simply adores your husband. Those workshops he's done with Karla's students are apparently a

hit with all the young people." Samantha cast me a sly smile. "Good dad material there."

"Hmm . . ." I couldn't disagree with Samantha. Richard was great with children, and I knew he wanted at least one of his own. But, despite being thirty-five, I wasn't in any rush to have a baby. Maybe in a couple of years . . . "Anyway, you go on to lunch. I can watch over the desk, and Denise is coming in later to shelve." I fiddled with the pencils stuffed in the desk holder. "I'd actually like to go out to the archives later, if you don't mind running things with Denise's help. I have some research to do."

Samantha arched her dark eyebrows. "Something to aid Zelda? I won't argue with that. She needs to have her name cleared, sooner rather than later."

"I totally agree and, yes, I hope I can find something that will help."

"Speaking of that, and before I forget—I wanted to mention someone who might be able to provide some information about Zelda's involvement in the chamber choir. I heard the victim might've been associated with a rival choral group that attended some of the same competitions." Samantha shot me a sidelong glance. "It seemed to me there could be a connection."

"Agreed, and I would love to talk with anyone with any information."

"It's my aunt, Lorraine Harris. She's a few years younger than Zelda, so she was only fifteen when Leeland's chamber choir won the state competition. She didn't make it into the chamber choir until her senior year, so she wasn't part of the group that won, but she did follow them pretty closely and

knew a few of the members because they sang in her church choir."

"So she might have some inside scoop?" I asked. "I would love to speak with her, if she's still in the area."

"Not far. She lives in Smithsburg, which is only a short drive. I'm sure I can convince her to stop by one day, if you want to talk to her."

"Just let me know what day and time work for her, and I'll be sure to be here." I offered Samantha a warm smile. "Now, I've kept you from your lunch long enough. Take as long as you need—Bill is coming in at five, so his volunteer shift will overlap with Denise's hours. I'm sure one of them will be happy to watch the desk if I'm still working in the archives when you leave for the day."

"I don't need too long for lunch," Samantha said. "Although I will take the opportunity to call Aunt Lorraine and see when she can stop by."

After Samantha returned from lunch, I headed out back, to the small stone building which had been built as lodging for Taylorsford's first library director. Converted into storage space, it now housed the town archives.

The windows cut into the stone walls were covered by metal shelving stuffed with archival banker's boxes full of print materials, requiring me to flick on the overhead lights even in the middle of the day. I shimmied past a row of metal filing cabinets to circle behind the large wooden table filling the center of the room.

Knowing that randomly digging through files and photographs was not an efficient research method, I sat in the wooden

chair to make a plan. Staring out over the rows of boxes and expanding file folders on the shelves, I decided my best bet was to start with any filed newspaper clippings from 1970, before moving on to town council meeting notes. There should be some mention of Leeland winning the statewide competition in one or both of those sources. The only question was—had there also been a news story or council comment about other events occurring at the same time, such as the peanut butter incident Kurt had mentioned?

I jumped up and headed over to the section of the shelves holding two boxes labeled "Clippings 1970."

People often assumed we'd digitized all of this material, but that was not the case. The truth was, digitizing documents required a lot of staff time and money, neither of which the Taylorsford Public Library had in abundance. While we didn't want to lose this history, the archives weren't used often, so we couldn't justify buying the necessary equipment, or hiring anyone, to undertake a major digitization project. We did store all of the clippings in acid-free envelopes, but that was far as we could go.

I carried the boxes over to the table and pulled on a pair of disposable white cotton gloves before taking out the clippings.

Since Walt had told me Zelda dropped out of the chamber choir halfway through her senior year, not long after the Leeland chamber choir had won a statewide competition, I assumed the event had occurred in the fall of 1970. Just to be sure, I began my search in August of that year.

It didn't take long to turn up a few articles. Most celebrated Leeland's win, but there were also two discussing the incident

Kurt had mentioned—the young man stricken after eating a cupcake that apparently contained peanut butter.

The first article didn't provide the victim's name, presumably to protect his privacy, but did cover the incident in some detail. I leaned over the desk to read the small print of the article. It seemed the young man who'd eaten the cupcake didn't know, or at least wasn't saying, who'd given it to him. Which struck me as odd. If he knew peanuts could be deadly to him, surely he'd be vigilant about accepting food from someone. Frowning, I read on, noting the victim had been rushed to the hospital and it had been touch-and-go for a time. But when he'd been interviewed a few days later, his main complaint was that he'd missed his opportunity to perform with the winning Leeland chamber choir.

I leaned forward, pondering this information. It seemed the young man had been a member of the Leeland choir, which meant Zelda had to have known him. I wondered if she also remembered the anaphylaxis incident.

Setting the first item aside, I examined the second article. It covered much of the same ground, except for one crucial detail—it identified the victim.

I sat back abruptly, clunking my head against the heavy wooden frame of the desk chair. The name had jumped out at me due to its connection to people I knew. The victim of the peanut butter cupcake incident had been Earl Blair, who I recognized from my acquaintance with his sister and nephew . . .

Jane Blair Tucker and her son, Chief Deputy Brad Tucker.

Chapter Eight

I called Sunny from work Wednesday evening to ask her if she knew anything about Brad's uncle and his brush with death back in high school. Sunny, who was preparing for a meeting with the Taylorsford town council, couldn't talk long. She told me she hadn't heard anything about this incident during the time she'd dated Brad but would be happy to ask Brad's mom, Jane Tucker, about it.

"We're still close, you know," she said.

"Of course you are," I replied, once again marveling at Sunny's ability to stay friends with the families of her exes. She was even chummy with Brad now, although I suspected his engagement to Alison Frye, a sheriff's deputy in an adjacent county, had something to do with his ability to regard Sunny as just a friend.

"I'll let you get back to your mayoral duties," I added, before wishing her a successful meeting and a good night.

Getting home after closing the library at eight, I didn't bother to call Aunt Lydia to see what she might know about the Earl Blair story. She and Hugh often chatted via Skype

on Wednesday evenings, especially when he was working on an out-of-town assignment. I didn't want to interrupt their conversation.

Richard was intrigued with what I'd found in the archives, but warned me about jumping to conclusions.

"Yes, it fits the time frame for the competition that links Zelda with the victim, but it's likely to have nothing to do with the current murder," he said as we snuggled up on one end of our living room sofa while Loie and Fosse were curled up together at the other end.

"I know, but it's a thread I want to pull." I laid one hand over his knee. "What if Claudia Everhart was responsible for giving Earl Blair the cupcake? It could be a motive."

Richard raised his eyebrows. "Several decades later? And he did live through the medical emergency, so why would he be angry enough to kill her now?"

"I don't know. It just feels like a weird coincidence. Maybe Earl didn't find out who gave him the cupcake until recently, which drove him to track down and then kill Claudia." I sighed and laid my head on Richard's shoulder. "But you're right—it's a rather weak motive for murder. Unless there's more to the story."

"I'm sure you'll unearth all the details, if there is more," Richard said, pressing his hand over mine. "Now, can we stop talking about murder for a moment?"

"Okay, okay," I said, glancing up at him from under my dark lashes. "By the way, is Karla still coming over to work with you on the choreography project Friday evening? I thought I'd make sure we had salad ingredients if she was going to stay for

dinner. But I know you have a full day of judging the dancing at the arts festival, so I wondered if you'd changed those plans."

"She's still coming over. I should be finished with the judging by four, so we'll have a little time to work."

I straightened, leaning back against the arm he stretched across the top of the sofa behind me. "You guys are so dedicated. It makes me feel like such a slouch."

Richard cast me a smile. "You know we love the work. That makes the difference. Anyway, I think managing a public library and assisting the authorities on numerous investigations over the last couple of years means you're something of a workaholic as well. Not to mention keeping me happy," he added, before sneaking in a kiss.

"My favorite avocation," I said, after the kiss turned into more.

Loie, lifting her head to stare at us with her emerald eyes, yawned.

"I'm afraid she finds our romantic interludes boring," Richard said with a grin.

"Good thing I don't," I said, before demonstrating my feelings with renewed enthusiasm.

Which effectively shut down any more discussions about murder, or anything else, for the rest of the evening.

*   *   *

Thursday was unusually busy at the library, and one of our volunteers had to call in sick, so I wasn't able to do any more research in the archives, or even online. Friday was the same. It was frustrating, but I'd made a promise to put my actual job

before any amateur detective activities, no matter how tempting it was to avoid statistics and spreadsheets for sleuthing.

Just as I was preparing to leave for the day, slipping out a few minutes early so I could get home to start dinner, I was waylaid by The Nightingale. Her eyes gleaming with excitement, she informed me she'd heard a news report about the recent murder.

"They matched the gun used to the exact kind Zelda Shoemaker's husband owned," she announced, her voice loud enough to carry throughout the main part of the library. "Seems like she's a pretty likely suspect."

"Please don't share that opinion with the entire world," I said, pressing a finger to my lips.

The Nightingale shrugged her boney shoulders. "It's all over the news so I 'spect everybody already knows."

"Maybe, but I really don't think shouting it out in the library is the nicest thing to do." I tried to keep the edge out of my tone, but failed. "Zelda's been a dedicated volunteer here for years. I think we should give her the benefit of the doubt."

"Volunteer or not, I bet she gets arrested soon," The Nightingale said, her eyes sparkling with excitement over this drama. "Still waters run deep."

I bit back a comment about The Nightingale's own rather murky past. "I wouldn't call Zelda a still anything. Anyway, I need to head home, so if you don't mind . . ." I glanced toward the desk, where Samantha was making a face that told me she didn't want to deal with this particular patron either. "Maybe you'd better run along for the day. We're about to lock up."

The Nightingale made a dismissive noise, but she did follow me through the glass main doors and into the lobby. Glancing over my shoulder, I caught Samantha giving a thumbs up sign.

"I heard Zelda knew the Everhart woman from back in their school days," The Nightingale said, as she trailed me outside. "So that's another thing. Might've been bad blood between them for years, and when they finally met again . . ." She curled her hand into the shape of a pistol, her forefinger pointed like a gun barrel. "Bang!"

"I really doubt that's the story," I said, fighting to keep my voice calm. "Anyway, here's where I have to turn left while you turn right."

The Nightingale looked me up and down. "Okay then, but you mark my words—Zelda Shoemaker's bound to be arrested soon. And there ain't nothin' you or anybody else can likely do about it."

I simply turned away and strode off without answering her. *There must be something I can do*, I thought as I walked the several blocks to my house. *For one, I need to get back in touch with Sunny and see if she found out anything about Earl Blair and the peanut butter incident from Jane Tucker.*

Although that would have to wait until later. Richard probably wouldn't want to drag Karla into a discussion of Taylorsford's most recent murder. At least, not over dinner.

Passing by my aunt's house, I spied a familiar car in the driveway. It looked like Hugh Chen had completed the assignment that had taken him out of D.C. and curtailed his visits with Aunt Lydia over recent weekends. Which also

probably meant Fred Nash would be free to attend the festival performance with Sunny after all. *She might not even answer the phone this evening,* I thought as I bounded up the steps to my front porch. I smiled ruefully, realizing I should probably shelve my curiosity until the next day. While I wanted to talk to Sunny, I certainly didn't want to interrupt my friend's romantic reunion.

I opened the front door to the haunting strains of folk music. A quick glance at the studio portion of our large front room revealed Richard and Karla marking out steps for one of the pieces they were creating for their folklore suite.

"Don't mind me," I called out as Richard lifted Karla off the hardwood dance floor. "I'm going to slip into the kitchen and start dinner."

Karla, poised in a position that reminded me of a bird in flight, flashed me a smile. "Hold on a minute and we can help." She slid out of Richard's arms in a single movement, smooth as water spilling over stone. "I think we're about done for the day."

Richard stepped back, raising his arms to clasp his hands behind his head. "Yeah, we just need to stretch out and cool down."

"Don't rush," I said. "It's nothing elaborate. Only a salad."

"But we can certainly help put it together." Karla grabbed a white towel draped over the barre and vigorously rubbed her damp brown hair. As she tossed the towel around her shoulder, several strands of copper-tinted hair flew up to halo her broad face.

Karla was tall and built like the goddesses depicted in Greek statuary. Her sienna brown eyes sparkled as she cast me a smile.

"Besides, as I told Rich earlier, I have some information that might interest you."

Richard groaned. "Not more murder talk during dinner," he said, pressing his palm to his forehead in a dramatic gesture.

Karla whipped off the towel and snapped it at him. "Come on, you should support your wife's efforts to help the authorities. Besides, you know Ms. Shoemaker pretty well. Don't you want to see her cleared of suspicion?"

Stretching out one leg, Richard flexed his foot. "Sure, but I'm not certain I want Amy mixed up in another murder investigation. It always seems to lead her into danger and"—he straightened and grinned—"I kind of like having her around, you know?"

"I never would've guessed," Karla said, with an answering smile.

As they shared a steady gaze, I sensed an unspoken connection some people might've mistaken for something more than friendship. But I wasn't worried. Sure, I knew they'd loved each other ever since becoming dance partners in high school. It was a relationship that had been interrupted for many years due to an unfortunate misunderstanding, but had instantly resumed once they'd finally reconnected.

But it was not a romantic connection, no matter how well they could depict those emotions through their dancing. Both only children, they'd formed more of a sibling bond.

"Finish your cooldown. I'm going to head into the kitchen to get things started." I glanced at Richard. "I assume the cats are out on the back porch? Is it safe for them to come in now?"

Richard nodded. "Now that we're done leaping about, they aren't as likely to get underfoot."

"They probably think it's a game, which is pretty cute." Karla rolled her shoulders. "But I always worry about stomping on one of them."

"More likely they'd trip you," I said with a wry smile. "Okay, carry on. I'll see you in a minute or two."

When I reached the kitchen, I immediately unlatched the cat door leading onto the screened porch, stepping aside to avoid two bundles of fur barreling through the flap. The cats skittered to a halt at the base of the kitchen island, spinning to face me with indignation clearly evident on their faces.

"I know, I know. You think it's terrible when you don't have the run of the house. But trust me, it's for your own good."

Loie narrowed her green eyes into slits and spat out a hiss, while Fosse waved his orange marmalade–striped tale like a battle flag.

"Perhaps a little treat might change your mood?" I strolled over to the cabinet where we kept a jar of cat treats. When I turned around. both cats were sitting up and slowly blinking their eyes as if I were an object of adoration. "Uh-huh, not so angry anymore, are you?" I fished out a few treats and dropped them on the floor. "Here you go, you little monsters."

The only reply was lip smacking from both cats, and a rumbling purr from Fosse.

After washing my hands, I pulled salad ingredients from the refrigerator and laid them out on the oak island, along with three cutting boards and knives. If Richard and Karla wanted to help prepare dinner, I wasn't going to argue. Besides, it

would give Karla time to tell me her news, while avoiding talking about murder at the dinner table.

When Karla and Richard filed into the kitchen a few minutes later, I noticed Karla's hair was damp again, especially at the temples.

"Forgive my dripping; your hall bath sink spat at me," Karla said.

"I'm sorry. We need to get it fixed," I replied, shooting Richard a significant glance.

Richard lifted his hands. "Don't look at me. I have many talents, but plumbing is not one of them."

"I wasn't asking you to fix it yourself, but I thought you said you were going to contact a plumber like . . . last week?"

Richard widened his clear gray eyes. "Did I? It must've slipped my mind."

"Okay, I'm writing it on the board of memory." I pulled a dry erase marker from the drawer we'd assigned to hold odds and ends and jotted down a note on the memo board affixed to the front of the refrigerator. We called it the "whiteboard of memory," because we used it to jot down appointment reminders or anything else we didn't want to forget. "There," I added, finishing off "CALL PLUMBER" with an extra flourish. "Now you'll be reminded without me nagging."

"A blessing indeed," Richard murmured to Karla, who laughed.

"I heard that." Dropping the marker back into the junk drawer, I grabbed a paring knife and waved it as I faced off with them across the island. "Now, make your sorry selves useful and chop."

"Yes, ma'am," Karla said, after another gurgle of laughter.

Richard circled around the tall oak table and threw an arm around my waist. "Forgive me. I shouldn't tease, especially"— he kissed my cheek before releasing me—"when you're holding a knife."

Karla offered us a sage smile. "Good point."

"Oh, I would never actually stab him," I told her, keeping my tone light as I sliced through a red pepper with more force than necessary. "Maybe just scare him a little. I like to do so occasionally, to keep him on his toes."

Richard rose up on the balls of his feet "It works more often than you think," he said, dropping his heels back down as he aligned several stalks of celery on his cutting board.

This time I laughed. "All right, enough fooling around. We'd better this get salad together if we want to eat before dark."

"Sun doesn't set until close to eight these days, but I get the point." Richard shot me a smile before concentrating on cutting up vegetables.

"What's this news you wanted to share with me?" I asked, focusing my gaze on Karla.

"I don't know if it's connected, but it does tie in with both Zelda and the victim having been in high school choirs at the same time." Karla dumped the leaf lettuce she'd torn into small pieces into a large wooden bowl. "My mom also sang in a choir participating in that competition. Another school, of course. Not Leeland or Stonebridge."

I laid down my knife to meet Karla's steady gaze. "She attended the same statewide arts festival fifty years ago?"

"Exactly." Karla plucked a cucumber from the pile of vegetables and placed it on her cutting board. "She didn't know

Zelda or the Everhart woman, of course, but she competed against their respective choral groups and remembers a couple of unfortunate incidents associated with the competition."

"I know about the situation where a kid was stricken after eating a cupcake," I said. "Was there something else?"

"Yeah." Karla's facial muscles tightened in concentration as she pared the cuke into paper-thin slices. "Mom said a lot of people thought the competition was cursed. That's nonsense, of course, but she claims many of the kids in her choir actually believed it at the time."

I shared a quick glance with Richard. "Why? Someone being rushed to the hospital for an anaphylactic attack was probably a bit scary, but the boy did recover."

"True, although he never had the chance to sing with his winning group, so I guess it seemed pretty tragic to a bunch of high schoolers. Everything's more dramatic at that age, you know." Karla looked up, her expression sobering. "But something else happened, about a week later, associated with the competition. Not directly, of course, but apparently it involved one of the choir members from Stonebridge, which was why it got bundled up with all the bad feelings from that event."

"Really? I haven't seen anything more in the archives." I dumped my chopped vegetables into the salad bowl.

"I guess no one but the chorus members would link the two things. I mean, they weren't actually connected, except for a singer being involved." Karla tapped her cutting board with the point of her knife. "Anyway, it seems one of the Stonebridge chamber choir members died in a car accident not long after the

competition. My mom says that's what sparked a rumor at the time that the event had been cursed."

"Sounds perfectly logical," Richard said, with a lift of his eyebrows. "And yes, I'm being sarcastic."

"Of course it wasn't logical. But it's a story the kids liked to share back then, according to my mom." As Karla tossed her head, her chin-length bob swung like a bell. "One of those spooky stories that grow in the telling."

"Interesting, though." I met Richard's amused gaze with a lift of my chin. "And yes, something I intend to research as soon as I find time."

"Never doubted it for a minute," he said, giving Karla a look of mock exasperation. "Now see what you've done?"

She just smiled and used the edge of her knife to slide the cucumbers off her board and into the bowl. "She would've found out whether I told her or not."

"I know." After dumping the vegetables from his own cutting board into the wooden bowl, Richard wiped his hands on a kitchen towel hanging from the oven door handle. "Now, what dressing should we use?"

Karla grinned. "Something rich and fattening to balance out all this healthiness."

"Blue cheese it is." Richard pulled a jar of dressing from the refrigerator and plunked it on the top of the island.

Puzzling over the information Karla had shared, I picked up the wooden bowl and tongs and headed for the kitchen table. "Your mom didn't happen to know the name of the teen who died, did she?"

"She honestly didn't remember. Only knew it was a girl, and some kind of gruesome accident." Karla set the jar of dressing on the table before taking a seat.

"Can we make a pact not to talk about this sort of stuff when we're eating?" Richard asked, as he sat down next to me. "I say we discuss something else."

"Like your folklore project, I suppose?" I winked at Karla. "Something we never hear enough about."

"Exactly," Richard said absently, looking up in surprise when both Karla and I broke out laughing.

Chapter Nine

With Richard spending the day at Leeland High School to complete the dance performance judging, I made plans to ride with Aunt Lydia and Hugh to the arts festival event on Saturday evening.

"Richard's going to meet us in the lobby outside the auditorium," I told my aunt as I perched on her bed while she chose the perfect jewelry to accent her lavender linen dress and white lace bolero. "I like the amethyst earrings best."

Aunt Lydia lowered the pearl drop earring she'd held up to one side of her face. "Better than the pearls? They're a classic look."

"Yes, but this is an arts festival. You can afford to be a little more daring, don't you think?" I jumped down off the bed and crossed to stand beside her, in front of her oval full-length mirror. "Also, then you can wear that beautiful necklace Hugh gave you. The one with the green jade beads and amethyst accents."

"True." Aunt Lydia patted her sleek silver bob. "You look very nice this evening. I like the bright print with your coloring."

"Thanks. I found this at the new shop downtown. I didn't realize they had clothes along with the garden décor and knick-knacks, but they carry some sundresses and that sort of thing." I fingered the silky fabric of my dress, which featured deep pink, amber, and coral flowers scattered across a black background. "And I did remember to grab a black jacket, as you suggested, in case it's cool in the auditorium."

"Good idea. In my experience, they always keep those places too cool." Aunt Lydia fastened the amethyst earrings before slipping the bead necklace over her head. "How do I look?" she asked, turning to face me.

"Gorgeous, as always," I replied. It was the truth. Although it was obvious my aunt was a woman of a certain age, she still looked lovely. She'd made aging gracefully into an art form.

"Well, let's not keep Hugh waiting any longer," Aunt Lydia said as she snatched up her small white leather purse. "I suppose Sunny and Fred are meeting us at the school?"

"Yeah, we're all gathering in the lobby, since Richard's holding all the tickets." I cast one last glance in the mirror, amused by the contrast between my aunt's fair coloring and relatively tall and slender frame, and my own dark hair and eyes and short, curvaceous figure. If someone didn't know we were related, they would never guess.

Which was true for my mother, Aunt Lydia's younger sister, too. *Rose White and Rose Red, indeed*, I thought.

We descended the stairs to find Hugh waiting in the front hall. Exactly the same height, and as slender as my aunt, he looked dapper in light brown slacks, a pale green shirt, and an ivory jacket that contrasted beautifully with his dark hair and

eyes. "Worth the wait, as always. Truly exquisite," he said, with a warm smile.

A sidelong glance at my aunt revealed a slight blush tinting her pale cheeks. I bobbed my head. "Thanks, although I can tell who's actually caught your attention, as she should."

Aunt Lydia tapped my arm as we joined Hugh in the hallway. "Don't be silly. Hugh and I are too old for such nonsense."

"I hope I never grow so old I can't recognize beauty when I see it," Hugh replied, gallantly offering her his arm as they walked out onto the porch.

I closed and locked the front door before following them to Hugh's car. Sliding into the back seat, I noticed my aunt's carefully applied pale pink lipstick was slightly smudged. But I just buckled my seat belt without making any comment.

As he drove to the high school, which was located a few miles outside of Taylorsford, Hugh entertained us with stories about his latest adventure.

"It was definitely a forgery," he said, after relaying information about a painting acquired by a New York art museum. "Fortunately, I was able to narrow down the list of forgers, and the local authorities came up with the most likely suspects. Then Fred actually tracked them down to a studio buried in a warehouse in Soho."

"Good for both of you. I hope it didn't involve too much danger?"

Hugh cast me a glance in the rearview mirror. "Not for me. I was safe in the lab. I think Fred ran into a few more difficulties, but he's equipped to deal with such things."

"No doubt," I said, thinking of the Fred's body-builder physique and background in law enforcement.

When we reached the school, we had to navigate a crowd to enter the lobby, but that didn't upset me. I was happy an arts festival could draw such a large crowd. Rising up on my toes, I spotted Richard near the double doors leading into the auditorium.

I waved a hand over my head. "We're here!"

Aunt Lydia cast me a glance and took a step to one side.

"Not behaving like a lady again, I see," said a familiar voice behind me.

I turned to greet Sunny, who was standing beside a man whose arms strained the seams of his beige suit jacket. Although Fred Nash was only an inch taller than Sunny, his muscular build dwarfed her slender frame. They made a gorgeous couple. Her pale skin, blue eyes, and blonde hair contrasted with, and complemented, his dark complexion, black hair, and chestnut brown eyes. "Glad you could make it, Fred. I heard your last assignment was a success."

"Not for the perpetrators." Fred shared a smile with Hugh. "But yes, justice was served."

"Always for the best," Aunt Lydia said, fingering one of the jade beads on her necklace. "Ah, here's Richard."

My husband slipped past a cluster of chattering young people to reach us. "Got the tickets." He waved a handful of cardboard strips. "And I was able to wrangle assigned seats near the front, since I'm a judge."

"The perks of celebrity," I said, bumping his arm with my elbow.

Richard grinned as he handed out the tickets. "Don't let anyone tell you there are no benefits to fame."

I shaded my eyes with one hand and made a show of searching the crowd. "So, wait, where are your screaming fans, exactly?"

"Amy," Aunt Lydia said with a cluck of her tongue.

But Richard laughed and threw his arm around my shoulder. "Right here, I hope."

"Always," I said, standing on tiptoe to brush a kiss against his cheek.

Sunny nudged Fred. "Can you believe it? Still lovebirds, even after the wedding."

"See, it can happen," Fred replied.

I glanced at Sunny, hoping she wasn't upset by this comment. I knew she worried whenever a romantic partner pressured her for a more formal commitment. But she appeared unfazed, which was an interesting development. Not one I would ever mention to her, of course. I glanced up at Richard, who seemed oblivious to this interaction, his attention focused on navigating us through the milling crowd.

Inside the auditorium, an enthusiastic young woman guided us to our seats, her eyelashes fluttering as she sneaked a few glances at both Richard and Fred. I smiled, thinking of my own teen years and the crush I'd had on a handsome English teacher, who thankfully had not paid me any more attention than my husband and Fred showed the young usher.

As Richard and I allowed the others to take their seats, a middle-aged man strode up and thrust out his hand.

"I must thank you again, Mr. Muir, for all your help with the dance students," he said.

"It's Richard, and no additional thanks necessary. It actually allowed me to scout some talent," Richard said, as he shook the other man's hand.

"For your studio at Clarion, I assume?" the man said, his gaze drifting to me. His hazel eyes were shadowed behind the lenses of his wire-framed glasses, but I could still sense him examining me with interest.

"Not just that, also for some of my choreographic projects. I'm always on the lookout for talent." Richard motioned toward me. "This is my wife, Amy. Maybe you've met? She's the library director in Taylorsford."

"I'm sorry to say I haven't had the pleasure." He offered me his hand. "Martin Stover, but please call me Marty. I'm the choral director and head of the arts programs at Leeland High School, so of course, also your host for the festival."

Martin Stover was about Richard's height, but skinnier. He had a wiry build and a thin face overshadowed by a full head of curly brown hair streaked with gray.

"Nice to meet you, Marty," I said, giving his hand a quick shake. "I guess you had the monumental task of organizing all of this?" I swept my hand through the air.

"It was a challenge. But it seems to have come together successfully, so I'm grateful. Tired," he added, with a warm smile, "but grateful nonetheless. Of course, having the assistance of people like your husband definitely helped."

"I'm sure," I said.

"Oh, one thing before I forget—my wife, Evelyn, and I wanted to invite the two of you to dinner sometime soon. If that sounds good, I'll have Evelyn give you a call to set a day and time."

"We'd be very happy to accept your invitation," Richard said after a swift glance at me. "I wonder if we could also bring along my dance partner, Karla Tansen? She's my collaborator on the folklore project I told you about, among other things."

"That would be fine. Perfect, in fact. I've actually wanted to meet her for some time. I've heard great things about her dance studio from some of my students." Marty studied us for a second. "You can let her know she can bring a guest, too. Unless you want Evelyn and me to rustle up a plus one?"

"Totally your call," Richard said, glancing toward the stage as the orchestra began tuning. "Karla doesn't require a date, but if you have a friend you want to include, I'm sure that would be fine with her. And us," he added, looking down at me.

I agreed, but then bobbed my head in a swift goodbye when the conductor called Marty over to the pit. "He seems like a nice guy," I told Richard as we sat down.

"I think so. I haven't had many dealings with him, but he's always seemed pleasant. And, more importantly, extremely competent at his job." Richard laid his fingers over the hand I placed on my knee. "By the way, you look lovely tonight," he added, lowering his voice to a whisper.

"You look pretty good yourself," I whispered back, giving his pearl-gray suit, charcoal dress shirt, and multihued blue tie an admiring glance. The combination looked especially nice on Richard, bringing out the gray of his eyes.

He started to reply, but as the overhead lights flashed on and off, warning the audience to take their seats, he pressed the recital program to his lips instead. I nodded and made a zipping motion across my mouth. I'd always known better than to

chatter once the lights went down, but I was even more careful these days. Richard considered it a mortal sin to talk during a performance.

The program interspersed musical pieces with dance performances and acting scenes, and included both groups and soloists. I was impressed with the level of talent displayed by the young people involved. Over the last couple of years I'd had a close-up view of the time and effort Richard put into his own career, so I knew how much hard work went into perfecting their craft.

After a stirring rendition of Aaron Copland's *Fanfare for the Common Man* by the Stonebridge orchestra, Marty Stover strode out from the wings of the stage, holding a portable microphone.

"Now we have a special surprise," he said, as scraping noises from behind the closed stage curtains hinted at risers being moved. "Fifty years ago, two local chamber choirs tied for first place in an arts competition similar to this one, although at the state level. We are fortunate enough to have members of both groups here tonight to sing for you. First, please help me in welcoming the fiftieth anniversary reunion Leeland Chamber Singers."

He stepped back into the wings as the curtains opened to loud applause. On the risers, a group of approximately twenty older men and women acknowledged the acclamation with synchronized nods. I spotted Gwen Ohlson in back and Olivia Rader up front before checking out all of the male singers. No one bore the slightest resemblance to Jane Tucker or her son, Brad, so I assumed Earl Blair had not agreed to rejoin his old choir for this performance.

Perhaps he lives too far away, I reminded myself as this observation raised questions in my mind. *You've attended events hosted by Jane Tucker and never met her brother, so that could easily be the case.*

I glanced past Richard to catch Sunny's eye. *No Earl,* I mouthed silently.

She gave a little shake of her head. *Talk later,* she mouthed back.

Richard tightened his grip on my hand as the choir began to sing. I shot him a look from under my lashes. He tapped his finger to his lips with his free hand.

I sat back in my theater seat, turning my head to take in the audience on the other side of the aisle. A familiar profile caught my attention.

What's Kurt doing here? I thought, narrowing my eyes. I knew he was a great supporter of the arts, but hardly thought a high school festival was his speed.

He seemed intently focused on the reunited Leeland choir, and it occurred to me that perhaps he knew one or more of the singers. As the foster son of Paul Dassin, he'd lived in Taylorsford when he was young. *He might have a close connection to someone on the stage,* I thought. *One he didn't share with me when we spoke the other day.*

Which was another thread I'd need to tug to unravel this latest mystery.

Chapter Ten

After the conclusion of the performances, we were directed to the school cafeteria for a reception. Tables and chairs had been shoved against the walls of the large room, and two long, linen-draped tables were placed near the entrance to the kitchen to hold snacks and beverages.

"There's a lot of talent displayed here as well," I told Richard, as we walked through the maze of portable gallery walls and display tables set up to showcase student artwork.

"Probably the real reason Kurt showed up," Richard said, motioning toward the older man, who was standing several feet away.

I frowned. Kurt was deep in conversation with someone, his head lowered and his lips close to the blonde woman's ear. *Gwen Ohlson*, I realized, when she lifted her chin to engage his intent gaze. They seemed comfortable with each other, as only close friends could be. *Or perhaps something more than friends*, I thought, as I caught the flirtatious lilt in Gwen's voice.

"It seems he does have another interest." I motioned toward the couple. "I wonder about the connection there."

Richard shrugged. "He did live in the area before. He could've known her when they were in school."

"Maybe, but since she must be around Zelda and Aunt Lydia's age, I suspect she's a good five years younger than he is. That doesn't matter now, of course, but it would've been weird for him to have dated her before he left Taylorsford at age eighteen. I mean, she would've been a kid at the time."

"True," Richard cast a thoughtful glance in Kurt's direction before looking back at me. "But he was in the area after that. Not openly, of course."

"Somehow I doubt he was hanging out with local girls when he was dealing drugs," I said dryly. "At least not any who could recognize him."

"Probably not," Richard said. "They must've connected more recently. He's involved in the D.C. arts community, and from what you told me, the lady in question . . ."

"Gwen Ohlson," I interjected.

"Right. Anyway, you said Ms. Ohlson doesn't live far from the city. Close enough to be involved in some cultural activities, anyway."

"I suppose." I slipped my arm through the arc formed by Richard's bent elbow. "Anyway, why don't we go over and say hello? Just to be polite."

"To allow you an opportunity to interrogate them, you mean," Richard said, with a chuckle. "All right. I'd like to talk to Kurt anyway."

"About your pet project, I bet."

"Guilty as charged." Richard gave me a wink.

When we strolled over, we were greeted warmly by Kurt, who introduced us to his companion.

Gwen patted Kurt's arm in a gesture confirming they were, at the least, close friends. "I recognize Richard, of course. You know I've been a fan of his dancing and choreographic work for some time. And I've actually met Amy before," Gwen added with a gracious smile. "Olivia Rader and I stopped in the library earlier this week, just to relive some fond memories of the place."

"I see." Kurt shot me a look, his bushy white eyebrows drawn together over his bright blue eyes. "Amy does have a knack for running into my old friends and acquaintances, it seems."

"Are you old friends, then?" I asked airily.

Richard tightened his grip on my arm. "Nice to meet you, Ms. Ohlson. I enjoyed your performance."

Gwen waved this compliment aside. "Thank you. I suppose it went as well as could be expected, given the age of most of the members, and the fact we haven't rehearsed together for decades. Until this week, of course."

Kurt frowned. "Don't paint yourself as too old, Gwen; that makes me ancient. And, to answer Amy's question—Gwen and I met at my Georgetown gallery. I don't know if she told you, but she's quite a celebrated interior designer in the District."

"No, she didn't say," I replied, looking Gwen over and concluding her fashion style fit her profession. Her tailored white silk blouse, cream-colored skirt, and carefully curated gold jewelry exuded understated glamour.

"Oh, not so very celebrated as all that," Gwen said, her blue eyes shining. "But I do have an avid interest in art. I often

convince my clients to invest in original pieces rather than reproductions, and Kurt's been a great help in locating some perfect pieces for certain projects."

"The high-dollar ones, I imagine," Richard said, with a grin. Gwen nodded. "Exactly. Which has aided his business as well as mine. And helped my clients, of course."

"A mutually beneficial arrangement." Kurt cut Gwen a look that did nothing to dispel my intuition that there was, or at least had been, more going on between them than business transactions.

Of course, it was not something I could ask. At least, not with Gwen Ohlson standing in front of me. "I imagine you were surprised to find out Kurt had resided in Taylorsford in the past. Did you remember him from when you lived here?"

Gwen's smile tightened. "Not really, but I was younger, you know. He'd graduated before I was even a freshman."

She's lying, I thought, but simply smiled in return.

Kurt narrowed his eyes as he caught my inquiring gaze. "I wasn't terribly memorable, it seems," he said in his usual urbane tone.

I raised my eyebrows. Kurt, who'd been known as Karl Kloss back then, had hardly been someone easy to ignore, or forget. At least according to Aunt Lydia, who'd told me the tall, blond, blue-eyed best friend of her future husband had been devastatingly handsome back in the day. *And a charming bad boy*, I thought, *the perfect catnip for any teen or preteen girl. Gwen must've remembered him, if only by reputation. Which means she knows he changed his name, and perhaps a few other things about his less-than-rosy past.*

"Funny thing is, I didn't meet Kurt until a couple of years ago myself, even though he and I have family connections. His foster father, Paul Dassin, was my great-uncle. Amy and I actually live in Dassin's former home." Richard tapped his chin with one finger. "I guess I should say, your old home too, Kurt."

"It looks much different now, which is a good thing," Kurt said. "You did an excellent job on the renovations."

Gwen, who'd been studying Richard intently, shook her head. "I thought you must've known each other forever, the way Kurt talks about you. Honestly, he was the one who first introduced me to your work, when he took me to one of your dance performances." She turned to Kurt. "That was at least six or seven years ago, wasn't it?"

I swallowed a comment as Richard dropped my arm and took a step forward. From a confidence he'd shared a while ago, I knew Kurt had followed Richard's dance achievements from high school onward, and had often anonymously contributed money to the scholarship and grant funds that had supported my husband's early career.

But Richard didn't know that.

"Really? Was it something Adele Tourneau was involved with?" he asked, raising his chin to face off with the taller man.

"Undoubtedly." Kurt's expression gave nothing away. But I noticed his hands, hanging loosely at his sides, were curled into fists. "You know I often provided financial support for her productions."

"That first show was absolutely glorious," Gwen said, her eyes shining. "Made me an instant fan."

Richard, relaxing his stance, cast her a smile. "Well, thank you. I'm always happy when someone likes my work."

"I adored it. I can still picture it in my mind. You danced in several repertory pieces but also debuted something called *Dimensions*, which, if I recall correctly, was one of your first choreographic works."

"Yes, but that was in San Francisco." Richard's bright gaze grew clouded. "Adele didn't have anything to do with that show, so I don't know how . . ."

"Oh look, there's Olivia Rader," I said, grabbing Richard's arm. "I met her when she and Gwen visited the library. I should go and congratulate her as well."

Gwen, her expression full of confusion, focused on me. "I'll come with you. If you'll excuse me, Kurt?"

"Of course," he replied, his gaze fixed on Richard, who'd struck a dramatic pose. *Brimming with coiled energy*, I thought, biting my lip. *Like he's preparing for a particularly explosive stage entrance.*

"You go, Amy. I want to stay here and chat with Kurt a little while longer," Richard said, without taking his eyes off the art dealer.

I cast Kurt a wide-eyed glance and a silent "good luck" before turning away.

Gwen and I caught up with Olivia, who was standing in front of a sculpture composed of twisted wire, chains, and bits of broken glass.

"What's it supposed to mean?" Olivia asked, with a tsk. "The title doesn't help."

I peered at the label, which said the piece was called *My Future*. "I think it's meant to evoke a feeling more than anything else," I said, my heart constricting as I thought about the student who'd created the piece. I prayed they were simply playing with ideas and didn't actually feel quite so hopeless.

"I never get this modern stuff," Olivia said, with a wave of her hand. "I like my art to look like something."

I bit back a sharp retort. Having majored in art history in college, I had my own opinions on such subjects. Fortunately, I'd learned through hard experience not to share them, especially with people I barely knew.

"I think it's quite good," Gwen said, as she walked around the pedestal holding the sculpture. "Not for everyone, of course, but it does have something to say." Half-hidden by the cage formed by the sculpture, she appeared lost in thought. She shook her head and locked gazes with me from the other side of the pedestal. "That's the main aim of art, don't you think?"

"One of them, anyway." I nodded, acknowledging my approval of her opinion. *No wonder Kurt likes her*, I thought. *She's attractive, but more importantly, she has the right kind of mind and personality to engage him.*

"I guess you haven't heard much more about the murder involving poor Zelda Shoemaker, have you?" Olivia asked.

I turned away from the sculpture. "Nothing that hasn't been in the news." I didn't care if this was entirely true. I wasn't about to share my research with a relative stranger. "But I'm convinced Zelda had nothing to do with the shooting. For one thing, she had no motive."

"Oh, I don't know if that's exactly true." Olivia's dark eyes sparkled as she furiously fanned her face with the festival program. "There was bad blood between them from way back, wasn't there, Gwen?"

Gwen circled around the pedestal to join us. "Oh, that. Don't be silly, Olivia. It was just a high school thing."

"What do you mean?" I asked, my curiosity overcoming my desire to shut down Olivia's obvious glee over sharing this gossip.

"She and Claudia dated the same boy." Olivia snapped her fingers. "At the same time!"

"Hardly a motive for murder, all these years later," I said mildly. "Especially since Zelda went on to marry someone else. Or at least I assume so," I added, realizing I didn't know much about Zelda's late husband.

"She did," Gwen cut her eyes at Olivia in a way that made me think she was also irritated with the dark-haired woman. "It certainly wasn't the same guy. He never married, from what I've heard."

"Anyway, I don't see how that worked," I said, as I puzzled over this latest revelation. "Didn't Zelda and Claudia attend different schools?"

"Yes, Zelda was at Leeland, and Claudia was at Stonebridge." Olivia crumpled the program between her fingers. "The boy in question attended Leeland with us, but he was in a church choir or Christian music group or something. That's where he met Claudia." She shrugged. "He was pretty clever, I guess. It certainly made it easier to juggle two girls when they attended different high schools."

"And who was this Lothario?" I asked, although I wasn't really interested. Surely a fifty-year-old love triangle had nothing to do with a current murder.

Olivia beamed, obviously thrilled to share her knowledge. "Why, only the uncle of one of the deputies investigating the case. Someone who should've been here tonight but never showed up for rehearsal . . ."

I shot Gwen an astonished glance. "Not Earl Blair?"

"I'm afraid so," she said. "He was quite a charmer when we were in school. Not that I was ever taken in. I always felt he was a little too . . . slick, or something."

"He was very stuck on himself." When Olivia tossed her head, not one strand of her lacquered hair moved. "Football star, you know."

"He was the quarterback," Gwen said, offering me a sympathetic smile. It was clear she wasn't terribly fond of Olivia Rader, whatever their long-term connection.

"Anyway, he was dating both girls at the same time, and they didn't find out until right before the choral competition," Olivia said. "You can imagine the drama that caused."

Gwen brushed a flyaway strand of her hair behind one ear. "But that was ages ago. I can't believe anyone would harbor enough hatred over some teenage betrayal that they'd kill their rival fifty years later."

"You never know," Olivia said. "Maybe there were long-term repercussions." She cast Gwen a look that made the other woman draw her lips into a thin line.

"It's still old news. Anyway, I think I'll go mingle a bit more," Gwen said. "Catch up with anyone I know in this crowd. Even

if we've all changed rather dramatically, I think I recognize a few people from high school." She waved her hand, jangling the gold bracelets encircling her tanned wrist.

"I'll come with you, but let's stop at the refreshments table first. I'm parched." Olivia raised her own hand in a casual good-bye. "Nice to see you again, Amy. Tell that handsome husband of yours he did a good job in picking the winners of the dance competitions. They were all splendid."

Gwen, who didn't look particularly thrilled about Olivia's continued company, offered me a pleasant farewell before they headed toward the buffet table.

I looked over the crowd, trying to spot Sunny and Fred. After Olivia Rader's revelation, I was even more eager to talk to Sunny about any information she had concerning Earl Blair. Not that I thought Zelda would've killed anyone over a man— she was far too well-adjusted and self-assured for that. *Besides*, I thought, *she went on to have a successful marriage, and now she's involved in a loving relationship with Walt.*

But before I could locate Sunny in the crowd, Richard came striding over. I swallowed when I spied the storm brewing in his eyes.

"Did you know?" he asked, before I could say anything.

"Know what?" I managed to squeak out, dreading where this conversation was heading.

Richard crossed his arms over his chest and rocked back on his heels as he loomed over me. "That Kurt has been following my dance career since I was in high school? And even helped to anonymously support some of the projects I was involved with?"

I opened my mouth and shut it again. His jaw was clenched so tight it made my own ache in response.

The muscles around his mouth twitched as he glared down at me. "Well?"

"Not really the best place to have this conversation." I cast a nervous glance at the people milling around us.

"Then let's go home," Richard said, before turning on his heel and heading for the cafeteria exit.

I followed, trotting to keep up with him. A few people called out to me, including Sunny, obviously wanting me to stop and talk, but I waved them off. "Later," I said, several times.

Hurrying across the lobby, I reached the main doors to the school, where Richard was waiting.

"I hope you know we will be discussing this matter, in depth, when we get home," he said, holding the door open for me to scurry outside.

"I'm sure," I replied, trailing him to the parking lot. *And what a delightful evening it will be*, I thought as I slid into the passenger seat of his car.

He shot me a thunderous look before turning the key in the ignition. "In case you couldn't tell, I'm very upset right now."

Snapping my seat belt buckle, I almost made a sarcastic retort, but decided, in this instance, discretion really was the better part of valor.

Chapter Eleven

We rode home in stony silence, my attempts to apologize or make any conversation rebuffed by Richard's comments about preferring not to have such discussions while driving.

When we stepped inside our house, we were greeted by both Loie and Fosse. They meowed and brushed up against our legs to remind us they hadn't had their nightly treats.

"Can you deal with them? I want to change out of this suit. I've been in the blasted thing all day," Richard said, before sprinting up the stairs to our bedroom.

I wandered back to the kitchen, trailed by the cats. "It's okay," I told them. "He isn't angry with you." I shook out a few treats and placed them on the floor. "Just me," I added quietly, as Loie and Fosse gobbled up their snacks.

Although, I thought, *it probably isn't just you. I'm sure he's ticked off at Kurt too.*

I headed back to the front room, and up the stairs, moving much more slowly than Richard had. I wasn't in a hurry to face the inevitable grilling I was sure I would receive.

Which you deserve. I paused outside our bedroom door to take a deep breath. I had to admit I'd never really considered how unfair it had been for me to keep Kurt's secret. *You should never have agreed to that.*

I stepped into the bedroom, prepared to apologize, but Richard was nowhere in sight. The sound of running water from our attached master bath told me he was probably brushing his teeth. His suit was thrown over a chair in the corner, so I assumed he'd already changed. I decided to take advantage of his absence to do the same.

Hanging up my dress in the closet, I debated whether I should wear one of my sexier nightgowns, but concluded it might look like I was trying too hard, and chose a well-worn loose cotton sleepshirt instead. As I exited the walk-in closet, I almost walked into Richard, who was wearing his usual nighttime attire—a T-shirt and boxer shorts.

I stepped back to look up into his face. "To start with, let me say I'm sorry."

He held up one hand, palm out. "No, I get to talk first."

"Okay." I crossed my arms over my chest, clutching my elbows with both hands.

Richard's fierce gaze softened slightly as he gazed down at me. "I do appreciate the apology, but it seems a little tardy, don't you think?"

"Very much so," I lowered my eyes. "You have every reason to be angry. I don't dispute that."

"Glad to hear it," Richard said, his voice losing its razor edge. "But I need you to know how much this really hurt me."

I gnawed on the inside of my cheek and glanced up at him from under my lashes. His face was drawn and pale. It broke my heart to see this, especially knowing I was one of the people who had caused him pain.

Richard exhaled a deep sigh. "Let's not stand here, facing off like we're in a boxing ring. Come and sit down," he said, as he walked over to the bed.

I waited for him to sit down near the headboard before perching closer to the foot of the bed.

"For heaven's sake, come closer." Richard patted the mattress next to him. "I'm not going to slug you or anything."

"I know," I said, scooting closer to him. "I thought you might not want me . . . well, near you right now."

He looked me over, his expression unreadable. "I will always want you, which actually makes this worse." He shifted his gaze to focus on the opposite wall. "Do you know how humiliated I felt when I found out someone had been helping fund my career without my knowledge? A man I hadn't even met until a few years ago?" He leaned forward, burying his face in his hands. "Then, to add insult to injury, I realized you knew and never told me."

"He made me promise not to," I said, my voice breaking. It was not a good excuse, and I knew it. But it was the truth.

Richard lifted his head, shifting his position so he could stare into my eyes. "And you decided your loyalty to Kurt Kendrick trumped your loyalty to me?"

"No, of course not." Unbidden, tears welled in my eyes. "I mean, it looks that way. But it was more . . . I don't know. Just feeling intimidated by him, I guess. And after a little while, the whole thing kind of slipped my mind."

Richard rubbed at his jaw with his fist. "How could you possibly forget something so important?"

"I guess I didn't see it as such a big deal." I squirmed under his intense stare. "I mean, you're closely related to Paul Dassin, the man who rescued Kurt from an orphanage and raised him as a son. I thought Kurt was repaying that generosity, that he simply wanted to help his foster father's grand-nephew."

Richard straightened, squaring his shoulders. "I hadn't really thought of it from that angle. I suppose it probably was Kurt's main motivation. But Amy"—he leaned in and clasped my hands—"don't you see how unnerving it is to suddenly discover someone's been shadowing you for most of your life? It's almost like having a stalker."

"When you put it that way, it does sound upsetting. But I really don't think that was Kurt's intention."

"I still don't like it." Richard gave my fingers a gentle squeeze. "It makes me feel manipulated. I mean, I guess he meant it to be supportive, but now I feel I'm in his debt."

"You're worried you owe him too much? And"—I held Richard's gaze as realization washed over me—"he might want to collect on the debt one day?"

"Exactly. Kurt's been good to us so far, but you know he has another side to him. A ruthless, calculating side. He's like a great bear—you may admire such a creature, and perhaps it even shows signs of liking you, but it's still a wild animal. You have to remain on your guard. You never know when a creature like that might turn on you."

"A good analogy," I said, mentally admitting not only the truth of this observation, but also my own underlying sense of

unease when dealing with Kurt Kendrick. "So, since I wasn't right there, what exactly transpired during your confrontation at the school?"

"I just told him I would appreciate more transparency in our future dealings, and asked him to cease sharing confidences with you. At least any concerning me." Richard dropped my hands and sat back. "Although, to be honest, I'd prefer it if he never shares any of his secrets and schemes with you. I don't entirely trust his motives and, more importantly, I'm afraid he might put you in danger."

"I don't think he wants that, but I see your point." I took a deep breath. "Okay, so I'm going to apologize again. Because I need to, for being such an idiot. My first loyalty should always be to you, no matter what. And I swear it will be, from this moment on."

Richard studied me for a moment. "Apology accepted. And you're not an idiot. Impulsive sometimes, and often stubborn . . ."

"Okay, okay," I said, waving off any more descriptions of my faults. *Of which there are plenty*, I thought ruefully.

"I think this was the first major fight of our married life," Richard said, his lips curving into a slight smile. "I suppose it was bound to happen sooner or later."

"Undoubtedly." I managed a weak smile. "I think we've handled it pretty well."

"Yes, but now we have to take the next step."

"What next step?" The tension drained from my body as I noticed the sparkle had returned to Richard's eyes.

"I think it's traditionally make-up something or other . . . Now what's that word?" he asked with a devilish grin.

I flung myself into his arms instead of replying.

*   *   *

The following afternoon, I caught a glimpse from our bedroom window of my aunt working in her garden and hurried outside to join her. Even though I was no longer living in her house, I liked to help with the upkeep on the property.

Aunt Lydia straightened and turned to face me as I passed through the rose vine–covered archway separating our two backyards. "I missed you at church this morning."

"We overslept," I said, keeping my expression as innocent as possible.

Aunt Lydia adjusted the ties on her wide-brimmed straw hat as she gave me a knowing look. "Hmmm, I'm sure."

I swatted a cluster of gnats away, using the opportunity to also fan my face. Typical for August in our area, the weather was hot and muggy. Within a few minutes of stepping outside, perspiration had already beaded on my upper lip, and the banded edge of my loose T-shirt was sticking to the back of my neck. "So where's Hugh? Don't tell me he already left."

"Unfortunately, yes. He got a call related to the forgery mess he and Fred recently worked on. Something about another witness who wanted to provide more evidence to bolster the prosecution's case. So, of course, he had to rush off to deal with that." Aunt Lydia shook her head. "Sometimes having a partner who's so dedicated to their job is difficult, as you well know."

I tugged on a pair of gardening gloves. "But you wouldn't have it any other way. You admire his dedication. Admit it."

"I do," my aunt said, without rancor. "By the way, I just want to tackle these two front beds today. The rest can wait, but these herbs are about to be choked out by weeds."

Casting a glance over the neat beds, I made no comment and grabbed the trowel Aunt Lydia had shoved into the soft dirt. "I guess Fred had to run off too? I bet that didn't sit too well with Sunny. She hasn't seen much of him lately."

"I'm sure she'll cope," my aunt said, as she knelt back down onto a padded kneeler. "Sunny has the lovely ability to be happy in her own company."

"It's true." I smiled as I thought about my free-spirited friend. Sunny, who'd never known her father, and whose mother had abandoned her to be raised by her grandparents, would've had every right to hold a grudge against the world, but she never did.

I crouched beside Aunt Lydia and began the delicate process of separating weeds from the herb plants. "By the way, I wanted to ask you something—a question concerning Zelda's past."

Aunt Lydia cast me a side-eyed glance. "You can ask. But I'm not going to break any confidences."

"I wouldn't ask you to. But I heard something last night I wanted you to corroborate. If it's true, that is." As I dug into the dry ground, a fine powder of dirt rose up in my nostrils.

"You heard some gossip, you mean."

"Maybe. It's why I want you to confirm or deny the story." I sneezed and apologized before I continued. "Remember the Leeland reunion chamber choir that performed at the end of the show last night? I met two women from that group earlier

in the week, and they told me they went to school with you and Zelda."

Aunt Lydia sat back on her heels, staring out over the lush garden beds filling her back yard. "I suppose they must have, if they attended Leeland fifty years ago. So who are they, and why haven't you mentioned meeting them before now?"

"Honestly, it slipped my mind in the midst of all the uproar over the murder." A monarch butterfly, dancing from the fuzzy leaves of a sage plant to the feathery blossoms of the beebalm, distracted me for a moment. "It was someone called Olivia Rader, along with a Gwen Ohlson, who's apparently one of Kurt's friends."

"Rader?" Aunt Lydia rose to her feet. "I don't recall that name."

"Oh, right, she said her last name back then was Bell."

My aunt pulled off her gloves and slapped them together, sending up a puff of dust. "Oh, that one. Yes, I vaguely remember them both. We were never friends. They moved in different circles."

I yanked one more weed before standing to face her. "I guess Zelda would've been more closely acquainted with them, since they were all in the chamber choir. And I did hear . . ." I plucked my damp T-shirt away from my ribcage. "That is, Walt told me Zelda was a bit distant from you both when she was part of the choral group."

"She dumped us, you mean." Aunt Lydia's thinned lips told me this memory still rankled.

"He also said she quit the choir in the middle of senior year, not long after they won the statewide award." I motioned

toward one of the white benches flanking the pea gravel path. "Was that because of her breakup with Earl Blair?"

Aunt Lydia strolled over to the bench and sat down before answering. "Did Olivia and Gwen spill information on that topic as well? They seem to have been quite talkative with a virtual stranger." She pulled off her hat and used it to fan her flushed face. "But then again, Olivia Bell always was a terrible tattletale."

I sat beside her. "To be fair, Zelda likes to gossip too."

"True, but she's never mean about it. Or at least, I don't believe she's ever intended to be cruel." Aunt Lydia shifted to look me in the eye. "What did they tell you, exactly?"

"That Zelda and Claudia Everhart were dating Earl Blair at the same time. Olivia seemed to think he'd chosen two girls from different high schools so he could successfully juggle them, but then the truth came out. It seems the two girls ended up meeting at the state choral competition and things didn't go well."

"That is true. I wasn't talking much with Zelda then, but I knew about her relationship with Earl. And after she broke it off and quit the chamber choir, I heard the whole story."

"The women—well, Olivia mostly—seem to have this idea that maybe there was still bad blood between Zelda and Claudia all these years later. They wondered if it was a motive for murder."

My aunt sniffed in derision. "Heavens no. Zelda was never that hung up on Earl. She enjoyed dating him off and on, but her heart was always with Walt, even if they couldn't interact much when we were in high school." Aunt Lydia met my

questioning gaze with a sigh. "Racial tensions were pretty high back then."

"Still are, unfortunately, but I guess it was worse, especially in terms of dating, when you were younger. I suppose Zelda and Walt being together was pretty much out of the question."

"In high school? Absolutely. Anyone who tried that was in for a world of hurt, and Walt didn't want to bring such trouble into Zelda's life." The sadness in Aunt Lydia's wan smile was echoed in her voice. "I think Zelda would've cast caution to the wind and dated Walt, despite any uproar, but he was much more careful. I suppose he had reason to be. He knew how discrimination actually felt. Neither Zelda nor I did."

"You don't believe Zelda held any sort of grudge against Claudia Everhart?"

"I know she didn't." A line creased Aunt Lydia's brow. "Of course, that may be difficult to prove, especially if someone like Olivia Bell puts in her two cents."

I patted her arm. "I wouldn't worry. It seems like a pretty feeble motive to me. Besides, there's also the issue of Earl Blair almost dying from a peanut butter–laced cupcake. A much stronger motive, in my mind."

Aunt Lydia sprang to her feet. "Right—he went into shock and had to be rushed to the hospital. I remember the drama that erupted over that incident." She stared out over her garden, her gaze fixed on the blue-tinted mountains rising up behind the strip of woods bordering her property. "There were rumors back then that Zelda had slipped him the cupcake, but she swore she had nothing to do with it, and I believed her. Still do." When

Aunt Lydia turned her gaze on me, her blue eyes shone bright as stars. "I always thought it was the other girl."

"Claudia Everhart."

"Right. Our victim." Aunt Lydia paced the gravel path in front of me, her hat swinging from her fingers. "Wouldn't it be more likely that the person who might want to harm Claudia was someone she'd hurt in the past? Someone like Earl Blair."

I frowned. "But it's been years and years. Surely no one would wait so long for revenge."

"Nonsense." Aunt Lydia stopped in front of me, jamming the hat back over her silver cap of hair. "Over the last few years, you've encountered plenty of people who nursed a grudge for decades before acting on it. Sometimes long-simmering rage resulted in a death, too."

I yanked off my gloves. I knew she desperately wanted to find another likely suspect to remove the shroud of suspicion from Zelda. But there were aspects of this theory that didn't make sense to me. "There's another sticking point, though. From what I've read and heard, Earl Blair recovered. It's not like he died and someone in his family set out to avenge him."

"But that's the thing—it did permanently harm Earl's life. You wouldn't know this, because most people don't. It was kept pretty hush-hush. But I learned from talking with Jane Tucker just the other day . . ." Aunt Lydia glanced over at me. "Oh, by the way, I told Jane you were doing some research into the past to see if you could turn up anything to help Zelda's case. I hope you don't mind."

I waved this off with a flap of my gloves. "It's fine, please continue."

Aunt Lydia pressed her fist to her heart. "Anyway, I found out from Jane that Earl suffered lingering effects after the anaphylaxis attack. She thinks it was psychological, but still, it left him with severe anxiety attacks that derailed his football career."

"You mean he had something like PTSD?"

"I guess that's what we'd call it today. He did almost die—in fact, Jane said he flatlined a couple of times and had to be brought back."

"It certainly would've been horrifying." I twisted my garden gloves between my fingers. "They didn't really know how to treat lingering aftereffects of trauma very well back then, either."

Aunt Lydia nodded. "The worst part was, Earl could only afford a university education because he had a sports scholarship. When he couldn't cope, and was kicked off his football team, he also had to drop out of college."

"What happened to him?"

Aunt Lydia lowered her golden lashes over her bright eyes. "That's the sad thing—no one really knows. He disappeared not long after dropping out of college. According to Jane, he only contacted his parents sporadically, and was constantly traveling, doing heaven knows what. When his mother and father passed away, he stopped almost all communication with his family. Jane hasn't heard from him directly in years, although she did receive a postcard a few years ago with nothing but an address. She assumed she could use it to contact him in an emergency."

"Did he ever say who gave him the cupcake?"

"Jane said he didn't know, although she always felt he had his suspicions." Aunt Lydia sat back down beside me. "She thought the most likely culprits would've been Zelda or Claudia Everhart, because they'd recently discovered his duplicity." Aunt Lydia shrugged. "He wasn't simply dating them at the same time. He also swore he was going steady with each of them."

I pulled a crumpled tissue from my pocket and wiped the sweat from my forehead. "But wouldn't Earl have seen who gave him the cupcake?"

"No, it was just left out, with a tag with his name on it. He assumed it was a good luck gesture from someone in the choral group, because they left tagged cupcakes for everyone else in the choir too. Earl didn't think there'd be a problem, because he'd made it clear to the group that he had a life-threatening allergy." Aunt Lydia pursed her lips. "Jane told me all the singers and their parents were aware of Earl's allergy, and were extremely careful to avoid providing snacks with even a hint of peanut products in them."

"So it had to be deliberate," I said thoughtfully.

"Definitely."

"But Claudia Everhart wasn't in his chamber choir. Wouldn't that rule her out?"

Aunt Lydia shook her head. "Not necessarily. Jane thinks she could've easily had access to the room where the snacks were left, and certainly could've tagged the cupcake specifically for Earl."

"And if they were dating, I'm sure she would've known about his allergy."

"Most likely."

I laid my gardening gloves on the bench beside me. "What if Earl Blair somehow realized it was Claudia who gave him the cupcake? I mean, more recently. He could've been trying to confirm his suspicion for years, and finally found someone who'd seen her carrying a tray of cupcakes or something."

Aunt Lydia glanced over at me. "If that were true, he might've heard about the choral groups reuniting this past week and decided to seize the opportunity to take revenge." Her eyes narrowed. "But why shoot Claudia in Zelda's garden?"

I sat back, staring up into the clear sky as I spun theories to explain this particular puzzle. "Perhaps he felt Zelda and Claudia's feud was the reason Claudia decided to take such severe action against him? If Zelda had escalated the situation to that point, Earl could've harbored anger against her as well as Claudia. So he decided to murder one woman and cast the blame on the other. Two birds with one bullet, so to speak."

"I suppose it's possible." Aunt Lydia wiped a tiny pearl of perspiration from her upper lip with one finger. "It's no more irrational than some other motives we've encountered in the past."

"That's certainly true," I said, thinking back to the other murders I'd stumbled over in recent years. "No one ever said killers were the most rational creatures on earth."

Aunt Lydia stood up, pulling on her garden gloves. "Typically, they aren't. Careful, cool masterminds are more common in books and media than in real life."

"Absolutely," I said, grabbing my own gloves before standing. "Now—how about we finish off these weeds and then pop into the house for a cool glass of something?"

"Good idea. I made some fresh lemonade earlier," Aunt Lydia replied as she moved her kneeler to another section of the herb bed.

I crouched down beside her. "I was thinking something a little stronger."

"I thought you'd want to keep a clear head for your sleuthing," Aunt Lydia said. "I mean, you're going to be scouring the internet for any mentions of Earl Blair later, aren't you?"

I yanked out a wild onion and waved it at her. "You know me too well."

My aunt smiled as she delicately pulled a sprig of grass from the bed. "I do, but it doesn't take close observation to know that about you. Everyone in town is aware of your obsession with solving mysteries."

I didn't bother to contradict her, since I was sure this was true.

Chapter Twelve

Since the library was closed on Sundays, I often scheduled both Samantha and Sunny to work on Monday mornings. It helped to have extra hands to check in and shelve all the materials returned late on Saturday or dropped into the outside book drop on Sunday.

"You'd think people would wait until today and bring things inside," Sunny grumbled as she hauled in another full tote from the book drop.

"Some of them probably don't have any other time." I stacked the returned items in piles on the circulation desk. "If they're working all week . . ."

Sunny huffed disdainfully. "We are open late some evenings."

"But if they have kids, that doesn't always work." Samantha, who was arranging checked-in books on a rolling shelving cart, cast a glance over her shoulder. "By the time you fix dinner, help with homework, and all that, there aren't many hours left for anything else."

"I suppose," Sunny said, her tone losing some of its sharp edge.

I cast her an understanding smile. "I guess Fred had to rush off again, didn't he? Aunt Lydia said Hugh was called back to work early too."

Sunny used both hands to sweep back her shining fall of blonde hair. "Yeah. Duty called, as it so often does."

"Thought so." I shared a look with Samantha, who mouthed *Oh, I see* back at me.

"If you're insinuating Fred's unexpected departure is the reason I'm a little cranky, you can think again," Sunny said, squaring her slender shoulders. "I didn't sleep too well last night, that's all."

"Understandable," I replied, fighting the urge to smile. I knew Sunny didn't like to admit she missed any man's company. That was too much like confessing a serious commitment.

Samantha spun around as someone called out her name. Following her gaze, I noticed an attractive older woman making her way toward the circulation desk.

The lady looked familiar. In a moment I realized why. She closely resembled Samantha, with the same warm brown skin and large dark eyes. The major difference, other than her age, was the silver tipping her close-cropped black hair.

Samantha ran her fingers through her own hair, which haloed her face like a dark cloud. "Aunt Lorraine, it's good to see you, but I thought when you said you'd drop by today, it would be later this afternoon." She waved her hand at the stacks of books and other materials piled on the desk. "Monday mornings are a little hectic, as you can see."

"Sorry, but I have an appointment later." Samantha's aunt offered Sunny and me a smile. "I'm Lorraine Harris, as you might've already guessed."

"Hello. Samantha mentioned you might drop by," Sunny said, before turning to me. "I think Amy wanted to talk to you, right?"

"Hi, Amy Webber." I leaned over the desk and extended my hand to Lorraine Harris. "I'm the library director for Taylorsford."

"And my boss," Samantha said, while Lorraine gave my hand a quick shake. "But I think it's actually Amy Muir now, isn't it?" she added, casting me a grin.

I pulled back my hand, using it to slap my forehead before dropping it to my side. "Yes, Amy Muir. I was recently married, you see. Since I was a Webber for so long, I keep forgetting the name thing."

"No worries," Lorraine said. "I've been divorced for years and still sometimes slip up and use my married name."

"That's why women should keep their original surnames, married or not," Sunny said.

I laid a hand on my friend's arm before she could expound on her strongly held views on this subject. "Anyway, it's very nice to meet you, Ms. Harris. Thanks for going out of your way to stop by. I know it was a bit of a drive from where you live."

"I don't mind. When you're retired, what's a little road trip?" Lorraine said. "Besides, I always like to see my niece. We don't get together as often as we should."

"That's my fault," Samantha said. "What with the job, and taking care of Shay . . ."

Lorraine waved one hand through the air. "I totally understand, dear. I don't see your mother often either, since she's a nurse and always working crazy hours." She shifted her focus

to me and Sunny. "Samantha's mom is my baby sister. There's a good fifteen years between us."

I seized the opportunity to pose the questions I really wanted answered. "You're my aunt's age then? Lydia Talbot, that is, although you probably remember her as Lydia Litton. Samantha told me you were in school together."

Lorraine nodded. "I remember her from high school, even though I'm a few years younger. I was just a sophomore when Lydia was a senior."

"But Samantha said you might be able to tell me something about the chamber choir, the one that had a reunion during the recent arts festival at Leeland?"

Sunny lifted her golden eyebrows. "Maybe not the best discussion to have right here," she said, motioning toward the other patrons approaching the desk. One of them was Mrs. Dinterman, who liked to share any "news" she overheard. There was also a young mother with two children, and one of our home-schooled teens. Heat rose in my face. I clamped my lips and bobbed my head in silent thanks. Sometimes my enthusiasm for amateur sleuthing overcame my common sense, not to mention my professionalism.

"Sunny's right, we should talk somewhere a little less public," I told Lorraine. "If you circle around the desk, we can head into the staff workroom."

Once I'd closed the workroom door, leaving Sunny and Samantha at the desk, I rolled the task chair away from the back-office computer workstation. "Here, sit in this. It's a lot more comfortable than those wooden chairs."

"But then you'll be stuck with a hard chair," Lorraine said, as she surveyed the room.

"It's fine. I think I'll stay on my feet." I leaned against one of the metal shelving units lining the walls. "Anyway, I don't know if Samantha told you, but Zelda Shoemaker is one of the library's most loyal volunteers."

"And a close friend of your aunt." Lorraine sat down before meeting my gaze, her dark eyes filled with curiosity. "I remember they were great pals, at least part of the time I was in high school. And Samantha did mention Zelda's connection to the library. So I'd already put two and two together and realized you wanted to speak with me to help Zelda's situation in some way."

"Can you?"

"I'm not sure. I wasn't really part of any of the groups Zelda was involved with. Not to mention I was a lowly sophomore, so . . ." Lorraine lifted her hands. "I only know what people whispered—tittle-tattle and such. Not all of which I believed. But I did hear something involving that lady who was killed."

"You mean you heard rumors about Claudia Everhart, even though she went to another high school?"

"Well, sure. The whole mess with Earl Blair almost dying was quite a scandal at the time." Lorraine tapped her foot against the hardwood floor. "He was our first-string quarterback, so everyone was really concerned. If not for him personally, for the team."

"Yeah, I guess football is usually a big thing in high school," I said, remembering how little attention I'd paid to my own

team. Never a sports fan, I wasn't part of my high school "in-crowd." Not that I'd tried to achieve such a goal. I'd always felt more comfortable hanging out with the book lovers and artsy outsiders.

"Football was super popular at Leeland, at least back then. So when Earl Blair almost died, well, it was all the talk for a while." Lorraine shifted in the task chair. "Anyway, there was a rumor going around that Zelda Shoemaker slipped him the cupcake that triggered his allergic attack."

"I don't think she was the culprit, but it is interesting to hear that a lot of other people did," I said slowly, pondering the implications of this old rumor.

Lorraine tilted her head and studied me. "Don't kill the messenger, but I'm not sure my recollections help Zelda's case at all. From what I remember, she and Claudia Everhart hated each other, and not just because of Earl."

"Really? What other reason could there be?"

"It had to do with the same competition where Earl fell ill." Lorraine wrinkled her brow. "Now what was that? Oh yes, Claudia Everhart accused Zelda of 'inappropriate behavior' or some such thing." Lorraine met my astonished gaze with a wry smile. "I never learned any details, but Zelda was kicked out of the chamber choir after that event, so something must've happened."

I sprang forward, pressing my palms against the top of the worktable and leaning forward to face off with Lorraine. "Kicked out? I heard she left of her own accord."

"That's not the tale I was told." Lorraine shrugged. "Of course, who knows the real story? It was all gossip, one way or

the other. I certainly wouldn't swear on a Bible that the version I heard was the truth."

I straightened, rubbing my forehead with one hand as if it would still my whirling thoughts. If Claudia Everhart had gotten Zelda dismissed from the chamber choir she'd worked so hard to get into . . . *That, combined with their rivalry over Earl Blair's affections, could look like a much stronger motive for murder, especially if bad feelings escalated into a fight when they met again, even many years later. It still seems unconvincing to me, but will it appear the same to the authorities?*

"That was the gossip spreading throughout the school? Everyone thought Zelda had been kicked out of the choir?" I asked, struggling to keep concern from sharpening my tone.

"It was definitely roaring through the rumor mill, although there must've been some kids who didn't hear the gossip. Come to think of it, I remember being in the cafeteria and overhearing your aunt ask a few chamber choir members why Zelda had dropped out. They didn't seem to know, or at least they weren't saying." Lorraine swiveled the seat of her chair from side to side in a nervous action that made me focus more closely on her face.

"Earlier you said you didn't remember much, but I'm not sure I believe you. It seems you were pretty interested in the whole business. Any particular reason why?"

"I guess Samantha's stories about you being an amateur investigator are true. You've certainly uncovered my secret in record time—there *was* a reason I was invested in this particular bit of gossip, and I do know more. Certainly more than I planned to say." Lorraine's lips twitched. "You see, I had a pretty big crush on Walt Adams at the time. Of course, he had

no interest in a skinny, silly sophomore, but I lived in hope, as they say."

"You were friends, though?"

"Casual, but yes—our families socialized and we attended the same church, so I talked to him from time to time. That's how I found out he was worried about Zelda, who he always claimed was simply a childhood friend."

"Along with my Aunt Lydia," I said.

Lorraine waved this off. "But Walt wasn't infatuated with Lydia. I knew that, just like I knew he was deeply in love with Zelda." The conviction in her tone told me she'd accepted this truth long ago. "Walt thought he hid it well, and I guess for the most part he did, but when you're crushing on someone, you're hypersensitive to their interest in anyone else, aren't you?"

"I can't dispute it," I replied, thinking back on my own unfortunate romantic relationships. *Before Richard, of course.*

"So naturally, I knew Walt was secretly in love with Zelda Shoemaker." Lorraine shook her head. "He was very upset when Zelda dropped out of the chamber choir and wouldn't tell him why. He confessed his concern to me, when I asked him what was wrong after one of our church socials. And I guess, even though I was jealous of Zelda, I was so hopelessly head-over-heels I still wanted to help him."

"By keeping your ears open to any information that would explain why Zelda left the choir?"

"Exactly. But sadly, despite my efforts, I never learned why. I did hear rumors about this Stonebridge student, Claudia Everhart, making some sort of accusation against Zelda. So"— Lorraine sighed deeply—"I told him."

This was a new wrinkle, for sure. *If Walt knew about the rumors, did he ever question Zelda to find out the real story?* I frowned. *If he did, he apparently never shared the truth with Aunt Lydia. And neither did Zelda.*

Which meant both of them might know more than they were saying about Zelda's connection to a murder victim.

I took a deep breath before daring to speak again. "Thank you for sharing what you know with me. Like you said, I'm not sure any of this will aid in lifting suspicion off of Zelda, but it does help my personal quest to gather more information concerning any events connecting Claudia Everhart to Zelda."

"You're welcome," Lorraine said, as she rose to her feet. "I just want to assure you I don't hold a grudge against Zelda Shoemaker." Her smile was genuine and warm. "Heavens, I've had a full life and barely thought about Walter Adams since he graduated from high school and went off to college."

"Don't worry, I can tell it no longer bothers you," I said, with an answering smile. "And anyway, both Walt and Zelda married other people, so . . ."

"I really had no chance?" Lorraine's wink told me she wasn't upset by this thought. But almost immediately her expression sobered. "The only thing is, I keep thinking . . . Well, are you sure Zelda and Claudia Everhart never met after their interaction in high school? Because I've wondered if maybe there was something going on between them over the years."

Crossing to the door, I halted and turned to look at her. "Why would you think that?"

Lorraine stared down at her clasped hands. "Because I saw them once, about five years ago. It was in Frederick, Maryland,

at a quiet restaurant. I spied Zelda first—it wasn't hard to recognize her, even after so many years—and almost walked up to say hello, but then I noticed her expression. She looked so angry and upset . . ." Lorraine twisted her hands. "Anyway, it didn't feel like a conversation I should break into."

"But how did you know the other lady was Claudia Everhart? You hadn't ever met her, had you?" I asked, as I clutched the doorknob.

"No, but I remembered the gossip from back when Earl Blair was dating both girls. Everyone said it was funny because they looked so much alike." Lorraine lifted her head and met my gaze without blinking. "And Zelda's companion that day could've been her twin, or at least her sister. It was uncanny, really. Then I heard Zelda say something like 'never again, Claudia,' so I figured that's who it had to be."

I swallowed a swear word as I read the honest concern on Lorraine's face. "It is strange. I can't imagine why they'd meet, but who knows? Zelda is very social. Maybe she met Ms. Everhart in a regional gardening group or something like that."

"I guess that's possible." Lorraine didn't look convinced. "Anyway, I should be getting along. I want to chat with Samantha for a moment before I leave, but I do have an appointment later . . ."

"Of course, of course," I said. As she met me at the workroom door, I tightened my grip on the doorknob. "Listen, I'd like to talk to Zelda before you share any of this with anyone else. Would that be okay?"

"Sure. I wasn't planning to run to the sheriff's department anyway, if that's what you're worried about." Lorraine stared

into my face, her dark eyes unreadable. "It's all gossip and hearsay, isn't it?" she added, in a lighter voice.

"Exactly." I laid a hand on her arm for a second. "Thanks."

Lorraine gave a little bob of her head. "No problem. I'm not so fond of authority that I'd share rumors, and besides . . ."

"You still care about Walt," I said, as this truth struck me.

"Yes, as an old friend, if not an old flame. He's an honorable man, and such a pillar of our community, he's earned that loyalty, don't you think?"

"Absolutely," I said before opening the door and stepping back to allow her to walk in front of me.

I left Lorraine chatting with Samantha and Sunny and headed into the stacks, where I was accosted by The Nightingale. She was standing in the middle of one aisle, with Mrs. Dinterman hovering nearby.

"Betcha haven't heard the latest, have ya?" The Nightingale said, her voice brimming with triumphant glee. "Just got the scoop before I came in, and was sharing it with Mrs. Dinterman here."

She looked too pleased for it to be anything but bad news.

"No, I've been working," I replied, steeling myself for her next words.

But Mrs. Dinterman beat her to the punch. "It's about Zelda Shoemaker," she said, ignoring The Nightingale's dirty look. "She's been arrested for murder."

Chapter Thirteen

After spending several hours at Aunt Lydia's house Monday evening, commiserating with her and Walt about Zelda's arrest, I was looking forward to a quiet evening at home Tuesday evening.

But it was not to be. Richard reminded me before I left for work in the morning that we had tickets to a poetry reading at Clarion University.

"It's Emily Moore," he said. "I didn't think you'd want to miss that."

I actually *did* want to skip the event, but decided I shouldn't. Emily Moore, who was the poet-in-residence at Clarion, had made several significant contributions to the library over the last year. As library director, the least I could do to show my appreciation was to attend her readings.

"If only it wasn't tonight," I told Richard, when we paused at the front door before heading off to our respective workplaces. "Zelda's hoping to make bail today. Maybe I should be available if she needs someone to talk to."

Richard grinned. "You mean you want to further your little investigation by asking her more questions."

"Not just that." I made a face at him. "I also want to listen to her concerns. You know, be a sympathetic friend. Although I do have some questions about the past . . ."

"A-hah, gotcha." Richard tapped my nose with one finger. "The bloodhound is on the scent."

"Very funny." I stood on tiptoe to kiss his lips. "Better move along, or you'll be late."

Richard glanced at his watch. "True enough. And, not being the boss, I don't get as much leeway."

"You really are in rare form today," I said, shaking my finger at him. "Just you wait, mister. I'm going to find some way to pay you back for all this teasing."

Richard pressed his hand to his chest. "I'm terrified."

"You should be. Because when you least expect it . . . wham!" I popped my fist into my other palm.

He pulled me in for a passionate kiss. "Save that fire for later," he murmured in my ear when he released me. "But I'm definitely going to be late if I allow you to distract me any further." He kissed me briefly again before heading out the door.

I watched him leave before stepping onto the porch and locking up behind me. My lips, still tingling from his kiss, curved into a smile. I'd waited a long time to find a man like Richard.

You should always remember your good fortune, I told myself, as I set off toward the library at a brisk walk. *Not everyone has such luck.*

I picked up my pace as I considered where to focus my next search for answers in the murder case. Counting my blessings had me made me vow to work even harder to clear Zelda's name.

*   *   *

Unfortunately, I wasn't able to do any research during the day. Sunny wasn't scheduled to work and Samantha called in, needing a day off because her daughter was ill. It was only Denise, one of our faithful volunteers, and me holding down the fort, and although I loved to play amateur sleuth, I knew my job, especially in terms of service to our patrons, had to come first. Digging through the archives would have to wait.

As soon as I arrived home, I rushed upstairs to change. As usual, I barely avoided tripping over the cats, who always seemed to materialize to weave around my legs as I climbed the steps.

"How can two cats create such an obstacle course?" I asked, eyeing an innocent-looking Fosse as he leapt onto the windowsill.

Richard finished buttoning up a white dress shirt before patting Loie, who'd jumped up on the bed. "It's one of their many talents. Now, what do you think? Am I good without a tie?"

I flashed him a cheeky grin. "You're good without anything, but yes, you look fine. This event isn't super formal, is it?"

"I don't believe so. Anyway, it's too hot for a tie." Richard slipped on a gray linen jacket. "Not sure how those businessmen do it. I don't think I could wear one of those darned things

every day." He tugged at his open collar. "I like to be able to breathe."

I smiled. Richard's typical work clothes were dance togs, which were a far cry from suits and ties. "I guess you get used to it, but I agree." I pointed the toe of one of my flat sandals. "I have the same issue with high heels. How women wear stilettos to work every day baffles me. I could never bear to wear them, even though they'd admittedly give my stubby self a little more presence."

"Don't worry, people know you're in the room, even if you are a bit short," Richard crossed to me. "Now, spin around so I can fasten you up."

"What do you mean?" I asked, as he tugged up the zipper on my full-skirted amber silk dress. I rolled my shoulders. The dress's short sleeves were a little tight, but since all I would be doing was walking and sitting down, I didn't think that would pose a problem.

"Oh, you have a certain . . . vitality that captures attention." Richard swept aside my hair so he could kiss the back of my neck. "And with those big brown eyes of yours—well, I'm pretty sure no one is going to overlook you."

"I think you're biased, but thanks." I turned to face him. "We'd better go, don't you think? I know parking at the university can be a nightmare."

"Don't forget, I have a designated spot," Richard said, as he leaned in close.

Aware that if he started kissing me we really would be late, I pressed my palm against his chest to push him a step back. "But that's halfway across campus from the English department, isn't it?"

"A little walk never hurt anyone." Richard patted his flat stomach. "Besides, I ate too much pasta at dinner and need extra exercise tonight."

I snorted. "Whatever you say. But let's get a move on. I don't walk as fast as you, and I don't want to be late to the reading." Grabbing my purse, I headed for the stairs.

Richard followed, muttering something about people who worried too much.

As I had suspected, we ran into some slow traffic during the drive to Clarion, which made Richard swear under his breath and me tap my fingers nervously against my bare knees. Once we were finally parked near the arts complex, we had to practically sprint across campus to reach the venue hosting the poetry reading.

"I probably look a sweaty mess." I combed my fingers through my hair as we paused in the lobby of the building that housed the English department.

"You look beautiful, as always." Richard leaned in to give me a peck on the cheek before taking my arm and escorting me into the lecture hall.

The auditorium was full, which surprised me. I didn't think poetry readings drew such large crowds. *Although*, I thought, as Richard and I paused in the center aisle to search for vacant seats, *Emily Moore is rather famous. And she's also an icon from the era of Andy Warhol and The Factory. That probably draws in some people, if only for nostalgia's sake.*

A waving hand from the side aisle caught my attention. I elbowed Richard. "Look, there's Marty Stover."

Richard squinted at the man. "And I guess the woman snuggled so close to him is his wife. Or at least I hope so."

Richard shot me a grin. "Anyway, it doesn't look like there are seats in their row, but I spy a few a couple of rows behind them. Let's circle around the back and grab those."

Marty met us as we walked down the side aisle. "Good to see you again. I'd introduce you to my wife," he added, motioning toward a slender woman with curly, light brown hair who glanced up at us with a smile, "but I think you'd better claim those seats while you can."

Richard nodded. "We'll catch up later."

We backtracked a few rows and slid past a couple of people to reach the two empty seats. They were off to the side and near the back of the auditorium, but since this was a reading, not a performance, I wasn't too concerned about the sightlines.

When Emily Moore took the stage, I observed, once again, how her appearance didn't match expectations for a poet who'd come to prominence in the psychedelic sixties. With her dark hair cut in a short bob, round tortoiseshell glasses, and stocky figure clad in a simple beige blouse and dark brown slacks, Emily didn't resemble the free-spirited flower child she'd been as a young woman. But, of course, it was decades later, and Emily now taught courses at Clarion, owned a Craftsman-style home in Taylorsford, and had—according to Zelda—recently joined the local garden society.

Poor Zelda. She and Walt would probably be here tonight, if not for all the notoriety. As Emily read one of her older pieces, my gaze wandered over the rows of heads in front of me. One in particular caught my attention—an ash blonde, artfully mussed cap of hair. I leaned forward in my chair as the woman turned her head and I instantly recognized Gwen Ohlson's distinctive profile.

Sitting back, I whispered to Richard. "Gwen Ohlson is here tonight."

He arched his dark eyebrows, murmuring, "And?"

"And I want to talk to her if I can," I replied, before a sharp look from the man sitting on my other side silenced me.

At the short intermission, I noticed Gwen leaving the auditorium and told Richard I needed to go to the restroom. He simply raised his eyebrows again.

I slid past the other people in my row, earning another dirty look from the man next to me, who'd stretched out his legs so I had to climb over them. Making my way into the lobby, I searched the crowd for Gwen, finally catching a glimpse of her waiting for entry at a main floor restroom.

"Always a line for the ladies, isn't there?" said the woman at the end of the queue. "You'd think someone would finally figure it out and build an extra one for us gals when they renovate these places."

I nodded without replying. Gwen had veered away and was making a beeline for an adjacent hallway. I immediately abandoned the line and crossed the lobby to catch up with her.

"Hi there, did you get a tip about another restroom somewhere nearby?" I asked, as she paused in front of a door marked with a stairway sign.

Gwen glanced down at me, puzzled, before her expression brightened. "Oh, hello, Amy. Yes, someone said there's another ladies' room upstairs. I thought I'd take a chance on that, since I didn't think I could even get into the other one before the reading resumes."

"Good idea. Mind if I tag along?"

"Not at all." Gwen pushed open the door. "I think it's the next flight up."

As we climbed the stairs, I mentally formulated questions about Gwen's past connection to Zelda and, possibly, Claudia Everhart. "I guess you heard Zelda Shoemaker was arrested yesterday," I said, huffing slightly as I struggled to keep up with Gwen's longer strides. Despite her high heels, she'd easily outpaced me.

"Yes, but I also heard she's out on bail." Gwen, balancing on the top step, glanced back at me. "I guess you know who helped her put up the money."

I realized she must mean Kurt, and opened my mouth to comment on this act of generosity before the lights went out.

Clinging to the handrail as inky blackness enveloped me, all I could see of Gwen was a solid form in the amorphous darkness. It seemed she was carefully making her way to the door leading onto the next floor, but I couldn't be sure.

The swish of that door and a scuffle of feet made me release the railing. I gasped as the shadow I assumed to be Gwen seemed to double in size before it teetered and tumbled down the stairs.

I lunged forward, grabbing the opposite side railing and bracing my feet against the rubber treads, my knees bent. Gwen's body, curled into a ball, appeared to bounce from step to step, like a child sliding down on its backside. When she hit me, the force knocked my feet out from under me, and her elbows slammed into my ribs, but the slowness of her descent thankfully halted our downward trajectory. I ended up in a seated position, still clinging to the railing above my head.

"Are you all right, Amy?" Gwen's voice was as tattered as late autumn leaves.

The lights flickered back on. I released the railing and scooted across the tread until I could lean my back against the wall. My shoulders felt like they'd been jerked from their sockets, but when I lowered my hands to my lap, I could tell nothing was seriously damaged. *Except for my dress*, I thought ruefully. I'd heard the rip of fabric as Gwen tumbled into me, and air tickled my underarms where the seams had given way.

"I think so." I glanced up at her. "How about you?"

"I'm fine. No doubt I'll be covered in bruises later, but nothing seems to be broken or sprained." She gripped the handrail and used it to pull her body to a standing position.

"Careful," I said, noticing her wobble. "What happened, anyway? Did you lose your balance?"

"No." Gwen met my concerned gaze with wide eyes. "Someone pushed me."

Chapter Fourteen

"Who in the world would want you to fall down a flight of stairs?" I asked.

Gwen fluttered her eyelashes. "I can't tell you. I never got a good look at them—they shoved the door open and gave me a push before I even knew what was happening."

I stared at her, surprised how calm she appeared after such an incident. True, the shadow had momentarily appeared too large to be one person, but then again, I knew my eyes could play tricks on me in the dark. Staring up into Gwen's face, I couldn't help but wonder whether she was telling the truth. I hadn't heard anyone else speak or make any sound. Had someone burst through the door and pushed her, or had she simply taken a wrong step and fallen?

But if she'd simply stumbled, why would she lie?

As I staggered to my feet, instantly aware I'd also be nursing bruises before too long, the door to the floor below us slammed open. "I heard a thump. Everyone okay up there?" asked the woman I'd spoken to in the restroom line.

I shared a look with Gwen, who shook her head. "If we make a fuss, we'll be caught up in a mess for hours," she said under her breath.

The fact that I knew this was the truth was the only thing keeping me from sharing Gwen's claim about someone deliberately trying to hurt her. "Yeah, we're fine," I called down to the woman.

"A fuse blew or something. You know how it is with these old buildings," the woman said. "Seems to be okay now, if you want to head back down."

Pressing my arms against my sides to hide my ripped dress, I forced a smile and gingerly made my way down the stairs, with Gwen following close behind. "Thanks," I told the woman, who was holding the door for us.

She examined me quizzically. "They're delaying the second half of the reading for an extra ten minutes, so you still have time to run into the restroom if you want."

"Good, because we never made it to the one upstairs," Gwen said, breezing past me as if nothing untoward had happened. She swiftly crossed the lobby to reach the ladies' room.

After once again thanking the woman holding the door, I followed Gwen into the restroom, which was empty except for the two of us.

"You want to explain what all that was about?" I asked.

Leaning over a sink, Gwen peered into the mirror. "As I said, someone pushed me. But I didn't want to make a big deal out of it because . . ." She shot me a side-eyed glance. "Well, I may have a few enemies, that's all."

"Ones skulking around Clarion University, waiting for you to magically appear so they can push you down a flight of stairs? That sounds a little too coincidental to me."

Gwen tweaked a few flyaway strands of her hair. "Ones who track me to various places, looking for an opportunity to do me harm."

"Is this connected in any way to deals you've made with Kurt?" I asked, massaging my sore shoulders with one hand.

Gwen straightened and looked me up and down. "Could be. Which should tell you why I don't want to make a fuss."

"I hope you inform Kurt then, if no one else. Because I'm sure if he knows, he'll do his best to protect you."

A splotch of color on Gwen's cheek told me she'd be sporting a bruise there soon. "Of course he would, under other circumstances. But, you see, I may have double-crossed him as well as one of his . . . associates. So I think I'd better manage this on my own." She flexed her wrist, which I noticed was slightly swollen. "Honestly, I'd appreciate it if you'd keep this incident between us. In terms of it being something other than an accident, I mean."

I met her cool gaze with a lift of my chin. "If you insist. Although I must tell my husband what happened. But"— I raised my hand, palm out—"I can say you claimed to have stumbled." I twisted my lips into a semblance of a smile. *Not that I won't tell him the whole story, or as much as I know of it, but Gwen doesn't need to know that.*

"I do, and thank you." Gwen turned back to the mirror, pursing her lips. "I should probably head home. It'll be difficult to explain this blossoming shiner if I stay."

"I'd better do the same. But first, I need to use the facilities." I crossed to the row of stalls and winced as I pulled open a door. "Just hope I can get back up once I sit down."

"Use the grab bar," Gwen called out, as I closed the stall door. I heard her footsteps on the tile and the swing of the outer door as she left the room without another word.

Thanks for your concern, I thought. A minute later, as I washed my hands at the row of sinks, I examined myself in the mirror. Although my hair needed smoothing, my face showed no signs of my tumble. My upper arms and ribcage would undoubtedly tell another story.

Richard was pacing the lobby when I emerged from the restroom. Catching sight of me, he strode forward. "Where did you go?" he asked, anxiety edging his tone. "I came looking for you as soon as I could after that trouble with the electricity, but didn't see you anywhere. Did you hole up in the ladies' room while the lights were out?"

I glanced around the lobby. Most of the audience had already headed back into the lecture hall, but I noticed Gwen slinking out an exit door. "Let's not discuss it here."

Richard's eyes narrowed. "Okay, now you've weirded me out. What's going on?"

"I'll tell you everything, but not here, and not now," I said, trying not to squirm as he intently examined me.

He threw his arm around my shoulders. "Just so you know, I was very worried."

My groan caused him to pull his arm back and stare down at me, his gray eyes brimming with concern. "Are you hurt?"

"A little. Nothing major." I offered him a wan smile. "I want to go home now, if you don't mind. I'll explain what happened on the way."

In the car I shared the details of the incident in the stairwell.

The lines bracketing Richard's mouth deepened as he stared out the windshield. "We should get you examined at the emergency room."

"Please, no. Can't you make sure nothing's broken or sprained when we get home? I know you have some experience with that sort of thing from working with your dancers."

Richard shot me a stern glance. "All right. But if anything feels wrong, off to the doctor we go."

"Absolutely," I said, although I had no intention of going anywhere before morning.

Richard rapped the steering wheel with his fingers. "You say Gwen Ohlson told you someone pushed her? Did you see who it was? Because if you did, I don't care what that woman says; we need to tell the authorities."

"But that's the thing." As I shifted in the passenger seat, pain from my right hip shot down my leg. I bit back a squeak of pain and took a breath before continuing. "I'm not sure I did see anyone. It was dark, and there were shifting shadows, so I can't swear anyone else was there."

"You think Gwen Ohlson threw herself down the stairs?"

"Maybe. I mean, she could've opened the door slightly and then just dropped and bounced down." I grimaced as I adjusted my position on the leather upholstery. "I've been thinking it over, and the truth is, she couldn't have fallen that hard, or she would've sent us both plummeting to the bottom."

"But what would be the point?" Richard laid one hand on my knee. "And how could she have arranged the blackout?"

"I don't think she did. But I wonder if she took advantage of the situation to set up a scenario where it looked like she was being attacked." I frowned. "Maybe to prove to me she was in danger, so she couldn't possibly *be* the danger?"

Richard tightened his hold on my knee. "You think she knows you're digging into the past to help clear Zelda?"

"It's possible." I pulled free of his grip. "Sorry, that's a little uncomfortable right now."

Richard made a disapproving noise. "I still say we should go to the emergency room."

"Come on, you know what it's like. I won't get seen for hours. I can't bear the thought of that right now." As he glanced over at me again, I widened my eyes and allowed my lips to tremble.

"Okay, enough of the theatrics. We'll head home for now. But if I think anything is sprained or worse . . ."

"Deal," I said, settling back against the seat cushions.

At home, the cats seemed to sense something was up and avoided being underfoot as Richard helped me climb the stairs. He then slipped off my torn dress before settling me on the bed and checking me over.

"Nothing seems to be broken, or even sprained," he said. "But you're developing some nasty bruises."

"At least they aren't visible," I said, grimacing as he manipulated one of my shoulders.

"That won't make them hurt any less tomorrow." Richard cradled my face in his hands. "Sorry, sweetheart."

"It's not your fault," I said, leaning my forehead against his.

"I know something that might help." He leapt up and padded over to our bathroom. "A nice hot bath will do wonders."

I slid off the bed and gingerly made my way into the bathroom, where Richard was liberally sprinkling Epsom salts into the water gushing from the faucet.

"Does that really help?" I asked, as I braced my back against the glass wall of the adjacent shower.

"It's proven beneficial when I've experienced bruises and sprains over the years." He glanced up at me from under his dark lashes. "Everyone thinks dancers look graceful, but a lot of pain goes into creating the illusion."

"I've seen you after some of your rehearsals, so I can certainly believe that," I said as he helped me climb into the tub.

"Now just relax and soak for a while," Richard said. "I'm going to give the cats their evening treat and then head back up to help you into bed. Don't try climbing out of the tub by yourself," he added, in a firm tone. "The last thing you need is to fall again."

"Yes, Doctor." I gave him a little salute.

"And there's the sass. Guess you aren't too bad off." Richard shot me a grin before leaving the room.

Once I'd soaked for a sufficient amount of time, and was toweled off—an activity that included some cursing and wincing on my part—Richard helped me pull on a loose nightgown and crawl into bed.

"Let me get this straight—you suspect Gwen Ohlson has a reason to worry about some indiscretion in her past." Richard cast me a puzzled glance as he climbed into bed next to me.

"But she told you her enemy or enemies had something to do with Kurt and art deals, so where's the connection to Zelda and Claudia Everhart?"

"There wouldn't be any, if she's telling the truth. But *if* is the operative word." I shifted, trying to find a comfortable position. Unfortunately, my ribs and shoulders informed me there probably wasn't one.

"Why do you think she's lying?" Richard exhaled as Loie leapt onto the bed and bounced off his thighs to reach a comfy spot between us. "Cat one has landed. Prepare for cat two in three, two . . ."

"One," I said in a strangled voice. Fosse had somehow managed to target one of the bruises on my hip. Ignoring my groan, he plopped down across my thighs, his purr rumbling like a lawn mower engine. "You can't stay there," I told the orange marmalade–colored tabby, who simply blinked his golden eyes in response.

"Come here, you." Richard lifted Fosse off my legs and draped him over his chest. "You've gotten a little too hefty to lie on anyone's sore limbs."

Fosse meowed in protest, causing Loie to lift her head. But as soon as she saw he was fine, she curled back up with her nose touching the tip of her tail.

"Sometimes I think we need a larger bed," Richard said, as he stroked Loie with one hand and Fosse with the other. "Or fewer cats."

"Well, that's not going to happen." A little squeak escaped my lips as my shoulders spasmed. "Sorry, can't seem to get comfortable."

"Understandable. But there are a few tricks . . ." Richard plucked Fosse off his chest and placed him next to Loie before rolling to face me. "It's mind over matter. You have to close your eyes and picture yourself in a relaxing situation, like resting in a hammock, or in a gently rocking boat, or something. Take the focus off the parts that hurt."

"Hmmm, not sure I have a good enough imagination," I stared into his beautiful gray eyes. "How about if I distract myself by discussing my theories on the whole Gwen Ohlson conundrum?"

"If that works, sure," Richard said, with a smile. "Discuss all you want."

"Okay, here's the thing—Gwen was in the chamber choir with Zelda and Earl Blair, and others, like Olivia Rader. She had to have seen the whole situation with Earl, Zelda, and Claudia Everhart go down, and she may even have observed the events connected to Earl's medical emergency. So maybe she knows more than she's letting on." I gnawed on the inside of my lower lip. "What if she saw Claudia leave those cupcakes for the Leeland choir? She could've been blackmailing Claudia for years."

Richard's expression grew thoughtful. "That's right, Brad and his team found a blackmail note on Claudia Everhart, didn't they?"

"And there wasn't any signature or anything, so no one knows who sent it." I clutched one corner of my pillow as a pain shot through my ribs. "It could've been Gwen Ohlson, as well as anyone."

"I guess. But why would she then decide to shoot Claudia? Isn't that like killing the goose that laid the golden egg? You can't extract more money from the dead."

"True, but they could've argued. If Claudia refused to pay, or threatened to confess everything to the authorities . . ."

Accompanied by a chorus of meows from the cats, Richard rolled over onto his back. "It seems odd they'd meet in Zelda's garden, though."

"Yeah, that's the weird part. Unless Gwen actually planned to kill Claudia and pin it on Zelda. I mean, she had to have known about the bad blood between Zelda and Claudia in the past. She could've decided to use it to her advantage."

"But, as you've mentioned before, Earl Blair could've used the same tactic."

"Which puts both of them on my suspect list," I said, absently petting Loie, who'd snuggled up against me.

Richard stared up at the ceiling. "If Gwen Ohlson did stage the fall on the stairs, it must've been a spur-of-the-minute decision. You were unexpectedly in the same location and then the lights just happened to go out. She couldn't have planned all that."

"No, but she could've taken advantage of a lucky chance. Making it look like she was being stalked and attacked, in order to make her appear a victim rather than a perpetrator."

"Because she knew you were digging into the past?" Richard snapped his fingers. "Of course she knew. She's Kurt's friend, and he could've told her how your research has assisted the sheriff's department in the past."

"Exactly," I said, admitting to myself that Richard had stumbled onto this explanation before I had.

"I think I need to have another talk with Kurt," Richard said darkly.

I inhaled a deep breath. "Maybe not immediately. Let me do a little more digging first." I laid a hand on his tensed shoulder. "You know it's best not to confront Kurt without having all the ammunition you can muster."

"Very well, but when it comes to your safety, I'm going to say something sooner rather than later."

"I know," I said, ignoring stabs of pain and protests from the cats to snuggle closer to him. "But let's worry about it another time. I think I'm actually feeling sleepy now."

Richard turned to face me. "All right," he said, caressing my jawline with his fingers. "You do need rest. We'll discuss this in more depth tomorrow."

"Mmm, sure," I said, with a yawn. Closing my eyes, I considered how to prevent Richard from doing anything rash. He had a good relationship with Kurt, and I wanted to keep it that way. Not to mention I didn't want him to do anything that might place him in danger.

Chapter Fifteen

I was scheduled to work the late shift on Wednesday, so when I lingered in bed, claiming I felt better but needed a little extra rest, Richard didn't have the opportunity to expose my lie. He had an early morning dance department meeting—one that could determine the performance calendar for the upcoming academic year—and was forced to leave the house before I got up.

When I finally crawled out of bed, my first challenge was deciding what to wear. My ribs and shoulders were still extremely sore, making the thought of fastening a regular bra painful. I compromised by choosing a loose black tunic top made from a slubbed, opaque cotton. Worn with a soft, worn sports bra, the tunic also covered the elastic band topping the white cotton slacks I pulled on without too much cursing.

Standing at the kitchen island, I stirred cream into my coffee, kept an eye on Fosse—who was crouched at my feet, poised to jump onto the counter—and contemplated my next move. I finally decided to make an end run around Richard's plan to confront Kurt and phoned the art dealer. While I didn't think

Kurt would ever do anything to harm my husband, I didn't want them to have a falling out, especially over concerns for my safety. Richard had never been close to his dad and had been very young when his great-uncle Paul Dassin had died. I didn't want another relationship with a father figure fractured.

"Why don't I drive into Taylorsford today?" Kurt suggested. "I'll even bring food. When's your lunch break?"

"I'm actually working until eight," I replied. "It's more of a break for dinner, from five to six."

"It's fine, I can do that too."

I shooed Fosse off the counter and Loie, curled up in a kitchen chair, opened one emerald eye as his paws thumped the floor. "Where are you? I don't want you to have to travel too far."

"I'm at the Georgetown gallery today, but driving is never a problem. I rather enjoy it, and I do want to talk to you." Kurt cleared his throat. "I have some information you might find interesting."

"That sounds promising. Okay, I'll meet you outside the library around five. Should I look for the Jag?"

"Of course. I may have money, but one expensive car is quite enough." Amusement colored Kurt's voice. "It's just me, after all. No need for multiple vehicles."

"Especially when the one you have is so grand," I replied, before saying goodbye.

Despite the good weather, I decided to borrow the car I shared with my aunt. "Only if you don't need it," I told her, when I stopped by her house.

She dismissed this with a wave of one hand. "Feel free to use it today. Walt's bringing Zelda by later so we can chat. We need to figure out our next steps."

I flinched as a needle of pain pierced my shoulder. Turning my head, I pretended to be distracted by the fern baskets Aunt Lydia had hung from the ceiling of her wraparound porch. "Tell them I'm still researching, hoping to find information that might help."

"I'm sure you are." Aunt Lydia tapped the edge of one of the sidelights framing her oak front door. "You look a little out of sorts today. Anything wrong?"

"Everything's fine," I replied, plastering on a smile when I met her questioning stare. "Anyway, I'd better get going if I hope to make it to work on time."

I waved goodbye, keeping my head down so my aunt wouldn't notice my grimaces as I descended her unforgiving stone steps.

Reaching the library in plenty of time, I parked in the gravel lot behind the building and sat in the car for a few minutes. I knew I couldn't hide my condition from Sunny, who was scheduled to work from eight to five. The question was how much to share concerning my suspicions about Gwen Ohlson.

In the end, I decided to tell her the whole story.

"Yikes, that's no good," she said, surveying the area near the desk. "I know you don't want to get into your theories about what really happened while we're at the desk, but you definitely need to tell me more later."

"If you aren't going out, I'll pop into the breakroom during lunch. Will that work?"

"Sure." Sunny fiddled with one of the golf pencils we kept at the desk for patrons to borrow. "You won't be alone tonight, I hope."

"No, Bill's coming in around four thirty. He'll be covering the desk for my dinner break and also staying with me
until eight," I added when I noticed lines wrinkling Sunny's
brow.

"Good. I wouldn't want you to be here all by yourself."

"I've done it plenty of times, as have you."

"I know, but I'm a little worried." Sunny fiddled with the
end of her blonde braid. "Face it, there might be several people
who don't want you conducting research to help Brad and his
team solve this latest murder."

"When has that ever stopped me?"

"Never, and that's what concerns me." Sunny laid her hand
on my shoulder, yanking it back when I flinched. "Sorry. Forgot
about the injuries."

"I don't know if I'd call them that. *Injuries* sounds far too
serious. It's really only a few bumps and bruises."

"Now you're splitting hairs, since you're obviously in pain.
Frankly, I'm surprised Richard allowed you to come in to work
today."

I arched my eyebrows. "Allowed? Since when do you speak
of a man having the right to control a woman's actions?"

Sunny swung her hand as if swatting aside my words. "Stop.
You're just being difficult now. You know what I mean—he's
always so concerned about your welfare. I thought he'd want
you to rest today."

"I may have told him I was feeling better than I really am."
I focused my attention on the circulation desk computer, deciding it was a good time to throw in a comment to divert Sunny's
attention. "Oh, I meant to ask sooner, but I assume you're going

to the party, a week from this coming Saturday? I mean Brad and Alison's engagement party, of course."

"Wouldn't miss it," Sunny said brightly, although her expression fell as she added. "Not sure Fred can accompany me, though. Which is a bummer."

"He has to work again?"

Sunny shrugged. "Maybe. He said he couldn't commit to the party yet. We'll have to wait and see."

"I hope he can go," I said, screening my interest with a casual tone. I didn't want my friend to realize I'd noticed her disappointment. "Anyway, getting back to work business—have you already run the overdue notices, or should I do that now?"

"Took care of it as soon as I arrived this morning." Sunny's voice brightened with her next words. "Hello, Hani, what can we help you with today?"

Hani Abdi's elegant face and figure reflected her parents' Somali heritage, but having been born and raised in Taylorsford, she had no accent. Other than the one we all shared, of course. "I wonder if you have any resources related to taxes? I want to educate myself a little more." She smiled brightly. "It seems the catering company's profits have increased this year, and I want to make sure I'm handling the tax implications properly."

"Well congratulations, and yes we do," I said, moving out from behind the desk. "The best resources are online. Let me get you started at one of the computers."

After walking Hani through the steps to access a few online financial resources, I rejoined Sunny. "Can I leave you to cover the desk for a while? I almost forgot I need to compile some

statistical reports for the town council," I said as I headed for the workroom. "I guess I'd better not overlook that. The mayor might not like it."

Sunny grinned. "No, she wouldn't, you slouch. Go ahead, I can take care of things out here."

Except for a short break to share the latest news with Sunny, I spent the remainder of the day completing book orders, compiling reports, and balancing the library budget. Fortunately, seated in a comfortable chair, with my mind occupied by new acquisitions, facts, and numbers, I didn't notice my pain quite so much. It was only when I stood up to tell Sunny goodbye, and to welcome volunteer Bill Clayton, that pangs from the soreness in my ribcage and shoulders assailed me.

"Are you sure you want to work until eight?" Sunny asked, as she collected her purse from a shelf in the workroom. "I could stay on if you want to head home."

"No, no, I'm fine. Besides, Richard scheduled a rehearsal with Karla knowing I'd be home late. I don't want to interrupt their work, and anyway, I'm meeting someone at five." As I glanced at my watch, I sensed Sunny's curiosity. "Someone who's bringing me dinner," I said airily, not wanting to bring Kurt into the conversation. Although Sunny got along with the art dealer, she was often skeptical about his motives—perhaps because Fred had occasionally joined Hugh in investigating Kurt's rather checkered past.

After making sure Bill was fine covering the circulation desk on his own, I slipped out the staff door and circled around the building to wait for Kurt. As always, he was on time, arriving in his gleaming black Jaguar at precisely five PM.

I strolled over to the car, attempting to keep my expression neutral when the toe of my loafer caught on a sidewalk crack and a wave of pain flooded my body.

Kurt leaned out the car window. "May I park around back? I thought we'd take a walk, if that's okay with you."

"Sure." I wasn't thrilled with this turn of events, but my curiosity about his information overrode my concerns over how far I could hike before betraying my current physical condition.

"Stay here. I'll walk around," Kurt said, before turning onto the narrow lane leading to our small parking lot.

When Kurt reappeared, he held up a large white paper bag. "Your dinner."

"Thanks. I assume it isn't fast food?" I asked, as he joined me on the sidewalk.

"Heavens no. I'm not a monster." Kurt flashed me a toothy grin before taking off at a brisk walk. He slowed his pace when he noticed I was falling behind. "Sorry, I forget others don't have my long legs," he said, as I caught up with him.

"Especially short people like me," I said with forced cheer, determined to hide any evidence of my pain from him.

Kurt shot me one of his laser-bright glances. "Anything wrong? You seem to be moving gingerly today."

"It's just the new sidewalks in this part of town. They're historically appropriate, but you do have to watch your step." I indicated the brick pavers Sunny had finally convinced the town council to install in the main part of town. Looking up, I noticed Kurt examining the façade of the new shop that had replaced Ruth "Rainbow" Lee's antique store.

"Pity everything's so bourgeois these days. I preferred Rainbow's eclectic collection of curiosities."

"It's actually not bad—mostly garden stuff, but with some trendy clothing and décor thrown into the mix," I said. "Not the worst option."

"I suppose not. It could've been turned into one of those dreadful shops that sell sofa-sized paintings." Kurt's smile twisted into something closer to a snarl. "As if one should choose art based on the size of a couch."

"I know that's anathema to you, but not everyone has your high standards," I replied mildly. "Where are we headed, anyway? I have to back at the library by six."

"Right here." Kurt pointed toward a narrow lane flanking the side of Bethany Virts's diner, the Heapin' Plate. "There a garden in the back, with a bench."

I frowned. "Bethany's kitchen garden? I'm not sure if we should be using it for dining al fresco."

"It's fine. I have an arrangement with Beth—she allows me to sit in her garden sometimes, and I supply her with exotic spices I pick up at gourmet shops in D.C."

"Always working the angles, aren't you?" I followed Kurt to the open space behind the diner, a small square of grass surrounded by flower and vegetable beds.

The wooden bench placed at the edge of one of the beds was weathered as gray as driftwood. Kurt took a seat on one end of the bench and motioned for me to sit at the other end. "We'll spread out our feast between us," he said.

After extracting a white linen napkin from the bag and draping it across the center section of the bench, Kurt pulled out

several small plastic containers. "Sushi, made by my George-town chef, who's quite an expert in the cuisine." He looked up at me, his blue eyes gleaming. "I hope you like this sort of thing."

"I do, actually," I said, taking the black enameled chop-sticks he handed me.

"Good, I thought you might." Kurt popped open the con-tainers to display a variety of glossy rolls. "It's all vegetarian or cooked fish, in case you were wondering. I was a little leery of bringing sashimi when I had to haul it in the car for an hour or so." He pointed his chopsticks at two small containers, one filled with a neon green paste and the other with thin magenta strips. "There's wasabi and pickled daikon if you want it."

"Richard will be terribly jealous." I plucked up a slice of white rice tightly rolled around a rainbow of ingredients. "He's quite the sushi fan."

"Really? Well, I'll have to bring some by your house one day." Kurt finished off a piece of the sushi before speaking again. "Now—getting to the real point of this meeting, why did you want to speak to me? I also have information to share, but I'd like to hear from you first."

I grabbed another slice of sushi. "It concerns your friend, Gwen Ohlson."

"Oh? What about her?" Kurt's tone was mild, but his eyes narrowed.

Between nibbles, I detailed what had happened at the poetry reading. "The weirdest thing is, Gwen first told me she'd been pushed by some stranger but then didn't want me to tell anyone else that version of events."

"Interesting." Kurt scissored his chopsticks in the air. "Let's cut to the chase. She actually told you she suspected it was retaliation from someone she'd wronged?"

"Yeah, like you," I said, noticing his face had gone still as stone. "What exactly did she do to you, anyway? Obviously not something that made you cut her off, since I saw you being friendly at the performance the other night."

"She made a backdoor deal with an artist I'd introduced her to, cutting me out of a commission." Kurt stabbed a piece of daikon with the end of his chopstick. "She got a better price that way, of course, so I have to applaud her chutzpah. But"— he flicked the chopstick, allowing the pickled radish to flutter down over a slice of sushi—"I wasn't too thrilled about her going behind my back."

"I guess not." I studied him for a moment. "You're still friends, or was the other night an act?"

"We are, but with the caveat that I no longer entirely trust her. I'll be watching her carefully if I broker any more deals for her." Kurt bared his large white teeth. "Of course, I doubt she entirely trusts me, either, so I suppose we're on the same page."

"You really didn't know her years ago, when you were Karl Klass?"

"No, like I said, she was just a child when I was in high school." Kurt expertly lifted the daikon-draped slice of sushi and chewed on it for a minute, his gaze never leaving my face. "I didn't even remember she'd participated in the community theater production of *Brigadoon* in 1970 until I saw that photo. I did attend one performance, since Andrew had painted the

sets, but she was simply part of the chorus and didn't make a big impression."

"The thing is, I suspect something must've happened around that time, or at least later that year, when Gwen, Zelda, and our murder victim, Claudia Everhart, were part of a choral competition. You told me Uncle Andrew was also involved with that event, so I thought maybe you'd attended those performances as well."

"He was only a judge for the visual art portion, so no." Kurt shrugged. "If it wasn't Andrew's work on display, I wasn't really interested."

I swallowed a tasty bite of rice, seaweed, and avocado before speaking again. "I was told Claudia Everhart accused Zelda of inappropriate behavior, which got Zelda kicked out of the Leeland chamber choir. Did you ever hear that rumor? Then, or"—I pointed a chopstick at him—"more recently? Because I'm sure you've sent out your little birds to pluck up any juicy tidbits."

"Sorry, no. Though you are correct—I have been attempting to glean whatever information I can to aid Ms. Shoemaker's cause."

I twiddled my chopsticks between my fingers. "Gwen intimated you'd put up Zelda's bail. Is that true?"

"It is, although I wish she'd kept that to herself." Kurt sighed. "She seems to be very free with sharing information on my activities. Another reason to watch myself around her, I suppose."

"Can I ask why you'd help Zelda in such a magnanimous way? I didn't think you knew her very well." Shifting my position on the hard bench, a flash of pain twisted my lips.

"Perhaps I simply hate injustice?" Kurt examined me more closely. "Judging by your face, you apparently find that hard to believe."

"It isn't that. I'm just a little sore from my tumble on the stairs. But I admit to being surprised by your generous gesture. Bail can't have been cheap."

Kurt squared his broad shoulders. "Honestly, I do like the lady, despite her tendency to chatter, but I must admit my main motivation was . . ."

"To help Aunt Lydia? I know you care about her more than you'll ever let on. My guess is, being aware of how close she is to Zelda and Walter Adams, you decided to do something to help alleviate her unhappiness." I jabbed my chopstick at him. "Admit it."

"Guilty as charged," Kurt said, with a wry smile. "I also know how fond you are of Ms. Shoemaker. So, having the spare cash, I thought I should offer my assistance."

"It is appreciated, believe me."

Kurt's smile broadened. "Good. Now, what I wanted to share is related to this." He slid something from his shirt pocket and held it out to me.

It was the photograph that had fallen from the Oscar Wilde book. After staring at it for a moment, I tapped the edge and looked up. "Your information has to do with this production of *Brigadoon*?"

"Yes, it's something I remembered the other day, when I examined the photo again. I was reminded of an anecdote Andrew told me over a bottle of wine. He made an amusing story out of it, but now that I think of the ramifications . . ."

Kurt laid down his chopsticks. "It has to do with the young ladies in that photo. A couple of them, anyway."

I stared at the picture again. Gwen and Olivia were posed in front of Andrew's beautifully painted depiction of the Scottish countryside, along with another girl. Squinting, I tried to see if the third girl resembled a teenaged Zelda. *Or Claudia Everhart*, I thought, remembering how closely she and Zelda had supposedly resembled one another.

But the third girl was willowy and dark-haired. No stretch of my imagination could turn her into either Zelda or Claudia. "Exactly what was this story Uncle Andrew told you?"

"A rivalry between a few of the high school girls in the cast," Kurt said. "Apparently, there was a fight that escalated when a couple of the girls were helping Andrew finish some of the scenery. It ended with them tossing paint on each other. The director was furious, but Andrew thought it was hilarious. 'Like a scene out of a Shakespearean comedy,' he said. 'Helena and Hermia trading barbs and blows.'"

Kurt's expression had softened, as it always did when he talked about my late uncle, who'd died over forty years ago. *But the love hasn't died*, I thought, with a little pang of sadness. "Did he name the culprits?"

"He did, although I didn't pay much attention to it at the time. That photo, and my own investigation into Ms. Shoemaker's case, brought it back." Kurt tapped his temple with one finger. "It takes a bit more effort these days, but the memories eventually resurface."

"Like you're mentally challenged in any way," I said, with a sniff of derision. "So spill—what were the names?"

"One was Olivia Bell, and her antagonist was Claudia," Kurt said, with obvious relish. "Ah, now I have your attention. You see why I wanted to speak with you, as well as give you the photo."

"Did Uncle Andrew know why they were fighting?"

"He thought it had to do with another young woman who was also part of the quarrel. Apparently, she was cast in a major role instead of either Olivia or Claudia." He leaned forward to touch the dark-haired girl's image with his fingertip. "I think it must be this one. I vaguely recall her playing one of the leads, but I'm afraid I don't recall her name."

"Gwen wasn't involved?" I asked, with a lift of my eyebrows.

"Come to think of it, she may have been," Kurt said dryly. "Andrew did mention her name. But he said she stayed on the sidelines, although she was backing her friend."

"Olivia," I said, my mind spinning with this new information. *If Gwen and Olivia had fought with Claudia Everhart, as well as some other, unknown girl during the summer before the choral competition . . .*

"Anyway, you can keep that photo to aid your research. I thought it might be useful to find out who the other girl was, and if she was involved in the recent choral group reunions."

I slipped the photo into the pocket of my tunic. "She could be another suspect."

"Along with that Olivia woman," Kurt said. "It occurred to me that it would help take the spotlight off Ms. Shoemaker if you could suggest a few other suspects to Brad Tucker and his team."

"Absolutely." I added Olivia and the unknown actress to my mental list. *Along with Earl Blair and Gwen*, I thought, but decided to keep that last name to myself.

"My other suggestion is for you to talk with Mary Gardner. She used to work for the school system, presenting special programs about area folklore. She might know something about any rumors or odd occurrences connected to Leeland High in the seventies."

I nodded. Mary Gardner was a woman in her nineties, but still sharp as a tack. She'd grown close to Kurt while working in the orphanage where he spent time as a boy, and was a great collector of local history and stories connected to the area. "You think she might know something related to Claudia, Olivia, or Zelda, or even this mysterious dark-haired girl?"

"It's possible. And if there's any truth to the story that Ms. Shoemaker was forced out of the choir instead of dropping out on her own accord, Mary is likely to have heard it." Kurt motioned toward the plastic containers. "If you're done, I'll pack this up." As he held up his wrist, light flashed off his gold watch. "Time's marching on, and I know you need to be back by six."

"Thanks, and yes, I'm done." I laid my chopsticks across the napkin.

Kurt covered all the containers and placed them back in the bag. "Come to think of it, you should take this with you. Share it with Richard. I'm sure he'll be happy to help finish it off."

"He's always happy to eat," I replied with a smile. "Of course, with all his physical activity, he actually needs the calories. Unlike me."

Looking me over, Kurt winked. "You look fine to me. Honestly, artists in the past would've loved you as a model."

"Come on now, no point in trying to charm me." I wrinkled my nose at him. "You know I'm not going to be swayed by such behavior."

"Alas, I've always known that, my dear." As he stood up, Kurt offered me another of his wolfish grins. "But you're right, I shouldn't try any of my tricks on you. For one thing, you're family. At least as far as I'm concerned."

I rose slowly to my feet, ignoring the complaints from my hip. "Found family, anyway."

"Often the best kind," he said.

Chapter Sixteen

Karla had already left before I got home, so she missed the lecture Richard delivered as soon as I walked into the kitchen.

"Really, I'm just a little stiff and sore," I told him, after allowing him to thoroughly express his displeasure over me going to work while I was still in pain. I held up the white bag as a peace offering. "I have leftover sushi. Kurt's chef made it."

Richard frowned. "You met with Kurt today too?"

I mentally slapped myself for having dropped Kurt's name into the conversation so soon. "Don't get bent out of shape. He simply wanted to share some information he thought might aid my research. You know, to help Zelda."

"I thought you understood I wanted to give him a talking to before you got tangled up in any more of his schemes." Richard plucked the bag from my hand and opened it. "Sushi, you say?" he asked, in a mollified tone.

"It's really good." I glanced at the white board on our refrigerator. "What's this about dinner Friday night?"

Richard moved to the other side of the island and began pulling the plastic containers out of the bag. "Oh, right. I hope

you don't mind, but I accepted an invitation for dinner with the Stovers for Friday evening. Marty's wife called earlier and asked if we could come, and since Karla was here to confirm she could make it, I went ahead and said yes." Richard looked up to meet my questioning gaze. "We're going to meet up at that new restaurant in Smithsburg, the Italian one we wanted to try."

"That's fine. One less meal we have to cook." I cast him a smile before grabbing a paper plate from one of the cupboards behind me. "Honestly, I didn't think you'd mind me meeting with Kurt if it could possibly help Zelda."

Richard popped open the top of one of the containers. "I suppose there's no harm in it, if it was just to give you information." He fished a pair of chopsticks out of one of the oak island's shallow drawers. "Do you want to save this, or can I have some now? Never had dinner."

"And you worry about me." I clucked my tongue and slid the paper plate over to him. "I bet Karla didn't eat either."

"She said she had leftovers waiting at home." Richard extracted several slices of sushi and placed them on the plate. "Any condiments?"

"There should be some small containers of wasabi and pickled daikon." I stepped back and leaned against the soapstone counter topping our whitewashed lower cabinets. "Anyway, Kurt suggested I talk to Mary Gardner. I thought I might call and see if I could stop by to see her Sunday afternoon. Or both of us, if you'd like to go."

"Sure, I always enjoy talking with Mary. Her recorded stories have been a great help with the folklore project."

"She definitely knows all the old stories." I cleared my throat. "The other thing Kurt shared was his knowledge of some sort of rivalry between Olivia Rader and Claudia Everhart. Back when they were teens, I mean. Apparently, Uncle Andrew witnessed a fight break out between them during that summer theater production I told you about."

Halting his hand halfway to his mouth, Richard arched his dark brows. "Gwen Ohlson wasn't involved?"

"Kurt says she was on the sidelines, but"—I shrugged— "I'm not sure if that's true of if he's covering for her."

Richard chewed and swallowed before replying. "You think he's fond of her? I didn't get that vibe when we saw them together."

"I don't know. It's hard to tell how much Kurt cares about anyone, don't you think? But it does seem like he's reluctant to support my theory that she could be a suspect in Claudia's death."

"Interesting," Richard said, before eating another piece of sushi. "This really is good. Hits the spot tonight."

"Finish if off if you want." I winced as I straightened and stepped away from the counter. "I think I'll head upstairs and take another one of those warm Epson salt baths. It seemed to help last night."

"You do that," Richard said, as he plucked a couple more slices from the containers. "I'll be up before too long, if you need me to rub on any muscle ointment or anything."

I headed for the hall, but paused in the doorway to look back at him. "Thanks for worrying about me, by the way. I know it just shows how much you care."

He flashed one of those smiles that always melted my heart. "Always do. Always will."

"I know." I blew him a kiss before leaving the room.

*   *   *

I felt much better on Thursday, which was a blessing because the library was flooded with teenagers in the late afternoon, all working on the same English project. After thirty aching minutes spent kneeling down and jumping up again to point out books, I finally gave in and filled a cart with every title I thought could be of use.

"Don't worry about reshelving that cart," I told Samantha before I left at five. "The project isn't due until Monday."

Samantha nodded sagely. "Which means the same books will be needed tomorrow and Saturday."

"Without question." I smiled at her before saying goodbye.

I almost regretted walking to work as I headed home, but at least the maple and oak trees canopying the sidewalk offered cooling shade. As I neared our block, I glanced at my watch. Richard wasn't planning to be back from campus until six, so I decided to stop by my aunt's house to find out how Zelda was doing.

Aunt Lydia was busy in the kitchen, layering noodles, sauce, and cheeses in a casserole dish. "Oh, hello, Amy," she said without looking up.

"Making lasagna?" I dropped my purse and soft-sided briefcase on one of the kitchen chairs. "Maybe Richard and I should come over."

She glanced up at that. "Sorry, this is for the weekend. I thought I'd make some things ahead so I wasn't cooking the entire time."

171

"Hugh will be here then." I plopped down in the chair next to my belongings.

"He's coming tomorrow evening." Aunt Lydia straightened and tucked a loose strand of hair behind her ear. "You and Richard are welcome to come over then, if you want."

"And ruin your romantic evening? I think not." I grinned as she made a shooing motion with her hand. "Anyway, we accepted a dinner invitation from Martin Stover and his wife. We're going to meet up at the new Italian restaurant in Smithsburg. Karla's joining us too. It's sort of a dance project–related thing."

Aunt Lydia carried the casserole dish across the room and popped it in the oven. "Something Richard and Karla are working on?"

"Not necessarily a specific project, although I guess they'll discuss the folklore suite. But I think Richard wanted to talk more broadly about collaborating with the school system. Marty Stover is head of the arts programs at Leeland, you know."

"Right, he was in charge of that recent festival, wasn't he?" After setting the timer on the stove, Aunt Lydia walked back to the table and sat down across from me. "I hadn't really met him before the other evening, although his name rang a bell for some reason. Then Zelda reminded me why I would've recalled that name." Her expression grew distant. "There was a horrible fire at a machine shop when I was a girl. I guess I was eight or nine at the time. I remember my dad mentioning the town council taking up a collection for the family of the man who died. There was at least one child, if not more."

"What's that got to do with Marty Stover?"

Aunt Lydia focused her gaze on me. "His mother was the widow. I only know because it was a topic of conversation in my mom's quilting circle about three years later. They talked about how nice it was that the widow had married again, and had another child. I remember the ladies mentioning a Mrs. Stover and her baby boy, Martin." Aunt Lydia shook her head. "Funny what sticks with you and what doesn't. I don't remember the name of the man who died in the fire, or how many children he had."

"That is a sad story, but I'm glad Martin's mother was able to rebuild her life." I fiddled with my aunt's pewter salt shaker. "Speaking of unhappy situations—how's Zelda holding up?"

Aunt Lydia lifted her hands. "Quite well, all things considered. Of course, she feels, being innocent, that she has nothing to fear."

"But you aren't sure," I said, as tension deepened the lines around my aunt's mouth.

"I've seen enough cases where innocent people were convicted of crimes. So no, I don't feel totally secure." My aunt rubbed her forehead, as if trying to banish a headache. "And, of course, Walt is beside himself with worry."

"I don't think we can be complacent. Which is why I plan to keep digging and uncover more evidence to help clear Zelda," I said. "Has she mentioned any more details about that day? I mean, why Claudia Everhart was in her garden, or anything?"

"No, she continues to claim she heard a noise and went outside to find the woman in her gazebo, already dead."

"It's odd, though, don't you think? Why would Claudia show up out of the blue?"

"But it wasn't totally unprecedented." Aunt Lydia drummed the tabletop with her fingers. "Remember, I saw Zelda talking to Claudia a day or two before. I asked Zelda what that was about again, and this time she said Claudia was simply trying to convince her to take part in the chamber choir reunion concert."

"It doesn't make sense." I set the salt shaker back on the table. "Claudia sang with the Stonebridge choir. Why would she care if Zelda rejoined a rival group?"

"I questioned that as well." Aunt Lydia jerked her shoulders as the doorbell chimed throughout her house. "Who could that be? I'm not expecting anyone."

I followed my aunt to the front door. When she opened it to reveal Olivia Rader standing on the front porch, I couldn't smother an exclamation of surprise.

"May I help you?" Aunt Lydia asked.

Olivia bobbed her head to acknowledge me before answering. "Actually I'm here to help you. Or try to, anyway."

"And you are?" My aunt's tone was glacial.

"Olivia Rader, although you might remember me as Olivia Bell." The dark-haired woman fumbled with the strap of her large purse. "I guess you don't remember me from back in high school, but Amy can vouch for me. We met at the library as well as the recent concert at Leeland High."

Aunt Lydia stepped back, still holding the door. "You were part of the chamber choir reunion? I guess that's why you look vaguely familiar, although I must admit I don't remember you from school. Come in, then."

Olivia bustled past both us, but waited in the hall until Aunt Lydia closed and locked the front door.

174

"Sitting room?" I asked my aunt.

"Probably the best option," Aunt Lydia said, as she led the way into the more casual of her two front rooms. "I will need to listen for my oven timer, though. Don't let me miss that, Amy. I don't want to overcook the lasagna."

Olivia sniffed. "Is that what it is? Smells delicious."

Aunt Lydia didn't respond to this obvious flattery, choosing to silently take a seat in her favorite armchair instead. "Please, sit down, Ms. Rader," she said, motioning toward the sofa and another armchair.

But Olivia was too distracted to join me on the sofa facing my aunt's chair. Making a beeline for one of the landscape paintings that filled a section of wall between two bookshelves, she clapped her hands. "Is this Andrew Talbot's work?"

"Yes, like all the paintings in this room," I said, as my aunt's eyes narrowed.

"Oh, right, you married him, didn't you?" Olivia turned to Aunt Lydia, her dark eyes brimming with curiosity. "Lucky girl. I had such a crush on him when I was a teen. He painted the scenery for a community theater show I was in the summer before our senior year."

Aunt Lydia arched her golden eyebrows. "Did he? I didn't really know him very well at that point. I encountered him a few times when he visited my neighbor, Paul Dassin, but that was when I was a child. We didn't start dating until I was out of high school."

Olivia sauntered over to the sofa and sat beside me. "You really don't remember me, Lydia? At the reception I recognized you right away. I guess you haven't changed quite as drastically as some of us."

Aunt Lydia settled back in her chair. "I'm surprised you connected me with that girl from the past. I didn't think any of the more popular students ever noticed me in high school."

Olivia fluttered her hands. "Of course we did. It's just . . . Well, you always seemed so distant. We used to call you 'the fairy princess.' Because you were so slight and fair and always seemed to be off somewhere else, floating along in your own little world."

"I was shy," my aunt said. "Fortunately, I got over that, in time." She primly rested her hands in her lap. "My younger sister was the outgoing one in the family, although she wasn't part of the in-crowd either. Too interested in science and other 'not-cool' subjects."

"Debbie, wasn't it?" Olivia turned to me. "That must be your mother. Come to think of it, you look a lot like her."

"So I'm told," I said, not mentioning the fact that both of us took after my great-grandmother, Rose Baker Litton. *Who was certainly memorable in her own way*, I thought, with a sarcastic smile. "Anyway, what information do you have to offer us, Ms. Rader? Does it have something to do with Zelda Shoemaker?"

"Please, call me Olivia. And yes, it does touch on the unfortunate incident that happened at Zelda's house."

"The murder," Aunt Lydia said.

I shot her a glance, surprised at her antagonistic tone. She didn't acknowledge my look. Her gaze was fixed on the woman sitting beside me. *She does remember*, I realized. *She just doesn't want to give Olivia the satisfaction of knowing she made any lasting impression.*

Which told me my aunt must've thoroughly disliked the woman when they were young.

Olivia blinked rapidly. "Yes, very tragic. Anyway, considering that horrible situation, and knowing how close you and Zelda always were, I thought I should warn you about a few things. Especially after I ran into Amy at the reception and realized that Gwen Ohlson was . . ." She coughed, covering her next words, then cleared her throat before speaking again. "That Gwen must be friends with some gentleman you both seem to know."

I cast a side-eyed glance at Olivia, who obviously hadn't recognized Kurt from his younger incarnation as Karl Klass. It didn't surprise me, since I doubted they'd ever moved in the same circles, even if Olivia had stayed in the area while Kurt was running his first, quite illegal business. But the trembling of her crimson-tinted lips still switched my investigative instinct onto high alert. *Why is she nervous, and why has she mentioned Gwen in connection to a warning?*

"What do you mean?" I asked. "If you have information that could help Zelda, you must share."

Olivia slid to the edge of the sofa. "I doubt this will actually help her, but I do think you should know. I mean, not to speak ill of Zelda, but she and Claudia Everhart were engaged in a pretty intense war back in the day, and not just one of words. Which means even though I'm sure you believe in her innocence, she may have had a motive to harm Claudia."

"Even if that were true, it's in the past. Besides, Zelda isn't the type of person who would hurt anyone." My aunt casually crossed one slender ankle over the other as she stared daggers in Olivia's direction.

Clutching her hands in her lap, Olivia tapped her foot against the hardwood floor. "Zelda may not have a temper now, but I saw plenty of it when she was in the chamber choir, believe me. And that Claudia . . . Well, she could definitely make a person want to shut her up, one way or the other."

"I admit Zelda has always been a passionate person," Aunt Lydia said in her haughtiest tone. "However, she has never been violent. Not in any way, shape, or form. She might shout someone down, but she absolutely would not shoot them."

"You are entitled to your opinion, but I know what I saw back when we were in the chorus together," Olivia said. "Zelda got into some fights then, believe me."

I swiveled to face her. "That's interesting. I've heard *you* were the one who got in a physical altercation with Ms. Everhart. When you were both in a community theater production of *Brigadoon*. Ring any bells?"

Olivia leapt to her feet, clutching her purse to her chest. "I have no idea what you're talking about."

I stood up to face off with her. "I have it on good authority that you were slinging paint at one another at one point. While Gwen Ohlson stood back and watched."

"That's ridiculous. Here I came to give you information— for your protection, I might add—and you treat me like this?" There was a full-on quiver afflicting Olivia's lips, although whether from nerves or anger, I couldn't tell.

She turned on her heel and stomped out of the room. "I'll show myself out."

"Not unless I unlock the door," my aunt said mildly. She rose gracefully and followed Olivia into the hall. I trailed both

of them, reaching the door in time to hear Olivia Rader's parting shots.

"As for Gwen Ohlson, let me clue you in." Standing on the porch, her chest puffed out like an angry pigeon, Olivia's eyes blazed with indignation. "Yes, we were friends in the past, but there's a reason we fell out of touch for many years, and our recent reunion has shown me she hasn't changed. She's still up her old tricks, spinning whatever story benefits her most."

"Thank you for the warning, but I think we can figure out who's telling the truth." Aunt Lydia attempted to close the door, but paused when Olivia stepped forward.

"You think so, do you?" Olivia said, jabbing a finger at my aunt. "I know you aren't inclined to believe me, but I'm a big enough person to still warn you—whatever else Gwen's told you is as untrue as that little fairy tale about me fighting with Claudia. Because, quite frankly, she's an incorrigible liar. Always has been, and probably always will be." Spinning on her heel, Olivia strode off, leaving Aunt Lydia and me speechless.

"Gwen didn't tell me that story," I said, once Aunt Lydia had closed the door.

Focused on securing the lock, Aunt Lydia didn't look at me. "Let me guess—it was Kurt."

"Bingo." I followed my aunt into the kitchen. "And, to be honest, he said he heard it directly from Uncle Andrew."

Aunt Lydia shot me a sharp look. "When Andrew painted the sets for the community theater production of *Brigadoon*?"

"You did actually know." I looked her over, a smile twitching my lips.

"I know a lot of things," she said with an answering smile. "Like how mean girls rarely lose their spite." She swept her gleaming hair away from her face. "And how one should never show a winning hand too soon."

Chapter Seventeen

On Friday evening we met Marty and Evelyn Stover at the Italian restaurant in Smithsburg.

"I really wanted to have you over to the house," Marty said, as Richard and I took our seats at the table. "But we've been having some kitchen renovations done and, as often happens, they didn't finish in time. The place is still a mess."

Richard took my proffered purse and set it between his chair and the wall. "No problem. We've talked about wanting to try this place out anyway." He glanced at his watch. "Karla should be here any minute, but I know she had a class until five. She warned me she might be a little late if she ran into any traffic."

"That's fine. We can peruse the offerings and chat while we wait for her," Marty said, as he picked up one of the large, faux-leather menus the waitress had brought to the table.

"I told Marty we should wait, but he was so anxious to speak with you and Ms. Tansen, he insisted we go ahead with the invitation." Evelyn fiddled with the gold clips holding back her curly hair.

She's nervous, I thought, as I examined her slightly flushed face. Her light brown eyes were watery behind the lenses of her ivy-green framed glasses. *I wonder if she's just shy, or if there's something else going on.* I turned my attention to her husband, who looked perfectly cool and comfortable in his robin's-egg blue polo shirt and navy slacks. *No wonder he's more at ease, though, since he is older and probably more experienced,* I thought. Even though their similar builds and coloring fit the stereotype of the married couple who resembled one another, I estimated that Marty was a good twenty years older than his wife.

Not that age seemed to be an issue between them. Whenever Evelyn Stover glanced at her husband, her adoration of him was blatantly evident.

"I admit I was determined to get together, sooner rather than later," Marty said, snapping his cloth napkin in the air to open it up before placing in his lap. "I have this idea for a summer program—for next year, of course—and wanted to get on your calendars before anyone else did."

Richard lowered his menu to look at him. "Too late—I already have a few choreographic gigs lined up for next summer, as well as one charity performance. But I'm still open to listening to your ideas."

"My husband is a workaholic," I told Evelyn with a grin.

Her answering smile was as limp as the ruffles on her white blouse. "Mine too, as you can see. In fact, he isn't satisfied with managing all the arts programs at Leeland and directing the choral groups; he's also spearheading a drive to renovate that old movie theater you may have seen when driving into

Smithsburg. The run-down one that still shows traces of its original Art Deco design."

"What can I say?" Marty lifted his hands. "It was going to be torn down if no one did anything, and I thought that was a shame. I'm not the only one involved in the reclamation project, but I am in charge. We've raised a reasonable amount of money so far, but still have a way to go."

As Richard closed his menu, his expression told me the gears were turning in his head. "Are you planning for it to remain a cinema, or do you hope to turn it into a theater for stage productions and concerts?"

"Both, actually. We're planning to install an actual stage and enhance the fly space, but also include a retractable movie screen."

"Interesting." Richard laid his menu across his plate. "I'd love to talk to you about that project sometime, Marty. The area could definitely use another venue for live theater, music, and dance."

"Especially dance," I said, with a smile.

"Hello," said a familiar voice.

I glanced over as Karla approached the table. Her draped ivory silk sleeveless top and linen slacks not only complemented her sienna brown hair and golden tan; they also made her look even more like a statue of a Greek goddess than usual. "Hi there. Good to see you again. Have a seat." I motioned to the chair next to me.

"Sorry I'm a little late," Karla said.

Marty offered her a bright smile. "Don't worry about it. Richard told us you were leading a class that ran until five."

He rose to his feet and stretched his arm across the table. I'm Martin Stover, by the way, but everyone calls me Marty. Nice to meet you, Ms. Tansen. I've heard a lot about you."

"Good things, I hope," Karla shook his hand before sitting down. "And please call me Karla."

"All very good." Marty gestured toward his wife before he also took his seat. "This is Evelyn, my better half."

Color rose higher in Evelyn's cheeks. "Hello, Karla. I'm glad you could join us."

"It's my pleasure." Karla glanced around me to catch Richard's eye. "I'm sure my erstwhile partner has told you I'm very interested in any ideas you have concerning summer dance programs."

"He mentioned something about that when we were both involved in the recent arts competition." Marty closed his menu with a snap. "He also told me your studio includes a focus on young dancers with disabilities, and that you're open to offering inclusive programs."

"Absolutely," Karla said as she picked up her own menu. "But I guess I'd better make a selection before we talk any more, as I see the wait staff hovering."

After the waitress took our orders, with Marty insisting on putting everything on one check he would cover, Richard slid his arm across the back of my chair. "I don't want to bore Evelyn and Amy with too much shop talk, so perhaps we could discuss your ideas before our meal arrives, then move on to other things."

"It's not a completely formed idea," Marty confessed. "I was just wondering if we could work together—the school system and your studios, I mean. Offer a few introductory classes to

interested students as part of a summer arts initiative. It would be free to the participants, but we'd get funding to pay for your time and expertise."

"I'd be interested in exploring that idea. I do have my regular students, but those classes don't fill all my available hours." Karla made a face. "Unfortunately."

"Part of the problem is that a lot of kids can't afford professional lessons. Or their parents refuse to pay for such a thing even if they can afford it." Richard sent me a sidelong glance. "I wouldn't have received any training if my great-uncle hadn't earmarked money in his will for that purpose. The idea students could explore dance for free is definitely intriguing."

Marty leaned forward, his eyes sparkling with enthusiasm. "My hope is, if we allow some of our students to experience real dance training, it will serve two purposes. First, it might encourage a few to pursue more formal instruction, and second, it could develop an appreciation for dance in others."

"Audiences for the future," Richard said thoughtfully.

"The other draw might be offering a performance opportunity." Karla glanced at my husband. "We're planning to include some of my students in the folklore project, as well as several dancers from Richard's studio. Why couldn't we also incorporate a few talented, hard-working kids from a public school arts program?"

"It might open up new grant opportunities," Marty said. "I'd be glad to help with that process."

Richard absently tapped his fork against the edge of his plate. "I'm definitely willing to discuss this further. But I think Karla should be the primary point person. I'll help any way I

can, but again, I already have some commitments lined up next summer." He laid down the fork and glanced at Karla. "If that's okay with you, of course."

"Sounds great. Right now the only thing on my schedule, other than our folklore project, are my regular classes. I certainly don't mind spearheading something with such potential." Karla placed her small purse on the table. "Let me give you my card, Marty, so we can stay in touch."

Our meals arrived soon after, leading Marty to declare his agreement with Richard's suggested moratorium on "shop talk." Our conversation over dinner shifted to more personal topics. Although Marty prompted Richard and Karla to share more details about their dance careers, we also discussed Marty's work at the high school and Evelyn's freelance job as an illustrator.

"She's an excellent artist," Marty said, pride evident in his tone. "But a little too shy about sharing her achievements."

Evelyn paused with a bite of pasta halfway to her mouth. "I don't like to blow my own horn, that's all," she said, laying down the fork.

"What sort of illustration?" Karla asked, her eyes bright with interest.

"Children's books, mostly. I work with some indie authors as well as a few smaller publishing houses. Nothing grand," Evelyn added, before finally eating her forkful of linguine.

"But that's perfect," I said. "Since I'm the library director in Taylorsford, and picture books are an important part of our collection, maybe you could speak about your work at the library sometime? I bet a lot of our kids, as well as their parents, would be interested."

Evelyn stirred her remaining linguine around on her plate. "Oh, I don't know. I'm not really comfortable talking in front of a large group."

"They would be welcoming and appreciative, trust me. Nothing to fear," I said, my enthusiasm causing my voice to rise in pitch.

Richard squeezed my knee under the table. "I get that, Evelyn. Some people prefer not to speak in public. I was like that when I was younger."

I shot him a look from under my eyelashes, unsure if he was simply trying to be sympathetic or if he was telling the truth. But thinking about his rocky relationship with his overbearing dad, I could imagine him being unsure of himself when he was a child. It was possible he may not have developed his current air of confidence until he was older. "Well, I certainly don't want to force you. I simply wanted to extend the invitation," I said in a calmer tone.

Evelyn ducked her head, staring at her plate. "And I appreciate that."

When the conversation veered off into a discussion of the area arts scene, Karla expressed her appreciation for Marty's efforts to expand the dance program at the high school level.

"Most schools don't even offer extracurricular dance activities, so the Leeland team is a lovely bonus for some of my students. It allows them to actually get some recognition, outside of my studio dance recitals."

"You can thank Evelyn," Marty said. "She's one of the sponsors of the team, and actually was the one who convinced Heather Abrams to coach."

"Oh, that is good work." Karla clapped her hands together, which only heightened Evelyn's blush.

"Abrams studied at Julliard, didn't she?" Richard pushed away his empty plate and settled back in his chair.

"Yes." Evelyn dabbed her corner of her mouth with her napkin. "She quit her professional career when she had her children, but she's kept up her skills. I was thrilled I could convince her to coach the team."

Richard shared a look with Karla. "Maybe we should bring her into the conversation about the summer program."

"Great idea," Marty said, as he motioned for the waitress. "Anyone want coffee?"

After the waitress took our orders, Karla mentioned a few of her students who were on the Leeland dance team. "They really appreciate your support for the program," she told Marty. "Apparently, some of the other regional high schools don't have an arts administrator who champions dance."

"There are a few," Marty said, with a broad smile. "But as Richard can tell you from judging the recent competition, the quality varies. Still, we strive to keep improving things, especially during our summer programs."

His words sparked something in my brain. *Marty conducted both reunion choirs at the arts competition, so he must've worked with Claudia, Olivia, and Gwen.* Seizing an opportunity to gather more information, I leaned forward and looked Marty in the eye. "What a shame your summer arts festival was overshadowed by the recent murder."

Evelyn let out a little squeak as Karla shot me a questioning glance.

"Yes, that was unfortunate," Marty said, his smile tightening.

Evelyn toyed with the fork she'd placed on the edge of her plate. "It was such tragic news."

"Yes, tragic," Marty echoed. "And strange. Since I led the rehearsals for the reunion choirs, I'd actually seen her earlier in the week."

"How had she seemed to you?" I asked, ignoring the tightening of Richard's fingers on my knee. "I mean, did she appear worried at all, or frightened, or anything?"

"I didn't notice anything like that." Marty's shoulders, obviously tensing, rose up closer to his ears. "But then, I wasn't paying close attention to any specific chorus member."

Richard gave my knee a squeeze. "Please forgive my wife, Marty. She often aids the local authorities with research related to their cases." He glanced over at me with a warning look in his eyes. "I'm afraid she sometimes gets a little too carried away."

Marty's eyes narrowed as he studied me. "Is that right? I suppose I can understand the interest, then, but I really prefer not to talk about the death of poor Ms. Everhart."

"Oh, sorry." I yanked my leg free from Richard's grip as I sat back in my chair. "I don't know what I was thinking. I keep forgetting you knew the victim, at least casually. I apologize for bringing it up."

"It's fine. I shouldn't be so sensitive. It was just such a shock to hear she was dead, after seeing her . . . Well, so recently." Marty relaxed his shoulders. "But here's our coffee."

"Again, I apologize," I said, as the waitress handed around white ceramic mugs.

Marty swept one hand through the air with a conductor's flair. "Think nothing of it. I suppose someone who has worked with the sheriff's department in the past might be intrigued by this new case."

"There's that, and also, Zelda Shoemaker is a friend of mine. Of ours," I corrected, when Richard shot me a glance. "She's actually my Aunt Lydia's best friend. That's honestly my real interest in the case."

"In other words, you think she's innocent?" Marty asked, with a lift of his eyebrows.

"I hope to help prove she is," I said firmly.

"Totally understandable." Marty studied me for a moment as he took hold of the clenched hand his wife had placed on the table. "Now, can we switch to another subject? My wife isn't fond of talk of murders and that sort of thing."

The tension sparking across the table evaporated as we drank coffee and chatted about other, more innocuous topics. But when I left the table to head to the ladies' room, Evelyn followed me.

She was still standing by the sink when I exited the stall. "Amy, please wait a moment. I'd like to explain that little . . . hiccup," she said, glancing at the door.

Drying my hands on a paper towel, I met her worried gaze with a lift of my chin. "We're alone, if that's what concerns you."

She briefly gnawed on her lower lip before replying. "I want you to know Marty doesn't usually snap at people like that."

"Don't worry, it was my fault for bringing up such a topic," I said, eyeing her. Evelyn's obvious concern intrigued me. She

seemed intent on defending her husband from any hint of displeasure. *But then again, it does appear that she's madly in love with him*, I thought, as I tossed the wadded-up paper towel in the trash can.

"The thing is, Marty knew Claudia Everhart before this week." Evelyn twisted her hands together at her waist. "Well, not exactly knew her. They were just chance acquaintances. But she was very kind to him once. He attended a local theater production when he was a kid and was so excited, he rushed backstage to congratulate the performers. As he tells it, he was stopped and told to get out of the way in no uncertain terms by everyone except Ms. Everhart, who took it upon herself to give him a backstage tour." Evelyn dropped her arms to her sides. "He never forgot that kindness. He claims it was the impetus for him focusing on the arts as a career, and then when she was killed . . ."

"It hit him especially hard? Understandable," I said, laying a hand on her arm. "I really am sorry I brought it up. Tell him I sincerely apologize."

"I will." Evelyn's smile was wobbly, and there was a hint of tears in her eyes. *She really is protective of her husband, which is sweet*, I thought. *Although maybe a little over the top. Marty Stover doesn't seem like a guy who requires that much coddling.*

We made our way back to our table, where the rest of our party were preparing to leave.

"Thanks again for picking up the tab," Richard said. "It's very generous of you."

"Yes, very," Karla echoed.

Marty flashed a bright smile "Least I could do. After all, I did rope you two into working with our summer programs.

Two such well-known names will surely draw a lot of attention and interest, not to mention grant money."

"Richard's fame might," Karla said with a chuckle. "I'm not such a hot commodity."

Richard pointed a finger at her. "You just wait. When the folklore suite gains its audience, everyone will appreciate you, for your dancing as well as your choreography."

"As they should." I nudged Karla with my elbow. "And don't try to downplay your contribution to the project. Richard tells me you're really helping him take it to another level."

"Totally the inspirational force," Richard said, as he linked his arm with mine.

Karla tossed her sleek bob. "Oh, come on now. We all know who's the choreographic genius around here. I only add a flourish here or there."

"But that can be the most important part," Marty leaned his upper body forward, sketching a gallant bow. "Anyway, thanks for joining us this evening. I look forward to working with both of you." He turned a sharp gaze on me. "And of course, I'm delighted to have gotten to know Amy a little better too."

"It was nice to talk to you and Evelyn as well," I said, before joining in the chorus of *good evenings* and *goodbyes*.

In the car, Richard waited until we pulled out of the restaurant parking lot before making a pointed comment. "You were coming on a little strong to Marty for a bit, don't you think?"

"I was simply trying to see if he knew anything that could help Zelda," I replied, staring out the side window. "But as it turns out, his overreaction probably had to do with a prior connection to Claudia Everhart." I shared what Evelyn had told

me, adding, "I guess it hit him extra hard because he associated Claudia with his love for music and theater."

"Could be," Richard said, in a thoughtful tone. "Or maybe he was simply concerned about his wife. She did seem a little fragile. Perhaps he was simply trying to shield her from unpleasantness."

I turned my head to study his handsome profile. "Like you do me?"

Richard flashed a sidelong grin. "Hardly. But then, you are a tough little cookie, as likely to shield me as I am you."

"Right," I said, patting his arm. "Equal opportunity care and protection. Isn't that what you want in a relationship?"

Richard laid his free hand over mine. "Wouldn't have it any other way."

Chapter Eighteen

R ichard and I drove up into the mountains on Sunday afternoon to meet with Mary Gardner.

After a bumpy ride over narrow gravel roads bordered on
both sides by dense forest, we pulled up in front of a compact
one-story house. The home's white siding was contrasted by
simple black shutters and a charcoal gray tin roof. A small concrete pad covered by a simple slanted roof comprised the only
porch.

"It's pretty isolated, isn't it?" Richard slipped his keys into
the pocket of his jeans and surveyed the property. "Surprised
she lives here all alone at her age."

"She does have help with the house and yard work." I joined
him on the beaten-down grass path leading to the porch. "Kurt
makes sure of that. I think he also pays for someone to bring in
prepared meals each week."

"That's right, he and Mary are good friends from back in his
orphanage days," Richard said.

"Yeah, she worked at the orphanage when he was there, and
took him under her wing."

Richard rang the doorbell. "One thing I'll say about Kurt—if you treat him well, he can be a very loyal friend."

But what if you don't, I thought, remembering Gwen Ohlson's betrayal. It was strange Kurt had apparently forgiven her for cheating him. *Unless she has some sort of hold over him . . .*

My musing was interrupted by a reedy voice calling out, "Come in, come in. It isn't locked."

I stepped into the house with Richard on my heels. The front door opened directly onto a small living room. White lace curtains framed the windows and a gallery's worth of paintings of flowers or landscapes hung on the polished wood-paneled walls. From a previous visit, I knew Kurt had gifted her most of the artwork, some of which was quite valuable.

"Don't get up," Richard told the elderly woman ensconced in an upholstered rocking chair.

The seated woman was tiny—the blue cotton blanket she'd draped over her floral print house dress swallowed up her thin body, and her feet, clad in heavy black shoes, didn't touch the floor. "Hello, my dears," she said. "How lovely of you to visit."

I crossed to her and clasped her gnarled fingers. "Very nice to see you again, Mary. I'm sure you remember my husband, Richard, from the wedding."

Mary looked Richard up and down while squeezing my hand in her surprisingly strong grip. "Remember him? Course I do. Hard to forget, isn't he." Her smile deepened her wrinkles, but lit up her hazel eyes.

When I moved aside, Richard took Mary's fingers and pressed a kiss against the back of her hand. "Glad to hear I'm somewhat memorable."

"Oh, go on with you," Mary said when he stepped back. "You've got about as much blarney in you as that sweet-talkin' devil, Karl."

Richard looked over at me with a wink. "Well, he is family, if only by way of my great-uncle taking him in as a foster child."

"Just hope you've got as much heart as he does," Mary said, a comment that almost made me laugh. *But then again, Kurt has always treated Mary like a queen*, I thought, as the older woman motioned toward a loveseat upholstered in sunflower patterned chintz. "Please, sit, sit."

As I followed Richard over to the loveseat, I noticed its delicate wooden frame. Carved in a floral pattern, the supports were as spindly as the legs of a newborn colt. "Do you think this will hold us both?" I whispered, as he sat down.

"Hopefully," he replied, patting the cushion next to him. "If not, we owe Mary a sofa."

I settled on the edge of the loveseat, keeping most of my weight forward. "Anyway, Mary, I don't know if Kurt . . ." I cleared my throat. "Karl, that is, mentioned why we wanted to see you today. Other than to visit, I mean," I added, when Richard nudged my foot with his.

"Which is always a treat," he said.

Mary waved off this attempt at gallantry. "I know he goes by Kurt now, although I'm not sure why. Anyway, he did mention something about you wanting information from the past. Around 1970, wasn't it?"

"To be more specific, it's the summer and fall of that year. I wonder if you remember anything significant happening, especially involving Leeland High, around that time."

"There was the poor boy who almost died from a peanut allergy." Mary snorted. "Seemed strange to me at the time. We didn't have so much fuss about allergies back then."

As I leaned forward, a lock of my hair fell into my face. "I know about the incident involving Leeland High's quarterback, Earl Blair. I wondered if there was anything else, especially related to high school students." Shoving the hair behind my ear, I studied Mary's still profile. "Since you were doing presentations in the schools around that time, I thought you might've heard things from the teachers or students. Even if it's only rumors, it could help . . ."

"Zelda Shoemaker?" Mary's piercing gaze fastened on me. "I'm aware that's what this is all about, child. Don't get out much, but I do still watch the news."

"You're right, I am trying to clear her name." I cringed as the loveseat creaked when I slid back from the edge. "She's a friend, as well as one of the library's most dedicated volunteers."

Mary clucked her tongue. "Think she's innocent, do you? Well, I suppose that's as likely as not. I remember her as a girl. Always bubbly and talking a blue streak, but I never saw no harm in her. Truth be told, I can't imagine her shooting anyone."

"I don't think she did," I said, gripping my knees with both hands.

Richard covered one of hands with his. "Unfortunately, Mary, the authorities felt they had enough cause to arrest her. I don't know if you heard that or not, but at any rate, we think it's a miscarriage of justice. She's out on bail now, but we're still trying to clear her and feel it would help her case if we could find other people with motives for killing Claudia Everhart."

"Hmmm . . . Let me think." Mary hunched her shoulders and stared down at her entwined hands. "I recall the Blair boy almost dying, for sure. That was all the talk at the time. Pretty much the only thing anyone was chattering about there for a while." She lifted her head to meet my inquisitive gaze. "But another thing happened around about the same time. I recall it being something tragic and thinking it should've gotten more attention."

"A tragedy?" Richard flashed me a raised-eyebrow look. "That sounds like it would've overshadowed the Earl Blair situation. I mean, he lived, even if it was touch and go for a few days."

Mary tapped her temple with one finger. "That's it— someone died. Not the football player, or that would've turned into an even bigger flapdoodle than it was."

"Someone who died around the same time Earl Blair suffered the anaphylaxis attack?" I asked, leaning forward again in anticipation of her response.

Mary bobbed her head. "There was a car accident right around the same time. A girl, I think it was. I don't remember any details, but I know it was a high school student. Not at Leeland, though, so it wasn't big news in the Taylorsford area. The Blair boy's story overshadowed everything else for a while. This accident was about a week after he got taken to the hospital, so it didn't get much attention around here."

I sat up straighter. This information confirmed the story Karla had shared. "You really don't remember the young woman's name?"

"Sorry, if I ever knew it, it's flown plumb out of my head. She was a student at Stonebridge, I think."

Just like Claudia Everhart. I tensed, hoping to hear something that would help exonerate Zelda.

Mary pulled the blanket tighter. "Wasn't no foul play or nothing like that, so I don't know what it would have to do with a current murder, but I remember thinking it was a shame to have two young people struck down within a couple of weeks."

I side-eyed Richard, who had shifted his weight on the loveseat a couple of times as if he too was excited. But he just looked puzzled. *Probably wondering why I even care about such a thing, since it doesn't seem to have any connection to Zelda. But if there's any possibility Claudia Everhart was involved in a crash that killed someone else . . .* "Who was at fault in the accident? Do you remember?"

"No one, except for the victim. Was one of those single-car crashes. The driver ran off the road and into a tree, best as I recall."

So not a reason for anyone to seek revenge. I shook my head. "That's sad, but I guess not related to anything that might've made someone hate Claudia Everhart enough to kill her."

"Laws, no. I can't imagine anyone holding a grudge over that, tragic as it was. It was an accident, pure and simple." Mary's gaze reminded me of the unblinking stare of a hawk. "Are you truly thinking the Everhart woman was killed over something that happened in the past?"

"That's Amy's working theory," Richard said. "And I guess the authorities think so as well, since they're looking at Zelda Shoemaker as the shooter. They've uncovered evidence that she and Claudia Everhart feuded in the past, and believe that might be a motive."

"Over that Blair boy, wasn't it? I remember some chitter-chatter about those two getting into it." Mary's thin lips quirked into a smile. "The high school girls liked to talk, even when I was giving my presentations, but I soon put a stop to that."

"Yeah," I said. "They were both dating Earl Blair, and supposedly found out about his two-timing behavior right before they all attended an arts event where their choral groups competed against one another."

"Seems to me those girls should've been angry with the Blair boy, not each other, but I know how such things go." As Mary straightened, she released the edges of the blanket and allowed it to fall away from her shoulders. "Now, can I get you all anything to eat or drink? I've got lemonade and cookies in the kitchen."

"You don't have to bother," Richard said.

"It's no bother. Ruth made up a platter of cookies and some lemonade this morning, when she dropped off my weekly meals. I confess the cookies came from a box, but they aren't bad." Mary scooted to the edge of her rocking chair. "Hold on—might take me a minute."

Leaping up, Richard crossed to her in a few strides. "Here, I can help," he said, offering her his arm to lean on as she struggled to her feet.

"Thank you kindly," Mary said.

Richard tucked her arm through his and pulled her closer to his side. "You're quite welcome. May I escort you into the kitchen, ma'am?"

Mary's eyes twinkled. "Well now, don't let it be said I'd ever spurn the attentions of a handsome young man."

I chuckled and followed them as Richard gracefully guided her into the kitchen.

With its robin's-egg blue solid surface countertops, gleaming stainless appliances, and pale yellow walls, the kitchen was as cheerful as the sunlight streaming through its windows. Knowing Kurt had paid for this renovation, and others, on Mary's 1940s home, reminded me he could be a very good friend indeed. *As long as you don't cross him*, I thought, while Richard settled Mary in a wooden rocking chair next to an electric heater.

That thought reminded me of Gwen again. "By the way, Mary, do you happen to remember a girl named Gwen Ohlson? She would've been in the same class at Leeland as my Aunt Lydia and Zelda Shoemaker."

Mary rocked back and forth for a moment before replying. "Was she tall and fair? I remember a girl who could've been Karl's sister, although of course they weren't related. But they had the same Scandinavian sort of looks, like those old-time Vikings."

I shared a conspiratorial look with Richard, who'd hauled over two chairs from the kitchen table. He and I knew Kurt's nickname when he been involved in drug dealing as a young man had been "The Viking." But I was pretty sure Mary didn't know about that, and I wasn't going to be the one to enlighten her.

"Yes, that was probably her." I plopped down in one of the chairs. "She was back in Taylorsford recently, for the special arts program at Leeland, and . . . Well, I wondered if you'd ever heard anything concerning her. Anything negative, I mean."

"Another one on your list?" Mary's thin eyebrows arched over her hazel eyes. She glanced at Richard. "Young man, since you're still on your feet, would you mind grabbing the plate of cookies on the counter?"

"I'll do better than that. I see some paper plates stacked over there too. Why don't I bring over some cookies for each of us, as well as the lemonade, which I assume is in the fridge?"

"It is. Thank you, my dear." Mary cast him an approving glance. "You'd better hang onto that one," she told me. "He's a keeper."

"Absolutely," I replied, catching a glimpse of Richard's grin before I turned back to face Mary again. "Now, about Gwen Ohlson—you do remember seeing her at Leeland, then?"

"Yes, but I can't say I recall hearing anything bad about her. There was this girl she hung out with some who did get in a spot of trouble. Little dark-haired gal. Nice and curvy like you, Amy."

I made a face as Richard handed me a small plate of cookies and mouthed *Very nice curves.*

Fortunately, Mary didn't notice this exchange. She simply took her plate of cookies from Richard and continued her story as he headed for the refrigerator. "Yes, that's the one. She got in a fight during one of my presentations. Just words, mind you, but I had to send her to the office. She didn't like that one little bit. Mouthed off at me something fierce."

"Olivia Rader," I said under my breath, adding when Mary shot me a questioning look, "You would've known her as Olivia Bell."

"That's right. I remember the name now, because I told one of the teachers I'd like to ring her like a bell." Mary's laughter

shook her bony shoulders. "Heavens, hadn't thought of that since I don't know when."

Richard returned with two glasses of lemonade. He set one on the side table next to Mary's rocker before handing the other to me. "Wait a minute, I'm going to grab mine," he said. "Keep talking, I can hear you."

"Better appreciate that. It's one of the blessings of youth," Mary called after him. "Along with romance and such," she added, shifting her focus back to me. "Always good to count your blessings in that area."

"Oh, I do," I assured her.

"So do I." Richard leaned in to kiss my cheek before he sat down. He gestured toward me with his glass of lemonade. "I waited a long time to find this one, but it was definitely worth it."

Heat flushed my cheeks. "Same," I said, before taking a gulp of lemonade.

Mary slapped her knees with her hands as she laughed again. "You two are cuter than kittens in a basket. Makes me happy just to see you, I swear."

Armed with information that could drive further research into the past, and convinced Mary probably didn't have more to share that might help the investigation, I switched the conversation to Richard and Karla's dance collaboration. "They've incorporated a lot of the folk tales you've shared through the library's oral history project," I told her.

"Glad I could help out," Mary replied, after finishing off the cookie she'd been nibbling on. "I'm also thrilled to pieces that the library's preserving all those old stories. I'd hate for a lot of the folk history of this area to die when I do."

"It won't, I promise. Anyway, I bet you're going to be around for many more years yet," I said.

Mary lifted her glass of lemonade with both hands. "From your lips to God's ears," she said, before taking a swallow. Lowering her hands, she smiled at us over the rim of the glass. "Truth is, as Karl often tells me, I'm too ornery to die anytime soon. He says the devil isn't ready to deal with me yet."

"I doubt it'll be the devil who greets you," Richard said. "I bet the angels will scoop you up first, anxious to hear all your fabulous stories."

Mary pointed her glass at him. "Now you're just sweet talking again. I won't be taken in by such flattery, young man. I'm too old to fall for that sort of thing." She turned to me with a wink. "But between us, we have to admit that's a lie, don't we, dear?"

"Yes, but we shouldn't let him know." I cast Richard a loving smile. "I wouldn't want to turn his head."

"You mean, like this?" Richard swiveled in his chair and leaned over to kiss me again, this time on the lips.

Mary's laughter rang out, tinny as a string of rusty bells. "You must promise me to bring him back for a visit soon," she told me. "Haven't felt so young in quite a while."

"Perhaps I should ask your friend Karl to accompany him," I said. "Then you could enjoy double the charm."

Mary pressed her hand to her breast. "Laws, child, I'm not so sure my heart could take that."

This time, it was Richard who laughed.

Chapter Nineteen

M onday was another busy day, so it was Tuesday before I could sneak out to the archives to do a little more primary sources research.

I'd already scoured the internet, and our digitized newspaper resources, for any news on the car accident both Karla and Mary had mentioned, to no avail. Since the accident had occurred in another county, I wasn't sure our archives would hold any clippings referencing it, but felt I had to at least make the effort to rule that out. According to Aunt Lydia, the typically sociable Zelda had holed up in her home ever since making bail, refusing to talk to anyone except Walt. If concern for her well-being hadn't been enough to drive my research, my aunt's haunted eyes would've done so.

Sunny agreed to watch over the library while I was in the archives. "The least I can do for Zelda," she said. "I really hope you find something to help her case."

"I'm afraid I won't. I already searched the clipping files from the early seventies and didn't see anything about an accident involving a high school student," I told her.

"But you weren't looking for that info at the time." Sunny said. "It's easy to skim past something when your focus is elsewhere."

"True. Anyway, I have to make sure, one way or the other." I thanked her for her help before heading for the library's back door.

Entering the archives, I was confronted by an entire corps de ballet of dust motes dancing in the sunlight spilling in from the open door. As I flicked on the lights before closing the door, I made a mental note to enlist our volunteers in a cleaning project. It was easy to forget the archives because it was so rarely used by the public, but I didn't want to neglect the space. It played an important role in preserving the history of the area.

I surveyed the shelves for any boxes that might contain information on nearby counties, finally discovering one possibility, marked "Miscellaneous Clippings, 1960–1980." The lid of this box was covered in a thick layer of dust, telling me it hadn't been pulled off the shelf in years.

I cleaned off the box with an old towel we kept on the worktable. Lifting the lid released an acrid odor that immediately told me this particular collection of clippings had never been transferred into acid-free envelopes.

"Not good," I said aloud, as I pulled on a pair of white cotton gloves. Paper from that time period likely contained acids, which meant the clippings could've yellowed and crumbled since being filed.

Since the labels on many of the folders had either curled back or fallen off, I decided to remove all the folders and lay them out, one by one, on the tabletop. I then slid any folders dating from the sixties or eighties to one side of the large table,

before gingerly opening each of the others to determine which ones definitely dated from the early seventies.

Only one folder remained after I completed this process. I wasn't surprised by this dearth of material—any clippings specifically related to Taylorsford or its surrounding county would've been filed in other boxes. This was the flotsam and jetsam someone had saved for unknown reasons.

The clippings were piled randomly in the folder. Some tore when I lifted them, no matter how gently I tried to pry them apart. Swearing under my breath, I wondered how this box had escaped processing when everything else had been placed in acid-free envelopes. Of course, that had happened prior to my tenure as library director. It was possible available funds, always tight, hadn't allowed for processing nonessential materials. I couldn't really blame my predecessor if that was the case—acid-free storage supplies were expensive.

I skimmed the materials shoved in the folder, looking for any mention of car accidents. After making my way through about two-thirds of the pile, I finally spied a crumpled piece of newsprint containing a short article referencing a "tragic one-car collision." Laying the small square of paper on the table, I smoothed out its wrinkles with one gloved finger, working delicately to avoid smudging the ink.

The article was only a few sentences, but it did offer a name—Patricia Johnson, known as "Patty" to her family and friends. The only other information provided was that she was an eighteen-year-old senior at Stonebridge High School, and that neither drugs nor alcohol were contributors to the single-car accident.

I peered at the article, as if the intensity of my stare could miraculously produce additional text, but there was nothing more, only a notation at the end that this was a "developing story." This sent me diving back into the pile of clippings, searching for subsequent articles covering the story, but my search proved futile.

Slipping the article into one of the empty acid-free folders we kept in a nearby file cabinet, I returned all of the pulled folders to the box. But I left the box on the table, planning to ask one of our volunteers to properly process it soon. After locking up the archives, I returned to the library with the acid-free folder in hand.

"Find something?" Sunny asked, as I joined her at the circulation desk.

"Not much, but I'm hoping I can discover more online now that I have a name," I replied, waving the folder.

Sunny fiddled with the scrunchie fastening her high ponytail. "A name for who?"

"It's probably not important, but you know how I like to trace every loose thread." I smiled when Sunny nodded. "Anyway, it's something Mary Gardner mentioned—an accident that happened right around the time Earl Blair was hospitalized."

"After the state arts completion, then." Sunny yanked the scrunchie free and shook out her glossy hair. "Sorry, that darn thing was giving me a headache. Happens sometimes."

"Which is one reason I don't grow my hair out quite so long," I replied. "But yes, soon after that event." I opened the folder and double-checked the date on the article. "About a week later, actually."

Sunny moved closer, peering at the article over my shoulder. "What's this got to do with Zelda?"

"Probably nothing." I slid the article back into the folder. "I thought maybe, if there was a connection to an old crime . . . Well, it's been known to happen."

Sunny shrugged. "Far too often lately. But this was a one-car accident, with no possible involvement of Claudia Everhart. I can't imagine anyone biding their time over the decades and finally seeking revenge."

It was such a perfect match to my own thought process that I chuckled. "Okay, got me. I was hoping I'd find something to link Claudia to a tragedy in the past."

"She might still have been involved in Earl Blair's near-death experience, though." Sunny made a face. "I forgot to ask Jane Tucker about that. Sorry."

"It's okay. I did get some information from Aunt Lydia, who had a recent conversation with Jane. And honestly, you aren't required to be my leg man, or I guess, woman."

Stretching out a slender but well-shaped, lightly tanned leg, Sunny said, "Darn. I wore a skirt today and everything."

"Very nice," I said, with a roll of my eyes. "Okay, let me put this folder in the workroom and then you can take a break from the desk."

Sunny flashed me a grin. "To shelve? Thanks for nothing, boss."

"No, a real break, silly. The volunteers can shelve later." I tapped her arm before I headed for the workroom. "Besides, you outrank me now. You're the mayor and preside over the town council. I'm just the lowly library director."

"Yeah, right." Sunny wrinkled her nose at me. "When I work here, I'm the assistant and you're the boss. That's how it's been, and that's how it always will be."

I pointed the folder at her. "Unless you become director one day."

"I don't have the proper qualifications," Sunny said.

"You have a college degree, and the experience."

"Not an MLS, though." Sunny's expression grew thoughtful. "I suppose I could get one, if I wanted. One of the state U's offers a mostly online program. I mean, if you ever wanted to leave, for some reason. Even if only for a year or two." Sunny made a cradle out of her arms and rocked them side to side. "I could hold down the fort."

I widened my eyes, realizing the implication of her gesture. The truth was, I hadn't really considered what I'd do about my job if Richard and I had a baby. I knew Richard wanted children, and I wasn't opposed to the idea, but hadn't thought through all the complications posed by his busy, erratic schedule as well as my career.

You're thirty-five. You don't have forever, my brain reminded me as I stared at Sunny, realizing she seemed to have given the subject more thought than I had. Taken aback, I flapped the folder at her and hurried into the workroom without replying.

The rest of morning went by without incident. With Sunny leading story hour in the children's room, and Bill happy to shelve several carts of books, I even had time to conduct some online investigation on Patty Johnson. Most of my searches were dead ends, until a photograph listing her name in its caption popped up on my screen.

I leaned in closer. The picture looked eerily familiar. There was something about the background, and the young, dark-haired woman featured in the forefront of the scene . . .

Letting fly a word not in the least professional, I stared at the photo again. It depicted a production of *Brigadoon*, just like the picture Uncle Andrew had given Kurt—the same community theater production that had included Olivia and Gwen as chorus members. I read the caption more closely. *Stonebridge high schooler Patty Johnson as Jean MacLaren*, it said, before listing the play's upcoming dates and details on ticket sales.

So there is a connection between Patty Johnson and Olivia and Gwen, I thought. *Not to mention Claudia Everhart, who, according to Andrew, got into a scuffle with Olivia during that production. All of them were involved, including a girl who later died.*

But Patty Johnson hadn't been killed until a few months later, after the state arts competition. Had she been a part of that event as well? I downloaded a copy of the page from the digitized paper and sent it to the workroom printer. Another avenue I'd need to explore, somehow.

Yearbooks. They always list activities, especially for the seniors. If Patty Johnson was in the Stonebridge chamber choir, I bet the yearbook will mention it. I jotted down a note to call the librarian at Stonebridge High School. Although school hadn't started yet, I assumed the teachers and other staff, like Richard at the university, were already at work, preparing for the fall term.

Of course, all of this research was moot if it didn't lead to anyone with a reason to kill Claudia Everhart many years later. But the coincidences were still striking. Patty Johnson, Claudia, Olivia, Gwen, and Earl Blair had all interacted in the past, at

least casually. *And Zelda too,* I reminded myself. *She was mixed up in the choir stuff, and maybe the play production too. Which is something I should probably find out more about.*

I grabbed my cell phone from my purse and put in a call to Zelda. She didn't pick up, but I was able to leave a message telling her I intended to stop by after work and begging her to talk to me. I made certain to mention my determination to uncover any information that could prove her innocence.

As soon as I completed my call, Sunny beckoned me back to the desk.

"This is so weird," she said, when I joined her. She was holding a book in one hand and a small envelope in the other. "Bill brought this to the desk. He found it lying on one of the tables in the reading room."

"The book or the envelope?" I asked.

"Both. The envelope was in the book, but with one corner sticking out, so it was very noticeable."

"That's not really strange," I said, as Sunny placed the book on the counter. "You know we find things in books all the time. People are always shoving items between the pages as bookmarks, then forgetting to remove them."

"But the book wasn't checked out. Someone must've pulled it off the shelf and placed this inside." Sunny waved the envelope in my face. "It's addressed to you."

"What?" I grabbed the envelope and stared at the block-printed letters that said: *Deliver to Amy Muir.*

"An admirer, maybe? I sure hope it's that, and not some stalker," Sunny said.

I ripped into the envelope. "Probably just a disgruntled patron who didn't want to make a complaint face-to-face."

Sunny circled around behind me as I unfolded the piece of plain white paper that had been placed inside the envelope. "What's it say?"

I opened my fingers, allowing the note to drift to the countertop. "Can you hand me a folder? I need to make sure no one else touches the envelope or the paper."

"What? Why?" Sunny grabbed a manila folder from a stack we kept on a shelf under the desk. "Don't tell me it contains a threat."

"I'm afraid so." I gingerly picked up the note by one corner and placed it and the envelope inside the folder. "It was a warning, telling me to stop digging into the past or investigating any other information connected to Claudia Everhart's death."

Sunny's blue eyes widened. "Or else?"

"Or I might find myself in serious danger." Feeling strangely calm, I took two steps back and crossed my arms over my chest, while my gaze remained locked on the folder.

"Good heavens, we need to call Brad immediately." Sunny moved closer and encircled my waist with her arm. "Was it handwritten?"

"Probably printed off a computer. I guess the authorities can still gather some information about the make and model of the printer, but there's no handwriting to analyze."

"Except on the envelope." Sunny drew me closer to her side. "Even though it's block printing, they might be able to decipher some clues. I guess there wasn't a signature?"

"No, but the writer obviously had to know I was conducting research in an effort to help Zelda's cause." I pressed my palm to my forehead. "But the truth is—a lot of people knew that, including the women involved in the recent choral group reunions."

"And Kurt, and me, and anyone with half a brain, since you've helped the authorities solve several murders over the past few years." Sunny gave my waist a final squeeze before she dropped her arm. "Who else?"

"Karla and Aunt Lydia, not that I suspect them. Marty Rader and his wife. Of course, you've probably mentioned it to Fred, and I'm sure Hugh is aware of what's going on. I mean, it's mostly people who I'm sure wouldn't harm me, but if they mentioned it to anyone else . . ." I snapped my fingers. "Jane Tucker would know, as well. Aunt Lydia talked with her about Earl recently, and mentioned something about my research, including uncovering information on his severe allergy attack at the arts competition. She told me Jane had a way to reach Earl in an emergency. What if Jane Tucker already had some suspicions about Earl connected to Claudia's murder, and decided to warn him? She could've shared that I was looking at him as a possible suspect."

"It's possible. Even if her son is the chief deputy, Jane may feel a sense of obligation toward her brother. She's really big into family. Which means we have to consider the fact that Earl Blair could be back in the area."

"And looking to silence anyone who could connect him with Claudia's murder, like me." I stared at the folder for a moment before meeting Sunny's concerned gaze. "Would you have recognized him if he'd walked into the library?"

"Maybe. I've seen photos at Jane's house, and Brad does bear a resemblance to him, so I might have noticed. But then again, I was so busy this morning while you were in the archives . . ."

"He could've slipped in and out without anyone seeing him," I agreed, with a gusty sigh. "Okay, I guess my best bet is to call Brad and have one of his deputies stop by to collect the envelope and note. I'm also definitely going to follow through on my plan to talk to Zelda after work today."

Sunny used both hands to flip her hair behind her shoulders. "She agreed to that?"

"Not really. I called and left a message, telling her I was coming by. But I think if I camp out on her porch long enough, she'll probably agree to see me." I shrugged. "I hope."

"Worth a try, anyway," Sunny said.

I stared out into the library. Someone had strolled in and pulled a book to leave that note for me. Either they didn't think they'd be noticed or they were familiar enough with the library's floor plan to surreptitiously reach the stacks and the reading room area. It was possible, if you knew your way around. *Or perhaps they simply waited until Sunny was distracted enough not to register their entry and exit*, I reminded myself.

In any case, someone had violated my workspace in order to threaten me. It had happened before, but not quite so blatantly. Not while the library was open and there were people in the building.

I squared my shoulders. It was one thing to threaten me, but I certainly didn't want any of my staff or patrons to be

placed in danger, if only by rubbing elbows with a possible murderer. Time to talk to Brad again and share my thoughts, no
matter how far-fetched they might appear. He needed to take
action and diligently investigate everyone on my list of possible
suspects.

I frowned. *Even if one of my top suspects is his uncle.*

Chapter Twenty

B rad wasn't exactly thrilled to get my call but grudgingly admitted that some of the information I provided might prove helpful.

"I just don't like the idea of you putting yourself in danger to collect any more info," he said, after promising to send someone to pick up the envelope and threatening note. "For one thing, I don't want to have to face you-know-who if anything bad were to happen."

"Richard knows what I'm doing," I replied. "He doesn't always like me taking risks, but he understands why I do. And realizes it would be difficult to stop me," I added with a little laugh.

"I meant Sunny," Brad said, in a tone that told me he was only half-joking.

The rest of the day proved uneventful, which I considered a blessing. I left work at five, after leaving a message on Richard's phone telling him I'd be home later than usual.

Since the weather had predicted possible thunderstorms, I'd driven to work. It was still dry when I left the library, but I

knew it was only a matter of time before the bottom fell out, as ominous clouds were clustered over the mountains like an anxious herd of Angus cattle.

I parked in Zelda's driveway, behind her cherry red sedan. Strolling up the flagstone path that bisected her neat front yard, I rehearsed a few opening lines I hoped would entice her to speak with me.

As soon as I climbed the concrete steps to the porch, the looming storm unleashed its fury. The hanging ferns swung wildly as rain pelted the porch roof above me and thunder rumbled like an approaching train. I pressed the doorbell repeatedly, all the while keeping an eye on the bolts of lightning illuminating the dusky sky.

After a crack of thunder rattled the boards under my feet, the heavy wooden door finally swung open and Zelda appeared, staring blankly at me through the screen door.

"You'd better come in," she said, in a voice with the monotone quality of an automaton.

From the wariness lurking in her light brown eyes, I realized the storm had been a blessing in disguise. I wasn't sure Zelda would've allowed me entry if she hadn't been worried for my safety.

Another shotgun blast of thunder followed me into the house. "Thanks. I'm not scared of storms, but loitering outside in one doesn't exactly thrill me."

Zelda didn't reply as she led me into her living room, which was a long, narrow space with a wall of windows opening onto the porch. Like Zelda, at least in her normal state, the décor in the room was bright and cheerful. Olive green and purple

pillows were scattered across the cream-colored damask covering the sofa and matching armchairs, an iridescent painting hung over the white-painted brick fireplace, and a bold hand-woven floral tapestry covered one of the moss green walls.

Zelda motioned toward one of the upholstered chairs. "Please, sit down. Would you like something to drink? I have water or iced tea—or coffee, of course, but it's too hot for that, don't you think?"

I examined Zelda with concern. Eschewing her typically vivid and stylish outfits, she was wearing a loose gray blouse over a pair of black yoga pants. *She's lost weight*, I thought as I studied her wan face. Gray roots betrayed an uncharacteristic lack of maintenance of her golden curls, and the color that typically blushed her cheeks had faded like the petals of a frost-blighted rose.

"I don't need anything, thanks." I placed my purse in my lap as I sat down in one of the armchairs.

Zelda sank into the cushions at one end of the sofa. *The one farthest from my chair*, I noticed. "Forgive me for not offering anything else," she said, her voice almost drowned out by another roll of thunder. "I simply haven't felt like cooking or baking lately."

"Totally understandable, and anyway"—I patted my abdomen—"I don't really need to eat anything extra today."

This comment seemed to rouse Zelda from her lethargy. "Now, lamb, you're perfectly fine as you are. My father used to say a man wanted something to grab hold of on a woman. Not everyone needs to be a stick."

I smiled, realizing Zelda was betraying her own defensiveness over this topic. Even though she'd recently lost a few

pounds, she was still plump. "That's never going to be my problem, but thanks." I drummed the chair arm with my fingers. "How have you been? I know the past few weeks must've been awful for you."

"I'm hanging in there." A flash of lightning illuminated the windows and turned Zelda's face into a macabre mask. "It's all I can do, really. Until all this mess is sorted, anyway."

I scooted to the front edge of my chair. "That's the thing—I want to offer my assistance. With the sorting, I mean. I've already done some research and uncovered additional people with connections to Claudia Everhart. That is, others who might've had some reason to shoot her."

"Oh, I don't know. It's all ancient history." Zelda glanced behind her as a low rumble filled the room. "Sounds like the storm's dying down a bit."

If she was dangling a lure for me to leave, I wasn't biting. "What I'm trying to say is, I may have uncovered a few individuals who had run-ins with Claudia in the past, or other reasons to hate her. Maybe even enough to drive them to murder."

"Surely the killer's motive had to be more recent."

"Not necessarily. Think about the murders I've helped investigate over the last few years. Long-term grievances definitely played a part in those. Which is why I wanted to ask a couple of questions about your relationship with Gwen Ohlson and Olivia Rader, and Earl Blair, of course."

Whatever color remained on Zelda's face vanished like sandy footprints swept away by a rising tide. "Heavens, why? I hardly knew them. Well, except for Earl. And that was a tempest in a teapot, you know. Everyone thought I hated Claudia

because she was dating Earl at the same time, but honestly, I wasn't overly upset." Zelda squared her shoulders. "Not at all, as a matter of fact."

I met her challenging gaze with a smile. "Aunt Lydia told me the same thing. She said you always had your heart set on Walt, and anyone else was simply a casual fling."

"Right as rain. I was never truly interested in anyone else, except for my husband, of course. He was the only other man I ever really loved. Earl Blair was just a distraction." Zelda toyed with one of her limp curls and glanced back out the window. "Definitely letting up outside."

I ignored this attempted distraction. "I assume that means you wouldn't have been angry enough to slip him a cupcake that would activate his peanut butter allergy."

"Absolutely not," Zelda said firmly. "I mean, I wouldn't have anyway, no matter how ticked off I was. I knew all about Earl's allergy and how deadly something like that could be."

"Who do you think did it, then—Claudia?"

Zelda bobbed her head. "That was my guess. She was a real drama queen, always flying off the handle over the least little thing. I could see her giving Earl that cupcake. Not wanting to kill him, mind you. Only to get a little of her own back when she found out he was two-timing her. I'd never have done such a thing, but she might have."

"Do you think Earl ever figured it out?" I asked.

"Hard to say. He wasn't the brightest bulb in the string, if you know what I mean. He was a looker, but not a keeper." The ghost of a smile flickered across Zelda's wan face. "Like I said, for me he was merely a distraction. I think Claudia

Everhart was more invested in their relationship, so it hit her harder."

"It does seem like she had a temper." I stared at the painting over the mantel for a moment, realizing it depicted a collection of seashells. "In fact, Kurt Kendrick told me a story he heard from my Uncle Andrew. Something about a fight during a production of *Brigadoon* put on by the community theater the summer before your senior year . . ."

Zelda cut me off with a wave of her hand. "I wasn't involved in that."

"But Claudia was, along with Gwen Ohlson and Olivia Rader, or Olivia Bell as she was known back then." I fiddled with the buckle on my purse as I studied Zelda's face. "I wonder if you ever heard anything about a fight breaking out between Olivia and Claudia. They apparently got into it at one point, at least according to my uncle."

"I heard some chatter, but figured it was one of those silly young girl things." Zelda shifted her position on the sofa and turned her face away from me.

"You did know both Gwen and Olivia, I assume? From the chamber choir, if nowhere else."

Zelda's entire body visibly stiffened. "Yes."

"Do you think either one of them could've held a grudge against Claudia? I know it doesn't seem like some minor high school feud from ages ago would lead to murder, but I've encountered stranger motives."

"I have no idea." Zelda sucked in an audible breath before turning to face me. "I'd say Earl Blair was the more likely suspect. Don't think I mentioned his temper yet, but he sure had one."

"Really?" *She seems awfully eager to push me off the subject of Gwen or Olivia*, I thought as I attempted to discern anything definitive from her expression. "Was that something you personally experienced?"

"I'm afraid so. He had a short fuse and liked to throw his weight around. Which was honestly another reason I wasn't broken up when I found out about Claudia. Good riddance to bad rubbish, I told people later." Zelda's lips twisted. "Although I'm afraid I did play up my indignation at the time. I thought I was supposed to, and was afraid the other girls would call me out if I didn't make something of a fuss." Zelda shook her head. "So foolish. It's what makes me look bad now, when at the time it was just me trying to fit into a clique."

I sat back against my chair cushions, weighing my next words. "Aunt Lydia mentioned you two weren't as close after you joined the chamber choir."

"That was the worst thing, me ignoring her and Walt for quite some time. My two best friends, and I treated them like dirt. All so I could be a part of something that made my life . . ." Zelda lowered her head and used her fingertip to sweep away the moisture seeping from her eyes. "That wasn't worth it, in the end."

"But you dropped out of the choir right after the arts competition," I said, keeping my tone light.

Zelda's head snapped up. "Because I wanted to. It was my choice, and not due to any so-called *indiscretion*, despite what that little alley cat Claudia Everhart said."

The fire in her eyes made me question, for the first time, whether she could've shot someone. "Why do you think she spread such rumors?"

223

"To implicate me as the one who gave Earl the cupcake, of course." Color had returned to Zelda's face, but in the form of two hectic red circles staining her cheeks. "It was a case of the guilty dog barking first, if you ask me."

"Trying to deflect from her own actions," I said thoughtfully.

"That's what I always believed." Zelda primly placed her hands in her lap and altered her expression. "Which is why I left the choir. Most of the members swallowed the rumors Claudia spread, hook, line, and sinker. They were happy to think the worst of me. So I quit."

I sucked in my cheeks as I studied Zelda's face. She'd probably hoped her change of expression read as tolerant resignation, but I'd spied something else. *Something like calculation*, I thought, wondering why she felt compelled to lie about the real reason she'd dropped out of the chamber choir. "I see. That does makes sense."

"I didn't like the way some of the girls in the choir talked about Lydia, either," Zelda said. "Just because she'd been orphaned and was being raised by that hoity-toity grandmother of hers. It wasn't Lydia's fault Rose Litton was, well, *strange*."

"That she was," I said, remembering everything I'd learned about my great-grandmother. "But, getting back to the question of who else could be considered a suspect in Claudia's death, what about Olivia or Gwen? I think Earl Blair is a given, but do you believe it's possible there was significant animosity between either of those girls and Claudia?"

Zelda fixed her gaze on me, narrowing her eyes as if she'd just realized what I was implying. "You're not thinking one of them might've shot Claudia, are you? Because I can't say . . ."

She covered her mouth and coughed. "Excuse me. Now, where was I? Oh yes, Gwen or Olivia as the shooter? I don't think so. No."

I met her intense stare without faltering. "There's not even a small possibility? It might help your own case if you could think of anything that might give them a motive."

"There's nothing," Zelda replied, before tightening her lips into a thin line.

She was blinking a little too much for me to believe her, but I decided not to push. "The deputies did find a blackmail note on Claudia's body," I said, keeping my tone light. "I don't suppose you know anything about that?"

Zelda shook her head so vigorously her curls bounced like tendrils on a windblown vine. "Heavens, no. I can't imagine what earthly reason would make her carry anything like that around, unless . . ." Her eyes widened. "Maybe it's something Earl sent her? If he ever did find out she was the one to slip him the cupcake, he could've been asking for money to keep his mouth shut about her crime."

She looked so triumphant I didn't bother to point out the fallacy in her argument. Responsibility for a nonfatal accident from years past didn't seem like the sort of thing anyone would pay blackmail to keep under wraps. *Unless*, I thought, my own eyes widening, *Earl was dim enough to think someone would, and he needed money, but Claudia refused to pay . . .*

"You know, you may have hit on something there." I jumped to my feet. "It could be the reason Earl took action now, so many years after his traumatic experience. If he recently discovered proof Claudia Everhart was the one who gave him that

cupcake, he could've decided to take advantage of that fact to blackmail her."

Zelda stood as well, but turned her back to me. "Could be," she said as she replaced the sofa pillows she'd tossed aside when she sat down.

"Well, I won't take up more of your time." I grabbed my purse from off the floor and slipped the strap over my shoulder. "I'm glad we got a chance to chat, though."

Zelda chopped her hand down onto one of the pillows to perfect her arrangement before straightening and staring out the window. "Looks like the storm's let up, for sure. It should be safe for you to drive home now." She turned to me, a broad smile plastered on her face. "Thank you so much for stopping by, Amy. You're such a dear to concern yourself with my little troubles."

"Any time," I said, before telling her goodbye.

I left, sincerely hoping my smile didn't look as fake as hers.

Chapter
Twenty-One

On the way to Brad and Alison's engagement party, Richard dropped the suggestion that we host a dinner party the following week.

"I wanted to invite Marty and Evelyn over, to thank them again for the other night," he said, as we turned onto the long gravel driveway of Jane Tucker's family farm. "I was thinking about a week from today. It's the Saturday before Labor Day."

I smoothed the full skirt of my poppy-print sundress over my knees. "How about Sunday instead, especially since Monday is a holiday. The thing is, with both Sunny and me taking off for this party, the volunteers have been forced to run the library on their own today. So I scheduled myself to work next Saturday. I felt it was only fair they should get the holiday weekend off."

"Sunday's fine with me. I'll be a week into classes, but as you say, Monday is a holiday, so I won't be teaching the next

day. Anyway, I thought we could invite Karla too, as well as Lydia and Hugh, if he's in town."

"I'm sure he will be, given the long weekend." I glanced over at Richard's handsome profile. "Anyone else?"

Richard side-eyed me before focusing back on the road. "Well, despite the fact he and Hugh sometimes clash, I'd like to ask Kurt to come. I think he and Marty could have some good conversations about the arts."

"You mean you think Kurt might agree to help fund the visual arts portion of an enhanced summer program?" I tapped Richard's shoulder. "I know how your mind works by now, mister."

Richard grinned. "You got me. But seriously, I want to support Marty's efforts to enhance the arts programs at Leeland and other schools in the area. It's honestly a bit self-serving—I need to recruit my dancers from somewhere. It would be nice to find some of them closer to home."

"I can't argue with that, especially since it could also help Karla's studio." I gazed out my window at the rippling field of orchard grass that bordered the lane. "And I'm sure Hugh and Kurt will be on their best behavior. if only because we're hosting." I glanced back at Richard. "I know the numbers are adding up, but I'd like to add Sunny and Fred to the guest list, if you don't mind."

"Why would I ever mind adding Sunny to the mix? And Fred, of course. Although I don't know him that well, he seems to be a good guy."

"He is, from what I can tell." I laid my hand on Richard's knee. "Between you and me, I think Sunny's a lot more invested in that relationship than she's willing to admit."

"Playing matchmaker, are you?" Richard cast me another grin. "Okay, we can do a buffet-style meal and set up a table on the back porch. Hopefully the weather will cooperate."

"Ten people," I said, as Richard pulled in behind a line of cars parked at the end of the driveway. "Maybe we should order some dishes from Hani. Not everything, but enough so we aren't cooking for three days."

"Sounds like a plan." Richard tapped his temple with one finger. "Always thinking, aren't you?"

"I just don't want either of us to feel overwhelmed," I said, as we climbed out of the car. "Grab the gift from the back seat before you lock up, please."

Gift in hand, we hurried across the newly mown lawn of Jane Tucker's sky blue two-story farm house, but paused at the porch steps. Although the covered front porch was decorated with gold streamers and silver balloons, the steps were blocked by a large banner printed with the words, *party this way*, and an arrow pointing to the walkway that led around the side of the house.

"Party in the back," Richard said, with a smile.

I bumped his arm with my elbow. "Hah-hah, very funny."

"Watch it, this gift is breakable, as I recall." Richard shifted the box to his other arm and crooked his elbow. "Shall we make a proper entrance, madame?"

"We can try," I said, slipping my arm through his. "But I don't know if anyone will notice. Sounds like the party's already in full swing."

A wave of voices mingled with music swept over us as we rounded the house and entered the back yard. In the center of the wide lawn, a large, white, open-sided tent had been set up

over a temporary wood floor. A significant portion of the population of Taylorsford and the surrounding county appeared to be already inside, clutching glasses and plates as they chatted, their voices rising to be heard over the music blaring from a DJ setup at the far end of the tent.

We brushed past several knots of people, acknowledging those we knew, and deposited our present on a table piled high with other gifts. Overhead, silver and gold balloons bobbed up against the white canvas ceiling, while multicolored streamers fluttered from the tent poles.

"Looks like Jane went all out," Richard said, as he guided me through the maze of guests.

I leaned in closer to his side to avoid bumping into another cluster of people. "I bet she's extra excited. Sunny claims Jane had almost given up hope of Brad ever marrying. He's in his early forties, you know."

"Even older than me," Richard looked down at me with a smile. "But like me, I think he was wise to wait for the right one."

"I couldn't agree more," I said, bouncing up on my toes to give him a kiss.

"Ah, there are our other pair of lovebirds," said a familiar voice.

We turned to face the speaker, a slender, dark-haired man in a tailored navy suit. He was holding two glasses of wine. "Hello, Hugh," Richard said. "I'd shake your hand, but it seems they are otherwise engaged."

"I'm waiting for Lydia. Again." The sparkle in Hugh's dark eyes removed any sting from his words. "It's not her fault,

though. She knows so many people here, I think she gets stopped every two seconds to chat with someone."

"That's what happens when you live in the same town your entire life," I said. "Wait, here she comes." I waved my hand over my head.

Aunt Lydia, looking elegant as always in a rose-pink silk dress and pearls, squeezed past two beefy men in polo shirts to join us. "Hi there. Quite a crowd, isn't it?"

I shrugged. "I guess it isn't every day the mother of the chief deputy, part of a family who've lived in Taylorsford for decades, throws an engagement party for him and his fiancée, whose family has lived here even longer. Just imagine the actual wedding."

"I'm sure it will be an enormous affair." Aunt Lydia took one of the wine glasses from Hugh. "But that's going to be held over near Smithsburg,"

"Right," I said. "At the bride's family place."

Richard released my arm. "I think I'll go and grab a couple glasses of wine for us. Stay here so I don't lose you in this mob."

"Will do," I said, as he melted into the crowd.

Hugh gazed into the milling group of guests as he sipped his wine. "I suppose one good thing is there's not likely to be any untoward behavior at this party, considering the number of law enforcement personnel who must be present."

"From two departments," I said. "Alison's also a deputy, but in a neighboring county."

"Ah yes, that's right." Hugh turned to Lydia. "You probably know both families."

"Not the Fryes; at least, not as well," she replied. "Of course, I'm friends with Jane Tucker. I've known her since we were both

girls. Even though she didn't live in Taylorsford proper, and was a few years older than me, we used to hang out together at church. She was always nice to me, despite the fact my grandmother could be rude to people like her parents."

"Because my great-grandmother thought our family was higher class for some reason," I told Hugh. "Jane's parents were farmers, like her late husband. I guess Jane has lived on one farm or another all her life."

"And she's the older sister of one of the people on your suspect list, isn't she?" Hugh smiled when I raised my eyebrows. "Your aunt may have mentioned your interesting theories concerning the murder of Claudia Everhart to me once or twice."

Aunt Lydia shrugged. "We don't have secrets."

"As you shouldn't," I said, holding out my hand when Richard returned with the wine.

"Navigating my way to the bar was like being backstage at a junior studio production of *The Nutcracker*," he said. "Too many bodies crushed into the same space, and half of them unsure what they're doing there."

"But you persevered. My hero." I winked before taking a swallow of wine.

"Grandmother wouldn't have been too pleasant to the Fryes either, of course." Aunt Lydia gestured with her glass toward Brad, who was helping Alison climb up onto the stage. "They lived too much like traditional mountain folk for her taste."

Hugh shared a conspiratorial look with me. "I often wonder what Rose would've thought of me."

"She would've probably fainted dead away," Aunt Lydia said dryly. "Even if you are a far better man than many of those she thought so grand."

Hugh smiled and slipped his arm around her waist.

"I'm sure a male dancer wouldn't have garnered her approval, either," Richard said, clinking his glass with mine.

Aunt Lydia shrugged her slender shoulders. "Very little did."

Feedback from the PA system crackled through the air, silencing the crowd.

"I think Brad's about to make a speech," Richard said. "Poor guy, he looks so uncomfortable."

I had to admit my husband was right—Brad's face was flushed red as a beet, and his short blond hair tousled into spikes. He clutched the microphone as if it were a tow rope pulling him to shore during a hurricane.

In contrast, the young woman standing at his side appeared perfectly calm. Alison Frye, who was ten years younger and at least eight inches shorter than her fiancé, looked especially lovely today, in a red dress that complemented her dark hair and eyes.

Brad's voice cracked as he welcomed everyone and thanked them for their presence and gifts. He only spoke a few more words, thanking his mother for the party, before handing the microphone to Alison, who offered her own words of welcome before they left the stage.

"Hello, stranger," Sunny said, laying her hand on my shoulder.

I turned to her, admiring her sleek blonde updo and the short azure dress that hugged her slender curves and complemented her blue eyes. "No Fred?"

Sunny made a face. "No. Work."

"Sorry," I said, as the DJ asked everyone to clear the center of the floor for dancing. Sunny shrugged and moved a few steps away. She was obviously trying to downplay her disappointment, but her tapping foot and laser focus on Brad and Alison, who'd taken the floor for a solo waltz before being joined by other guests, gave her away.

I leaned in to Richard. "Listen," I said, under my breath. "Could you take Sunny out for a spin on the floor? Fred isn't here to partner her, and you know how she loves to dance."

"All right, but you are dancing with me at least once before the day is out." Richard's tone dripped with mock sternness. "You're not getting out of that, not when I know you've learned enough steps to get by."

I pressed my hand to my heart. "I promise. But dance with Sunny first. And let me take your empty glass. I just spied Delbert Frye sitting over near the buffet table, and I'd like to say hello to him before he disappears. You know he's not much for these big social events."

Richard clasped my fingers for a second after handing me his glass. "Thank him again for his help with the folklore project."

"I will." As I slowly maneuvered my way through the crowd, I heard him mention the dinner invitation to Sunny, Aunt Lydia, and Hugh.

After tossing the plastic wine glasses into a bin marked *Recycling*, I crossed to a seating area set up next to the edge of the tent and made a beeline for one of the older men hanging out there.

Delbert Frye was a short, wiry man in his eighties, whose full beard still bore traces of the russet hair that must've once covered his now bald head. He lived alone in a cabin up in the mountains and had something of a reputation as a hermit, even though he'd become more social in the last few years, sharing his love of folk music. Alison was his grand-niece and, I suspected, his favorite relative, which was probably the only thing that had compelled him to attend such a crowded function.

"Hello there," I said, as I took a seat beside him. "I don't think I've seen you since my wedding. How have you been?"

Delbert's sharp-featured face brightened when he looked at me. "Very well, thank you. Keeping to myself, as I like to do, although I have seen your husband once or twice."

"Yes, and he said to thank you again. Your assistance with the music for his dance project is much appreciated."

"Glad to help. I like knowing classic folk music will be getting some attention for a change." Delbert shifted in his chair. "Not like this stuff they're playing now. Not even sure what it is."

I listened to the music filling the tent for a moment before replying. "Sounds like pop songs that have been adapted into instrumental pieces for dancing."

"Neither fish nor fowl," Delbert grimaced. "I told Alison I'd help with the music today, but that fiancé of hers is apparently friends with this DJ."

Since Delbert's musical expertise lay in building and playing dulcimers and other traditional instruments, I could see why Brad and Alison had gone in another direction. But I knew better than to share that thought, and changed the subject instead. "I never really asked, but were you acquainted with

Brad's family before he and Alison started dating? I know both your families have extensive roots in this area."

Delbert shot me a suspicious look from under his lowered eyebrows. "Heard tell of the Tuckers, because they always ran one of the biggest farms around, but I didn't really know any of them personally. Had a few more dealings with the Blairs. That's Brad's mama's kin."

"Yes, I know," I said, tempering my voice to keep from sounding too eager. "You knew Jane, then, and her brother?"

"Not really. They were just kids when I did some business with their parents. Blair had a good stand of timber, you see. I used to get some of my wood from him."

A break in the crowd allowed me a good view of the dancers. I caught sight of Richard and Sunny and halted my questioning of Delbert long enough to admire what a lovely couple they made. They were close in height, and Richard's dark hair was the perfect foil for Sunny's blonde tresses.

"Your husband's dancing with Sunny Fields, I see." Delbert cast me a sharp look. "Reckon it's okay, though. She's a trustworthy sort of gal, in my experience."

"My husband's trustworthy too," I said mildly. "Anyway, I was wondering if you knew anything about Jane Tucker's brother, Earl Blair. I thought maybe he'd show up for this party or the wedding, even though he's stayed away for so long. It's a shame, don't you think? Jane's been all alone since her husband passed years ago, except for Brad, of course. But he's so busy with his own life . . ."

"Fishin' for information, are you?" Delbert's eyes crinkled with humor. "I may live alone in a cabin up in the woods, but I

do know things. Like how you've helped out Brad with some of his investigations recently. So you needn't go all wide-eyed and innocent with me, missy. Stop beating around the bush and ask your dang questions."

My folding chair squeaked as I sat bolt upright. "Okay, then—what do you know about Earl Blair, before and after his traumatic experience? I mean, when he almost died from his peanut allergy?"

Delbert stroked his beard for a moment. "He was a right royal little brat even before he almost died. I always thought Jane was a sweetheart, but her brother had too high an opinion of himself. He was a good-looking kid, and a great athlete, so his parents, and most other folks, treated him like he was the prince of Persia or something." Delbert shook his head. "It wasn't good for his soul, to my way of thinking. I wasn't around him much, but the few times I was, I overheard him say some downright cruel stuff, even to his mama."

"Was he violent?" I asked, pleating the fabric of my dress between my fingers.

"He could be." Delbert's lips thinned. "I once saw him mistreat a dog just because it barked too much. When I told him to stop, he threatened to hit me. But I laughed in his face and he backed down. Not like he could've managed to hurt me, even though he was a generation younger." Delbert straightened, puffing out his hollow chest. "I might look like a bent sapling a big wind would blow away, but I'm actually tough as barbed wire."

"I don't doubt it." I clasped my hands in my lap. "Did Earl change after his terrible medical ordeal? I heard it was quite serious—that he even flatlined a couple of times."

"He just got quiet. Still mean, though, from what I could tell. Almost dying didn't mellow him, it only made him more withdrawn and sullen." Delbert met my questioning gaze with a tight smile. "I always said it was a good thing, him up and leaving town like he did. He wasn't sweet before, but after he came home from the hospital, he had a look in his eyes that reminded me of a trapped badger, and that's nothing you ever want to see."

"There you are." Richard, his forehead glistening with perspiration, jogged up to us. "Oh, hello, Delbert. Good to see you again. How have you been?"

"Fine and dandy, especially since I've been enjoying a little chat with your missus." Delbert stood to shake hands with Richard. "Nice to see you again too, but if you'll excuse me, I think I'll go and talk to Allie and Brad and then head home. This mob is a little too much for me."

We offered our goodbyes before Delbert wandered into the crowd.

"So, did you pump him for information?" Richard asked as he pulled me to my feet.

"I did."

"And did you get what you wanted?"

"Maybe. He did help paint a better picture of one of my top suspects," I said.

"Good." Richard slipped his arm around my waist. "Now that you've done your daily sleuthing, Nancy Drew, it's time to fulfill your promise to dance with me."

I wrinkled my nose. "Just make sure I don't fall on my face."

Richard looked down at me, his dark brows arched over his gray eyes. "Dancing with me? Never. If you so much as stumble,

I'll lift you up and transform it into a spectacular move. Everyone will think we planned it."

"You can't pick me up so easily," I scoffed.

"Oh can't I?"

Before I knew what was happening, Richard swept me up in his arms and lifted me off the ground. Thankfully, he'd grabbed me in a way that kept my skirt pressed against my legs, so I wasn't flashing everyone. Applause erupted from the crowd as Richard carried me into the middle of the dancing couples, who all backed away. Then he spun around and lifted me a little higher before setting me down in the center of the dance floor, right in front of an obviously bemused Brad and Alison.

"Good grief, man." Brad, his arm around Alison's shoulders, looked us over, amusement sparking in his blue eyes. "Way to set the bar too high."

Chapter
Twenty-Two

I was surprised by a visit from Brad on Wednesday morning. He stopped by the library as I finished leading story hour in the children's room, so he had to dodge a herd of excited kids and their weary parents before reaching me.

"Let's head into the staff breakroom," I said, motioning to a door off the children's room. "Samantha's covering the desk for another thirty minutes, which means I don't need to get back right away."

Brad clutched his hat in front of him like a shield. "Good, because I want to talk to you about some of this information you've been sharing with the department."

"Nice party the other day," I said, as I led the way into the breakroom. "I hope you didn't mind Richard making a bit of an exhibition."

"Not at all. I thought it added a certain element of fun missing up to that point." Brad flashed a grin as he took a seat across the table from me.

I waved this off with one hand. "It was one of those married people things. I questioned his abilities and he had to meet the challenge." I mirrored Brad's grin. "You'll learn all about that soon enough."

"You bet. Alison is quiet, but that doesn't mean she's a pushover."

"I'm sure she's not. But then, you seem to like women who can hold their own," I said, thinking of his former relationship with Sunny.

"Seems like it, doesn't it?" Brad's smile faded as he placed his hat on the table. "Now, getting down to business—I wanted to assure you the department is looking into everyone you seem to think could be a suspect in the Everhart case. Some were actually on our radar before you contacted me, to be honest."

My chair legs squealed against the tile floor as I pushed back from the table. "Including your uncle?"

"Yes, including Earl Blair. In fact, he's suspect number one on my list."

"Mine too." I tapped my foot against the hard floor. "Do you have any idea where he is?"

"You mean, has he been seen in the area?" Brad hooked two fingers over the knot of his tie and tugged to loosen it. "To be frank, he has been spotted. One of his old pals reported running into him in a bar in Smithsburg. Which means it's entirely possible he may also have been in the area at the time of the Everhart murder. But I'd like you to keep that between us, if you don't mind."

"Of course." I studied Brad's face for a moment, noticing the lines fanning out from the corners of his eyes and bracketing

241

his mouth. He looked tense, which was to be expected when a family member was a person of interest in a murder investigation. "Has he tried to contact your mom?"

Brad shook his head. "Not yet. I've warned her to be on her guard, but I don't know if she'll follow my suggestion and refuse to meet with him. You know how family-oriented she is. I'm afraid Earl might be able to talk his way around her defenses."

"So you've placed a watch on her house, just in case? Discretely, of course."

"Of course." A wan smile flitted across Brad's face. "Anyway, I wanted to make sure you were also being careful. Since Earl seems to still have a few contacts in the area, he might've heard about your research. You haven't exactly been subtle about it, you know."

"Well, to be fair, I've been digging into the backgrounds of other people as well, but I get your point."

"Just contact me or the department if you see him, okay? Don't try to talk to him on your own. Leave that to the professionals." Brad's stern expression told me he wasn't going to be happy if I disobeyed this request. "And not just Earl. Even though we haven't determined who wrote it yet, that note you got the other day is a warning you shouldn't ignore."

"Will do. Even though I'd do a lot to help clear Zelda, I promise I won't willingly place myself in jeopardy."

"It's the *willingly* part that worries me," Brad said, with a frown. "You've found yourself in trouble before, even without rushing into danger."

"I remember. Pretty hard to forget things like that." I scooted my chair closer and leaned over the table. "Have you

discovered anything to tie Gwen Ohlson or Olivia Rader to the crime? I still think that's worth investigating."

Brad raised his eyebrows. "Because they had a spat with the victim over fifty years ago? That's a pretty flimsy motive, Amy."

"No weaker than the evidence your department used to arrest Zelda."

"Her house, her garden, likely her gun," Brad said, ticking off each item on his fingers.

I crossed my arms over my chest. "It was her husband's gun, which Zelda says she never used. After he died, she didn't even know where he'd stashed it."

"Maybe that's true, and maybe it isn't, but whatever the case, her husband's gun wasn't found in the house when we turned the place upside down. And the make and model match the ballistics of the weapon that killed Ms. Everhart." Brad jabbed his forefinger in my direction. "You have to admit it's damning evidence."

"But again, what was Zelda's motive? A feud over some boy who was two-timing her and the victim fifty years ago? Doesn't sound any more solid than what you call Gwen and Olivia's 'flimsy' motives."

"I know, I know." Brad rubbed his forehead with the back of his hand. "That's definitely the weak link in our chain. Although there was the note found on the body. I still think either Zelda was blackmailing Ms. Everhart, or the other way around. Why, who knows? Zelda's certainly not saying."

"Which is strange." I pursed my lips as I considered this aspect of the case. "It could've been a note sent to Claudia Everhart from someone else, though, couldn't it? I mean, someone other than Zelda."

"Possibly, but if so, why confront Zelda in her garden?"

"I don't know." I sighed. "Maybe she wasn't even meeting Zelda there. She could've chosen that spot to meet someone else, because . . ." I paused, my mind drawing a blank on any reason for such an action.

"Yes, because why?" Brad grabbed his hat and rose to his feet. "That's the hundred-dollar question."

I stood up to face him. "Zelda hasn't changed her story at all, has she?"

"No, she keeps insisting she knew nothing about Claudia Everhart's visit until she heard a noise like a gunshot and ran out into the garden to find the woman dead in her gazebo. But her story doesn't hold water. Why was Ms. Everhart there, with a blackmail note in her pocket, if not to meet Zelda?"

"There has to be another reason," I hesitated for a moment before adding, "If Earl was the killer, he might've wanted to frame Zelda for the murder. Hit two birds with one stone, so to speak."

Brad's eyelashes fluttered, telling me my words had hit home. "Anyway," he said, as he strode to the door of the break-room, "you need to watch your step, Amy. I appreciate all the information you've shared with us, but there's still a murderer on the loose. Regardless of who they are, a lot of people know you've been conducting research to help the investigation. Judging by that threatening note, the killer could easily know that too."

"I'll be careful, but I can't promise to stop digging," I said. "I can't let Zelda, or my aunt, down. I have to do everything I can to help clear Zelda's name."

"I know." Brad's smile was sad, but sincere. "Just keep me in the loop, and I mean the minute you uncover anything else, okay?"

"Cross my heart," I said, making that gesture. "And thanks again for allowing me to help."

Brad paused in the doorway and cast me a rueful smile. "Could I stop you?" he asked, before striding into the children's room.

*　*　*

I decided to take a walk at lunch, hoping to clear my mind. I needed time to concentrate so I could pull together all the threads of information I'd collected concerning Claudia Everhart's murder.

The day was warm, but the light breeze ruffling my hair also evaporated any sweat from my skin. I strolled a few blocks in the direction of my house before deciding to cross the street to examine a particularly beautiful flower bed.

Overflowing with orange and crimson zinnias and tall spikes of purple thistles, as well as bell-like blue lobelia blossoms, the flower bed offered a perfect spot to take a deep breath of perfumed air. As I raised my gaze, I realized I was standing in front of Emily Moore's Craftsman-style home. Instead of grass, she had planted sweeping banks of flowers that formed colorful waves set off by a curving flagstone path. I paused, admiring this design, until I caught the flicker of movement out of the corner of my eye.

Assuming a fellow Taylorsford resident was approaching, I turned to greet them. But as soon as they saw me move, the

other person, who was wearing a dark sweatshirt with the hood pulled up despite the summer heat, fled in the direction of Emily's detached garage.

Finding this strange, I pulled my cell phone from my pocket and followed. I turned on my camera. If the stranger was planning to steal anything from Emily's property, I was ready to catch them in the act.

Ready to call 911 as well as snap a photo, I crept up to the garage. But the hooded stranger darted away before I got too close. They sprinted across the neighbor's back yard, which bordered the cemetery behind the Lutheran church.

Knowing a tall black iron fence enclosed the cemetery, I decided to return to the sidewalk and circle around the church to reach the graveyard's main gate. Even if the stranger found a way into the cemetery from the woods, there was a chance they'd try to exit through the main entrance. All I had to do was wait.

I debated about preemptively calling the sheriff's department, but decided to bide my time. After all, I hadn't seen the stranger steal anything, even if they had trespassed on private property. I had to consider the possibility that it was merely a kid enacting some sort of dare. I didn't really want to get a young person in trouble over such a minor thing, but I also didn't want to allow a stranger to tramp across local properties. I decided if I could catch a glimpse of their face, I'd know what to do.

I slipped through the half-open gate and walked far enough into the cemetery to be able to look out over its rows of graves. The only problem was this was an older graveyard. Unlike the

low headstones found in more modern cemeteries, it included several large-scale family monuments.

One of the most dramatic soared up from the center of a family plot enclosed by a short wrought-iron fence. Carved from white marble, it featured a square column topped by an angel. No cherub, this heavenly creature appeared poised for flight, one foot pressed against the flattened top of the pillar, while its other leg and robe swirled out behind it like a flag. The tapered horn the angel held to its chiseled lips still bore traces of the gold leaf that once gilt its surface. Carved into the pillar was one name—*Baker*.

Some of my mother's ancestors were buried here. That explained the extravagance. The Bakers had once been the wealthiest family in Taylorsford, owners of a large lumber yard and mill, among other things.

I cast another glance around the area but didn't catch even a glimpse of the hoodie-clad stranger. Perhaps they'd run into the woods instead, which actually made more sense for someone trying to escape. Pocketing my phone, I moved closer to the Baker monument. Even though the Lutheran church sat directly across from the library, I'd never bothered to wander through this cemetery before. In all honesty, I'd never known that part of my family had been buried there. I guess it hadn't occurred to me because they'd always been Episcopalians, not Lutherans.

But I bet this was a community cemetery back in the day, before the new one was built outside of town, I thought, noticing the name of another local family, who I knew to be lifelong Methodists, on a nearby headstone.

Intrigued, I decided to examine the Baker plot more closely. But as I approached the monument, footsteps thudded against the hardpacked dirt path behind me. Before I could spin around, a hand was thrust into the small of my back, shoving me forward.

I stumbled and fell, my palms and knees smacking the short grass simultaneously. I let out an exclamation that probably made my proper ancestors roll over in their graves. Stunned, I jerked away as my assailant shoved their hand in my pocket before dashing away. By the time I gathered enough of my wits to sit back and struggle to my feet, the stranger had vanished.

Brushing off bits of dirt, I stared in despair at the knees of my beige linen slacks, now streaked with green grass stains. *Ruined*, I thought, as I flexed my wrists, grateful nothing felt broken or sprained.

I shambled out of the cemetery as if I were a revenant, so preoccupied I almost ran into Hani Abdi.

Hani's thick black lashes fluttered over her dark eyes. "Heavens, Amy, what happened to you?"

"I slipped and fell," I said, not really sure why I was lying. Gazing at Hani's concerned face, I realized it was probably a reflex action—I instinctively didn't want to involve her in a messy, and possibly dangerous, situation.

"Poor thing, you look like you really took a tumble. Come, follow me to the shop. I can fix you some herbal tea to help ease any aches and pains."

"Thanks, that sounds lovely," I said. "And if you have anything for these slacks . . ."

Hani glanced down at my knees as she measured her stride to match my shorter steps. "I think my mother has one of those sticks that are supposed to remove stains. We can give it a try."

We reached Hani's home, which was located only a few blocks from the library. One of the few remaining fieldstone buildings in town, her house butted directly up against the sidewalk. There was no front yard, and only a stone stoop for a porch, but its four-square design, as well as the mottled white and gray stones, lent it a simple beauty. Attached to the main structure, a smaller wood-frame addition sheathed in white siding housed Hani's catering business.

A bell attached to the heavy wooden door jangled as we entered the shop, drawing Hani's mother from the kitchen located behind the plain wooden counter.

"Amy, so good to see you again," said Mrs. Abdi, as she dusted flour from her hands. "But what's this? Are you injured?"

"No, no, I'm fine, thanks. I took a fall in some grass, that's all." I pointed to my knees. "My slacks got the worst of it."

"Oh dear." Mrs. Abdi's dark eyes widened. "Wait, I have just the thing."

As she bustled back into the kitchen, Hani gave me a wink. "I told you she'd have something. Now—let me get you that tea." Hani pulled up a hinged portion of the counter and stepped behind it. "Oh, I meant to ask—are we all set for Sunday? Any changes to your order?" Hani asked as she turned on an electric kettle.

"No changes," I said. "But I was going to call and let you know Richard's planning to stop by Saturday afternoon to pick up the dishes, since most everything is meant to be eaten cold.

That way you don't have to hang around here on Sunday, waiting for us."

"Great. I don't have any events on Sunday, so that will give me a rare day off." Hani offered me a smile. "Not that I'm complaining about having an abundance of work, but it's nice to have a free day every now and then."

"I'm sure," I said, as Mrs. Abdi reentered the room.

"Found it," she said, brandishing a stick of something that looked like deodorant.

I jumped up and crossed to the counter. "Thanks. I'll give it a try. Anything is better than going back to work looking like a kindergartner coming in from the playground." I grabbed the stick and vigorously rubbed it over my knees.

"Is it working at all?" Mrs. Abdi leaned on the counter as Hani brought over a steaming mug of tea.

"A bit. I mean, it's better, for sure," I said, holding out one of my legs.

"Much less noticeable." Hani pointed to the mug. "Your tea."

Lines creased Mrs. Abdi's brow. "Oh, Hani dear, I meant to tell you, that man came back while you were out."

"Thanks again." I dropped the stain removal stick and wrapped my hands around the mug, pulling them back when the heat stung my scraped palms. Carefully clutching the handle instead, I took a sip of tea as Hani shared a worried look with her mother.

"Again? What did he want this time?" Hani asked.

"Same thing as before. Kept asking when the library closed for the evening."

I looked up from my tea. "What man was this?"

"I don't know. I've never seen him around before," Hani said. "Although he does look a little familiar for some reason. He's been in a couple of times, asking about the library's hours." She shrugged. "I guess that's not so strange, although you'd think he could walk down the street and find out, since the schedule is posted on the lobby window."

The hair rose on the arms. "What does he look like?"

"An older guy, but tall, and broad-shouldered, with that sort of ruddy complexion some fair-haired men have. I suspect he was a blond when he was younger, although his hair is gray now," Hani said.

Mrs. Abdi lifted her hands. "Reminded me of someone too, but I can't think who. All I know is he had a look in his eyes"— she pressed one hand to her heart—"like a wild creature in a trap. Made me nervous, especially with him asking and asking about the library hours, as if he was planning something."

I shivered, despite the warmth of the tea. "Did he, maybe, resemble Chief Deputy Brad Tucker a little?"

"That's it, that's who he kind of looks like," Hani shared a glance with her mother, who nodded vigorously, affirming this statement.

Earl Blair, I thought. *Asking about library hours because . . . he's tracking my movements? Maybe he was the one who shoved me too, except . . .* I gnawed the inside of my cheek. *That person seemed to have a slighter build, so maybe not.*

"Thanks for the tea and everything, but I really must get back to work." I set down my half-finished mug. "And as for that guy—I think you should call the sheriff's department if he shows up again. Just to be safe."

I told both women goodbye and left the shop, pausing outside with the intention to phone Brad and tell him his uncle might be lurking around the area near the library. *Along with some other hooded stranger, so two possible suspects instead of one.*

But as I thrust my hand in my pocket, my fingers encountered a crumpled piece of paper. I pulled it out, realizing the stranger who'd pushed me in the cemetery must've shoved it in my pocket.

It was a piece of paper torn from the bottom of a receipt. I couldn't tell what store it was from, the date of sale, or any other identifying information. Bemused, I flipped it over and gasped when I read the text scrawled across the back.

Stop your digging, it said, in a shaky hand that told me it had been written on the fly, *if you don't want to find yourself sleeping here with your relatives.*

Chapter
Twenty-Three

I called Brad, bracing myself for the "I told you so," but thankfully he didn't admonish me again. Instead, he immediately sent a deputy to collect the note and take my statement concerning the stranger who'd shoved me to the ground.

Not that there was much I could tell them, other than a vague description of someone wearing a dark hoodie. "A rather slender person," I said. "Could've been male or female; I couldn't get a good enough look to determine which. But I don't think it could possibly have been Earl Blair, even though he has been seen in the area." I provided the information about Earl that Hani Abdi and her mother had shared, which the deputy jotted down while muttering something like "the chief won't be too happy about this."

When I got home, I waited until Richard and I were settled on the sofa in the living room with an after-dinner glass of wine before describing my encounter in the cemetery.

"Another threatening note?" Richard's eyes narrowed as he plunked his wine glass down next to mine on the coffee table. "This is getting out of hand, Amy. You know I make it a practice not to tell you what to do, but in this case . . . Well, I won't order you, but I will beg—please stop pursuing this amateur investigation. For the sake of my mental health, if nothing else."

"I think I can still do a little more research," I said, placing two fingers against his downturned lips to silence any further protest. "Who will know about that, as long as I just collect information and share it directly with Brad? I'm even willing to tell a white lie and publicly state I've stopped looking into the case if it makes you feel better."

When Richard pulled my hand away, he pressed it to my chest. "Will you swear?"

"Yes," I said, covering his clasped fingers with my other hand. "And you can share that fib with people too. If the murderer is keeping tabs on me, that should reassure them. Hopefully, they'll believe I've stopped any snooping into their business. Somehow, I don't think they're sophisticated enough to be tracking my online research, or what I'm looking up in the archives, or anything like that."

"Probably not," Richard said, before leaning in closer. "To be clear, I'm not trying to run your life. I just want you to stay safe," he murmured, before kissing me.

Since I knew this was true, I didn't hesitate to reassure him again, before concentrating on more pleasant things.

* * *

I kept my word, and limited my sleuthing to some online investigation during the rest of the week. This unfortunately turned up nothing of any value, although a phone call I placed, to the librarian at Stonebridge High, did garner a promise to return my call when he had a minute to check through the yearbooks the school kept on file.

I didn't really have much time to think about the Claudia Everhart case, anyway. In addition to working every day, including Saturday, I had to dive into yard work and cleaning every evening. I wanted to make sure that by the time Sunday, and our dinner party, rolled around, the house and yard would be in good shape. Of course, Richard also helped with these chores, but since he was equally busy with his teaching, both of us ended up scrubbing bathrooms late Saturday night.

Fortunately, Sunday turned out to be a warm, dry day, which meant we could set up a folding banquet table on the back porch and use the kitchen counters and island for a buffet. This was our usual practice because, since Richard had turned half of the front room of the house into a dance studio, we didn't have a formal dining room. Our plan was to eventually enclose the screened back porch to create one, but that was something we needed to save money to accomplish.

The doorbell rang right as I finished setting the table. I hurried back into the kitchen to look over the buffet setup, making sure we had the proper number of plates and serving utensils. Since it was summer, we'd ultimately decided to have Hani supply dishes that could be eaten cold, including a spicy couscous salad laced with dried fruit and nuts, and green beans and mushrooms in a vinaigrette. She'd also provided some of

her delicious hors d'oeuvres, a chickpea-based vegetarian main course, and an almond-studded vanilla custard dessert. All Richard and I had to prepare was a green salad and grilled tuna fillets.

While I pulled the covers off some of the dishes, Richard answered the door, welcoming our guests.

"Cats securely stowed?" I heard Karla ask.

"Upstairs, in the bedroom," Richard said. "Which pretty much guarantees some sort of retaliatory destruction, but what can you do?"

Karla's laugh rippled through the house as she crossed the hall and stepped into the kitchen. "Hello there, Amy. Wow, this looks great. You must've been cooking for days."

"Not exactly," I said. "We cheated and bought some things from Hani Abdi, the lady who catered our wedding."

"Then I know it will be delicious." Karla pressed her hand to her mouth for a second. "Oops, didn't mean to imply it wouldn't have been if you'd made it all yourselves."

I waved a serving spoon at her. "Don't worry, I know what you meant."

"Is my date being difficult?" Kurt asked, as he entered the room and threw an arm around Karla's shoulders.

Karla shot him a look from under her lashes. "Am I your date today? I wasn't informed of that honor."

With a grin, Kurt pulled her a little closer. "I think you're my plus one, since I don't think either of us are here with a date. Isn't that right, Amy?"

"You are both our guests; what you decide after that is your business," I said dryly.

Kurt's laughter filled the room as he released Karla and moved closer to me. "Touché, my dear." He leaned down and kissed me on the cheek. "You always seem to know how to put this old man in his place."

"Who's an old man?" Sunny asked, as she bounced into the kitchen. "Surely you aren't talking about yourself, Kurt."

Behind her, Fred Nash shook his head. He caught my eye and grinned as Kurt acknowledged Sunny, who was looking adorable in a sleeveless turquoise top and matching shorts, by kissing her hand.

"Old perhaps," Kurt said, "but fortunate, for sure, to be surrounded by so many beautiful women. In any case"—he lifted his hands—"I can't complain."

A dismissive huff announced the appearance of my aunt and Hugh. "Really, Kurt," Aunt Lydia said, "no need to lay it on so thick. I know how you like to flatter, but perhaps you should save your charm for those who don't know you quite so well."

"Hello, everyone," Hugh said, with a bob of his head. As he raised his gaze, I noticed the sharp side-eyed glance he cast in Kurt's direction.

This didn't surprise me. Hugh had investigated Kurt's art sales and purchases many times in the past, hoping to prove the art dealer was involved in shady business practices. The fact that Hugh hadn't yet found any conclusive evidence didn't mean he'd given up this quest. He'd also enlisted Fred to help with some of his investigations. Which was probably why Fred was also surveying Kurt with a dubious expression.

But I knew both men were gentlemen and unlikely to cause a scene at a dinner party. Or at least, I hoped so.

"Here we are," Richard said, leading Marty and Evelyn Stover into the room. "Everyone piled in the kitchen, as usual."

Sunny grabbed a celery stick from a platter of raw vegetables and shook it at Richard. "Haven't you heard? It's the hub of the home. Which is why all those design shows go for the open concept style these days."

"Pretty hard to do here, without destroying the entire floor plan." Richard turned to Marty and Evelyn. "Some people think I've done that already, installing a studio in the front room. But I did try to retain the original 1920s bones of the structure in the rest of the house."

"I think it's charming," Evelyn said, ducking her head.

Realizing her shyness might be compounded by not knowing some of the guests, I quickly made introductions all around.

"So you're related to Richard?" Marty asked Kurt.

"Not exactly, although I do consider him family," Kurt replied, ignoring a raised eyebrow look from Aunt Lydia. "Richard's mother is the niece of my foster father, Paul Dassin, the man who actually owned this house for many years."

"Is that how you came to live here?" Marty asked Richard.

"Yes, my mom inherited the house from Great-Uncle Paul. My parents rented it out for a while, but when I could afford to take it over and do some necessary renovations, they transferred ownership." Richard glanced over at me. "My good fortune, in more ways than one."

Sunny smiled brightly at Marty's quizzical expression. "You see, Amy was living right next door, with Lydia, who's her aunt, when Richard moved in here."

"And that's how you met?" Marty's gaze swept from me to Richard. "How interesting. One of those wonderfully serendipitous occurrences life sometimes offers."

"Good luck, indeed, like me coming to Taylorsford on a case involving some mysterious artworks." Hugh slid his arm around Aunt Lydia's waist. "A fortuitous happenstance, as it turned out."

Aunt Lydia didn't say anything, but her smile was response enough.

"Looks like everyone's here," Richard said, "so I'd like to ask our guests of honor, Marty and Evelyn, to kick off the meal. We're doing this buffet-style, so please, grab a plate and fill up and then head out to the back porch. We have a table set up out there."

Once everyone was seated, and Richard and I filled glasses with their beverages of choice, I kicked off the party by filling in the guests about Marty and Evelyn's artistic skills and achievements. Then Richard shared some details about an upcoming choreographic gig that would take him out of town at the end of the next week, while Hugh talked about his latest discovery— a forged painting mistakenly attributed to John Constable and hung in a place of honor in a small museum. After that, conversation continued to flow, focusing, not unexpectedly, on dance, music, and art, until Fred mentioned something about the death of Claudia Everhart.

"I guess it was a shock to you in particular, Marty, since she was supposed to be a participant in one of the reunion choirs. Had you already worked with her in rehearsals?" Fred asked, before he jerked like he'd been stabbed with a hot poker.

Probably Sunny, stomping on his foot under the table, I thought, as Evelyn Stover's mouth trembled.

"Yes, but really, between the two choirs I was conducting, there were so many people," Marty said smoothly. He speared a green bean and studied it for a moment. "I barely remember seeing her."

"I'm sure the authorities will find the true culprit soon." Hugh pressed his fingers over my aunt's hand, which she'd clenched on the table. "Of course, Lydia and I are certain it wasn't Ms. Shoemaker."

"But can you truly be sure?" Marty laid down his fork and gazed around the table. "I suppose everyone here thinks Zelda Shoemaker is innocent, but the facts don't seem to support that belief."

Aunt Lydia lifted her chin, her blue eyes bright. "I don't just think it, I know Zelda is innocent. Her arrest is a miscarriage of justice."

"That's the thing, though." Marty shrugged. "Justice isn't always served, in my opinion. Sometimes the innocent suffer, while the guilty go scot free."

"Unfortunately, I have to agree," Fred said, turning his gaze on Kurt and ignoring Sunny's hiss of disapproval.

The object of his scrutiny simply sat back in his chair with a smile. "In my experience, justice simply works according to its own timetable," Kurt said.

"If it works at all," Marty said, with a bitterness that made me share a confused look with Karla.

"Anyway," Karla said, her tone bright as the sunlight still streaming in through the porch screens, "we all hope the case will

be solved soon, so Ms. Shoemaker can be exonerated. But, if you'll allow me to change the subject, I wanted to thank you again, Marty, for your support of our future plans. Richard and I will be working with some regional high school dancers next summer, thanks to Mr. Stover," she added, addressing the other guests.

Feeling a sudden lessening of tension, I rose to my feet. "Excuse me, I'm going to grab some more beverages. I'm sure everyone could use a refill."

As I headed into the kitchen, Marty told Richard and Karla he'd received some money from an arts grant and had a check he wanted to give them, in support of the folklore project as well as planning for the summer dance program. *That should keep the conversation on happier topics*, I thought, yanking open the refrigerator door to retrieve a pitcher of water.

"May I help?" Evelyn asked

I turned to face her over the kitchen island. "It's not really necessary, but thanks. If you can carry in the water, I'll get the iced tea."

Evelyn didn't move. "I will, but first, I wanted to apologize for Marty's little outburst."

I stared at her for a moment, taken aback by the anxiety shadowing her eyes. "No need. I'm sure no one was offended by what he said. I mean, it was just an opinion. We all have those," I added, with a tense laugh.

"The thing is"—Evelyn pressed her palms against the polished surface of the island—"Marty doesn't really trust the sheriff's department, or any other authorities, for that matter. He had some bad experiences when he was younger, and it soured him."

"I'm sorry," I said, my fingers tightening on the handle of the glass pitcher. "Was he accused of something he didn't do? I'm sure that can be traumatizing. Seeing Zelda these days . . ."

"No, no, nothing like that," Evelyn said, cutting me off. "In his case, it was more the inaction of the authorities. He was in foster care for a while, you see, after his mom had a nervous breakdown." Evelyn stared down at her white-knuckled hands. "His dad had already disappeared from their lives by then, and there was no one left . . . well, there wasn't anyone to care for Marty. So he ended up in the system."

"And endured some bad experiences there?" I offered Evelyn a sympathetic smile. "Problems the authorities ignored?"

Evelyn nodded. "Pretty much. He told me that he even went to the police once, to report one of his foster parents, and the authorities did nothing. Just referred it back to social services, whose solution was to quietly move Marty to another home. Which helped him, of course, but left several other foster children he'd grown fond of abandoned in that bad situation. That's why he doesn't have the highest opinion of law enforcement."

"It's definitely understandable," I said, right before a crash from the living room made us both jump.

"What was that?" Evelyn's eyes widened. "It almost sounded like glass shattering."

"I know, but I can't imagine . . ." I moved toward the hallway. "I'd say it was the cats getting into mischief, but they're locked in upstairs, and this came from the front of the house."

As I headed down the hallway, Evelyn called after me, "Hold on, I'll get Richard and some of the other men."

I almost told her the other female guests would offer as much protection, if that's what she intended by her remark, but simply shook my head and dashed toward the front of the house.

It didn't take long to realize what had caused the noise—a rock, surrounded by glass shards, marred the meticulously maintained wooden dance floor in Richard's studio. I stood in the living room, staring at the offending object for a moment while my mind attempted to process the reason for its presence in my home.

Did someone throw that rock? But why? I thought, as I crossed to the front door. Opening it, I was met with a shout from a man standing on the sidewalk in front of our house.

"Amy Muir," he called out, "hustle yer butt outside unless you want me to break another window."

Hanging on the edge of the door, I stared blankly at the stranger, who was a tall, large-framed man with a full head of gray hair. *Earl Blair*, I realized, noting the shape of his jaw and nose, which both betrayed a familial connection to Brad Tucker.

"What do you want?" I asked, as footsteps thudded behind me.

"Get away from the door, he could have a gun." Richard's hand landed on my shoulder, pulling me to the side. He quickly inserted his body between me and the open doorway.

Gun, my brain repeated. *And Richard is a perfect target.*

I tried to slide closer to Richard as Earl yelled, "I want you to stop smearin' my good name, that's what I want."

My attempt to squirm around Richard to make sure Earl wasn't leveling a gun at him was halted by another hand

263

gripping my upper arm and yanking me back. "Let us handle this," Kurt said, in a tone as deadly as it was calm.

Locking my pleading gaze onto Kurt's stony face, I stammered, "Make sure he doesn't shoot Richard."

"I don't see a weapon, which doesn't mean he doesn't have one stashed somewhere. But for now, he appears unarmed." Kurt jerked his head toward the hall. "Go reassure everyone else things are under control."

I turned to see our other guests crowded together in the hallway. "It's okay," I said, in a voice shaking a little too much for that statement to be perceived as the truth. "Please, wait in the back while this is sorted out."

"Okay, but I'm calling the sheriff's department," Sunny said.

I gave her a thumbs-up as she herded everyone back toward the kitchen.

Everyone except Fred. He stormed forward to join Richard and Kurt on the porch.

I crept up behind him so I could hear what was going on. Kurt, who was speaking in a tone that would've given a cobra pause, flatly informed Earl he was an idiot.

"If you're innocent, this is no way to prove it," Kurt said.

"Only way to shut down that interfering little . . . woman," Earl replied, obviously changing his preferred terminology when Richard leapt toward the porch steps, fists clenched.

Kurt threw out his arm to keep my husband from descending the steps. "In my experience, someone with nothing to hide doesn't need to fear any sort of investigation," he said.

That comment elicited a bemused glance from Fred, who was flanking Kurt's other side.

"I got people tailing me and checking into all my business now, when I ain't done nothin' wrong," Earl said, his anger melting into belligerence.

"You thought throwing a rock through my window was the way to solve your problems?" Anger vibrated through Richard's words.

"Only way to get the attention of your wife, it seemed like." Earl crossed his arms over his chest. "I sent a nice enough note to her at the library, but she didn't pay no mind to that."

I stepped out on the porch. "And slipped me another note in the cemetery?"

Richard wheeled around to face me. "Amy, I thought you were told to stay in the house."

I was too struck by Earl's reaction to protest—he dropped his arms to his sides as confusion washed over his ruddy face. *I was right—he didn't have anything to do with the cemetery message*, I thought, as Richard moved toward me.

"Come on, let's go inside," he said, taking hold of my shoulders and backing me into the house. "Kurt and Fred can handle that creep, and hopefully the authorities will be here soon, if anyone thought to call them."

"Sunny did," I said, smiling when approaching sirens outside confirmed this fact.

"Sensible girl, unlike someone I know." Richard's weary expression told me he was no longer angry.

Just relieved you're okay, I realized, as he wrapped his arms around me. I buried my face in the folds of his soft cotton shirt, muffling the noise outside.

Glancing up at the sound of footfalls hitting our wooden plank floor, I caught a glimpse of Kurt tugging down one of his

sky blue shirt sleeves. "He ran off at the first wail of the sirens," he said. "I was going to give chase, but Fred Nash beat me to it."

"Probably for the best," I said, pulling free of Richard's embrace. "He's got a few less years, and certainly more time spent engaged in professional training, over you."

Kurt's bushy eyebrows rose up to meet the fall of his thick white hair. "So I'm being put out to pasture now?"

"Certainly not," I said, earning a smile from Kurt before I added, "Wolves may hunt in pastures, but they never live in them."

"Uh-oh," Richard said, his lips twitching. "I'm pretty sure I don't want to get caught in the middle of this. Maybe I'm better employed reassuring our other guests."

I tipped up my chin to meet Kurt's sardonic gaze. "Please do. I'm sure they're concerned. Kurt and I can probably answer the sheriff's department's preliminary questions on our own."

"It is something I have plenty of experience with." Kurt's grin displayed his large white teeth. "But then again, so do you, my dear."

I was saved from formulating a proper response by Fred bursting through the half-open front door. "Jerk got away from me, but now the deputies are on his tail, so I expect they'll track him down soon enough." He fished a tissue from his pocket and wiped away the sweat that had beaded on his forehead and upper lip before adding, "He did have a good head start, but I must admit I'm a little slower than I used to be."

Kurt turned to me with a wink. "See—younger doesn't always mean better."

Chapter
Twenty-Four

Monday was another blur of activity, punctuated by a visit from a deputy who was following up on my encounter with Earl Blair.

"No, we haven't tracked him down yet," the deputy said, shaking her head. "We don't know if he's left the area or is holed up somewhere. We are aware he still has a few friends in Taylorsford, so we're keeping them under surveillance to see if he makes contact. But so far, no luck."

"I'm sure you'll find him eventually," I told her. "Your department is very efficient, from what I've seen."

"We do our best." The deputy tipped her hat with a smile. "You just give us a ring if Blair contacts you again, and we'll be right on it."

"Thanks. I hope he believes he's put a stop to me helping with the investigation and won't bother me again."

"Have you stopped?" Amusement glinted in the deputy's dark eyes.

"Oh sure," I replied, with a wink. "And you can quote me."

"I'll be sure to do that," she said, before wishing me a good day.

After the interview, I left Samantha in charge of the desk and headed into the workroom to process new orders and generate a budget report for the next town council meeting. But as soon as I sat down, the phone extension in the workroom jangled.

Samantha stuck her head around the door. "For you. A librarian from one of the local high schools."

I jumped up and crossed the room to answer the wall-mounted telephone.

"Hello, is this Ms. Muir, the library director?" the voice on the other end of the line asked. "This is Tony Sexton, the librarian at Stonebridge High."

"Thanks for returning my call. Were you able to discover anything about Claudia Everhart in the school yearbooks?"

"She definitely was a member of the chamber choir, which I know was your primary question. Not only was that activity listed with her photo, but she also appeared in pictures of the choir in the volume documenting 1970 and '71."

"Great, exactly what I needed. Thanks so much."

"Sure, no problem. Always happy to assist another librarian's research." Tony cleared his throat. "There is something else. It's not related to the yearbooks, or any of our print materials, though. It's more of an oral history kind of thing."

I wrapped the long coil of phone cord around my hand. "I never discount that source of information. Is it related to Claudia Everhart's time at Stonebridge?"

"In a way." There was a rustle of shuffled papers before Tony spoke again. "I jotted down the story so I would get all the details right. To be perfectly honest, it's a tale my grandmother told me when I mentioned doing some research on the latest Taylorsford area murder victim."

"Your grandmother knew Ms. Everhart or her family?"

"Not really. But back in the seventies, Grandma was a nurse at the county hospital. She worked in the emergency room, and was on duty when a Stonebridge student was brought in. That was around the time of some statewide choral competition your Ms. Everhart was probably involved in."

A Stonebridge student, so not Earl Blair. I dropped my arm, allowing the phone cord to unspool off my hand. *But there is someone else.*

"Was the victim Patricia Johnson? She went by Patty, I think."

"That was the girl. Terrible car wreck. Grandma said it really shook her up, even though she'd experienced plenty of awful things working in the ER. But apparently, my grandmother had seen this girl perform in a play a few months earlier and believed she had a bright future. Anyway, Grandma thought it was a particularly tragic loss, which is why it stuck with her all these years."

"Wait, I'm confused—what does an accident have to do with Claudia Everhart?"

"That's the really strange part of the story. My grandmother said this other high school girl showed up at the hospital, asking about Patricia Johnson. She seemed frantic, so Grandma took her aside to calm down. That's when the girl, who gave her

name as Claudia Everhart. said something so odd my grand-mother never forgot it."

I switched the phone receiver to my other hand and shook out my fingers, which had cramped from the tightness of my grip. "What in the world did she say?"

"She claimed the wreck wasn't really an accident."

The phone slipped from my hand, banging against the floor. I swooped down and grabbed it, apologizing to Tony as soon as I pressed the receiver back to my mouth and ear. "That doesn't make sense. All the reports said Patty Johnson somehow lost control of the car and hit a tree. According to what I've read, she wasn't driving under the influence of anything, and no other vehicles were involved."

"That's what my grandmother said too, but Ms. Everhart told her the victim could've blacked out because she'd hurt her head earlier in the week." Tony expelled an audible breath. "She wanted Grandma to tell the doctors to check and see if Patricia Johnson had a prior head injury."

"And did they?"

"No, because . . . Well, my grandmother said it would've been almost impossible to tell, given the victim's trauma from the acci-dent. Anyway, Grandma did mention this to some of the offi-cers investigating the wreck, but she said nothing ever came of it. Apparently, no one could verify that the victim had recently suffered a bad fall, and then Ms. Everhart retracted her story."

"She said it didn't happen?"

"That's what the deputies told my grandmother when she asked about the case. So it was officially listed as an accident, probably due to distracted driving, and that was that."

"But your grandmother always had doubts?"

"Yeah, which is why she remembered Claudia Everhart's name when I mentioned my research. Grandma told me she always felt Ms. Everhart was telling the truth at the hospital and, for some inexplicable reason, lied later."

"Wow, thanks for sharing," I said, my mind racing as I attempted to slot these new clues into place.

"I didn't know if it would be helpful, but it was such an interesting story, I thought you'd like to hear it," Tony said. "Librarians always like to compile all available information, right?"

"Absolutely." I thanked him again before saying goodbye.

Clicking the receiver back onto the phone base, I stared blankly at the wall for a moment before making another call.

"Hello, Aunt Lydia," I said when she answered the phone. "I wonder if you could do me a favor?"

"I'll do whatever I can," she replied. "As long as it doesn't involve cooking. I've already done way too much of that today, prepping some garden vegetables for the freezer."

"No, this is connected to Zelda's case. Could you please ask her and Walt to come by your house around five or so? I'll stop by on my way home from work."

"To do what?" Aunt Lydia's voice held cautious undertones.

"Ask a couple of questions." I took a deep breath. "And see if we can finally get Zelda to tell us the truth."

*   *   *

I walked home at a faster pace than usual, anxious to speak with Zelda. I wasn't sure she would agree to explain everything—after

all, she'd maintained her silence so far, even with the threat of a murder conviction hanging over her head. But armed with more information, I felt it was worth a try.

When I opened Aunt Lydia's front door, I heard voices sailing down the hall from the back. Locking the door behind me, I made my way to the enclosed sunporch, which stretched across the back of the house.

Aunt Lydia, seated in her favorite wooden rocker, looked up as I entered. "Why, hello, Amy," she said, signaling me she'd simply invited her friends over and hadn't mentioned my planned ambush.

I grabbed the arm of a fan-backed wicker chair and turned it to face the glider, where Walt and Zelda were seated next to one another. "Hi, guys." I plopped down onto the chair's rose-patterned chintz cushions. "How are you both today?"

"Tolerable," Walt said, his dark eyes narrowing. He had obviously noticed the tenseness in my posture, or perhaps the overabundance of enthusiasm in my voice.

Zelda's pink-tinted lips twitched into the semblance of a smile. "Oh, I'm fine, dear, really. I think everyone else is more worried about my situation than I am." She swept one of her hands through the air, her gesture including Walt and Aunt Lydia.

"As well we should be," Walt grumbled. As he sat back, the glider banged into the stone wall behind him. "The sheriff's department still seems to be focused on Zel as their main suspect, even though it's clear as crystal she had nothing to do with that woman's death."

"Yeah, about that." I placed my hands in my lap and squeezed them together to disguise a slight tremor. "I heard

something today I wanted to ask you about, Zelda. Not that it necessarily ties into the case, but it made me wonder . . ."

As Zelda squirmed on the cushions of the glider, Aunt Lydia shot me a glance as acidic as vinegar. "What's this all about, Amy? No sense hyping up the mystery. This isn't an episode of *Murder, She Wrote*—ask your question and be done with it."

"Okay." I took a deep breath before plunging into dangerous waters. "There was a young woman who died in a car accident not long after the vocal competition where Earl Blair suffered anaphylactic shock. Her name was Patricia Johnson, and somehow, she had a connection to Claudia Everhart. Or, at least, Ms. Everhart showed up at the hospital after Patty Johnson's wreck, so there had to be something going on there."

Zelda's face blanched until her skin looked as fragile and pale as the blooms of a paper-white narcissus. "Where did you hear that?" she asked, in a strangled voice.

"From the grandson of a nurse who was on duty when Patty Johnson was brought in to the ER," I said, ignoring the icy daggers Aunt Lydia's eyes were casting my way.

"What's all this?" Walt draped his long arm around Zelda's shoulders and pulled her closer to his side. "Why are you so upset over this old story, Zel?" He shot me a fierce glance. "Of course, I remember hearing about it at the time, but that was nothing but a tragic accident."

"It was tragic," I agreed, as my fingernails bit into my clenched palms. "But Claudia Everhart apparently claimed it wasn't precisely an accident. Or at least, she told the nurse it might have been precipitated by another event—a fall of some

kind that could've led to Patty Johnson later blacking out in her car."

Zelda dropped her head into her hands and burst into tears. As sobs wracked her body, Walt patted her back and sent Aunt Lydia a silent plea for help.

She immediately stood and crossed to the glider, sitting down on Zelda's other side. "Now then," she said, laying her hand over Zelda's knee. "It can't be that bad. Just tell us what's going on."

"You don't understand," Zelda managed to sputter out. "My dad was a doctor."

Aunt Lydia shared a confused look with Walt. "We know your father was in general practice, but what does that have to do with anything?"

Zelda choked back another sob and sat up with a jerk, dislodging Walt's arm. Fishing in the pockets of her black tunic top, she yanked out a cotton handkerchief. "It means I should've known better. I *did* know better," she added, wiping the tears from her face.

"About what, darling?" Walt kept his voice low, but I could hear tension vibrating through his words.

"Patty Johnson." Zelda blew her nose before balling up the handkerchief in her fist. "I should've insisted she get looked at by a doctor or some other medical professional."

"Hold on." I slid to the front edge of my chair. "Patty Johnson did experience some sort of head trauma before her car accident? And you knew about it?"

Zelda's curls bounced as she bobbed her head. "Yes, I knew. And so did Gwen Ohlson and Olivia Bell. And Claudia Everhart, as it turned out."

I sat back, bumping my head against the high back of my chair. "How did this happen?"

Zelda straightened and crossed her legs, throwing off Aunt Lydia's hand. "The actual fall happened at the music competition where my choir tied for first place with Stonebridge. But I have to go back a little further to explain." She sniffed. "You see, even though Gwen and Olivia and I went to Leeland, and Claudia and Patty attended Stonebridge, there was another connection between some of the girls."

"The summer community theater production of *Brigadoon*," I said.

"That's right." Zelda dabbed under her nose with the wadded handkerchief. "I wasn't involved with that show, but the others were. The main actress was already chosen—she was a girl from the theater program at Clarion—but there was another role they were all vying for."

"Jean, the secondary lead," I said, remembering the photo Kurt had given me.

"Yes. I was trying my best to get into the Leeland chamber choir at the time, so I'd already cultivated Gwen and Olivia's friendship." Zelda cast Walt an apologetic look from under her dewy lashes. "It was when I was so rude to you. And you," she added, glancing at my aunt.

"I remember. You were running with that crowd all summer," Aunt Lydia said.

"I was so foolish. I was so desperate to be a part of their clique." Zelda shook her head. "Don't ask me why. But anyway, I knew from Gwen and Olivia that Patty Johnson from Stonebridge had snagged the part. They were not happy."

I caught Aunt Lydia's eye. "Kurt told me Uncle Andrew worked on the *Brigadoon* production, designing and painting sets."

"Did he?" My aunt lifted her golden eyebrows. "That was before my time, but I suppose Kurt might've known."

She's still pretending she didn't know, I guess for Zelda and Walt's benefit, I thought. But I couldn't let that stand in the way of the truth. "Kurt also said Uncle Andrew witnessed a fight between Olivia and Claudia, with Gwen on the sidelines." I shifted my gaze to Zelda. "Did you ever hear anything about that?"

"Oh dear, yes," she replied. "Apparently, Claudia was defending Patty. They weren't close friends, from what I was told, but because they both went to Stonebridge, and the schools were rivals, Claudia took Patty's side."

The lines creasing Walt's forehead deepened. "But what does any of this have to do with Ms. Johnson's death?"

"I'm getting to that," Zelda said, with a trace of her usual feistiness. She primly placed her hands in her lap. "There were a lot of bad feelings boiling between all those girls—Gwen, Olivia, Patty, and Claudia. Unfortunately, their feud hadn't been resolved by the time we attended the competition that fall."

"And then there was the whole mess with Earl Blair dating both you and Claudia," I said. "I guess it didn't help matters."

"It didn't, although as I have said before, I wasn't really in love with Earl, so it didn't upset me much. It kind of hurt my pride, since I actually loved someone else . . ." Zelda leaned into

Walt, who smiled. "But Olivia and Gwen already had it in for Claudia, so they spread a lot of rumors about her, which led Earl to break up with both of us at the same time."

"She slipped him that cupcake, didn't she?" Aunt Lydia asked.

"I always thought so, but Earl wasn't convinced. Like I told Amy, he accused me as well as Claudia. There was never any proof as to who it was, of course, so no one was ever brought to justice."

"Which is a good reason for Earl Blair to choose your garden when he lured Claudia to her death. He wanted to frame you in addition to killing her," Walt said grimly.

"Maybe, although . . ." Zelda took an audible breath. "He's not the only one who had a motive." She met my questioning gaze. "I think Amy has an inkling as to the other likely suspects."

"Gwen Ohlson and Oliver Rader? Was one of them blackmailing Claudia and she finally refused to pay?"

Zelda shook her head. "No. She was blackmailing them. And me," she added, meeting Aunt Lydia's exclamation of surprise with a wan smile.

Walt massaged his temples. "I'm confused. What could Claudia Everhart have on any of you?"

"Although we didn't know it at the time, she saw something we wanted to keep a secret." Zelda squared her shoulders. "You see, before the competition, when everyone else was distracted by the incident involving Earl, I walked in on an argument between Patty Johnson and Gwen and Olivia. Apparently, Patty had lost an earring on the risers during her choir's earlier

rehearsal, and had come back to look for it. She ran into Olivia and Gwen, and words were exchanged. Somehow, everything escalated and"—Zelda looked from Aunt Lydia to Walt—"Olivia shoved Patty off the top riser."

"She hit her head when she fell," I said in a hushed voice.

"She did, poor lamb. So hard she was knocked unconscious for a short time." Zelda's sigh was echoed by my aunt. "I ran to her while the other two were climbing down from the risers. There wasn't any blood, but I knew"—tears welled in Zelda's eyes—"I knew she should be checked out. My dad had dealt with head trauma before, and I'd heard him say how dangerous it could be, especially if someone blacked out."

Aunt Lydia pulled a clean tissue from her pocket and passed it to Zelda. "But Olivia and Gwen didn't want to tell anyone, I guess."

"No, and they swore me to silence. Stupidly, I went along with them—partly because we likely wouldn't have been able to compete with our choirs if we told anyone, and partly because I knew if I went up against Gwen and Olivia, my membership in the in-crowd would be over."

"But what happened to Patty? She must've been okay if things proceeded as planned," Walt said. "I mean, the choirs obviously did compete."

Zelda's light brown eyes glazed over as she stared at Aunt Lydia's lush garden, which was framed by the windows behind me. "She came to, seemingly okay. Only had a slight headache, she said. But I knew something was wrong. She didn't remember the argument or being pushed, so when Olivia told her she'd simply fainted and fallen, Patty believed it."

"Olivia and Gwen convinced Patty it was an accident?" Aunt Lydia frowned. "And you went along with that?"

"To my eternal shame and regret," Zelda sniffed back another sob as she focused her gaze on my face.

"Claudia Everhart saw you," I said, not bothering to frame this as a question.

Zelda nodded. "We didn't see her because she was in the wings. I think she was hiding there because she had given Earl the cupcake and wanted to steer clear of the commotion over that, but, at any rate, she saw everything."

"Which is why, when Patty had her car accident, Claudia rushed to the hospital. I think she initially wanted to expose what had happened at the competition, but changed her mind later." I snapped my fingers. "She decided to blackmail the three of you instead."

"Not exactly the best way to honor her friendship with Patty," Walt said with a grimace.

"I don't think they were really friends, dear." Zelda patted his hand. "And I guess Claudia saw a way to turn the whole disaster to her advantage."

"She blackmailed you all this time?" My aunt's eyes widened.

"Yes, but not regularly, and not for large sums at any one time. It was never enough to make my husband suspicious, or make me dip into my savings, anyway." Zelda pursed her lips. "I always suspected she just hit us up when she was a little short, or wanted to take a trip, or something. Anyway, that was why you saw her leaving my house that day, Lydia. She was in the area, so I guess she thought she should try to squeeze a little more money out of me. But, for once, I said no."

"Which is why she came back," I said, piecing together the likely sequence of events in my mind. "She was in your garden, planning to ambush you again whenever you came outside, or working up the courage to bang on your door again, or something like that."

Zelda nodded. "I imagine so. It was about the blackmail again, which is why I was so evasive with the authorities when they asked whether I knew her or had encountered her recently. I thought if I said anything, the whole story would come out."

"But why wouldn't you tell the authorities?" Aunt Lydia crossed her arms over her chest. "She was the one at fault. Blackmail is illegal."

"So is what we did, covering up an accident that led to a death. Or, if not illegal, certainly morally repugnant." A tear rolled down Zelda's cheek. "The truth is, I was so traumatized when I heard Patty had died, I wanted to bury the entire incident. I knew she could've blacked out due to lingering effects from that fall and I . . . Well, I know it sounds cowardly, but my guilt paralyzed me. I simply wanted it to all go away."

"And now?" I asked, fighting to keep disapproval from coloring my tone. "You must tell the sheriff's department everything you just told us, Zelda. They need to know there are others, like Gwen and Olivia, who could've wanted Claudia Everhart dead."

"I know." Zelda turned to Walt. "And before you say anything, I realize I should've confessed this from the beginning. But I spent years hiding the truth, and I thought, maybe . . ."

"You'd be cleared without dredging up past transgressions?" Walt took hold of Zelda's shaking shoulders. "I understand,

Zel, but it was incredibly foolish. What did you think, that I'd love you less if I knew the truth?"

Zelda bobbed her head. "You and Lydia. I was ashamed I'd treated you both shabbily around that time, and then I'd done something so horrible . . ." She burst into tears again.

Walt pulled Zelda into a close embrace while Aunt Lydia wrapped her arms around her as well, until they were all three tangled in a hug. I rose to my feet, knowing it was time for me to leave.

"I'm heading over to my house," I said, as I crossed to the door. "But promise me you will talk to Brad as soon as possible, Zelda. For your own sake, as well as providing new leads for the investigation."

"Tomorrow, I promise," she told me, between hiccups.

I left then, certain if anyone could work through the fallout from this confession, these three lifelong friends surely could.

Chapter
Twenty-Five

When I got home, I was greeted by two cats but no husband. Checking my phone, I saw Richard had sent a text saying he'd be a little late, so I set to work preparing dinner—after petting Loie and Fosse, of course.

"What do you think, guys?" I asked the cats, who'd taken up bookend positions on the wide windowsill that overlooked our side yard. "Was the murderer really Earl, or was it Gwen or Olivia?"

Loie yawned, displaying her pink tongue and sharp white teeth, while Fosse stared at me, his golden eyes narrowed into slits.

"Lot of help you are." I scraped chopped onion into a bowl and reached for a stalk of celery, all the while pondering the information Zelda had just shared. Each chop of my paring knife brought up a new thought.

Why would the killer have followed Claudia to Zelda's garden, unless it was Earl seeking to harm both women? If the murderer

was either Gwen or Olivia, what would've been the point in involving Zelda? Of course, they probably suspected Claudia was blackmailing Zelda as well, so was it merely a way to frame her to cover their own tracks?

But since Claudia had blackmailed Gwen, why was Gwen shoved down the stairs, and by whom? It couldn't have been Claudia, since she was already dead, and Earl shouldn't have had any beef with Gwen. Or was my first theory right? Did Gwen fake the tumble to look more like a victim than a perpetrator?

I stared down at the pile of celery for a moment before sweeping it into the bowl. Dinner would have to wait. I had something else I needed to do first. Grabbing my cell phone, I called someone who might provide a few answers.

"Why hello, Amy," Kurt said. "To what do I owe this honor?"

"To your ability to keep things close to the vest," I replied, before sharing Zelda's confession. "But you knew, didn't you? You knew Claudia Everhart was the one who targeted Gwen."

The long pause on the other end of the line told me Kurt was calculating whether he could continue to stonewall. "I did. I didn't have the whole story, as Gwen was rather vague about the reason for the blackmail, but she did tell me it was happening. Sorry for not sharing that information sooner, but I'd promised Gwen to keep it under wraps."

"I see. When did she tell you about this?"

"A few years ago, actually. We were . . . closer for a while, and she confessed it after getting another demand for payment from Ms. Everhart. Seeing her distress, I agreed to help Gwen put an end to the nonsense."

"This was before Gwen double-crossed you, I take it."

"It was. I might not have been so amenable after that." Irony sharpened Kurt's tone.

"Wait"—I crossed to the side window—"you said you helped Gwen deal with the situation. Do you mean you confronted Claudia Everhart?"

"Not personally. But I did send her a message, through an acquaintance."

I stroked Loie's head before petting Fosse. "You threatened her."

Kurt snorted. "I don't know, is threatening a blackmailer really a thing? They're the one initiating an illegal action, after all. Anyway, let's just say Ms. Everhart stopped asking Gwen for hush money, and no one was harmed. I call that a win."

"I'm sure you do," I said, as Fosse bumped my hand with his nose, demanding more attention. "Did you share any of this information about Claudia's blackmail activities with the authorities?"

"No, because I was afraid it would hurt rather than help."

"Make Gwen Ohlson appear to have a motive, you mean."

"Not at all. Gwen was already out of the mix. No, I was thinking about Zelda Shoemaker. The sheriff's department already had her in their sights, and I felt if they knew she was definitely being blackmailed by the victim . . ."

"I see your point, but you've forgotten one thing." I stared out at the birdfeeder we'd set up in the side yard, in a place the cats could watch. It offered them amusement, without allowing any harm to come to the birds. "It wasn't only Zelda who was being blackmailed. Even if, as you say, Gwen was no longer being harassed, there was another person involved."

Kurt inhaled sharply. "Olivia Bell."

"Or Rader, as she's now known. And by keeping quiet, you and Gwen may have allowed her to escape the investigation's notice."

Kurt spat out a word not typically a part of his vocabulary. "I really am slipping. Mea culpa. I should've certainly considered the implications of that before now."

"Well, Zelda is spilling the whole story to Brad or someone else at the sheriff's department, so Olivia will finally be on their radar." I gave Loie another pat before walking back to the kitchen island. "By the way, you might want to alert Gwen. Tell her to talk to the authorities as soon as possible. Otherwise, she might come under suspicion as well."

"I'll call her now. Of course, I may ask her to leave out my involvement in the matter."

"I wouldn't expect anything else." I picked up my paring knife and examined its sharp blade. "But Gwen may not agree to that, especially if she needs to confirm she was out from under Claudia's thumb long before the murder."

"She will. She owes me," Kurt said, his voice edged with frost.

"Okay then." I jammed the point of the knife into the cutting board. "I suppose I should let you go so you can call her. Just remember—Zelda's confessing everything tomorrow."

"Then I'll be sure to tell Gwen to call the department early enough tomorrow to confirm Ms. Shoemaker's statement. But I'll also suggest she not call tonight, so it doesn't paint Ms. Shoemaker in a bad light. That is, as if she is only responding to being outed. You might want to consider that if you're contemplating calling Brad Tucker tonight."

I yanked the knife free. "You really have done a lot of this sort of maneuvering before, haven't you?"

"Goodbye, Amy," Kurt said. "Thanks for the heads up."

I didn't even get a chance to say goodbye before he ended the call.

* * *

On Wednesday afternoon, Brad stopped by the library to let me know Zelda had confessed her past involvement in the cover-up of Patty Johnson's fall.

"I don't know why all these people thought they had to keep such a thing secret. There's honestly no way to know if that fall contributed to Ms. Johnson's car accident," he said.

"Guilt." I met his questioning look with a shrug. "I think that was why Zelda stayed silent. She carried the guilt so long, it had become a part of her. It was a dark side she didn't think she could ever expose, for fear of losing people she loved."

"I suppose. All I know is it's muddied the waters in the case. Knowing that Ms. Everhart blackmailed Ms. Shoemaker, Ms. Ohlson, and Ms. Rader . . ." He rubbed his temples, as if trying to banish a headache. "Well, it's not only about them, is it? If she was the sort of person who resorted to blackmail, she might not have stopped with that incident, or those three women. Let's face it—there could be any number of other people out there who might have wanted her dead."

"I hadn't thought of it like that." I fiddled with the pencils in the wire mesh holder we kept at the desk. "Did Gwen Ohlson contact your department as well?"

"Yes, and told the same story as Ms. Shoemaker, although apparently Ms. Ohlson was able to shut down the blackmail scheme some years ago." Brad tapped the top of the counter with one finger. "You wouldn't know anything about that, would you? Ms. Ohlson's story was a little light on the details."

"Me?" I plucked out a pencil and twirled it between my fingers. "Why would I know anything concerning Gwen Ohlson?"

Brad made a dismissive noise but didn't press the issue. "Of course, we're trying to talk to Ms. Rader now, but she isn't answering our calls. I've made plans to send some deputies to her house to ask questions."

"According to Zelda, she was the one who shoved Patty Johnson off the risers, which means she may feel she has more to hide," I said, dropping the pencil back into the holder.

"And maybe had more of a motive to silence her blackmailer? Yeah, we're considering that, especially with the matching statements we've received from Ms. Shoemaker and Gwen Ohlson."

"I assume you're still trying to locate Earl Blair, as well."

"Absolutely. He's not off our list yet." Brad fixed me with the stare I was sure he'd perfected to intimidate suspects. "You're still keeping your head down, I hope? No chasing strangers into graveyards or anything?"

"No sir," I said, giving him a mock salute.

"It's not funny, Amy. Like I said before, I don't want to have to face either Sunny or Richard if anything were to happen to you. Or your aunt, if it comes to that."

"Yeah, Aunt Lydia might be the fiercest in that pack," I said with a smile. "Look, you don't need to worry. Didn't I urge both Zelda and Gwen Ohlson to come clean to your department

before I took any steps to research their stories? I left it on your plate, where you always say such things belong."

"Hmmm . . ." Brad looked me up and down as he jammed his hat back over his short blond hair. "Let's keep it that way, okay?"

"Absolutely. Besides, I've probably exhausted my research avenues in this case. At this point, I think you have all the information I'm likely to uncover."

"Honestly, I'm grateful for what you've found, and shared. But I agree—time to leave this with me and the rest of the department."

"Just don't hesitate to ask if you need me to search for any background information online or in the archives," I told him, before wishing him a good day.

After Brad left, I welcomed Sunny back from a stint in the archives. She'd volunteered to help a local resident conducting genealogical research. We'd both agreed the archives was the best place to start.

"Was that Brad I saw leaving?" she asked.

"Yes, he was updating me on the Everhart case."

"Which means you can fill me in," Sunny said. "Not only because I'm nosy, but also because I promised Fred I'd keep him in the loop. I mean, he did chase after the bad guy, after all."

"So he did. Although, sad to say, he didn't catch him."

"Don't I know it. I heard all sorts of excuses, believe me." Sunny tossed her long, single braid behind her shoulder. "Honestly, I had to soothe his battered ego for some time. 'No, honey, thirty-eight is *not* that old,'" she added, in a sugary tone, before

continuing with wicked grin, "It took some doing, but I did convince him he still has what it takes."

I laughed, drawing a frown from Mrs. Dinterman, who was approaching the desk, her arms laden with books.

"I'd like to check these out," she announced. "If you're done with your girl talk, that is."

Mrs. Dinterman kept her head down while she stacked the books on the counter, allowing Sunny to shoot me a look that drove me into the workroom before I started laughing again.

Since the rest of the afternoon passed without incident, I was able to leave right at five. Sunny had agreed to cover the evening shift, as this was Richard's last night at home before he took off for his choreography gig.

When I entered the house, a loud thump vibrated the ceiling of the front room. Dashing up the stairs, I discovered Richard standing by our bed. He waved his hand toward the bedroom closet, where a suitcase lay, splayed open.

"Little stinker jumped up before I could stop him." Richard pointed an accusing finger at Fosse. The ginger cat peered down at me from the closet shelf, his eyes like golden orbs.

"He looks a bit like the Cheshire Cat perched up there, doesn't he? Only without the grin."

"I'm sure he's grinning inside, having ignored all my demands to avoid that leap." Richard motioned toward the suitcase. "He knocked the case onto the floor; probably broke a clasp."

"I doubt it." I crossed to one of our nightstands to deposit my cell phone before hurrying back to the closet. Leaning down, I grabbed the handles and pulled them together. "Let's see how

much trouble you're in, Fosse." The suitcase closed with a satisfying click. "Looks okay, which means you can continue to live, buster." I straightened and carried the empty case to the bed.

"As if we'd hurt him, regardless. And he knows it, the monster." Richard, taking the suitcase from my hands, leaned in and kissed me. "Good evening, sweetheart. Want to help me pack?"

I wrinkled my nose at him. "Is that a real question?"

Richard opened the suitcase and tossed it onto the bed. "I thought you'd want to spend a little extra quality time together. You know, before I take off."

"For three days," I said. "You said you'll be back late Saturday night."

Richard cast me a grin. "Yeah, but it's two entire nights. How will you manage?"

"How indeed?" I moved behind him and slipped my arms around his waist. "I may simply wither away," I said, pressing my face against his back.

"We can't have that." Richard spun around with the agility I always forgot he possessed. "I'll have to make sure to call and remind you I'll be back before you turn into a wrinkled crone." Placing his hands at my waist he lifted me off the floor before plopping me on the bed beside his suitcase. "Or I could take you with me. There's room to pack you, don't you think? I mean, who needs socks and underwear?"

"You do, unless you want to acquire a very strange reputation," I said, trying and failing to keep a smile off my face. "Besides, in addition to there being no way I could fit in that case, I have to work tomorrow and Friday."

Loie, who'd apparently been hiding under the bed, crept out and jumped up, landing in the suitcase.

"Nope. If Amy can't go, you can't either," Richard said, shooing her off. He stared down at a pile of folded clothes lying on the bed. "I guess I only need my dance stuff, and maybe something for dinner out after rehearsals. Nothing too fancy, though. It's not like I'm going to be dining at the Ritz."

"Not without me, anyway." I picked up a pair of tights. "Are you dancing? I thought this was simply you teaching the choreography. Or polishing it, or something."

Richard glanced over at me, his dark eyebrows arched. "Or something? Am I never going to teach you all the technical terms?"

I leaned back on the pillows stacked against our headboard. "I'd rather you teach me moves, not terms."

Richard held up one finger. "I'll respond properly later," he said, as my phone jangled. "You'd better answer that."

I rolled over and grabbed the phone from the nightstand.

"Amy, it's Brad Tucker again. I hope I'm not calling at an inconvenient time."

"No, no, it's a perfectly fine time to call," I said, pulling a face that made Richard chuckle.

"Well, I didn't want to interfere with your dinner or anything, but I thought you should know—Olivia Rader has vanished."

I sat bolt upright. "As in, she's on the run, or something has happened to her?"

"We don't know yet. When the deputies checked out her residence, some of her neighbors said they hadn't seen her since

yesterday. And apparently, that's odd. The neighbors claimed she always takes a morning walk with her dog, and often works in her yard in the late afternoon and early evening. But no one has seen her do either today. And when one of the deputies approached the house, he heard a dog barking, yet no one ever came to the door."

"That is strange." I met Richard's quizzical gaze and mouthed *Tell you later.* "If she did run off, why wouldn't she have taken the dog?"

"Maybe she thought it would slow her down. I mean, if she's really on the run. But anyway, we're getting a warrant to investigate the property, and of course we'll make sure the dog is taken care of." Brad cleared his throat. "I wanted to let you know, so you can take precautions. If she appears at your house, or the library . . ."

"I'll alert you immediately, of course," I said.

"Better yet, call 911. You might not always be able to reach me directly, and I don't want you to take any chances, since this erratic behavior might mean Ms. Rader is our killer."

"I understand," I said, waving off Richard's grab for the phone. "Thanks for calling, Brad."

After I hung up, I shifted on the bed to face Richard. He had his arms crossed and his eyes narrowed—never a good sign.

"Do I need to stay here?" he asked.

"Of course not. Brad was simply bringing me up to date on Zelda's case. You know, I told you about her confession concerning the Patty Johnson tragedy from the past. It was just more stuff related to that."

"You're not in any danger?"

"No, I'm not." I pointed toward the suitcase. "You finish packing. I'll go put together something to eat." As I hopped off the bed, I smiled up at him. "We want to have time to relax after dinner, don't we?"

Richard glanced from Loie, who had jumped up onto the other nightstand, to Fosse, who was still crouched on the closet shelf. "I guess we have to assume everything is okay, don't we, guys? I mean, she wouldn't let me leave town if she was in danger or anything, would she?" He turned his intense gray-eyed gaze on me. "Would she?"

"She would not," I replied, standing on tiptoe to kiss him. "Now get to work, mister. The sooner you're packed, the sooner we can have dinner. And the sooner we have dinner . . ."

Richard pulled me close. "The sooner we can enjoy dessert?" he asked, returning my kiss before I could reply.

Chapter
Twenty-Six

With Richard out of town, I was happy to accept Aunt Lydia's invitation to dinner on Thursday.

After a relaxed meal at the kitchen table, we retired to the sunporch, opening the windows to enjoy the evening air through the screens. The light wind was warm but not sweltering, and laced with the intoxicating scents wafting from Aunt Lydia's garden.

"I won't keep you too long," my aunt said. "I'm sure you don't want to miss Richard's call." She cast me a smile. "As I'm sure he will."

I took a sip of my white wine before replying. "No problem. He was scheduled to run rehearsals all afternoon and into the evening. He probably won't get back to the hotel until eight, and then he'll still have to grab something to eat."

"Which piece is this, anyway?" Aunt Lydia leaned back in her rocker, which she had positioned so she could look out

not only over her garden, but also the woods and mountains beyond.

"One of his earlier ones, *Dimensions*. The one utilizing dancers of all shapes and sizes. It doesn't get performed as often as he'd like, so he was eager to support this company adding it to their repertoire."

"He's not dancing this time, though?"

"No, he's not performing with them, just setting the piece on the company and making sure it's ready for their performances later in the month." I placed my wine glass on the tile-topped table I'd pulled up next to my chair. "Switching subjects, how's Zelda doing?"

"Better, I think." Aunt Lydia's sidelong glance was pensive. "It was a great relief for her to finally admit her guilt over her past actions." She frowned. "Well, it's really inaction, I guess. She said she's been tormented for years over her failure to insist Patty Johnson get checked out after her fall. And, even though we are supposed to be her closest friends, I'm ashamed to say neither Walt nor I ever recognized her pain."

"It's not your fault. She'd buried that incident deep. If she wouldn't even share the story when it might've helped her to avoid a murder charge, I don't imagine there was anything you or Walt could've done to draw it out of her."

"I suppose you're right." Aunt Lydia pulled her phone out of the pocket of her loose cotton slacks. "Speak of the devil, there's Zelda now. Hold on, let me get this." She said hello, then held the phone to her ear for a few minutes before speaking again. "Can I put you on speaker, Zelda? Amy's here, and I'd like her input, if you don't mind."

Zelda must've agreed, because her voice sailed from the phone. "Hi, Amy. I would appreciate your opinion."

I stood and moved closer to my aunt's rocker. "Glad to help. What's the issue?"

"It's Olivia Bell, I mean, Rader. She sent me a text a few minutes ago."

"She had your number?" I asked, sharing a raised eyebrow look with my aunt.

"I guess she found it somewhere, like my Facebook page. I don't keep such things secret; never saw the point. You're supposed to be connecting with people there, right?" Zelda sniffed. "Anyway, she sent me a text, asking me to meet her."

"You can't do that," Aunt Lydia said. "Delete it."

I was about to agree when another idea crossed my mind. "Wait, maybe she should respond."

My aunt huffed and shot me a sharp look. "You told me yourself, Olivia could be the killer. And you want Zelda to meet up with her?"

"Not alone," I said. "But if she agrees to meet Olivia somewhere quiet, but out in the open, like the garden behind the Heapin' Plate, it could make a good trap. I mean, we'd make sure there were several deputies present. The garden backs up to the woods, so they could easily remain hidden until they had Olivia in their sights."

"What a splendid idea." Zelda's tone brightened. "I could tell her to meet me tomorrow. That would give Brad Tucker and his team time to set things up."

"The diner would be closed by two, but you'd have to give Bethany an hour to clean up and leave before you arrived," I suggested.

"Around five, then, don't you think? It will still be light out, but not as many people will be roaming around downtown," Zelda replied.

Aunt Lydia's blue eyes widened with concern. "Now wait, you two. Perhaps you should run this by Brad first. What if he can't put together the proper arrangements in time?"

"Oh, pish-posh, Lydia. You know Brad Tucker can rally his troops by tomorrow evening. Besides, they'll drop everything else for this, since they're pretty desperate to talk to Olivia." Zelda's voice took on a wheedling tone. "And you know how anxious I am for them to find her. It might be the thing that clears me of all suspicion. Come on, Lydia, let me do this. It won't be dangerous, not with the sheriff's department providing protection."

"All right, I suppose it is the best way to force her out in the open." Aunt Lydia sighed. "But promise me you'll call the sheriff's department as soon as you can."

"I will. And, Amy, thanks so much for the idea."

"Glad I could help," I said. "Let Aunt Lydia know what you hear from Brad about the arrangements. She can fill me in once everything's set up."

"Alright, dear." Zelda clucked her tongue. "Now turn off the speaker, Lydia. I want to talk with you privately for a few minutes."

With Aunt Lydia absorbed in her phone conversation, I decided to make my exit. Waving goodbye to my aunt, I carried my wine glass into the kitchen before leaving the house, careful to lock the front door behind me. As Brad had said, there was still a killer on the loose, and while I didn't think Aunt Lydia was on their list of future victims, I wasn't taking any chances.

Back home, I poured another glass of wine and settled on the sofa to stream a rom-com I didn't think would interest Richard. The cats soon joined me—Loie snuggled between the sofa arm and my left side, and Fosse on the right, one paw pressing into my thigh as if staking a claim.

I'd finished my wine and watched about half of the movie when my cell phone rang. Grabbing it off the coffee table, I was happy to see it was Richard.

"Hello, sweetheart," he said. "How are things?"

"Fine. I'm just sitting here watching TV. Surrounded by cats, of course."

"That goes without saying."

I heard the sound of liquid being sucked through a straw. "Are you chowing down on fast food, or what?"

Richard chuckled. "You caught me. Yes, I'm being very wicked this evening. But in my defense, I did work off a ton of calories today."

"Teaching the choreography? I didn't think it required as much effort as actual dancing."

"You'd be surprised. I had to demonstrate quite a few passages. Although, to be honest, I think some of that was the troupe wanting to see me dance."

"I bet. You do have quite a reputation." I gently lifted Fosse's paw so I could cross my legs. "Fess up—you enjoyed it."

"I did, but then I always love a reason to dance." Richard took another slurp of his drink. "There was one dancer in the company who really impressed me, too. I may ask her to perform with me sometime in the future."

"Uh-oh, should I be jealous?" I asked, in a teasing tone.

"Don't be silly." Richard's reply was sharper than I'd anticipated.

"I was only kidding," I said quickly. "You know I trust you."

"I should hope so." There was a slight pause before Richard continued. "Sorry, I shouldn't have overreacted. It's just, well, I've dealt with a lot of that sort of thing in the past. Everyone always thinks if two dancers perform well together, there must be something between them. More than professional respect or friendship, I mean."

"I know you and Karla have had to deal with that sort of gossip."

"It's not only Karla. Every time a partner and I really click, the rumors start to fly. Male, female, it doesn't matter." Richard sighed deeply. "But I know you don't think that way, so I shouldn't have jumped all over you."

"Well, now, I wouldn't really mind, if you were here," I said, hoping to lighten the mood.

It seemed to work. "Good to know," he replied, with a chuckle. "Oh, before I forget—I got a text from Marty Stover. He wanted to drop off the check he mentioned the other day. I reminded him that I was out of town, but said I'd see if you were planning to be home tomorrow. After work, of course."

"Sure. I have no plans, so I should be here unless some sort of emergency springs up." The thought of Zelda meeting up with Olivia Rader crossed my mind, but that operation didn't involve my participation. "Tell him I'll be at the house around five thirty PM. Any time after that is fine."

"Great. Just so you know, he did mention it might be Evelyn who drops off the check. Apparently, Marty's waiting to hear if he needs to attend a meeting concerning the restoration project he's involved with."

"Oh, right. The old cinema building they hope to convert into a venue for live theater as well as movies." I absently stroked Loie's sleek fur. "It's fine. I'll be here, whoever comes by."

"Okay, I'll text him back and let him know. I'll also give him your cell phone number, in case he needs to reach you about any change in plans." Something rustled. *Probably food wrappers.* "So what are you doing this evening, besides watching TV?"

"Nothing, really, although the cats are demanding my attention, as usual." Fosse batted my leg with his paw, so I switched my phone to my other hand and petted him. "I had dinner with Aunt Lydia. That was nice." I considered mentioning Zelda and the plan to trap Olivia Rader but decided such information could cause undo concern. Richard might worry, even if I assured him I wasn't directly involved.

Because he knows how often you've gotten entangled in such things in the past, I thought ruefully. *Even when you swore it was something that couldn't possibly involve you.*

"I'm sure Lydia enjoyed the company as well," Richard said. There was a moment of silence before he added, "I miss you."

"Miss you too," I said. "But it's only a few days. We've been apart longer than this before."

"Yes, but not since we've been married."

"I know." I stared at the paused image on the TV, which was two people, mid-kiss. "But I also know you need to keep taking

on these dancing and choreography gigs. You're not going to be happy only teaching, admit it."

"It's true. I need the creative outlet," Richard said, his tone warming. "I am glad you understand."

"If I didn't, I wouldn't really know you, would I?" My lips curved into a smile. "It's such an essential part of who you are. How could I say I loved you if I didn't comprehend that? I wouldn't ask you to abandon your love for dance, any more than you'd ask me to change important parts of myself."

"Like your need to be a sleuth?" Richard asked lightly. "Even though it does worry me from time to time, I know it's part of what makes you you."

"Which is just one of the many, many, many reasons I love you," I said.

"Now, that's what I like to hear. Although maybe you could add another 'many'?"

"Hey, don't push it," I said, with a giggle.

I head a sound—a squeak, like a mattress complaining when someone plopped down on the bed. "Alright, so the TV show, what is it? We can do a buddy watch."

"Not sure it's anything you'd like," I said, stopping my movie and flipping back to the TV channel guide. "And I was streaming it, so that might not work. But there's an old musical starting up on one of the movie channels soon."

"I see it. *An American in Paris*. One of my favorites."

"Of course it is," I said indulgently. "All that dancing."

"All that great dancing," Richard replied. "Alright, let's pretend we're together and watch with comments and all that."

"But sadly, the *all that* doesn't include snuggling up with you. Or any kisses."

"Only a raincheck," Richard said. "Save up and I'll collect on Saturday night. Deal?"

"Deal," I replied, and settled back with the cats while I enjoyed Richard's commentary on the show.

Chapter
Twenty-Seven

Arriving home on Friday, I realized I couldn't follow my usual routine. I was stuck wearing my coral silk blouse and black linen slacks—no changing into my comfortable shorts and T-shirt until after one of the Stovers dropped off that check. I did switch from loafers to sneakers, though. Surely they wouldn't look askance at casual footwear.

I fed Loie and Fosse before rummaging through the refrigerator, looking for leftovers for my own dinner. As I pulled out a container of hummus and some vegetables, my cell phone chimed.

That meant a text. Grabbing the phone off the counter, I noticed the caller was Marty Stover.

So sorry, it said. *Evelyn got called away to help a friend, and I'm at the old movie theater in Smithsburg. Could you come pick up the check? Don't want to carry it around too long.* An address followed.

I sighed and placed the food back in the fridge. I didn't really want to drive to Smithsburg, but I knew Richard would want me to pick up the check. *And,* I thought with a smile, *I could stop by the pizza place and pick up a slice or two for dinner on the way home.*

Since pizza sounded much more appealing than hummus, I texted Marty back, agreeing to meet him at the movie theater.

"Well, guys," I told the cats. "I'm off again. But I'll be back soon. Don't get into too much trouble while I'm gone."

Perched on the windowsill, both cats turned unblinking stares on me.

"Yeah, right. Anyway, please don't destroy the house."

I tossed my phone back into my purse and headed outside, exiting through the back porch to reach Aunt Lydia's driveway. I didn't think my aunt would need the car this evening, but to be sure, I texted her to let her know I was taking it for a short trip. She sent me an "ok" before I even started the engine.

The trip to Smithsburg was a pleasant drive, at least. Once I left the Taylorsford historic district, I quickly passed the string of small strip malls, drive-ins, and car dealerships outside of town before reaching a stretch of road bordered by rolling farmland and thick stands of trees. On one side, the Blue Ridge Mountains rose in a tapestry of trees whose color changed as I glanced upward—a watercolor wash of emerald melting into forest green and then misty blue.

Like Taylorsford, the outskirts of Smithsburg were marked by an increasing number of gas stations, fast food joints, and drug or grocery stores. As these faded in my rearview mirror, Victorian homes and two-story brick shops signaled my arrival

at the older part of town. I glanced at my directions, remembering the theater was supposed to be close to the Italian restaurant where we'd met the Stovers.

Actually, it was hard to miss, once I knew what I was looking for. Situated on the main street, the cinema building definitely appeared abandoned. Its marquee was empty of any lettering, and most of the globe lights were broken or missing. Still, a swirl of Art Deco decorative flourishes betrayed the building's former glory.

I found a parking spot on the opposite side of the street and locked the car before dashing across the road, dodging a couple of cars that were blatantly ignoring the speed limit. Pausing in front of the old cinema, I examined the decorative niches on either side of the double doors. Obviously meant to display film posters, the niches were empty, except for a building permit taped to the glass.

The doors, featuring large windows cut in diamond patterns, still retained flecks of the crimson paint and some of the chrome geometric accents that must've made them the height of fashion in the past. I tugged on one of the door handles, surprised when it swung open.

I guess Marty left it unlocked for me, I thought as I stepped into the lobby.

It was instantly apparent to me why Marty and others wanted to save the building. Marble columns flanked the doorways leading off the lobby, and the soaring pale blue ceiling created the illusion of a summer sky, even with its flaking paint. A tiered chandelier, still gorgeous despite lacking some crystals and being festooned with dust, hung over the center of the

lobby, where a chipped tile mosaic evoked the floor medallions of ancient Rome.

I allowed my gaze to wander, taking in the faded glamour of the interior. There was a definite Roman theme, with an elaborate proscenium-style arch enclosing the concession area, but the Art Deco style still won out. It was obvious in the silver and gold flourishes, geometric elements, and the layered arch motifs.

Good on you for trying to save it, Marty, I thought, as I surveyed the various doors, wondering whether I should try to track him down, or simply wait in the lobby. *Duh, silly, maybe ask?*

Pulling out my cell phone, I texted Marty again, letting him know I was in the building.

Doors to your right, marked auditorium and balcony, the answering text said.

I frowned, wondering why he was insisting I meet him upstairs, instead of him bringing the check down to me. But I shrugged this off, dropped my phone back in my purse, and headed for the labeled doors.

The stairwell clearly showed the building's age and state of disrepair—the gold and silver embossed wallpaper hung in tatters off the walls, curled like the skin of an orange. I glanced over to my left, through the arch that led to the lower portion of the auditorium, before climbing the stairs, which were scuffed and even splintered in spots. I hung onto the chrome railing, its shine dimmed by too many hands and too little polish. A fine mist of dust filled the air, making me sneeze as I walked onto the balcony.

At least there were a few lights illuminating this area, even though the main portion of the auditorium remained dim. Peering down, I made out curved rows, their missing seats gaping like lost teeth in a crooked smile. The large movie screen, covered by velvet drapes so dusty I couldn't tell if they were gold or gray, was surrounded by an elaborate pseudo-Roman frieze I assumed was plaster painted to resemble marble.

As I admired the beautiful bones of the dilapidated structure, a shadow stretched across the short wall fronting the balcony. "I can understand your enthusiasm for restoring this," I said, assuming I was talking to Marty.

"Get over here," said a harsh woman's voice.

I turned to face Evelyn Stover. "Hello," I said, forcing a smile.

A squeak of protest made me cast a swift glance up the tiered rows of the balcony. Huddled on seats in the back corner were two people.

I looked back at Evelyn, finally noticing something I'd missed.

The gun in her hand.

"I said, move it," she barked.

"Excuse me, what's this all about?" I shot another glance up at the two figures, my eyes narrowing. They were both women, I realized. One was Zelda, and the other was our missing suspect, Olivia Rader. "Why are they here?" I asked Evelyn, fighting to keep a tremor out of my voice.

"For justice," she said, pointing the revolver at my heart. "Now, drop your purse and join them, please."

Your cell phone is inside, I reminded myself, as I placed my purse on the floor. *You need to find a way to get it back, sooner rather than later, but for now, leave it.*

As I climbed the steps flanking the rows of seats, the thud of footsteps told me Evelyn was behind me. *With the gun.*

"Sit," she commanded, waving the revolver toward the end of the row.

I slid into the seat next to Zelda, who pressed her fingers against my bare forearm. "So sorry," she murmured. "I lied."

"Seems like something you do a lot." Evelyn's eyes were hard as amber behind the lenses of her glasses. Her gaze swept over the three of us. "I need to send another text, which means moving to a spot with better reception. But I'll be keeping my eyes on you the whole time, so no one better make a move, or it won't be good for the other two." She backed down the steps until she was standing at the front edge of the balcony again, facing us.

I shot a glance at Zelda and Olivia. "What are you doing here?" I asked under my breath.

Zelda tightened her grip on my arm. "Like I said, dear, I lied. After we had everything set up, Olivia texted me again and asked me to meet her here, instead of the garden behind the Heapin' Plate."

"And you never told Brad or his team about the switch?"

"No. I thought . . ." Zelda looked at Olivia, who appeared so listless I wondered if she were in shock. "I hoped Livy and I could work things out, without the authorities getting involved. I really didn't believe she'd killed Claudia. I was sure the shooter was Earl."

"But it wasn't," I said, speaking to myself as much as to Zelda. I stared down at Evelyn Stover, who was texting but still

alert enough to cast me a warning glance. "I'm confused. How did you end up here?"

"I was fooled. It wasn't Olivia texting me at all. It was that one, using Olivia's phone."

Just like she'd used her husband's phone to text Richard, and then me, I realized. But why? I took a deep breath to still my racing thoughts. I had to make sense of this. If I understood what was going on, I might have some leverage. "Olivia was here already?" I whispered to Zelda.

She nodded. "She's been trapped here since Wednesday. Evelyn Stover wanted us together, so she could exact justice. That's what she told Olivia, anyway."

I gnawed the inside of my cheek. "Justice for what?"

Zelda released her hold on my arm and used two fingers to wipe the drops of sweat from her upper lip. "It has to do with Patty Johnson. That's all she's told us, so far. I assume she tried to get Olivia to confess to shoving Patty off those risers, and wants me to admit to covering it up."

Staring down at Evelyn, I struggled to reconcile my original impression of her with this angry, vengeful woman. She'd seemed so reserved and gentle. A devoted wife . . .

Deeply in love with her husband, I thought, as the gears turned and clicked into place in my mind. *Marty, who suffered in the foster system after his mother had a breakdown and his father disappeared. But what could Patty Johnson have to do with the Stovers? Unless . . .*

The seat of my chair, once plush velvet, was now so tattered that a spring pierced my slacks, scraping my skin as I shifted position to lean closer to Zelda. "Marty's mother lost

her husband and remarried. Aunt Lydia said there was at least one other child, from her first marriage. Do you know anything about that?"

Zelda's eyes widened. "Patty Johnson did have a half-brother or sister. Do you think that means anything?"

"Hey, pipe down up there," Evelyn called out, waving the revolver. "If you think you can plot an escape, remember I have the gun. And I don't think Ms. Rader is in any condition to make a run for it."

As if startled out of a stupor by the mention of her name, Olivia turned to Zelda, her eyes wide and wild. "Patty," she croaked, "had a little brother."

I jerked, banging my head against the hard rim of the seat back. *A younger brother*, I thought. *That could be the connection.*

"I think I might know why you're both here," I told Zelda and Olivia, as Evelyn pocketed her phone and climbed back up to stand in the row below us. I lifted my chin and fixed her with the fiercest stare as I could manage. "Patty Johnson was your sister-in-law, wasn't she?"

Zelda gasped, but Evelyn, keeping the gun trained on us, simply looked me up and down. "She would have been," she said, her lips twitching into a manic smile. "But she died when Marty was only ten."

"And his mother had a breakdown. Understandable, given all her terrible losses. I suppose his dad couldn't handle it and took off before his wife was committed to a mental institution?"

"Exactly. Leaving his son behind, with no family to care for him." The hate flaring in Evelyn's eyes made me wonder what

had eventually happened to the elder Mr. Stover. Was he gone now too, and had it been a natural death?

I sucked in another ragged breath. "And Marty suffered when he was thrown into the foster system. He didn't have a good experience, you told me that."

"It marked him forever. He still has nightmares, even after all these years." Evelyn pointed the gun at Zelda, and then Olivia, before swinging it back where she could easily target any one of us. "If any of you had cared more for another person than for yourselves, maybe Patty wouldn't have died. If you had gotten help after her fall, she wouldn't have had that blackout and crashed the car. If you had possessed an ounce of human feeling"—Evelyn used her other hand to steady her grip on the gun—"maybe my darling husband wouldn't have had to endure the trauma that's tortured him for most of his life."

"How do you know any of this?" Zelda asked. "About Patty's fall, and us being there, I mean?"

"I found Patty's diary when Marty and I were cleaning out his mom's old house a year ago. She went back there, you see, after getting out of the institution. Too late for Marty, of course. The damage was done." Evelyn sniffed back what sounded like a sob. "Anyway, after she passed, we inherited the house and had to get it ready to sell. That's when I found the diary, shoved behind Patty's old bed."

"She mentioned the fall?" I asked, keeping my tone as mild as possible.

"Yes, and who was there. She didn't think anything was wrong at first. She bought the story she was told, about her fainting and falling accidentally. It wasn't until a few days later . . ."

Evelyn's expression hardened. "She wrote she was having head-aches, and feeling dizzy. So she made an appointment with a doctor to get checked out. That was where she was headed when she blacked out and crashed her car."

Tears welled in Zelda's eyes. "I'm so sorry, really I am."

"Lot of good that does now." Evelyn motioned toward Olivia. "You might want to give her a poke. I may have hit her a little too hard before you got here. She seems to be experiencing a few blackouts herself."

Zelda turned to Olivia, who'd slumped forward, while I kept my gaze fixed on Evelyn. "Patty also wrote something about remembering her fall, didn't she? Before she headed out for her appointment. I bet she made a note about Olivia shoving her off the risers."

"You're something of a junior Miss Marple, aren't you?" Evelyn studied me for a moment before adding, "Yes, she obvi-ously remembered what really happened and jotted down the truth, before slipping the diary back into its hiding place. She also planned to talk to the sheriff's department, you see. Right after she saw the doctor."

"You didn't tell your husband about the diary," I said, not making this a question.

"No. He's dealt with enough trauma in his life." Evelyn lev-eled the revolver at each of us in turn. "I decided I'd spare him the ugly truth. But I also vowed to exact justice. For him, as well as for Patty."

"You want everyone involved to admit to their wrongdo-ing. Are you recording their confessions?" I asked, sharing a concerned look with Zelda, who mouthed *Olivia's in bad shape.*

Evelyn's right eye twitched. "Of course. I almost messed that up, when I took action before thinking things through, but then decided to make a compilation tape. A greatest hits collection, if you will. Something I will share with the authorities, so they can see justice was served."

"But you'll be in trouble too," I said. "For kidnapping, and for Claudia Everhart."

At that, Evelyn's stony expression cracked. "I didn't mean to kill Claudia," she said, her voice shaking almost as violently as the hands gripping the gun. She swung the revolver to target Zelda. "That's your fault. I thought she was you."

She didn't know about the blackmail, I realized. She thinks she killed Claudia, an innocent victim in her eyes, by mistake. I wondered if there was a way to use that for leverage. "You saw her in the gazebo, and just took the shot on the spur of the moment?" I asked conversationally. "Well, that's not premeditated murder or anything, so if you were to let us go and talk to the authorities . . ."

"You, shut up," Evelyn said, leveling the gun at me.

Zelda laid her hand on my arm. "What now?"

"Now we wait for the final member of the clique," Evelyn said.

I met Zelda's glance, widening my eyes, praying she knew better than to speak the truth, silently begging her not to say anything about Gwen Ohlson's connection to Kurt.

Evelyn had overstepped. She may even have made a fatal error. It was something I clung to as tightly as my fingers gripped the armrest of my chair—the knowledge that if Gwen Ohlson had just received a text from Olivia's phone, there was hope.

Because there was a chance she wouldn't show up alone.

Chapter
Twenty-Eight

Time passed. I had no way to tell how much, since I wasn't wearing a watch and my cell phone was still in my purse, which was sitting several rows below me.

I pulled free of Zelda's compulsive grip and kept my eyes on Evelyn, who had moved back down to the front of the balcony. She was alternately stealing glances at her phone and glaring at us while brandishing the gun, as if to remind Olivia, Zelda, and me she still had a weapon. Not that Olivia was aware enough to care. As Zelda had observed, the dark-haired woman was in bad shape. Her eyes, when her lids fluttered open, were unfocused, and her arms and legs drooped, limp as cooked pasta. I didn't know what Evelyn had hit her with, but I suspected it had been the butt of the revolver, or something just as solid.

"That looks like my husband's old gun, the one I thought was lost," Zelda whispered to me. "I don't know how she got her hands on it, but however it happened, it means . . ."

"She definitely shot Claudia. Yeah, I'm afraid it does," I said softly, placing my hand on Zelda's tensed arm. "But that doesn't mean she intends to kill us all. She's admitted that killing Claudia was a mistake."

Zelda turned to look me in the eyes, her lips trembling. "You know that's a foolish hope, Amy. Mistake or not, the woman has already murdered someone. I doubt she'll hesitate when it comes to killing again."

I bit my lower lip and looked away. Zelda was right—Evelyn Stover had little to lose, which made her dangerous. Even worse, she didn't appear to have an exit strategy, other than killing us before attempting to flee.

But does she even desire escape? I thought, as Evelyn paced in front of the balcony wall. *She wants to record Zelda, Olivia, and Gwen confessing their culpability in the accident and cover-up that led to Patty's death. Once she has that, and can turn it over to the authorities, I'm not sure she even cares what happens to her. Which makes her even more of a threat. She isn't thinking about saving her own skin, simply revenge.*

I tapped Zelda's arm. "I think maybe you should confess. Let her record your statement. At least then she'll feel her plan is working. It might keep her from doing anything rash before"—I squared my shoulders as I met Zelda's concerned gaze—"Gwen Ohlson arrives."

"If she does," Zelda muttered.

"I think she might. I just hope . . ." I laid my finger to my lips as Evelyn jerked her head up and glared at us.

"Too much chatter," she said.

"I thought you wanted me to talk." Zelda's short blonde curls bounced as she tossed her head. "I'm ready to do so, if you wish."

"And you'll speak the truth?" Evelyn used one finger to shove her glasses up the bridge of her nose.

Zelda rose to her feet. "I will. I think it's time."

"All right. But you should be aware I'll be recording you," Evelyn said, as she bounded up the steps to reach our seats.

I stood up as well. "Do you want Zelda to step out of the row? I can move out of the way," I added, as a plan blossomed in my mind.

Evelyn gave a sharp nod. She had paused on the tier below our row, so I sidestepped to allow Zelda to slide over and stand in front of her.

"Remember, I have the gun," Evelyn said, as she held out her phone with her free hand. "I can still shoot any of you in a second."

I clasped my hands behind my back. "Understood."

Evelyn pressed a tab on her phone. "Okay, talk," she ordered, thrusting the phone closer to Zelda.

"Just a minute. Let me think how best to say this." As Zelda cleared her throat, I glanced over at Olivia, who had slumped deeper into the chair, her head thrown back. It looked like she was staring at the ceiling, but her eyes were closed.

She can't be moved. Not safely, I thought, pondering this dilemma. I didn't want to leave Olivia to Evelyn's mercy, but there might not be any other option. Not if I wanted to give Zelda, and myself, any chance to escape.

"It was during the statewide vocal competition, fifty years ago," Zelda said, her voice resonating throughout the empty theater. "I walked in on Gwen Ohlson and Olivia Bell, who's known as Olivia Rader now." Zelda cast a swift glance at the

comatose woman. "They were standing on the risers that had been set up for performances taking place later that day."

"And they were fighting with Patricia Johnson," Evelyn said. "Don't forget that part."

The hand gripping the revolver was lowered. Yes, she might be able to raise it quickly enough to shoot one or both of us, but I couldn't help but notice her flushed face and glassy eyes. She was so totally engrossed in capturing Zelda's words I doubted she was thinking of anything else.

Like her balance. I unclasped my hands and dropped them to my sides.

"Well, arguing, but yes," Zelda said. She cast me a glance from under her lowered lashes. "Then there was this flurry of movement, and I saw Patty fall backward off the risers."

"You mean you saw Olivia push her." Evelyn tapped the gun barrel against her thigh.

Nervous energy, the kind that could make for an unsteady aim, I thought, flexing my fingers.

"Yes, although I don't think Olivia meant for her to hit the floor," Zelda said.

"Doesn't matter." A froth of spit bubbled at the corner of Evelyn's mouth as she bent her head over the phone, fiddling with the volume. "Her actions still caused the fall. Exactly like your inaction led to Patty's later accident."

"Inaction can be just as deadly," I said, shooting Zelda a glance. "Be ready," I murmured, as Evelyn lifted her head.

Zelda opened her mouth but snapped it shut as I leapt forward with my arms raised and bent at the elbows. I used all my strength to thrust them out like two pistons.

Right into Evelyn's shoulders.

The phone went flying, sailing up over our heads as Evelyn stumbled. She still had a grip on the gun, but before she could level it on us her back foot slipped out from under her and she fell, tumbling and landing in a heap at the bottom of the riser steps.

"Run, now!" I yelled at Zelda, who was frozen in place. "Across this row and over to the other aisle."

"Olivia," Zelda whispered.

"No time. We have to get out. Alert the authorities," I said, shoving Zelda forward. "Only way to help her now."

We dashed to the other end of the row, passing Olivia, who was still slumped in a chair in the row above us. Racing down the tiered aisle on the opposite side from Evelyn, I forced Zelda through the exit door before making a dive for my purse.

Evelyn, on her knees, fumbled around, obviously looking for her glasses as well as the gun. "You could've killed me," she said, her voice jagged as shattered glass.

"Just like you tried to do when you pushed Gwen down the stairs at the poetry reading," I said, shoving my hand into my purse. "You were there; it had to be you."

Slipping on her glasses, Evelyn's fingers searched the area around her. "She deserved it, just like Zelda Shoemaker. Now, if you want to live, call her back," Evelyn said, her fingers closing over a dark object.

"No. She's going to get away. And alert the authorities. And end all this."

Evelyn pointed the revolver at me. "Not before I end you."

Curling my fingers around my phone, I used my other hand to yank the purse free and hurl it at Evelyn.

It hit her square in the face. She squawked and dropped the gun again. I considered trying to grab it, but decided I was better off running away. I had my phone. I could call for help.

Hurrying down the steps so fast I almost tripped, I was startled to run into Zelda at the bottom of the stairs.

"Door won't open," she said, casting a wide-eyed glance at me over her shoulder.

I motioned her aside and tried the doorknob, but realized Zelda was right. Whether it had locked behind me or was simply stuck, it wouldn't budge.

I punched 911 into my phone, but the reception in this enclosed area was apparently too weak to send my call. Shoving my phone into my pants pocket, I glanced up and spied Evelyn's shadow falling across the top landing. Whatever minor injuries she might have sustained in her fall obviously weren't enough to keep her off her feet. She'd soon be on our heels.

With the gun.

"Into the auditorium," I told Zelda in a hushed voice. Following her into the dark, cavernous space, I touched the armrest of the chair at the end of each row to feel my way until my eyes adjusted to the lack of light.

A loud rattle told me Evelyn was trying to open the door to the lobby. That was good—it meant she'd assumed we'd fled toward the main entry. When the noise stopped, I stepped up and grabbed Zelda by the shoulder. "Into the aisle, and stay down," I whispered in her ear. "If we can sneak to the other side, we might be able to reach an emergency exit."

Zelda nodded in response. Hunched over, we crept along the row, while the sound of metal banging against metal resonated throughout the silent theater.

Evelyn, knocking the gun barrel against the frames of the seats, I thought, as the noise repeated, louder this time.

"You can't really get away," Evelyn called out. "For one thing, I know this building better than you do. I've accompanied Marty on many evaluation visits. Besides, what makes you think any of the exterior doors will open? This place has been locked tight for years. Most of the exterior doors are chained from the outside."

Zelda froze in front of me. I nudged her upper thigh, forcing her forward. Evelyn might be right, or she might be lying. I was willing to take a chance on the latter, especially since there really wasn't any other choice.

"And I still have this handy-dandy little revolver," Evelyn said. "Thanks for leaving it out in the garden shed where I could find it, by the way, Zelda." She tsked loudly. "Not very safe, storing a gun in an unlocked shed, although I guess you meant to latch it and simply forgot. I suppose that sort of stuff happens when one grows old."

Zelda stopped short again. I gave her another shove.

"But it was a useful mistake, at least for me. I was able to hide in the shed the first time I spied you outside, talking to that friend of yours."

Aunt Lydia, I thought.

"I'd finally tracked down your address, after a few tries. Your name had changed with your marriage, like Olivia's. Made it a little harder. But I found you, just like I'll find you in here. Of

course, I had to duck out of sight once you both walked into the garden. And there was the shed, door ajar. It was simply a lucky bonus when I found the revolver and bullets, stuffed behind some clutter. I decided maybe I should take both, along with a pair of gloves, and slip away. That way I could plan a more productive encounter, another day."

Her voice was drawing closer. Reaching the end of our row, I motioned for Zelda to stay low and turn left so we could creep down the aisle to a door I thought might lead outside, since it was in the location of emergency exit doors in most movie theaters.

"And it all worked out, except it wasn't you in your garden the next time. It was Claudia, who I never wanted to harm. So her death's on you, just like Patty's."

Glancing through one of the open rows, I spied Evelyn striding toward the front of the theater. I swallowed back a swear word. If she reached the screen and circled around the front row before we ran out the door, she'd have us trapped.

Scuttling up next to Zelda, I laid my hand on her arm, forcing her to look at me. "When I open that door, jump up and head out," I mouthed.

She started to protest, but I pressed my fingers to my lips. Unfortunately, my cell phone tumbled from my pocket and slid under a seat as I leapt to my feet, but I decided to abandon it, especially since it had displayed no signal earlier. I couldn't take time to grab it; I had to reach the door.

"Got you!" Evelyn shouted.

I twisted the door handle and shoved. Thankfully it opened, just as a bullet whizzed over my head. "Run!" I yelled at Zelda,

clinging to the handle and ducking as another bullet pinged the wall above the door.

Evelyn wasn't a good shot. At least, not from a distance. That was a point in our favor. With Zelda safely behind me, I slammed the door as Evelyn stormed toward us.

"We aren't outside," Zelda said, in a shaky voice.

"And this door doesn't lock," I muttered, thoughts tumbling as I considered our options. I cast my gaze around the dusty space, which was basically a vestibule. I noticed a metal-framed sign propped next to the door. There was also a narrow spiral staircase leading up to heaven knew where, as well as another, heavier door. "Check that one, maybe it's an exterior exit," I told Zelda, as I grabbed the dilapidated sign and shoved it up under the door handle. It wouldn't keep Evelyn out for long, but it might slow her down.

"Locked," Zelda called out, before rejoining me.

The door to the auditorium rattled, making the metal sign rumble like thunder.

"We have to go up," I said quietly, pointing to the stairs.

Zelda cast me a panicked look before sucking in an audible breath. But she took a few steps upward anyway, and I followed.

The staircase swayed slightly as we climbed higher. I steeled myself to keep going, ignoring my fear the entire metal spiral might crash to the ground. When Zelda reached the top, she peered down at me. "There's a metal walkway that stretches from one side to the other," she said.

"A catwalk." I met her concerned gaze with what I hoped was a confident smile. "It should be safe. We can use it to cross to the other side."

Zelda nodded and disappeared from view. When I reached the top of the staircase, she'd already taken a few tentative steps onto the catwalk.

We were behind the screen, surrounded by a maze of metal scaffolding. I glanced up into the rafters. *There is enough fly space for live theater. Richard will like that*, I mused, before shaking my head to clear my thoughts. I knew my mind was trying to minimize our danger by focusing on unimportant details, but I couldn't allow my attention to wander. A bang followed by a crash from below told me Evelyn had pushed her way through the door, dislodging the metal sign. She'd be tracking us up the staircase soon enough.

"We need to cross," I told Zelda, who was gripping both sides of the narrow catwalk for dear life.

"Must we?" Zelda asked, her eyes widening.

I didn't discount her fear. The floor of the catwalk was a wire mesh—sturdy enough, I hoped, to hold us, but also offering a clear view of the long drop to the floor. "Look forward, not down. And go."

To her credit, Zelda complied, albeit slowly. "Faster," I urged, as the spiral staircase squawked under Evelyn's footfalls. If she reached the top before we descended the staircase I'd spied on the other side . . .

"We have to keep going," I said when we reached the middle of the catwalk. Granted, Evelyn's aim wasn't so great that she was guaranteed to hit either of us from a distance, but I didn't want to take that chance.

Or the chance of a bullet ricocheting off all the metal beams and guywires up here, I thought grimly, before a new sound startled

me. This one, a voice, rose from the auditorium to drift down over the top of the curtains and screen.

"Whoever is here, you'd better show yourselves," Kurt called out. "The sheriff's department has the building surrounded. I'd advise against doing anything foolish."

Evelyn, appearing at the top of the spiral staircase, fired off a shot in the direction of the voice, piercing the screen.

Kurt's calm voice sailed up again. "Now that wasn't just foolish, that was downright stupid."

Chapter
Twenty-Nine

Evelyn fired off another shot in the direction of the auditorium, giving Zelda and me enough time to scuttle to the other end of the catwalk.

"Take the stairs," I told her. "Step by step. Don't look down."

This admonition was meant for me as much as her. It was one thing climbing up a spiral staircase, and another climbing down, especially into a space that yawned black and forbidding as a cave.

Even the faint light we'd enjoyed on the other side was lacking, so staring down these stairs was like peering into a well. A thought that made my hands flutter like wild birds caught in a cage. *Not again, not again*, my mind whispered, as I gripped the stair railing. Everything in me fought against descending into that darkness, not knowing how sturdy these stairs were, or what might wait at the bottom. But thank goodness, Zelda, despite her age and obvious fear, resolutely clambered down, lending me the courage I needed to follow.

At the bottom of the steps, I felt my way in the darkness. My searching fingers encountered a wall ridged with conduit that must've been installed to carry electrical wires, but try as I might, I couldn't find a light switch.

"There has to be a door," Zelda said, as my hand landed on her shoulder.

"Hold up, let's not get frantic. I bet this matches the vestibule on the other side, so if the stairs are in the same place . . ."

"The door to the auditorium would be off to one side," Zelda said, stepping away from me. "I think that's better than trying to get outside right now, don't you agree?"

I inched forward, following the sound of Zelda's voice. "Definitely. The exterior doors are probably chained shut, like Evelyn said." I ran up on the heels of Zelda's shoes. "Sorry."

"No problem, dear." Zelda fumbled around before clutching my hand. "I think we've reached the side wall. The door must be here somewhere," she said, releasing her grip.

I moved forward with my arms outstretched, stopping when my palms smacked up against a hard surface. "Wait, I'm feeling the edge of something, like a doorframe."

My fingers danced over the molding, landing on the raised panels of what had to be a door. I swept my hands in wide circles until they finally bumped into a piece of metal. "Handle," I crowed triumphantly. But my happiness was instantly tempered by squeaking and rattling above us.

Zelda bumped into me. "Evelyn's coming down."

"She can't see any better than we can," I said, frantically fiddling with the door handle. It didn't seem to be locked, yet also didn't move.

"She can still shoot, and might, if blasting wildly through that screen is any indication." Zelda laid her hand over mine. "Up or down?"

"Down, I think, but it feels stuck."

"Well, we can put some power behind it, if we both try," Zelda said, flinching when another blast from Evelyn's gun rang out and ricocheted off the walls. "How many was that?"

"What?" With Zelda's hands wrapped around mine, we both shoved down on the handle. It shifted slightly, but not enough to open the door.

"Bullets," Zelda said, flexing her fingers. "That revolver doesn't hold an unlimited supply, you know."

"I hadn't thought of that." As we grabbed the handle again, I counted the shots I'd heard in my head. Unfortunately, my counts were punctuated by Evelyn's feet hitting the steps of the spiral stairs. "Five, I think, so she might be running out. But we can't count on that."

"So let's give this all we've got," Zelda said. "One, two . . ."

"Three!" I shouted, as we slammed down the handle and threw our bodies into the door.

It flew open, sending us both cascading onto the worn carpet of the auditorium.

"Don't shoot!" yelled a familiar voice.

A scramble of feet filled my sightline. "She's right behind us. With a gun," I told the deputies' shoes.

"We're taking care of that."

I sat back on my heels and looked up into Brad Tucker's stern face. "So glad to see you," I said, as I took hold of his

outstretched hand. Glancing over at Zelda, I noticed Kurt helping her to her feet. "Both of you."

"Lucky for you Ms. Stover felt compelled to invite Gwen to her little soiree," Kurt said.

"She told you." Swaying a bit, I didn't push away the arm Brad had slipped around my waist.

"Yes, although she thought it was Olivia doing the texting. Which we considered equally dangerous at the time," Kurt said.

"And he told us," Brad said, shooting Kurt an approving smile. "Sharing information with the authorities, for once."

"Oh, now, I've done it quite often." Kurt, supporting Zelda with one arm, gave Brad a mock salute. "When it suits."

"Hmmm . . ." Brad looked Kurt up and down before turning his attention to the open door.

"She's headed up and crossing back over," one the deputies called out.

"Shut down the other side as well," Brad barked out, before thrusting me toward Kurt. "Make yourself useful, Kendrick, and escort these ladies outside." He jogged off, heading for the other vestibule.

"With pleasure," Kurt said, although I was sure Brad couldn't hear him.

"I'm fine now." I shook out my tensed arms. "You help Zelda. I'll follow."

Kurt raised his eyebrows. "You'd better, or I'll come back and drag you out."

"Don't worry, I have no interest in dealing with that woman again," I said, trotting beside him as he led Zelda up the center aisle of the theater. "She wanted revenge mainly for her

husband, you know. Because she felt he'd suffered due to stuff that happened after his sister died, and she blamed Zelda and the others for that."

"I guess she truly loves him," Zelda said with a sigh. "Strange what love can do."

Kurt released his grip on her shoulders, but crooked his arm so he could still offer his support as we left the auditorium. "Sounds more like obsession to me."

"Maybe so," Zelda said, taking his arm. "I mean, I love Walt, and I would die to protect him, but I don't think I'd shoot anyone to avenge something in his past."

"Speaking of Walt." I pointed to the entrance doors as we entered the lobby. "I think he's out there, waiting for you, Zelda."

Zelda let out an adorable squeak of excitement and pulled away from Kurt. She took off at a fast clip as Walt shoved open the outer doors and dashed inside. They met in the middle of the lobby in a flurry of hugs and kisses.

"It's like those perfume commercials." I cast a sly glance up at Kurt.

"Without the sappy music," he replied, grinning down at me before gazing out over the lobby. "And there's Lydia, of course. Anxious to see how the both of you have fared. You'd better go and reassure her."

I caught a glimpse of my aunt's pale face through the windows that flanked the front doors. "I will, but I do want to thank you again."

Kurt shrugged. "I didn't do that much. Just alerted the cavalry to come to your aid."

"You put two and two together when Gwen told you about that text. That's something."

Kurt squeezed my shoulder. "You would've done the same, my dear. That's why we get along so well."

I shot him an amused glance. "Do we?" I asked, as Aunt Lydia entered the lobby.

"Of course we do. Which makes sense. I've always thought we were quite like-minded." He gave me a wink. "Birds of a feather."

He strode off to greet my aunt before I could think of an appropriate response.

*　*　*

By the time I was able to contact Richard, I'd already given my statement to two of Brad's deputies, one of whom also retrieved my cell phone from the auditorium, and been assured that Evelyn Stover was in custody.

"You can't say I was trying to interfere or involve myself in the investigation this time. All I did was go to pick up that check," I told him when he sputtered out his horror and relief over the phone.

"I'm coming home now," he said, once I'd told him the whole story.

I stroked Loie, who was curled up in my lap. "No, you're not. You should complete your work with the dance troupe. I'm fine, and the killer is safely behind bars. There's nothing to worry about."

"But you're alone at the house . . ."

"Nope," I replied, patting Fosse, who was snuggled up beside me on the sofa. "I have the cats for company. And Aunt Lydia only recently left, after fussing over me for hours."

"I should be the one fussing over you."

"You can do that when you get home. Right now, you should simply tell me about your day."

"It's a lot less exciting than yours. A bit boring," Richard said, his tone finally losing its anxious edge.

"Good," I said, dropping my head back against the sofa cushions. "Boring actually sounds delightful. Tell me all about it."

Chapter Thirty

Aunt Lydia decided to throw an impromptu garden party on Sunday afternoon. "To celebrate Zelda being cleared of all charges," she told me. After calling Richard to confirm, I volunteered our backyard as additional seating space. Aunt Lydia's garden was beautiful, and she did have benches scattered throughout her beds, but there wasn't much room in her yard for seating a large group of people.

I spent Saturday helping Aunt Lydia prepare some food for the party, a welcome distraction from thinking about the events of the previous evening.

"We can arrange chairs and tray tables on our side of the fence," I told her, as I chopped some onion for a vegetable salad. "That way, we can set up the buffet table on the gravel path in front of your herb beds, without having to place chairs in the same spot. The guests will have plenty of space to move around."

"Thanks, that will definitely help with the traffic flow." Aunt Lydia stuck a wooden toothpick in the center of a freshly baked cake layer. "Done. Now I just need to let these cool before assembling and frosting."

I glanced over at her with a smile. "You really are the queen of cakes. And yet you stay so slender."

"Always had the good fortune of a fast metabolism," Aunt Lydia replied. "And, of course, I usually bake for other people more than for myself."

"True." I looked up from my cutting board. "Speaking of other people, where is Hugh? I saw his car earlier, but it's gone now. Don't tell me he's left already and will miss the party."

"No, he's doing a grocery run for me. To several different stores, so I'm not surprised it's taking him a while." Aunt Lydia set the three cake pans on a couple of large wire cooling racks. "Richard will definitely be back by tomorrow, I hope?"

"He'll be home late tonight," I said, slicing a green pepper into rings. "He could've stayed over another night, the company would've paid for it, but . . ."

Aunt Lydia cast me a sidelong glance. "He was anxious to get home to you?"

"Yeah, I think so," I replied, with a grin that swiftly faded as I added, "He was pretty worried once he heard what had happened."

"I'd imagine so. Walt was really shaken up too."

"And you weren't?" I asked, with a lift of my eyebrows.

Aunt Lydia turned to face me, wiping her hands on a kitchen towel. "Of course I was. My niece and my best friend were in peril, trapped in a building with a killer. I was so shaken after the fact, Hugh had to ply me with several glasses of wine before I could even think about falling asleep last night."

I grabbed a tomato to add to the salad. "It's kind of sad, don't you think? Evelyn Stover going off the deep end, I mean.

She obviously loves her husband deeply, and couldn't bear the fact that past action, or inaction, by Zelda and the rest of that crew had led to his childhood trauma. Once she pieced together the real story from Patty Johnson's diary, it seems she felt compelled to avenge what happened to him, as well as his sister."

"Not a very sensible way to go about it," Aunt Lydia said. "And I think Kurt is right. He was saying last night that in his opinion, it was obsession, not love, because real love wouldn't drive someone to do such things."

"I suppose." I tapped my paring knife against my cutting board. "It's too bad that Marty had to suffer as a child and teen, but he seems well-adjusted now, at least to me."

"Well, we don't know what goes on behind closed doors, but he does appear stable. Even last night, when we were outside the movie theater, waiting for news, he didn't fall apart." Aunt Lydia twisted the towel between her hands. "But I do feel sorry for him. He's basically lost his wife, on top of everything else."

"And has to deal with the fallout from a trial and all that. She's going to be charged with murder, as well as attempted murder in Olivia Rader's case. And kidnapping, of course. At least, according to Brad, the doctors think Olivia will pull through, although she may need ongoing treatment for her head injury." I frowned. "Anyway, who knows if there will actually be a trial? They are committing Evelyn for a psychological evaluation, from what Brad told me this morning. I wonder if she'll even be judged competent to stand trial."

"Hard to say." Aunt Lydia turned to hang the towel on a hook over the butcher block counter. "At least Jane Tucker can

breathe a sigh of relief now, along with Brad, since Earl has been cleared of any involvement in the murder."

"He did send that threatening note to me and throw the rock through our window. It seems he heard about my snooping from some of his local friends, and was angry I was targeting him in my research."

"He wasn't the one who attacked you in the cemetery, though," Aunt Lydia said.

"No, that had to have been Evelyn. Another strike against her, I'm afraid." I glanced over at my aunt. "I decided not to press charges on Earl's threatening note, by the way."

"I'm sure both Jane and Brad appreciate that."

I shrugged. "I didn't see any point in making a big deal out of it, especially when Brad told me he was asking that Earl get mandated counseling as part of any sentence."

Aunt Lydia pulled down a saucepan from her pot rack. "I'm glad to hear it. Maybe he can turn his life around. I think Jane and Brad will do their best to help him, if he'll let them."

"Yeah, there's the rub." I absently rolled the tomato across the cutting board. "People have to want to improve their own lives, don't they? Nothing their loved ones can do, otherwise."

"That's a truth, if ever there was one," Aunt Lydia said, her tone tinged with sadness.

Before dicing the tomato, I studied her pensive face, guessing she was thinking about her late husband, who she'd loved deeply, but couldn't save from addiction. "It does let us off the hook a bit, though. We don't have to fault ourselves if we try our best to help someone, and they still can't get it together. I mean, all we can do is try."

"I know. But it's hard to watch someone you love suffer. You want to do more, to take the pain away." Aunt Lydia cast me a wan smile. "I understand Evelyn Stover's desire to do that, you know. Just not her method."

I dumped the chopped tomato into the mixing bowl before reaching for a bottle of apple cider vinegar to pour over the vegetables. "Which, sadly, has only brought her husband more pain."

Aunt Lydia sighed. "Revenge tends to do that. Especially when violence is involved."

"One of the many reasons why I prefer real justice," I said. "Which Evelyn could've sought, if she'd just gone about things in a more reasonable way. I think Zelda and the others would've confessed, and even made a public apology, if only Evelyn had explained the situation in a reasonable fashion."

"I believe Zelda would have. Not so sure about the others. But you're right—the truth should have come out, but in a way that didn't cause more harm." Aunt Lydia reached up into a cabinet to grab some more ingredients. "Now, let's change the subject and focus on prepping for this party, shall we? I want to think about celebrations and freedom, not guns and death."

"Sounds good to me," I said, as I seasoned the salad with some herbs as well as salt and pepper. "Let's just hope this is the last murder in or around Taylorsford for the foreseeable future."

"I'll second that," my aunt said, before shooting me a warning glance. "Maybe you should send up a prayer or two, asking that your future research is limited to more pleasant, and less dangerous, topics."

"Well, I can always ask," I replied, with a wry smile.

*   *   *

Sunday afternoon was a typical early September day in our area, which was to say, warm and humid. Summer had yet to release its hold, making me debate between wearing a sundress or a nice pair of shorts and a top.

"Shorts," Richard said, as I dithered in our closet. "Shows more leg."

"I'm not dressing just for you," I called out.

"Really? I'm crushed." Richard poked his head around the closet door. "Crushed, I tell you."

I waved him off. "Have you finished setting up all the chairs and tables in the yard?"

"I have. Just as you commanded," Richard said.

I moved closer and kissed him before saying, "Good. Now please go so I can finish getting ready." I grabbed a pair of mint green shorts off a shelf.

"Perfect. Match those with that watercolor blouse I like so much," Richard said before dashing off.

I shook my head. It didn't help that he was right—the silk top he'd mentioned was a subtle wash of greens and blues that complemented the green of the shorts perfectly. *Of course,* I thought, as changed my clothes, *he's a choreographer, and that's such a visual medium, it's not surprising he has an artist's eye for color and design.*

By the time I made it outside, most of Aunt Lydia's guests were already milling about in our yard, chatting.

"There she is," Sunny said, handing her glass to Fred before running up to me. "So glad you're okay," she murmured as she wrapped me in a fierce hug.

"Perfectly fine. Not a scratch on me," I replied.

"For once," Richard said, over my shoulder.

Sunny stepped back, holding me at arm's length. "We do need to find a way to keep this one out of trouble," she told Richard.

"What do you suggest?" he asked. "Should I lock her in a tower, or what?"

Shooting him an exasperated look, Sunny released my arms. "Okay, make fun. I thought you, of all people, would understand my concern."

"I understand it, I just don't know what we can do about it." Richard slipped his arms around my waist. "You know she doesn't respond well to being told what to do."

"Hey, I'm right here," I said, leaning back against Richard's chest.

He kissed the top of my head before replying. "Thankfully."

Glancing past Sunny, I noticed Zelda bustling toward us, followed by Walt. "Oh, my dears, how lovely to see everyone without a dark cloud hanging over everything," she said.

"We're certainly happy all that suspicion has been lifted off you," Richard said, before acknowledging Walt. "I'm sure you're both ecstatic."

"Absolutely." Walt draped his arm around Zelda's shoulders. "It's a bright new day after so much gloom."

"You should've seen Zelda," I told Walt. "You would've been proud."

"I'm always proud," he said, pulling her closer to his side.

"Yes, but she was so brave. Keeping calm and climbing up onto that catwalk, and down again without faltering." I beamed at Zelda, who was blushing. "She was like a ninja."

"Oh, I wasn't calm. Not really." Zelda pressed one palm against her cheek. "I was terrified. But Amy was keeping it together so I felt I had to follow suit."

"In my opinion, you were both splendid," said a deep voice.

I turned my head to meet Kurt's amused gaze.

"Leading that woman up and down those spiral staircases—genius," he said.

I stepped forward, slipping out of Richard's hold. "I don't know about that. It was really our only option."

"Whatever the motivation, it worked, and kept her from firing off a clean shot at either one of you. Not that she was much good with a revolver." Kurt lifted his shoulders. "I think she only hit that poor Everhart woman because she was standing close to her at the time."

"I, for one, am happy she wasn't a crack shot," Richard said.

"Me too," said Walt.

Sunny pointed toward the rose vine–draped archway that separated my aunt's yard from ours. "I think Lydia is trying to get our attention."

"She wants you to know that there's food that needs to be eaten," Fred held up a plate piled high with various goodies as he approached us. "I'm doing my part."

"I see," Sunny said, with a lift of her golden eyebrows. "Did you leave any for me?"

"Plenty," he replied. "But you better make tracks. Brad Tucker just showed up, and I have a feeling he can put away his fair share of food."

"Unlike you?" Sunny asked dryly. She linked her arm with Fred's and cast a glance over her shoulder. "Let's go, everyone. You know Lydia spent hours on this spread. We need to show our appreciation," she added, before they strolled away.

"Not hard to do, when it's Lydia making the food," Walt said.

"Wait a minute." Zelda looked up at him, her tea-brown eyes sparkling with mischief. "Are you saying Lydia is a better cook than I am?"

"Heaven forbid. You are both kitchen goddesses." Walt slid his arm away before making a little bow.

Zelda laughed and clasped his hand. "Silly man. I can see right through your flattery. But I appreciate it all the same. Now, come, let's sample all of Lydia's delicacies."

"I helped," I muttered under my breath, earning a wolfish grin from Kurt.

"In that case, I definitely must check out this spread," he said before loping off.

Richard and I followed more slowly.

"This is a good day," he said, taking my hand.

"Very." I smiled up at him. "Zelda's cleared of all suspicion, she and I are safe, and a murderer is behind bars."

"And I'm here with you," Richard said, with an answering smile. "That's always a good day."

I gave his hand a little squeeze. "It certainly is."

As we walked under the arbor, Hugh looked up from his conversation with Fred and Sunny. "There you are. Finally, everyone's

in the same spot." He swiftly moved to join Aunt Lydia, who was standing at the end of the table, ladling punch into small crystal glasses. "Let's set that down for a moment, dear," he said, taking the ladle from her fingers. Still holding her hand, he led her out from behind the table to join Fred and Sunny, before raising his other hand to motion another guest forward.

"You're on," he told Walt.

"All right, Zelda, let's make that announcement," Walt said, pulling her into the center of the circle formed by the guests.

I shared an astonished glance with Richard. "They are going to . . ."

"Announce their engagement," he said, as Walt did just that.

The ensuing cheers and claps drowned out any further conversation for a few minutes. Richard and I hurried forward to offer our congratulations and hugs.

"So when's the wedding?" Sunny asked. "And can I help arrange it?"

"Thank you for the offer, dear, but it won't be anything fancy. I think we may simply sneak off and tie the knot quietly," Zelda said, acknowledging Brad and Alison with a smile. "We won't be trying to outdo your upcoming celebration, that's for certain."

"All the same, congrats," Brad said, laying one hand on Alison's shoulder. "It's nice to hear some happy news, especially after these past few weeks."

"Amen to that." Aunt Lydia turned to Hugh. "I think there might be a few bottles of champagne tucked away in the refrigerator. At least, there was last time I checked," she added, with a smile. "I had my suspicions something like this might happen, sooner or later."

"All right, let me go grab those," Hugh said.

"I can lend a hand too," Fred said, setting down his plate.

As the two men took off for the house, I turned to Richard. "This is definitely a very good day," I said, throwing my arms around him.

"One of the best. Next to meeting you," he replied, pressing a swift kiss against my lips. "And getting engaged to you," he added, with another kiss. "And of course, marrying you."

I pressed my fingers against his lips. "For me, it's every day with you," I said, before I kissed him back.

When we broke apart, Walt and Fred had already returned with the champagne. I hurried over to the table to help fill some of the small punch glasses.

"So, who's next?" I asked, when Sunny joined me. "Hugh and my aunt, or you and Fred?"

"Don't be foolish. I'm never getting married, you know that," Sunny said, while sneaking a glance at Fred. She downed a full glass of champagne before refilling her glass. "Need to have some for a toast," she said, in response to my questioning look.

"Uh-huh." I patted her arm. "Don't worry, your secret is safe with me."

"Silly, I don't have any secrets." Sunny tossed her head, swinging her shining fall of hair, before grabbing two glasses of champagne and walking over to join Fred.

"I give it twelve months," said Kurt.

He was standing at my elbow. As he reached around me to pick up a glass of champagne, I looked up into his lined but still handsome face. "You think Sunny and Fred will break up in a year?"

"No, I believe they will be engaged by that time," he replied, with a sardonic smile. "Or married. I see them as the type to elope, like Walt and Zelda."

"And what about you?" I asked

"Me?" Kurt's bushy eyebrows disappeared under the white hair falling over his brow. "I'm no longer in the game, my dear." He spread wide his hands. "These days, I find sufficient joy basking in the happiness of others."

I pursed my lips. "Not sure I believe that."

The amused expression on Kurt's face melted into something else—something I might've called sadness if it were haunting anyone else's visage. "But it's true. Although"—his gaze drifted to my aunt—"perhaps there is always hope. I'm glad Lydia and her friend Zelda discovered their happy endings, at least."

I tapped him on the arm. "Happy beginnings, I'd say."

He looked down and gave me a wink as Richard appeared at my side. "Ah yes, a new start. Something to consider," he added, saluting us with his glass before walking away.

"What was that all about?" Richard asked.

"Not sure," I said. "A cynic expressing a glimmer of hope, maybe?"

"That sounds like a good thing." Richard caressed the side of my face with the back of his hand. "Have I told you today how much I love you?"

"Yes, but you can tell me again. I really don't mind. So—how much?" I said, with a little smile.

A smile he kissed away with a thoroughness that left me in no doubt as to his answer.

Acknowledgments

B ooks don't come into being without the assistance and support of many people. While I appreciate them all, I have to single out a few individuals and groups for special thanks:

My agent, Frances Black of Literary Counsel.

My editor at Crooked Lane Books, Faith Black Ross.

The Crooked Lane Books team, especially Melissa Rechter, Madeline Rathle, and Rebecca Nelson.

Critique partners and fellow authors Richard Taylor Pearson and Lindsey Duga.

My husband, Kevin, my mom, and the rest of my family.

My friends—both online and in real life.

My author colleagues, as well as bookstores and libraries. (Without you, what would I read?)

The bloggers, podcasters, YouTubers, and reviewers who have mentioned, reviewed, and promoted my books.

And, as always, readers!